The Stolen Child

The Stolen Child

A Novel

LISA CAREY

HARPER PERENNIAL

NEW YORK • LONDON • TORONTO • SYDNEY • NEW DELHI • AUCKLAND

The Stolen Child is a work of fiction. While the inspiration came from true stories of evacuations of Irish islands such as Inishark and the Blasket Islands, St. Brigid's Island and its inhabitants are imagined and not intended to represent any real place or people. Any mistakes are mine, either out of ignorance or artistic license, and I apologize for them in advance.

HarperCollins books may be purchased for educational, business, or sales promotional use. For information please e-mail the Special Markets Department at SPsales@harpercollins.com.

P.S.™ is a trademark of HarperCollins Publishers.

Originally published in the United Kingdom in 2017 by Weidenfeld & Nicolson.

FIRST EDITION

Designed by Leydiana Rodriguez

Library of Congress Cataloging-in-Publication
https://lccn.loc.gov/2016032315
Carey, Lisa, author. The stolen child : a novel / Lisa Carey. First edition.
New York: HarperPerennial, [2017]
  pages cm
  PS3553.A66876 S76 2017
  ISBN: 9780062492180 (paperback)
  9780062492203 (ebook)

ISBN 978-0-06-249218-0 (pbk.)

17 18 19 20 21 LSC 10 9 8 7 6 5 4 3 2 1

For Liam and Timothy,
who don't hold back any love.

Come away, O human child!
To the waters and the wild
With a faery, hand in hand,
For the world's more full of weeping than you can under-
    stand.

"The Stolen Child," William Butler Yeats

The Stolen Child

PART ONE

St. Brigid's Island

I will arise and go now, and go to Innisfree,
And a small cabin build there, of clay and wattles made:
Nine bean-rows will I have there, a hive for the honey-
   bee,
And live alone in the bee-loud glade.

"The Lake Isle of Innisfree," William Butler Yeats

PROLOGUE

May 1960

The day of the evacuation, the first of May, 1960, dawned cloudless and still, weather so fine the islanders said it was stolen.

St. Brigid's Island perched like a jagged accident above the water, all grass and rock, no beach to ease the passage of a boat, no harbor to shelter it once there. Twelve miles west of Ireland, at times nearly impossible to get to and just as deadly to try to leave. It was the whim of the wind and the swelling sea that determined who landed there and who was let go. The islanders were apt to say that it was not the weather at all that decided such things. Something else, they believed, turned the world to suit itself.

So they said it was stolen, that morning's passage, from the good people, the fairies. They did not give such gifts, or lend them. Someone must have tricked it out of them. The islanders muttered their gratitude at the same time as they crossed themselves, in the name of their saint, against it.

Had it not been the day they were scheduled to leave, the women would have put off their chores, set chairs outside their houses, and turned their doughy faces to the sun. Lashing rain and gales had

battered the island for most of April, the sort of weather that abandoned them. Many had speculated that this day would not come at
all—that it would be put off, perhaps until midsummer—and the
thought of another month like the last few set the women gasping
at the ends of their sentences with disapproval and fear.

Two sisters, twins who looked more like strangers sharing the
same bed, noted during the night exactly when the weather let them
go. Emer breathed deeply, the invisible band that gripped her neck
and tethered her loosening enough for a sigh. Rose pressed her lips
together, too angry to allow a breath of concession. She had nothing
packed. The other women had been ready for weeks, but she hadn't
even brought the crates in from the shed.

Rose got up and stirred the hearth, feeding dry rushes to the
orange spots of heat that had crouched, waiting, beneath the ash
during the short night. The same fire had burned on St. Brigid's
Island for generations, some said since the time the saint herself had
lived there. Glowing clumps of turf were buried and reawakened;
whenever a new house was built, the first fire was brought over on
a neighbor's spade. Evacuation or no, Rose would not be the one to
extinguish it.

By dawn the boats were already there, anchoring out from the
island because the rocks and current made approaching the slip impossible for anything larger than a currach. Four boats—the mail
boat, two fishing trawlers and a Galway hooker—all piloted by men
from the mainland and the neighboring island. Rose, watching
from her doorway, grumbled over the attendance.

"Sure, when we're leaving, the vessels come out in droves; if only
they'd been so keen in February." She heard the slight change in the
silence of her sister. As though the mention of February had actually stopped her breathing.

A dozen men rowed in, along with the priest who had been es-
sential in bringing the evacuation about. More men than had stood

on that island in years. They shared a pipe together before starting the first load. All day long, families walked their belongings down to the quay, the borrowed men carrying dressers and bedsteads roped to their backs, the women lugging baskets of linens and dishes, the children gathering cats and hens and cattle and ushering them toward the water. The dogs bullied sheep into cramped, panicked flocks that tried to stay together in the moving boat. The cows and the one bull were made to swim, as well as a donkey, tied by their necks to the back end of a currach, their eyes huge and shining white with panic. One girl put her cat into a cast-iron pot, tying the top down slightly off-kilter so there was a slit to let the air in and the wails of protest out. Then, every once in a while, a nose, a paw with claws extended. Soon every covered pot on the island held a cat or a duck or a hen, and they lined them up on the grass, like a parade of badly tuned instruments, to wait for their turn on the boat.

In the house above, Emer and Rose moved, barely speaking, through the morning routine of breakfast and chores and getting children ready. Since there were plenty of children, this took until the sun was high above the boats waiting below. The children ran back and forth from the quay to the house, reporting on whose family had loaded what, whose cat was in a pot and who was arguing about what to bring and what to leave behind. Rose's oldest, Fiona, told them that Jimmy Moran, eighty-six years old and the only male left on the island over the age of eleven, was refusing to leave. He was parked on a kitchen chair outside his door and was striking with his cane the knees of anyone who tried to get in.

"The old fool," Emer said. "As if they'd let him stay."

Rose stiffened. "That's grand," she said. "Coming from you."

Emer narrowed her one eye. The memory of the other eye was hidden under a brown leather patch. She opened her mouth to say something further, but Rose turned away.

Emer, who had her own house down the road that she no longer lived in, had only one trunk, which had been packed for weeks. She was leaving the rest to the birds. Rose, who was more likely to want to bring everything, still hadn't packed a bag and was washing the breakfast dishes and putting them away in the press as if it were any other day.

"Will I put the delph in a crate?" Emer said. Rose gave her a look that was enough to stop any further suggestions.

Emer went outside. Their mother was propped on a stool against the stone house, one limp arm tucked beneath her breasts, her head covered in wool as though the sunshine and sea air were insults she needed to guard against.

"She'll take her time about it, sure," she slurred, the left side of her mouth as useless as her arm. Emer ignored her. Though her own opinions often leaked out of her mother's half-paralyzed mouth, she refused to commiserate. Only Rose had the patience to answer her anymore.

Emer walked the two cows and their calves down the road to the water. The man who took the rope from her did so with caution, taking care, as they all did, not to brush against Emer's hand.

In the early afternoon, when a man from the boat told Rose it was time—hers was the last house to go—she nodded at Emer, and they began to collect things. It was all done quickly; within an hour, a house that had seen life for two hundred years was empty. Their mother rode down on the last donkey, led by the men, like a tired child. Rose stayed behind, sweeping at the cobwebs and dust blossoms that had appeared when the furniture was moved. Emer, who had walked the children down, came back up with one of the babies on her hip and found her sister feeding the fire from the pile of turf on the hearth.

"Rose," Emer said, not trying to keep the sharp annoyance from her tone. "What does that matter now?"

"No fire, no moon, no sun shall burn me," Rose muttered, the incantation of Saint Brigid that children were taught to say when lighting a fire or climbing into a boat. It was meant to protect them.

"It's a little late for that carrying-on," Emer said. She left her sister, going down to the water to wait with their mother and the children.

Rose washed the floor, wiped down the windowsills and polished the thick glass of the tiny windows. "No lake, no water, no sea shall drown me. No arrow of fairy nor dart of fury shall wound me." She fed the dust and dirty rags to the fire with tears running down her cheeks, swiping at them as though they were something not related to her, like a bee too close to her face. She cleaned and cried and burned what was left, and when the house was spotless and the fire was as hot as it could get, she blew her nose and stood in the open doorway. She took the Saint Brigid's cross from where it hung on the wall, woven from rushes last February by a woman she missed more than she cared to admit, and briefly imagined igniting it in the fire and touching the flames to the thatched roof. The fire would make short work of the dense straw, it would leap from one roof to the next and feed itself long after the boats were gone. From their new council houses on the mainland, in such fine weather, they would be able to see that fire, burning on top of the sea.

If she must go, she thought, why not leave the whole place ablaze?

But she was a sensible woman, a mother, a sister, a guardian of the fragile leftovers of her family. Emer was the one who could get away with setting fires, burning hope away with her hands, like a possessed, grief-stricken witch. But Emer was done with all that, and Rose had never been allowed.

She nestled the cross in the basket instead, along with the last treasures she found in the secret crevices of the house. She put on her good coat, usually worn only to Mass. In its pocket she slipped her kitchen knife, the tool every island woman kept at hand, as the men had once carried their spades. She said three names softly and closed the door.

She saw women gathering in the graveyard, nestled in a promontory above the quay, a patch of jutting purple stones, the first and last thing you saw when pulling a boat into or away from the island.

Rose wouldn't bother with that.

She walked the long road instead, up north to the cliffs, past the clocháns that had stood for centuries, solid as beehives mortared with honey, since the time when the island was a convent of loving virgins. When an island of women alone was a pilgrimage to God rather than a death sentence.

There was too much to remember here, at the cliff's edge, where even on a calm day the wind skinned her ears. The memories licked like fire at her throat, her groin, her heart: screaming to save her sister, lifting her skirt for a lover, building fires to cry out for help in the darkness. She could not separate the love from the terror. She listened for the trickle of water she knew ran quietly beneath the grass, a holy well hidden where few would think to look for it. She half-expected to see a fiery-haired woman with a red dog at her heels, coming to seek the water. But that woman had left the island already, following the same watery road as those who had gone before. They had trickled away, for storms, war, emigration, careers, to a handful of souls, and today was the last day people would ever live here.

The story was that Saint Brigid swindled this island away from a king. He agreed to give her for free whatever land she could cover with her cloak. When she unfurled the blue fabric, the wind carried it in every direction, until it grew and spread and darkened itself over the entire island. The king, angry at being codded, warned her that the place was rotten with fairies, called "good people" only to placate them, for they were anything but good. Brigid, the story went, only smiled and said: "That will suit."

She wasn't a Christian saint but a Celtic one—born in the doorway between two worlds, named for a goddess, suckled on the milk

of fairies, ordained as a bishop—she was a woman who feared nothing, with both God and the good people on her side.

Now the islanders were being given a village, on the mainland,
for the price of leaving this story behind.

The same cove that once protected the nuns, isolated them in devotion, was a curse in the modern world. A dangerous inlet that was
not a real harbor, a rocky hollow and narrow cement quay where
men risked their lives pulling a boat in. Or they used to. Now there
were no men to risk it. Now there were only women, save old Jimmy
Moran and a few young boys. Women not willing to pretend they
had the strength of saints any longer. They knew this evacuation
was coming: they've known for almost as long as they've fought
against it. They asked the government for a harbor; the government
gave them a cul-de-sac on the mainland instead.

On that last walk down, down the green road that had been
carved by nuns and trampled by the bare feet of children, Rose
turned her mind. Now that she was packed, she would go without
once looking back, let the fire go out, leave the holy water in the
ground, not carry it with her in a tiny vial as the other women surely
would. She would busy herself making her new council house, with
electricity and a water tap and a gas cooker and a toilet and a key for
the front door, into a home, and be kind to her sister, who seemed
not to care that they were losing their entire lives because she had
already lost far more than the boats could take away. She would
build a fire in her virgin chimney, the hearth so small it was meant
only for pleasure, and light it with a match.

Rose didn't think that morning's weather was stolen. The fairies wanted them gone as much as Emer did. Even Saint Brigid had
abandoned them. They, too, had had enough.

On the last run, the mail boat brought a reporter from Galway,
who snapped a few photographs for the sensational story that would
appear in the weekend edition. He took pictures of the women

kneeling in the children's graveyard, and one of Jimmy Moran being carried, chair and all, down to the boats. The photograph that made the front page, and was used afterward whenever the subject of evacuated Irish islands came up in the news, was one of Rose and Emer, sitting in a currach, each holding a baby in her lap. Both of the sisters wore the traditional island head covering, brown sheep's wool knitted into a tube, which could be worn over the head to block the wind, or draped as a scarf on finer days. The wool was knit in a continuous circle, a spiral, so once you put it on, it was impossible to lose it to sea air or the hands of needy children. It was said to be the same head covering, the reporter wrote, that Saint Brigid knitted for each of her new postulants.

With this wool draped over their heads, their hair hidden, and in black and white, which smoothed Emer's complexion and dulled Rose's, you could see a physical resemblance that was rarely there when you looked at them in life. The set of their jaws, perhaps, the worry lines, deeper than they should have been for women still young. Though they had always been opposites, in the photo they were reversed; Rose, who had always been sunny next to Emer's dark scowl, looked snuffed out, while Emer, who had spent a lifetime being asked to smile like her prettier sister, was lit from within, glowing, as if something had just been whispered to her, handed to her, stolen and then returned. As if Emer, the one who was bringing nothing, was the one most looking forward to the future. As if, the eagerly dire reporter suggested in his article, leaving the island might put to rest all the terror and sorrow that trying to remain upon it had borne.

CHAPTER 1

The Yank

May 1959

ONE YEAR EARLIER

The Yank arrives on the first day of summer, with the pigs. She comes in Festy's boat, which has to drop anchor and wait for the island men to row out in a currach. They hand her over the side, along with the mail and two squirming sacks. Rumor has it the Yank has been waiting on the mainland for two weeks, staying in the room above Oliver's bar as the last of the spring storms battered the quay and made it impossible for anyone to approach the island.

Emer's son, Niall, has been watching the quay all morning. His father and uncle rowed out early to purchase this year's piglets. Every May, during the festival of Beltaine, which marks the beginning of the summer, each family on the island gets a new pig. They are raised into the autumn and slaughtered one by one over the winter, so fresh meat can be shared among them. Pig day was a favorite for Emer and Rose when they were children, and now it is her son's turn to be excited.

"They're in," Niall comes running to tell her, though she has already seen it from the window. "They're helping Festy bring that Yank."

"*Amadan*," Emer's mother hisses from her perch by the fire. Fool. No one responds. Their mother is used to complaining to the air.

Emer, who has been peeling potatoes at the kitchen table, slips her small knife into the pocket of her apron and dries her hands. Normally, Emer would send Niall down alone, to avoid Rose's husband, and the other islanders who avoid her. But she wants a look at this Yank. She wants to know what sort of woman she is, coming here all on her own. Americans, the islanders know, are used to modern conveniences that St. Brigid's Island is not able to provide. Emer wants to see for herself if it takes something more than a fool.

Niall runs back outside, twirls downhill in the sunshine, then circles back for his mother to catch up. Emer should call in the other direction to Rose, invite her to come along, but she walks quickly to keep up with Niall, without looking back. No women will be clamoring to meet the Yank, she knows. They'll keep their distance, wait to see if she is staying a decent stretch. Emer wants to meet her first.

Emer is tall, like most St. Brigid women, sharply angled and awkward, nothing soft to ease the protrusion of bone. She keeps her dark hair trimmed to the length of her jaw and banished behind her ears. Her skin is decent enough, sallow, with olive tones left over from Ireland's collusion with Spanish pirates. As if reinforcing that theme, she wears a calfskin patch over a stolen eye. Beneath the patch is the fat worm of a keloid scar that seemed to widen long after the rest of her stopped growing. The eye she has left is striking, always wet, lipping over, like a dark blue stone sitting at the bottom of the water, far too deep to reach.

They say Saint Brigid pulled her own eye out, to repel a man sizing her up for a wife. When he was gone, she popped it in again, and her beauty was restored. No one dared propose to her after that. The fairies took Emer's eye, but the one they left suggests she is capable of doing something similar. Of ripping away what is precious should you look at her the wrong way.

The men have rowed out in two currachs to meet the boat, transferred all the Yank's bags and trunks, and are hauling her up onto the quay, one man for each arm, grunting and apologizing. She has a fierce lot of bags and wooden crates from the shop in town. Piled on the quay along with all her things are supplies for the island, which hasn't had a delivery in three weeks: mail, flour, sugar, tea and tobacco, and two sacks that are bulging and emitting the muffled squeals of terrified baby pigs. Niall skips over to them and nudges the lumps in the brown fabric with his bare feet. Emer stops just before the stone quay, to look at the Yank from a distance.

The young men are already taken with her. Rose's husband, Austin, and his cousins, Malachy and Michael Joe, are slagging her about the pigs; apparently she sat down on one of the bags on the way over. She seems able for it—hooting at their jokes, throwing her head back with a big American laugh. She isn't bothered by them grabbing her around her long arms and jostling her breasts as they settle her on the quay. Her hair is loose and frantic with wind, auburn with streaks of fiery red, the curls springing every which way about her head like they are trying to get away. She is wearing a massive yellow jacket and matching trousers the men are praising as American genius. (*Won't that stay bone dry in a wetting rain, now.*) She pumps the hand of old Jimmy Moran too fast and eager, not seeming to realize that he would prefer a simple nod and wink of welcome. She catches sight of Emer and smiles, revealing dazzling white teeth, so Emer is forced to step forward. She holds her hand out as Emer approaches, and Emer hesitates before taking it.

"I'm Brigid," she says, pronouncing her own name wrong, hard on the last *d* instead of softening it to barely there. Emer takes the woman's hand and wraps her fingers around the palm.

Nothing happens. Brigid seems to have no aversion to Emer's hand. Instead of Brigid pulling away first, it is Emer who lets go. She doesn't do what most strangers do, look back and forth indecisively between Emer's remaining eye and the patch over the other. She looks at Emer straight on, as if both eyes are still there. Brigid's eyes are auburn and match the darker streaks in her hair. Even after Emer lets go, she can still feel the woman's palm, pulsing, relentless, like a child chanting the same demand over and over again. Emer flushes and tells her name.

Brigid makes her repeat it twice. *Ee-mer.* She is not only loud, but also asks other people to speak up, as if she is slightly deaf. Most Americans are like this.

"Brigid and Mary be with you," Emer mutters automatically.

"Everybody keeps saying that," the Yank booms. "My mother used to say that too. When I was little I thought it was about me, but then I found out it's about the saint."

Emer gives no response to this. She makes no effort to nod and smile while others are speaking, or fill awkward pauses with chatter. *Like talking to a stone*, islanders say about her.

Niall skips over to them.

"Mammy, may I have my pig now? Austin says I can choose. I want a spotted one."

"Where have your manners gone to?" Emer says. She often chides him in front of others, out of an attempt to appear herself. She is a different person altogether when they are alone.

Brigid winks at him. "What's your name, handsome?"

"Niall," he says. He has to say it twice, *Nye-l*, then spell it.

Brigid holds her hand out and he takes it. Emer has to quell the instinct to stop him, to prevent her son from touching her at all.

"Look at those eyes," Brigid croons. Emer crosses herself quickly. Brigid notices, flicking her eyes quickly back to Niall.

"They're a fairy's eyes," Niall says, mimicking what the islanders say about him. The outer ring is a cloudy, feverish blue, the inner area, around his pupil, as orange as a hot ember. Emer can be feeling her worst, cold and damp and scatterbrained and trapped, hating the island, Patch, her bright, smiling sister, her sullen, crippled mother, who divides her time between Emer's and Rose's houses, and she only needs to look at Niall's eyes and the burning settles her right down.

Where he got these eyes, however, she can't think about for too long or she forgets how to breathe. He didn't have them when he was born.

"It's only an expression," Emer attempts.

"I have fairy ears, myself," Brigid says, hauling her hair back to reveal them: cold-reddened, protruding a fair distance, slightly pointed at the top. "Wanna trade?"

Niall beams. This is the sort of teasing he is used to; the Yank wins him over instantly, and Emer isn't sure she likes it.

"Mammy?" Niall nags.

"Go on and choose your pig, then," she says.

Austin unties the sack and holds it open for Niall, who sticks his head and arms right down into the screaming pit. He emerges with his hands full of squirming pink and gray flesh and tucks it into the front of his sweater, crooning and stroking it until it settles against his small chest like a contented baby.

The men whistle and hoot at Brigid to get moving, they've loaded as much as they can onto the donkey and are carrying the rest. Niall joins the procession, walking next to Brigid. The piglet, a spot like coal dust around its eye, falls asleep. Niall twirls around and winks at Emer, daring his mother to follow them.

"What will you name it?" Brigid is asking. Emer walks just behind them.

"We'll slaughter it come autumn." Niall explains this kindly, a bit condescending, as if Brigid is a child and he is the adult.

"Can't it have a name in the meantime?" Brigid says.

"You might name it Rasher," Emer says. No one responds to this.

"How old are you, Niall?" Brigid says. He looks at her oddly, this is not the way they ask in Ireland.

Emer translates: "She wants to know what age you are."

"I'm six," Niall says. "Today."

"Is it your birthday?" Brigid beams. Niall nods. "And I didn't bring you a present."

That's when Emer realizes that her husband is not among the men hauling her gear.

"Where's Patch?" she asks Austin.

"He'll be along later, sure." Austin evades her eye.

Not likely, she wants to quip. He's at the pub and won't be back for three days, not until his brother bodily collects him.

Niall has run ahead, but he circles back to bestow a curative squeeze to her hand. He knows what it means that Patch is not there, but it doesn't bother him, beyond regretting that it bothers her.

"Were you named for the druid Brigid or the saint?" Austin calls out to the Yank.

"What's the difference?" Brigid says.

"Some say there isn't one." Austin is flirting with her. He wouldn't speak to her at all if Rose were around.

"The first Brigid was a druid goddess, daughter of the original fairy race of Ireland." Austin, who finished secondary school, is showing off now. "The one who lived here was a Christian nun. Some think that it was one woman who changed camps when it suited her."

"Even Britain is named after her," Niall adds.

"I didn't know that." Brigid smiles politely. "But I think my mother just named me after this island. Because she missed it."

Emer makes a quick gasping noise in her throat, a noise particular to island women, a noise that makes Niall look up and wonder what has his mother so peeved.

They make their way up the west road. Brigid is explaining to them how she wrote to the priest to say she was coming to live in her uncle's house after Old Desmond died, but they all know this already. The priest's housekeeper couldn't resist such gossip and told them months ago. Desmond's is the last cottage before the road ends, and only sheep paths continue up and around to the cliffs. The view from one side is of the open Atlantic; from the other, the house looks out on the mountains of Connemara and the neighboring island, Inis Muruch, which has four times the population, the priest's house, a church, a shop and a pub and gets mail delivered year-round. No one has lived in this house in the year since Desmond died, unnoticed for long enough that the body had started to turn. He hadn't spoken to another islander willingly in forty years.

Emer watches for the Yank's reaction as they get closer. The house looks no better than derelict, whitewash worn away to gray stone, one window broken into a circle of jagged teeth, thatch on the roof half–eaten away, wrens rising in commotion as they approach. When Austin halts the donkey in front of it, the Yank stops for a beat and blinks, but presses on, stepping over the fallen stones and crushed barbed wire of Desmond's wall. The men mutter and apologize, prop the door open to let in the air, reassure her she'll have it sorted in no time, unload her belongings and pile them neatly inside. They scurry off like startled mice, promising to bring down a load of turf, leaving Emer and Niall alone with the Yank in the house. It smells of damp that has been let to win, urine and the old, bitter man who died inside it. If she were that Yank, she'd walk straight back to the quay. She imagines she sees a dip in the woman's broad shoulders, a weary release, as if the state of the place is a last straw. But Brigid puts her hands on her hips, which are square and strong on top of lean legs. She is almost as tall as the doorway, taller than most of the men who hauled her things up, though St. Brigid men are not strangers to being towered over by women. She blows a stray cluster of red curls away from her eyes. It bounces up and back like a live, opinionated thing. Her complexion is as bright and as varied as her hair, milk-white cheeks giving way to a wave of auburn freckles across her nose. She might be Irish, except for the teeth.

"Well, this is even worse than I thought," she says blithely, taking off the yellow costume and pushing up the sleeves of her equally mannish but more familiar woolen sweater. Though Emer hates to clean house, as her sister, mother and husband can attest to, she can't really bring herself to walk away. Women are expected to do such things, just as the men were expected to unload her belongings and take off for another chore. Emer suspects that it is no different in America. There is something about this woman—her resolve seems to border on desperation—that fires up Emer to help. She wants to see what she might do next.

Niall goes back outside to let the pig run around on the hill behind the house. Within a few minutes he has taught the thing to play a version of tag.

Emer and Brigid open three of the four windows, pick the last one free of broken glass. They sweep out the cobwebs and mouse droppings from the cupboard, clean the ashes from the hearth, and start a new fire with the turf Austin brings back in the donkey's creel. For luck, Emer knows they should borrow from another fire to start it, but she doubts the Yank knows or cares about this, so she uses a whole box of damp matches that Brigid brought from the mainland to get it lit. Emer tells her how to bury the fire at night and dig out the embers in the morning so the fire will never go out and no more matches will be needed.

"My mother used to do that," Brigid says. "There's a chant you say, about Saint Brigid."

"*No fire, no moon, no sun shall burn me.*" Emer's recitation is quick and without feeling.

"That's it," Brigid says. She jerks her head, as if flicking aside an unpleasant memory like one of her curls.

Niall comes in to check their progress. He has found a bit of rope and fashioned a leash for the piglet. It trots beside him happily, the screaming emigration over the water in a canvas sack wiped forever from its mind.

"What about Saint Brigid's well?" Brigid says. "The holy well the island was named for. Is it nearby?" Brigid says this casually, but Emer can tell she is holding her entire self in check awaiting the answer. There is that feeling from her hand again, a pull, a frantic grab, though her face remains prettily detached.

She's come for a miracle, then.

"The island was named for the saint, not a stream," Emer says. "You'll hear a lot of nonsense about what she could and could not do. But there's plenty of wells," she says. "You won't want for fresh water." Niall, who has been trying to get the piglet to sit on command, looks pointedly at his mother.

"Take that creature outside," Emer says, to stop his tongue. They don't share the well with outsiders. Not anymore.

She sends Niall out for ordinary water. He takes the job on like a game, cheerfully bringing them the bog-stained liquid and pouring the dirty buckets into the dike when they've used it up. If Brigid can hear his chattering, the back and forth of a half-invisible conversation, she doesn't say so. Perhaps she thinks he's talking to the pig.

Emer marvels at the groceries, luxuries they only see on a holiday: store-bought milk, butter and yogurt, white sugar in a paper bag, sliced bread and potatoes scrubbed so spotless they look sickly. Rashers sliced thick and ready to fry. Chocolate, currants, soap wrapped like a gift.

"I guess I wasn't thinking," Brigid laughs uncomfortably. "I was expecting a fridge."

"We haven't been given the electricity like some places," Emer says. She shows Brigid the low, dark shelf where she can store the perishables.

"I'll bring you milk and butter until you sort out a cow," Emer says. "You can buy mackerel from the lads at the quay. They set aside some before selling the rest on the mainland."

Brigid nods and smiles, taking it in as if she's lived on a remote island in Ireland before and it's just a matter of remembering how to do it. There's a tension to her smile since she asked for the well, a tight crack in her face.

"Are you from New York?" Niall asks when he whirls in again. He has tied the pig outside and it squeals painfully for him.

"No," Brigid says, "Maine." She has to explain where this is. She ends up saying it's above New York and below Canada.

"What's it like?"

"Like this," Brigid says, gesturing to the sea. "Rugged, rocky coastline. But with trees."

"Like a forest?"

"Yes. We call it the woods."

"Have you got fairies in it?"

"I used to make houses for them." Brigid smiles warmly now. "Don't you?"

Emer is glaring at him with one cold eye.

Niall sees this and shrugs.

"Em," he says. There is a pause where all they can hear is the pig still crying for him. And for a beat longer than is comfortable, Niall is gone. His pupils contract, making the fiery ring around them look larger. Emer darts toward him, alarmed, but it is over quickly, he pulls himself out of it, whereas often he needs to be hollered at, or shaken. Still, it is a few painful seconds before he speaks again. "We've tree roots in the bog," he says, as if there was no pause at all. "They're massive."

Brigid smiles, but Emer can see that she noticed. Noticed his absence, and Emer's reaction. She probably thinks he is simple.

Emer tells him to go outside and silence the pig.

"Is he your only child?" Brigid asks when he's gone, and Emer sets her jaw.

"He is," she says, ready to defend herself.

But Brigid only nods, as if this answer is acceptable.

"You must have had him fairly young," says Brigid.

"I'm twenty-three," Emer says defensively. Brigid chuckles and shakes her head.

"I'll be forty in February," she says. Emer forgets for a moment to hide her thoughts, letting her mouth hang open in shock. Her own mother is forty-two and looks ancient compared to this tall, glowing, barely wrinkled woman.

"I'll take that as a compliment," Brigid says.

"Are your children grown?" Emer asks.

"Haven't had any." She says this nonchalantly, not even looking at Emer, as if she might just change her mind and start a family next week. But that smile again. So tight it has begun to quaver.

That's what she wants the well for. The stories were that Saint Brigid used the water to heal sick children, or to revive barren wombs. The islanders guarded it, though there was no evidence that it still worked. Emer could discourage her. "They tried it on my eye," she could say. "I lost it regardless." But she holds her tongue.

Emer says she needs to go, so they walk outside. Brigid squints out over the view, the mountains on the mainland, the sea like a calm blue walkway pretending as though it never tries to trap them in rage.

"It's beautiful," Brigid says, but she doesn't mean it. Emer sees it in her face, in the set of her shoulders. Looking at the sea brings her something other than peace.

"What was my uncle Desmond like?"

"A bit touched," Emer says. Brigid doesn't need to ask what this means, like most Americans would.

"Did any of them come back?" she asks Emer. "Of my mother's family? Anyone before me?"

"No one comes back here once they've gotten away."

"Why not?"

"Can you imagine a more desolate place?" Emer scoffs. Brigid raises her eyebrows.

"We're to be evacuated," Emer blurts. "The priest on Inis Muruch is trying to get the county to give us land in town. We'll have new houses, council houses." She almost pulls out the planning sketch the priest gave her, which she keeps in her apron pocket, of the council houses, painted in cheery pastels, concrete paving around them. But she decides against it when she sees Brigid's face.

"Sounds like you want to leave," Brigid says. Emer shrugs.

"We'll be gone by the time Niall is seven, please God," she says.

"What's happening when I'm seven?" Niall says, coming around the side of the house, piglet in tow.

"Whisht, you," Emer says.

Brigid shakes her head, as if she can shake Emer and her pessimism right off her like she does her curls.

"Well, I've come to stay," she says. Emer says nothing. Let's see how long you last, she thinks, with no phone, no electricity, no doctor or priest, no newspaper unless the weather permits it, and weeks on end with no contact whatsoever from anyone but the same people you've seen every day of your life.

"Mammy!" Niall calls. Both the Yank and Emer turn to where he is pointing.

A dog is crouching in the weeds to the side of the house, a low growl in its throat, the skinny red body arched as if to run or attack.

"Mind that dog," Emer says to the Yank. "It won't take to anyone since Desmond died."

"I'm supposed to mind it?"

"That means be careful of it. The lads drowned her litter before you came. Couldn't catch herself, though. Too clever for death, sure."

"How cruel," Brigid says.

"You won't say so after she's bitten you," Emer says. Just like a Yank, she is thinking. Fussing over dogs as if they are children.

"Sure, she's only a mongrel who couldn't feed her pups," Emer adds, for Niall's sake. Despite what he says about slaughtering the pig, he is on the touchy side about animals as well.

Brigid goes inside and comes out with a plate and two of the precious store-bought rashers. She puts it just below the stone wall. The pig squeals. The dog looks at the pig, then the plate, and growls low in her throat.

"That's a waste of good rashers, that is," Emer says. Niall laughs and jumps up and down, clapping his hands.

"You're like Saint Brigid," he says. "Giving bacon to the dogs."

"She's not taming lions, for pity's sake," Emer scolds.

"Thanks for all your help," Brigid says. She has learned to direct her smiles to Niall already. He's the one who returns them.

"See you tomorrow," Niall chirps. Emer takes his hand. She has to pull to get him to turn away from Brigid and start walking home.

The pig trots beside them, stumbling every once in a while on the uneven ground. Niall's hand is in hers. She squeezes it lightly and rubs, milking the comfort. He leans briefly against her, and she allows herself a quick brush of her lips against his glossy ink hair. She mutters an endearment in Irish: *A chuisle mo chroí*, and he whispers it back. She never lets others see this sort of thing, but there's no one watching now but the pig.

They walk the long way round the field to check on the sheep. Niall sings softly, as he often does while walking, to himself or to something else, Emer is never sure. The pig seems to join in, squealing and grunting the same rhythm.

The wind is gusting when they round the cliffs, and the pig stumbles. Niall picks him up, buttoning his sweater around it once more.

"I like the way she talks," Niall says. Everything he says to Emer is a thread from one long, uninterrupted conversation.

"Do you now," Emer mutters.

"Is Brigid our cousin, Mammy?" he asks.

"She's not. Desmond was no relation to us."

"Is she our friend, then?" he says hopefully. Niall hasn't started school yet. When he does, he will be related to every child in his classroom. The concept of friends is as foreign as the Yank herself.

"Would you like her to be?"

"I would," Niall says. "She's lovely."

Emer bristles, though she has been thinking the same thing. Thinking how ruined she must look in comparison.

"I'd say she's fond enough of you," Emer says.

"Her smiles have frowns in them," Niall says.

"And what do you mean by that?" Emer says, but she already knows. It was in Brigid's hand as well. Emer couldn't put anything bad into it, there was so much pain already there. Still, a charge comes off her, as lively and invading as the copper glint of her hair. Emer finds herself thinking ahead to tomorrow, and the next day, of the moments between chores that they might find a way to see her again. Chance a greeting from that fiery hand.

"Will you not tell her about the well?" Niall says.

"I won't. And don't you go blabbing it either."

"Auntie Rose says it gives you babies."

"Your Auntie Rose could do with fewer herself."

The wind turns and assaults her with a whiff of the pig at her son's neck.

"That thing is ripe," she scolds halfheartedly. "And now you will be as well."

"Sorry!" he laughs, letting go of her hand and running ahead to chase the sea birds. When he runs to the left, toward the cliff, he vanishes from her limited vision. Her neck grows tight and she yells for him to mind himself. She misses the days when she still carried him everywhere, bound to her chest with a woolen shawl, and she didn't have to rely on her faulty vision for vigilance.

"Mammy, can I bring the pig in the house?" Niall says. "So he can sleep by the fire?" Emer grunts but knows she will let him. Her mother has gone to Rose's house, and there is no sign of Patch returning. No one is there to remind either of them not to get too fond of something that will only be taken away.

Inside Emer's mind, she still sees with both eyes. The image of Brigid's bright new face burns there now. With the wind from the cliffs screaming memories into her ears, Emer can't decide what she is feeling. There is a striking similarity between anticipation and dread.

CHAPTER 2

Mongrel

It takes three days, all the rashers and half a chicken before Brigid gets the dog to come in. Most of the dogs on the island look like some mix of sheepdog—long dirty fur, black or brown patches on white, chunks missing from their ears and tails. Brigid's mutt is an auburn shorthair, with the long face and droopy, apologetic eyes of a hunting dog. She moves the plates of raw meat closer to the back door each day and on the third day it is sitting there, haunches tucked in tight, trying to make itself as small as possible. She holds the door wide and moves aside. The tail wags once, then it looks at her again, eyes as auburn as its fur.

"Well, come on," she says and the dog half trots, half wriggles inside, excitement almost bending it in two.

She leans down to run her hand over the sleek head. The smell almost gags her.

"Boy do you stink," she says. The dog wags its whole body in agreement.

She takes down the metal dish tub and pours water from the enormous black kettle, warm on its hook by the hearth, and adds a squirt of dish liquid. She has to lift the dog into the tub, but it freezes and lets her. The dog stands, tail between its legs, eyes rolled so far sideways the whites are shiny with panic, while she pours the water over its back and shoulders, soaps and pours again. She knows how to do this. She has bathed grief-stricken women and tense newborns, coiled into themselves, unwilling to let go and return to or enter the world. This dog requires the same firm consolation of her hands. One leg is crusted with dried clots of blood. The stomach is a slack pouch, nipples extended, raw and empty. The memory of puppies still in her skin. Brigid croons and speaks softly to it while she massages away dirt and blood, and the dog doesn't take its eyes off her. When she rinses it a third time and the water at its sinewy ankles is brackish and foul, she uses the one bath towel she has to dry it off, then folds it into a little mat in front of the fire. The dog turns around six times in a tight circle, then lies down, curled up as small as she can get, her chin touching the base of her tail.

"I don't believe you've bitten anyone," Brigid says, pulling each of the ears through her hands like she's smoothing the pigtails of a child. "No one who didn't deserve it." She dumps the water outside into the drainage ditch that lines the road and by the time she returns the dog is deeply asleep, not even stirring when she pulls the rocker up so she can share the heat of the fire. She makes more tea—the amount of tea she drinks here has quickly climbed to the unfathomable, she drinks it like she once drank water—and eats some brown bread with butter and marmalade. She cannot be bothered to figure out how to cook on the open turf fire, so she spreads things on the bread Emer brought her and calls it a meal. Soda bread, butter and jam, brown bread, butter and smoked fish, brown bread, butter and a soft egg. She is afraid to eat the unrefrigerated meat and used it all to seduce the dog. She swallows enormous vitamins with glasses of lukewarm milk from Emer's cow.

She rinses her mug, plate and knife with the last of the water.

She pokes at the turf fire—slow burning clods of earth that often, if the wind is wrong, fill the house with smoke—and buries the red nuggets with ash. In the morning, they will still be there. Fire seems to last longer here, like the sun. The sun doesn't fully fade until midnight, the twilight stretching on for hours, and comes blaring up again at 4 a.m. Her sleep has been riled by all this daylight. Though she covers the windows with sacking, she still senses the light, and there is a part of her, a child she remembers from a long time ago, that seems like it is sitting up in bed all night, eyes wide open, hair tingling with fear, listening for the moment it is safe to get up again.

She goes into the bedroom, changes into her chilled, slightly damp nightdress, laying her clothes on the trunk for the morning. She gets into the low bed and burrows under three blankets and the eiderdown bedspread she auspiciously purchased in Dublin. After a minute she hears the dog get up, stretch and click its toenails along the floor, pausing at the door to the bedroom. She folds the covers back in a triangle of welcome and it climbs in, turning once and flopping down so Brigid is spooning its back. She covers it up with the blankets and smiles at the thought of Emer, with her lyrical voice that is punctuated with disapproving noises, telling the islanders that the Yank sleeps with her dog.

She came here planning to keep her hands to herself. She wants to be finished with touching, and everything that gets smothered and resurrected between fingers. The dog is a nice compromise. It warms the bed; she can stroke it because it expects nothing more from her hands.

THE FIRST TIME BRIGID shakes Emer's hand, she knows the girl is trying to put something inside her. Brigid can feel it, something stronger than the grip of her palm, which is weak really, passive, the sort of handshake she despises, someone presenting their hand but unwilling to contribute any pressure to the exchange. The jolt is not what Emer is trying to insert as much as the resistance Brigid is able to muster, as if whatever Emer is handing out, a dark uneasy germ, has met its match in the calluses on Brigid's palm. It cannot penetrate her, and Emer, who doesn't meet eyes easily, widens her one eye in surprise.

"You won't try that again, will you?" Brigid wants to say. But she doesn't need to. Emer takes her hand and its intentions and buries them away in the pocket of her apron. Her fist bulges in there, balled up in anger at the defeat.

They're not unfamiliar to Brigid, hands that do damage. Her own parents had them, and used them frequently enough.

THE MEN ON THE boat won't even admit the well exists, let alone tell her where it is. They speak Irish on the row over, hard guttural and lilting, her mother's secret language in the mouths of these rough, thin-lipped men. She knows it wouldn't be wise to let on that she understands them. She lets them speak about her and around her, not catching it all because though they called it a calm day, the wind is still there, relentless and mournful, right at the entrance to her ears.

"She'll not be long if she's looking for a miracle," one man says.

"She's quare enough," the other man says. "Like all the Darcys."

"She'd better be hard as them as well," the man replies.

Her stomach drops a bit, as the currach rises high on a wave. This is where it began for her mother, the hardening, the carapace, the shell she had needed to escape and then survive. Brigid hasn't come here for that. She's been so many places already that required her to be hard. She wants this one to crack her wide open.

Once she is settled, the men on the island are helpful and friendly and wink a lot, until she mentions the well, and then they evade her eyes, drop their voices even lower than usual, mouths barely moving, dismissive mumbles lost in their beards or the wind. Some of them blush, as though she has asked something improper, or feminine, like where she might purchase sanitary napkins. Others smile, cock their heads and look delighted, as if she is a child and keeping this secret from her is an enjoyable game. This is infuriating, but she can't afford to anger or insult them. She is not sure how this magic will work, but she may need one of these men in the end. She sizes them up with this in mind. Austin: handsome, seems intelligent, but she is suspicious of him. He held her hand too long, and left a film of oily sweat she had to wipe on her trousers. Malachy: sweet, dim, solicitous, he might fall in love with her if she is not careful. Festy, the mainland man who runs the mail boat, who told her without preamble, as if they'd known each other for years, to send word when she was ready to leave, seems the least complicated. Imagining having to decide between these options leaves her anxious and slightly repulsed. She did not come here for a man.

SHE SEARCHES FOR THE well every day, walking the island in the mornings after breakfast, at midday, which stretches on for longer than it should, no shelter from the merciless sun, and in the bright evenings, up around the west road past the cliffs and down again by the east end. The dog accompanies her, taking the lead, bounding in front along the green road. Half the houses are abandoned, thatched roofs long since decayed, spiky weeds and wildflowers growing as high as the walls inside. Occasionally she sees women in the occupied houses, if they catch her eye they will nod and cock their heads, but then look away, not inviting her to talk. They are nothing like the Irish women she met on the mainland, who called her "Pet" and were eager for conversation. Here the women keep to themselves, or at least keep themselves from her. She catches the names they use for her, which she knows from her mother mean "blow-in" and possibly "madwoman," she can't be sure. The men call happily as she goes by, often stop and talk to her for longer than she would like. They wear the same woolen coats in the fields and on the water and marvel over the Grundens oiled canvas jacket and overalls she brought from Maine. She is not sure why she is accepted by one gender and snubbed by the other, but since she came here to escape the complications of women, she is not complaining. Though she does wonder, do they avoid her because she is a blow-in, or because her mother was not?

She climbs narrow paths made by sheep to the highest point of the island, where circular stone buildings sit abandoned by a sheer drop to the sea, listening for the trickle of fresh water beneath the earth. She turns over stones, squats down to smell the ground, plunges her fingers into boggy soil that leaves a stain she can never fully remove from beneath her fingernails. Everything is wet here, even on dry days the very earth is soaked to the core. She has found seven wells so far, not man-dug holes but natural crevices in the earth, marked with circles of purple rock, one so deep it has slate steps leading into it and a tin dipper held by a chain nailed into the earth above. She drinks from every one of them, trying not to think of land runoff and primitive latrines and disease. She gulps the cold liquid, clear or bog-stained, and waits to feel something, but they are just wells. None of this water can come close to addressing her thirst.

Though she is not overly fond of nuns, she prays to the saint as she trudges the steep hills, where slivers of slate layer with dirt that crumbles if you step on it at the wrong angle. She whispers to her as she investigates small coves, pocketing cowrie shells while following the rivulets in sand, the veins where freshwater runs to meet the sea. She recites the fireside chant of her mother, the prayers she once muttered in obligation as a girl. She calls her own name over and over as she lies on swathes of moss so varied and intricate they look woven by tiny beings. *Saint Brigid, hear me. Saint Brigid, have mercy on me. Saint Brigid, save me.*

She doesn't really know what she is doing. She is not familiar with the magic she is looking for, and isn't sure if it is a saint she is calling to or something older and darker, the sort of spirit that makes islanders cross themselves in fear. She didn't even know where this island was, or that it shared her name, until she received that letter from the solicitor. All her mother ever told her of this place were stories she didn't intend to be taken as true. Stories of fairies and changelings and enchanted water and the superhuman strength of threatened children. Brigid wasn't even certain the well from the stories was real, until she saw the reactions it caused in the shifting fishermen and awkward, bitter Emer. They don't want her to find it, and this fact more than anything lets her know that it is her answer. Being so close fills her with an almost unbearable anticipation, she wants to scratch the eyes out of every local who mutters and looks away and pretends not to know what she is asking for.

She calls the dog Rua, which she remembers means red-haired. She says it over and over when they're walking, until the dog learns to bend her ears to the sound.

AFTER TEN DAYS, THE women still won't speak to her, beyond a murmured *God bless*, or a *Soft day*, a phrase that apparently means "it's raining, again." Most merely nod and look away before she can speak. Their children come closer but then giggle and run away if she tries to talk to them, or look blankly as if she is speaking a language they have never heard. They run back to their mothers and Brigid feels the familiar remorse, the stab that occurs whenever she witnesses the thoughtless gestures that occur between mother and child. The swift easy lift of a toddler onto a hip, the blind swipe to clean a nose or cheek, even the yank of an arm to warn of danger or disobedience. A mother's hands are not careful, they don't need to be. They are efficient, harried, solid, quick and tender extensions of the bodies that are poised to react, with their strong arms, thick middles, full breasts. Mothers' bodies are not their own. The happiest ones seem to have forgotten what it is like to want themselves back at all.

The patient anticipation she came with has surrendered to a frantic anxiety. She barely sleeps, she walks the island until her legs are on fire, until the sky darkens with charcoal and the rain soaks through every layer of clothing and claims her skin. She turns over boulders, rips at bracken and heather and, during one violent hailstorm, crawls into a strange, child-sized hut of stone to weep and fall asleep, holding the warm consolation prize of a mongrel dog. The dog whines as if she knows exactly what Brigid is grieving, and presses her body right into her middle, as if she can fill the void for her. Brigid wails a visceral, unself-conscious keen, enormous inside the hive of stone, while a part of her waits to cry herself out, hoping that no one but the dog can hear her above the cliff wind.

She cannot find it on her own.

If she keeps this up, she will go mad. She has ripped her arms bloody on nettles, her pants have worn down at the knees. She hasn't bathed in too long and when she squats looking for water the smell between her legs assaults her. She has tended to women who let themselves go like this, who smelled like they were rotting from somewhere inside, because to freshen up was to start over and they couldn't bear that.

She needs to calm down. She won't find it this way. It's hidden, it's a secret they don't want to share. She is acting like a child, she could ruin the last chance she has by exposing such blatant need. She must behave like the mature woman she is, deliberate, methodical yet gracious, not some teenager who grasps at chances because she still has some vague hope that adulthood will be so much easier than being a child ever was.

She hasn't laid eyes on her mother in almost thirty years, but now she hears her accent daily in the words of the islanders. When she dares to remember herself that young she is now reminded of Emer, needy, barely grown girl who is an adult already whether she wants it or not.

When she goes to sleep that night, she dreams of Matthew, of his long, slender, feminine hands on her body, caressing her belly as it swelled and emptied over and over again. Her darling, guilt-ridden Matthew. She was a child when he fell in love with her, and he tried to make up for this crime for the rest of his life. He died after failing again and again to give her the only thing she wanted. If she does not find this well, she will have let him die for no reason at all.

She wakes early the next morning and takes her tea outside to watch the mountains. She is almost forty years old, but she is no longer racing against time. It is not her body she must rely on, her only hope is a miracle, or a curse. She doesn't care which one. She wanted to do this alone, she imagined that being here would be similar to her childhood, where there was no one but herself to rely on. A place so quiet she could have conversations with the rocks, the trees, the sea, and no one would hear them. But this place has no trees, and they won't let her find it alone. She will go back to her original, less attractive plan, to the exhausting bright conversation, to flirting, to pretending she has come to be a part of this place instead of merely taking from it.

She looks at the cottage, derelict, the weeds grown high as the miniature windows, yellow lichen eating its way through the stone. The roof leaks so furiously when it rains, she has to move her bed to an odd angle in the center of the room to avoid it. She will ask Austin and Malachy about their offer to repair the thatch. The next time Emer comes by with bread or milk, though she is exactly the sort of desperate girl Brigid has vowed to stay away from, she will invite her inside. She has seduced what she wants out of people before, though she no longer has the same enthusiasm for it.

Instead of searching for the well, she spends the morning heating buckets of ordinary water, for herself, for dishes, for her underwear and the filmy sheets. In between batches, she tidies the place up; she has neglected the inside of the house as much as herself. She squats in the lukewarm tub and lets the water slough off the layers of her first weeks here. In her mind, she makes a list of the things she will need to turn this abandoned nest into something resembling a home.

Neither of them is in any condition to welcome a baby.

CHAPTER 3

Changeling

Saturdays have always been bath days. On Sundays, if the weather allows, the islanders all go over to Inis Muruch for Mass, so Saturday is the chance to wash the week away. Even if the weather looks fierce, and Mass unlikely, children are washed of their sins regardless.

The Saturday after the Yank arrives, Emer heats bathwater for Niall, then herself. Her husband is still "on the tear," which is both a relief and an embarrassment; when he does arrive he will need three times the bathwater to wash it away.

Niall has never whined or resisted baths, but sits happily playing with the soap while she scrubs and rinses his body with a gentle touch no islander would suspect of her. She knows every inch of him and cannot imagine a day when she won't, so though he is old enough to bathe himself, she has never suggested he try. Niall has never felt anything but love come out of Emer's hands.

Emer's own ablutions are rough, quick, she doesn't like to linger over her body, which is like a girl's, strong but too thin, without the curves men admire on Rose. Even after pregnancy, she shrunk immediately to her former bony self. Aside from breast-feeding,

Emer's body hasn't participated in much pleasure, nor been the object of any desire. Sometimes Niall will peek around the curtain she fashions over twine to ask her a question (the notion of privacy still baffles him), and gaze at her small breasts as if trying to figure something out. Then the fiery ring in his eyes will grow and she'll have to bark at him to leave her be. She worries, when she sees that ring in his eyes, that he is remembering something far more dangerous than suckling milk.

Once they are both bathed and dressed, they walk up the road to Rose's house, Niall's pig trotting alongside him, so Emer can help bathe their mother. Rose's oldest girls, Fiona and Eve, are outside feeding the hens. They call Niall over to them. Emer doesn't like to let him out of her sight for long, but Fiona has a head on her shoulders, and can be trusted to yank him back if he starts to drift away. The other girls are too young to be of use, and Eve seems to have nothing but wool between her ears.

Rose bears her children in litters of two, all girls with her red-gold hair and the names of saints. She is currently working on her fourth pair of twins in eight years, during which she has always been pregnant or nursing or both. That many pregnancies without a break makes other women look knackered, but Rose looks better with each one, as if the babies are adding something to her body instead of taking it away. "More's the pity," they say on the island, "that her sister has only the one." There is a rumor that Emer is barren, that something went wrong during Niall's birth in the hospital on the mainland. Emer started this rumor.

Rose has just finished up with the toddlers, Clare and Cecelia. She sends them outside with Teresa and Bernadette, who are six, and instructions to comb their hair.

"Emer, pet," Rose says brightly. "The day's fine enough, is it not?"

"It's lashing over on the mainland," Emer reports. "It'll come our way if the wind changes."

"Where have *you* been?" their mother slurs. "You went missing and Rose had to come collect me." Rose pours the contents of the kettle into the metal tub, then adds a bucket of tepid water.

"Is Patch home, Emer?" Rose deflects.

"Not yet."

"Useless bastard," their mother mutters.

"Language, Mammy," Rose chides, but she winks at Emer.

"Austin says you wasted a whole day settling that Yank," her mother says. "He had to milk your cow, you could hear her keening from the field."

"Austin wasn't bothered, Mammy," Rose says.

Emer moves over to her mother's chair and begins to take her hair out of its pins, too quickly to be gentle, and her mother bats at her ineffectually with her better arm.

"What's she like, so?" Rose asks. She lifts their mother under the arms and supports her standing, so Emer can pull down the woman's skirt and remove her stockings and bloomers. Her mother's thighs are like strangers to each other, one heavy and pocked with cellulite, the other loose skin swimming around bone. Her pubic hair has shed away in the last few years, and what is left is as sparse and colorless as the hair on her head. Rose removes her top and woolen undershirt. Clodagh stopped wearing a bra a long time ago.

"She's like most Yanks," Emer replies. "Bold."

Together they help their mother shuffle the few steps to the bath, guiding her useless leg over the metal lip and lowering her slowly into the murky water. Emer takes charge of her hair, while Rose starts soaping her limbs with a scrap of flannel.

"If she's at all like her mother she'll put your heart crosswise," Clodagh slurs.

"Oh, hush," Rose chides, pouring water over her hunched, soapy back. "You didn't know any of them besides Desmond."

"I know the stories. Changelings and whores and good men twisted to evil."

"Leave the stories, so. I want to know about the actual woman."

"She's here for the well," Emer says. Their mother makes a noise like she's amused. Emer pours the rinse water too sloppily over her head and her mother ends up sputtering and cursing her, wiping at her good eye.

"Poor thing," Rose says. "Did you tell her, Emer?"

"I didn't."

"I don't see why we keep it secret," Rose says.

"We can't be giving away our miracles," Emer imitates the thick accent of an older island woman.

"Nonsense. As if Saint Brigid herself would be so stingy!" Rose says. She accompanies this with a quick sign of the cross that inspires an eye roll from her sister. "It's not as if you believe in it. And you're not the loyal one. Why not tell?"

Emer shrugs. She didn't keep the well from Brigid out of loyalty to the island or belief in the legends or anything so grand. The longer Brigid looks for it, the longer she will be there. Emer already wants her to stay.

"She'll bring us nothing but sorrow, sure," their mother says. "She'll want to change things. Yanks always do."

"There's no panic," Rose quips. "We're able to stand a bit of change. Isn't that so, Emer?"

"Will you not get me out of this tub," their mother says. "I'm after freezin' me arse off."

They lift her to a standing position and Emer holds her steady while Rose swipes her dry with a ragged towel. They get her dressed again, pushing the useless half of her into sleeves and leg openings while her working side pushes itself, knocking into them without apology. Even Rose, viciously bright minded, looks knackered after wrestling their crippled mother into clothing. They've been caring for her most of their lives, physically since her stroke the year they were twelve, and though she grows weaker each year, her temperament hasn't eased at all. A woman almost as angry at life as she is at her inability to leave it. Emer is often tempted to use her hands, to press all the anger she has at this woman into her ruined body, but it would only create more that she and her sister would be required to tend to. They plop her clumsily back in the rocking chair and empty the tub in the ditch.

"I should call in to her," Rose says, visibly relieved to be finished with this chore. "I've a fresh batch of scones."

"Don't bother," Emer says, trying to sound nonchalant. "She won't invite you in. She's as batty as Desmond was."

Niall and Fiona come inside, announcing that they've seen Brigid with the dog, walking up over their Uncle Aidan's back field.

"Can I go say hello to her, Mammy?" Niall asks.

"No," Emer and Rose say together. Rose will say that Emer fusses over her only child too much, but even she knows there are places on their island that Niall should not be let to go alone. Their uncle Aidan's back field is one of them.

"Stay with your cousins in sight of the house," Emer says, and Fiona takes Niall's hand and leads him, dejected, outside. Rose looks out the open top half of the divided back door.

"Poor woman," she mutters. "What do you suppose she's after?"

"I didn't ask her," Emer says.

"Do you not think it's a baby?" Rose asks.

"You think every woman wants a baby," Emer scoffs. "And she brought no man with her, so I'd love to see her manage that."

Rose smiles, caressing her own belly, just beginning to swell with the latest pair.

Austin comes in then, and Emer blushes. He looks so hard and handsome in the small house usually full of women and children. He drops a bloody lamb leg on the table.

"Did I miss your bath, ladies?" he jokes, and Rose grins, and before he can steal a kiss, and send their mother into complaints of impropriety and Emer into a hot rush just being close to it, Emer walks out on the lot of them.

She shades her eyes from the fierce sun and watches the Yank trudging up a steep green hill. Emer has watched her every day, on the road, on the cliffs, across the bog. Every stone Brigid turns over has a memory attached to it, every place she looks is already lodged beneath Emer's uncomfortable skin.

THEIR MOTHER WASN'T ALWAYS like this. She was once as young as they were, a dark beauty their father would grab in the middle of the kitchen, sending the children out of doors for an hour. She doted on her husband, and on their older brother, Dónal, her first child and her only boy. Boys were the only true children on the island. Girls were just small women, expected to behave before they could even speak. If their mother wasn't glaring at five-year-old Emer and Rose in disapproval, she was nodding at them with a sort of solemn recognition. The girls were there to help her; her son was there to please her. Until he died.

Her husband and son were taken by the sea in a storm that claimed twelve, half the island's able men. Island women were rowed to the mainland to identify the bodies, laid out on pallets like fish at a market. The boy's body was never found. His coffin was laid empty in the graveyard.

For a month their mother refused to leave her darkened bedroom, where she ripened daily in the bedclothes, the vinegar smell of her an onslaught when her daughters opened the door to bring her tea. Then she rose one evening, put on her scarf, and brought them to the cliff.

EMER KNEW SOMETHING WAS wrong while strapped to her mother's back, wrapped too tightly in a damp flannel shawl—she was five and far too big to be carried this way. Rose was made to walk beside them, cheerily enough, until it began to rain and she asked their mother where they were going.

"There's none of our sheep this way," Rose said. They were following an old narrow sheep path, barely the width of one of her mother's calloused brown feet, up over the hills of grass and gorse and heather and dead wild flowers. There was nothing in this direction but the cliffs, where the wind was so strong the birds dove and rose without needing to flap their wings, wind that got in your ears and bruised your brain. No island child was meant to go there alone.

Their mother didn't answer, just changed hands, pulling Rose behind her like part of a set dance. Rose met Emer's eyes, and looked daggers at her. Emer turned her head. She didn't often help her sister. She preferred to slip away, or put a face on as if she didn't fully understand what was being asked of her. This was why the islanders said that one twin got more than her share of brains in the womb. They said this in front of them, as if Emer was not even bright enough to understand the language. She obliged them by blinking at such comments. Not scowling, but not smiling either. She didn't smile the way her sister did. She got less of that inclination in the womb as well.

Emer, her ear pressed against damp wool, could hear her mother's heart beating, quick and rushing, not from the walk—their mother walked up hills all day—but from some excitement. Her heart was hammering with this thrill and every few minutes it skipped, and Emer recognized this as something she had felt before in herself, this skip that was like a little interruption of dread.

They crested the last hill and the ocean appeared in the distance;

she couldn't see how close it was because of the sheer drop that was the cliffs.

She meant for them to go over it. Emer knew this. Heard it like a short, brutal sentence through her mother's back, though it was not said aloud.

Rose struggled to get her hand free. "Let me go, Mammy," she said, but all Emer could hear was the tone of it, words blurred by wind. Her mother's voice, booming inside her chest, was clear.

"We're almost there."

Rose had given up walking and was trying to pull her mother back. Their mother leaned over to lift her, but Rose was writhing, slippery, impossible to catch, like a fish leaping about on a boat. They moved closer and closer to the ground in this struggle and finally their mother lay right down on top of her, upending Emer, pinning Rose down under bosom and belly. Rose began to cry.

"It'll be done soon," their mother said, and the last word was swallowed with a sharp inhalation of breath. It was the same musical gasp all the islanders used, to indicate agreement or horror or finality, much like the way her mother's heart skipped, a pause you could get lost within.

Emer could see the cliff edge from her perch on top of them both, how it looked just like any swath of thick grass, how deceiving it was, you could put your foot forward sure there would be something beneath it and fall straight into rock and water and wind. The birds would sweep away from you, no help whatsoever, they would barely look as you fell right through. That was where they were headed, over that edge, and Rose, crying, raging, pinned to the ground, knew it now.

"I won't, Mammy!" she screamed from underneath her mother's soft weight. "I won't allow it! I won't! Emer!" Her mother tried to muffle her voice with pressing hands; when that didn't work, she put her mouth on Rose's in a crushing kiss, like she could swallow the noise. It had no effect. "I won't go, Mammy, I won't." It sounded like her throat was ripping on each *won't*, like such determination would permanently scar her voice.

"It will be done soon," their mother said again, but the assertion was missing. Emer could tell that her mother thought it sounded wrong now, this phrase, when it had sounded almost reasonable a moment ago. "Please," she said instead, and Emer heard it through her chest like wind. "Please, Rose."

That's when Rose spat in her face. Their mother rolled off her in shock, and Emer, jostled and dizzy, expected her mother to strike. She had seen it before, the rough red hand rushing at her sister's lovely cheek.

Rose was holding a knife. She'd taken it from the pocket of her mother's apron, the small, wood-handled paring knife that all the island women kept near, given to them as girls, their age revealed in the wear of the blade. Their mother's blade was not as worn as her face; she was only twenty-three years old.

"You'll leave us, so," Rose said, breathing heavily from the effort of screaming. "You'll leave my sister."

That was when their mother began to cry, pressing her face to the wet ground, keening with the same raw wail as the day she buried an empty coffin. Rose watched her with a look of superior disgust.

Emer was whispering, so softly it sounded like no more than her breath. Whispering encouragement, but not for her sister.

She turned her head, her damp hair catching in the fibers of her mother's back, and saw the clochán, a beehive of stone with one small opening. The ruins of Saint Brigid's abbey were all over their island, and the children liked to play in them. Emer had never seen this one, completely intact, perched on the edge of the cliff like an offering.

Emer saw a hand. A hand coming out, not from the clochán but the air. It pried its way from nothingness and hovered there, wriggling its joints as if shaking off sleep. Then it pinched its fingers and pulled the scene of wind and grass and gray sky aside, like a veil. A curtain that looked exactly like the world. The hand was attached to a woman, who ducked and stepped through the opening she had rent in the sky. She was dressed all in white, robes of fabric whipping in the wind like untethered sails. Her hair was as orange as flames leaping above her head. She reminded Emer of the stained glass window in their little church, which portrayed the rising soul of Saint Brigid. The woman looked right at Emer and smiled, and Emer knew she was not a saint. Her teeth were too sharp. A saint wouldn't smile like that, Emer thought, when it was quite clear she knew exactly what Emer was thinking. A saint would have come to help Rose, not stood there grinning wickedly in destructive collusion with Emer. In her other hand she was clutching some sort of fabric or pouch, blue as a jewel, and she held it toward Emer like a gift.

She didn't point the woman out to Rose or to her mother. She didn't want to be told, as she was quite sure she would be, that only the clochán was actually there.

She closed her eyes, counted to three and turned back again. The woman was gone. All that was left was the beehive hut and the wind and the knowledge that everything she saw could be as thin as that veil.

They sat by the cliff's edge, sliced by rain and wind, Rose holding tight to her mother's trembling hand, kinder now, now that she had won, the knife hidden in the pocket of her small dress, ready to help. Emer was still strapped to her back, her burning eyes closed, her whispering, which was fierce and fast only moments ago, gone, as if her little voice was the only part of them that managed to throw itself over that edge. She didn't know if anyone, other than that woman, heard her during the last moments. For while her sister screamed and saved them, Emer had been murmuring encouragement into the warmth of her mother's neck, "Go on," she had whispered. "Go on, go on."

For a long time, Emer would think this day was the beginning, that it defined her, that she alone had inherited her mother's pervasive, bitter despair. That Rose would be the fighter and Emer would give up, let the worst of it, the strongest things, pull her over, and it would be like this time and time again, so surely they would grow to depend on it and design their lives to fit inside. Emer would see things her sister never could, but they wouldn't save her. They would only mortar her more immutably in herself.

Even after she had Niall, which banished forever the option of merciful cliffs, she would refuse to forget how she let herself be pulled toward a death of wind and rock and sea, not from giving up so much as to see what would happen if she let go.

AFTER MASS ON SUNDAY, Rose sends Austin to the mainland and he comes back with Emer's husband. After nearly a week of drinking in town, sleeping it off in fields when the pubs were closed, Patch needs Austin to help him walk up to the house. Emer stands outside her doorway, ready to collect him, and sees the fiery-haired shadow of Brigid above on the green road, dog at her heels, looking down on Emer's embarrassment. Emer almost raises her hand in greeting, but clenches it in her apron pocket instead and turns her eyes to her fetching brother-in-law and his foul-smelling failure of a brother.

Patch avoids her gaze, but she can see he is sober enough, just too knackered to walk on his own. Austin brings him into the house, sits him down on the hearth bed and ruffles the dark head of Niall on his way out. He doesn't look at Emer either.

"Hello, Da," Niall says, out of obligation, but his eyes go to his mother, gauging her mood. She manages a smile for him, and a wink, and gestures that he take the pig, sleeping by the fire, outside before Patch gets his bearings enough to notice it.

She heats water and draws him a bath. Patch undresses behind the curtain and drops his clothes to the stone floor. She scoops them up, turning her head and trying not to gag at the smell. She takes them outside and scrubs at them angrily in the washbasin, watching Niall run around giddily with the pig. Once the foul chunks and smears and a tinge of cosmetics have been washed away, she hangs it all on the clothesline. She wants to stay outside long enough that she doesn't risk seeing him in the bath. She does the milking, since evening is coming on, though the sun is still high in the sky. Mass today had been full of questions about the Yank, and since Emer was the only woman who had spent any time with her, she had gotten a lot of attention. Away from her island, Emer is a bit easier to talk to, as long as they stay away from her hands. She is always sorry to row back home.

When she finally goes in again, Patch has finished, and put on his spare trousers and flannel shirt, combed his long hair, the leached color of dried turf, and shaved the week's worth of dirty whiskers from his neck and face. He sits at the table, avoiding her eyes, holding on to a mug of tea tightly to disguise the tremor of his hands. He looks young enough, still. Emer has a flash back to a less ruined version of his face and their first awkward, dogged kiss. She hasn't kissed him, or anyone, unless you count the small willing mouth of her son, in five years.

"Will you have a bite?" Emer says roughly and Patch nods, so she slices some cold chicken and heats it up with the leftover spuds, adding a dollop of butter and pinch of sea salt. When she puts the fire-warmed bowl in front of him, he leans away to avoid an accidental brush with her hands.

"*Go raibh maith agat*," he says, *Thank you*, his voice rusty from little use. As she turns away, he adds, so softly she almost doesn't hear him, "*Logh dom.*" Forgive me.

"You're all right," Emer says, with a smidgen less vehemence than her normal tone.

Emer is not fond of her husband. He is a daily reminder that she plays second fiddle to Rose, married to the better brother. She resents his failure to follow through on the few promises he has made. But this is not, she knows, entirely his fault. He has never fully recovered from the time when he was still willing to put his hands on her and be touched by her in return. The few times her husband entered her was enough to turn him off the whole business, even though she tried, for a while, to touch him in other ways.

Every person on the island, except Rose and Niall, stays away from Emer's hands. Even strangers can sense something in her, beyond the scowl and the plainness, that makes them shy away. As if standing too close to Emer is like choosing to grasp the hand of a fairy and be pulled into the dark, boggy, merciless ground.

EMER NEVER FORGOT THAT hand. As a girl, she looked for it in all the places on the island where children were forbidden—the fields where corncrakes nested, the green road that rose past Old Desmond's house, a cluster of ancient piled rocks by the cliffside. In any of these places, they could be stolen, snatched away, a husk of a child left in their place. They would live in an eternal world of gluttony, lust and dancing, and they would never see their families again.

Emer went to all the forbidden spots, looking for that woman, the curtain to another world. She wanted to fall into her clutches, be stolen away. Lose herself. Like the stories of women and children who fell under the world and refused to return, leaving a fairy changeling in their place.

The cave that hid Saint Brigid's holy well also harbored a shelf carved into the walls of the cliff that held one heavy rock—*an clocha breacha*, the cursing stone—left by the fairies and linked to tales of murder and revenge. Emer went there, but refrained from actually touching the stone. She didn't want to accidentally kill herself in the process of being saved.

It was two years before the hand came back for her, in the bog. It was turf-cutting time and the whole island was at work, children and women outnumbering the men, who had either drowned or left the island in search of employment. At seven, Emer and Rose ran the household. Their mother had crawled into her grief and would not budge. If she could not die, she refused to live either. She left the house only for Mass.

Emer was slicing the earth into floppy dark logs and laying them in rows to dry. When the smallest hand imaginable came poking out of the bog wall—a hand the size of a newborn's but with long delicate nails iridescent as oyster shells—and handed her a knife, Emer didn't scream a warning as a sensible child would have, but took the knife eagerly, a little disappointed when it made the hand sink away.

She used the knife, with an engraved silver handle much finer than any she'd ever seen, to slice away the turf, and the amount she cut was much more than what she was able to do before. Only Rose noticed her sister's sudden fervor for the chore and the expectant flush on her normally pallid cheeks.

Later, when the hand came back and Emer set down her knife to hold and caress and tickle it, Rose snuck up behind her, picked up the blade and lopped the fairy hand off with one swipe. There was a squeal of angry horror that only Emer could hear, and the stump of wrist, clean as a sliced turnip, no blood or flesh or anything so messily human, pulled back and closed itself off in the earth. The little hand rolled to rest at Emer's bog-stained feet and shriveled upon itself, curling and shrinking and turning whitish green, until it resembled nothing but a loose clump of lichen. When Emer tried to lift it, it crumbled in her fingers and left a fine green-gray dust on her apron.

"What did you do that for, Rose?" she cried and stood up to face her sister, stomping her feet like a toddler in a tantrum. Later, in the loft bed they shared at home, Rose would apologize, spooning herself into Emer's rigid back, and whisper how she would never, ever let her be stolen away. But in the moment, in the sun-warmed bog, a fairy blade glinting in her hand, Rose said, "Don't be a fool," and walked away.

She didn't even want to know what the knife could do. She marched straight up the cliffs and tossed it over, scattering a flock of birds from where they'd been hovering within the wind of the sharp cliff's sides. Emer was sure that Rose, who had no idea what it was like to desire something else, to *be* something else, even if it was deformed and threatening, had ruined any chance of her being invited under the ground again.

THE BEES TRIED NEXT, when she was nine. In a high back field that belonged to their uncle Aidan stood a tree stump left from another time, when the island was covered in enormous oak trees, before they were cut down, burned and ultimately swallowed into the bog. The stump was so wide around that two children couldn't circle it, five feet tall, a forest of moss and purple thistle on top, and deep inside the hollow base lived a writhing colony of honeybees. Their auntie Orla used turf to smoke them into a trance, and gave tiny jars of honey as Christmas presents. The honey was a luxury, and never offered to children unless they were ill, when a dollop was set on their tongue to cure a swollen throat or cough. Children on the island longed for sickness so they could be given a taste of that honey.

Only Rose and Emer knew what it was like to gorge themselves on it. Not even their auntie Orla had ever swallowed more than a judicious teaspoonful. Emer let it dribble from her thickly covered fingers into her sister's waiting mouth.

Emer could lull the bees more effectively than the sweetest turf smoke. Rose would stay back, lying in the spongy grass, while Emer approached the log, the bees growing quieter the closer she got, the hum subsiding as they dropped off to sleep. She would dip a jug into the opening—dark with crowded, furry bodies—picking off the small corpses that had sacrificed themselves to the sticky sides. The honey was amber brown and flecked with bits of comb, lost bee legs and ancient chips of bark that stuck like chips in their teeth. It tasted like the scent of wildflowers and was thick enough to chew. They scooped it into each other's mouths, giggled and sighed and lay down, because they could barely stand up with such sweetness coursing through them. It was dishonest and gluttonous and a little bit lustful, all things they'd been raised to avoid and confess as sin, and, to Emer's surprise, Rose didn't call on Saint Brigid for help to resist it. Emer loved what the honey did to her sister, normally so sharply tuned to what was safe and what was right. Rose didn't hear the threat, as tangible as the magic blade of that knife, buzzing underneath.

Emer felt the difference one day as she leaned in, as if the bees were only feigning sleep, as if every fuzzy body were just closing its eyes and waiting for the cry of Now! before they came awake and snatched her.

What Rose saw was this: her sister reaching in and being pulled, yanked with a force that seemed merciless, a gulping swallow that left no regret about what it might leave behind. She leaned into a space only large enough to fit her head and shoulders and disappeared as if she were stepping off a cliff. The bees rose in a swarm of angry victory, and Rose ran screaming and crying over the fields for help.

All Emer saw was the little hand. The one her sister had sliced, grown back, slightly smaller, like the severed arm of a starfish. A little hand coming out of the honey, ready to pull her away. She remembered nothing after that moment of decision, where she chose the cruel promise of that hand, and as she did so, felt the bees wake up, or rise from pretend slumber, and cheer callously as she was yanked under the world.

She wasn't gone for seven days, or seven years, like the stories told. She wasn't even gone for an hour. By the time Rose's hysterical crying was deciphered and the women ran up the fields, aprons whipping up at them, their hair wild with maternal ferocity, Emer had been spat back up again. She lay on the rough grass, her throat puffed up to the width of her face, her eyelids ballooned shut, her mouth a smear of bruises. Bees fell out of her nose and mouth and she coughed and retched and tried to answer the worried questions of the women who lifted her. They carried her back home, bees shedding behind like husks of dead skin. She was wrapped in flannel soaked with holy water, and the men rowed the doctor over from the mainland when it was clear that her breathing, the way it kept catching, then stopping, then starting again, was not quite right.

The doctor calmed her wheeze and removed hundreds of stingers, properly, so no more poison was poured into her. He wasn't there when the infection began in her left eye, and by the time he returned and discovered it, despite a visit to Saint Brigid's healing well, it was already too late. She was taken to the hospital on the mainland, where a surgeon removed her ruined eyeball.

When Emer came home from the hospital, the place where her left eye had been sewn tightly shut, she tried to see if she'd been changed in some other way. But all that remained from being pulled under the world was a thick, buzzing band of anxiety that gripped her neck, a swarming that would follow her into adult life. It was as if, instead of stealing her, the beings under the ground had taken a good long look, flipped her over, then decided, as the human world had, that she wasn't much to fuss about, and sent her back. She was not a changeling after all, but simply Emer, dipped into a pool of bees and found not sweet enough to keep. Expelled, rejected by the very world she so longed to abduct her. She would never be invited again. All that would stay of her trip below was the brown circle of leather held over the memory of her eye, and the power to make others feel as ugly as she did. The good people had left some fire in her hands, but it did nothing to warm her.

ALL THESE YEARS AFTER her trip beneath the world, darkness still rises up in Emer like water filling to the top of a well. It swells up from deep inside her, forming a thick, immovable plug that settles in the hollow of skin below her throat. Every time she looks in the mirror she expects to see it there, an ancient, gnarled fist waiting for the chosen moment to unfurl. People's faces make it rise, and bright sunshine, a bee snarling inside the cup of a flower, that unbearable millisecond between when she calls her son's name and he answers her. Life threatens daily to close her throat.

She puts it into people. She folds their hands inside her own and presses and something bites into their souls. Her hand can reach into them, find where there is a doubt or a guilt or a fear, a small hole in their fabric, and catch it, pull and widen it, until someone who was feeling just fine about their day or their life or their choices will be almost doubled over with a hopelessness, a yawning weight that makes them question their former happiness. It only lasts a few minutes, but afterward, for days, or weeks, they will shudder at the memory of that place underneath who they believe they are. Women who have birthed children liken it to labor, a contraction of pain in the mind that is only bearable in retrospect, when it is all over. People like Emer's mother find the feeling familiar, and assume it comes from their own grief-laden hearts. Emer drags them under the water and pulls them back up just when they've forgotten how to breathe. It doesn't make her feel any better, but it does, while she grips them, make her feel less alone.

It doesn't work on Rose. Emer tried for years, when their bodies developed, (Rose's prettily and Emer's in an embarrassing, odorous, hairy way) when Rose was praised in school, or noticed by a boy, or laughed with other girls in a way that made Emer suspect it was at her expense.

Emer despises her sister. She hates Rose for loving her. "She's not as bad as all that," Rose will say, when others criticize her. Emer can see that Rose will never really see her, will never believe the worst, will stand beside her whether she feeds her stolen honey or tries to strike at her with the fire of her hands. Emer knows this is some sort of blessing, unless of course it is a curse, that this person who will always love her is the one who knows her least of all.

Niall is the only true antidote. Only with her child are her hands able to soothe rather than repel. The fairies she once invited terrify her now. She has gone from a girl begging to be stolen by something dark and exciting to a mother who must guard her child. All she has wanted for years is to leave the island and the good people far behind.

But then the Yank resisted her hands. Unlike Rose, who just can't be penetrated, or Niall, who diffuses it, something came back from Brigid's hand, a response that burned Emer's darkness away like dried moss tossed on a turf fire. There was strength in there, alongside the need. Brigid is damaged, but not easily harmed.

The Yank, true to her mother's gloomy predictions, has already changed things. Now Emer is thinking less about fairies and evacuations than she is about what might happen if Brigid's hand touches her again.

CHAPTER 4

Nesting

May 1959

It's not until Brigid decides to fix the house up that she notices how much is missing. She has been drinking tea out of the same cracked mug, eating off her only plate—thick pottery with a sponged pattern of red, bell-shaped flowers. She often licks the one fork and knife clean instead of bothering to wash them. The sheet on her bed is worn thin and stained with a man-sized yellow sweat blotch; she has been using her rolled-up fisherman's sweater as a pillow. At first she assumed this was the austerity of her bachelor uncle, but then she wonders. According to Malachy, this house has raised generations stretching back centuries. It must have sheltered women and children and all the necessary accessories that go along with them. What happened to it all?

In the narrow, catch-all drawer of the kitchen press, she finds various treasures: a bankbook, a Mass card with the names of what she assumes are her grandparents, various handwritten receipts for the purchase and sale of sheep and wool, a fountain pen and a bottle of clotted ink. A brown envelope with a neat stack of birth certificates, school reports, confirmation and communion cards. A white envelope with an American stamp on it, a short letter written in careful schoolgirl's cursive.

Dear Desi,

I made it to America. I live in Maine now, in the northeast, where it snows in the winter and some trees lose their leaves and others don't and are like dark green giants that walk over the land. My village is by the ocean and the men here trap lobsters and catch herring just like they do at home. When I first arrived I lived in a boardinghouse for girls, but now I have a husband. He is a light-keeper and we will be moving to his first posting this spring.

I miss the fuchsia and the mountains, the sheep, even the corncrake. It makes me sad to think I will never see them, or you, again. To think of you alone in that house now, all of us gone. I wish you would consider emigrating, yourself.

I won't be able to post much from the lighthouse, as it's very remote, but I will write you often and send them all together in large parcels when I can. I hope you can find someone to read them to you.

I have a baby girl. I named her Brigid. She looks how I imagine Mam must have looked, with furious ginger hair. She is a great comfort to me.

Your loving sister,
Nuala

After reading this letter, Brigid looks all over the house for more, but that is all. She goes back to bed in the middle of the day, the worried dog pressed to her aching middle, and cries for her mother with a freedom that seems childlike, except she never allowed herself to cry that way as a child.

"MOST OF IT WAS stolen, I suspect," Emer says when Brigid invites her in for tea and asks about the lack of necessities. She opens Brigid's press and finds it bare of anything but long, spindly-legged spiders and their cotton candy webs. "People help themselves when a house is abandoned." Brigid has a brief image of shawl-laden women flapping down on the place like vultures. "I can ask around, bring some of it back."

"That's all right," Brigid says. She should have guessed. Her mother told her about stealing from the neighbors. Running around the island in the dark, ransacking abandoned houses for tea leaves and sugar. They were that poor.

"Your mother was the youngest?" Emer asks.

"I don't know," Brigid says.

"The one who went to America on her own?"

"Yes," Brigid says. Though her mother didn't tell her directly, she believes something ugly and unforgivable occurred here. Something that should have made Brigid wary of crossing that water at all.

"Did she tell you what it was like?" Emer asks. Brigid cannot meet Emer's eye.

"She told me fairy stories."

Emer makes a gasping sound in her throat and for an instant, Brigid is in a dark, dirty kitchen with her mother. It is the same noise, the noise she thought was her mother's own: a gasp of surprise and agreement but also despair, humor superimposed onto dread. Emer's phrasing, her accent, the hard glint of her eyes, all of it brings her mother back like a slap to the face.

"You'd have to look long to find love in this house," Emer says. "Ten children, and their father drank, and hit them more than was prudent. The mother died in childbirth. The children were sent to the orphanage on the mainland, all of them caught fever and never left. Desmond was the eldest, he stayed to care for the old man and the baby, your mother. She was the only one to get away."

She wonders if that is all that Emer really knows. It's a hard story, but it's only the surface. Nothing about what her mother could do. Brigid had worried that people would know, and she would be driven away. But apparently it has just become a simple story of poverty, and the failings of the human world.

Brigid looks at Emer now, who shifts a bit in her chair.

"Have I shocked you? It was a hard place. Still is. It's not the saint's paradise they write about. She left us to our own defenses a long time ago."

"No, I'm not shocked."

"Desmond was the last of them. There's none of yours left here."

No family, no crockery, the furniture pulled apart and the place ransacked. Barely a chair left behind. The memories of whatever happened here smothered like the fires they bury at night.

"Everyone's wanting to know why you've come," Niall says to Brigid. Emer looks daggers at him.

"You're not the only ones who can keep secrets," Brigid says, winking. He beams, but Emer narrows her one eye in warning.

EMER RETURNS SOMETHING TO her every day. Plates, bowls and mugs in the same spongeware pattern, three caned chairs and a bedside table, thick cotton sheets bleached white by the sun, mismatched cutlery, a washboard, cast-iron pans. Delicate, cracked lace doilies far fussier than Brigid would ever use. An apron like all the island women wear, a smock she must pull over her head and fasten at both sides of her waist. Emer always carries a small knife in the front pocket of this apron. Brigid finds a similar knife in the deep back of Desmond's drawer, the wooden handle worn to the soft curves of another woman's hand, the blade narrow from generations of sharpening. She finds it useful to keep in her pocket, for cutting the wildflowers she collects on her walks, or clearing away nettles looking for the origin of a bubbling spring. She still looks for the well, but with less furious desperation. She is waiting for the right time to ask again.

She hopes the answer will be given to her, the way Niall brings her a canvas sack filled with stolen belongings, as if they are gifts.

Another week passes before she finds out about her cows. Emer has been bringing her fresh milk, and one day Austin is there, stopped on the road talking to Brigid in her doorway. Emer comes up quietly, behind him, as if she hopes she can slip by without being seen.

"Howaya keeping, Emer," Austin says, nodding. "Niall." A little wink for the child, but his eyes avoid Emer.

"Austin," Emer says, with more disdain than should be able to fit into one word. He is a handsome man, but Emer doesn't seem impressed. Niall hands Brigid the jug of milk he's been sloshing up the whole road.

"Thank you," Brigid says. "I just drank the last of it."

"What are you getting milk delivered for, when you've a cow up in that field?" Austin says. Brigid is confused, but Emer shakes her head, and glares pointedly with her one eye.

"I suspected as much," she murmurs when Austin has gone.

She walks Brigid up over the field and they speak to Michael Joe, who behaves as though she's known all along that she has cows and he's been waiting for her to collect them. She is apparently the owner of two brown cows and a calf, and Emer and Niall help her move them over to the field directly behind her house. Emer tells her to leave one cow separate for milking. Brigid hasn't milked a cow in years and finds she enjoys it, resting her forehead against the cow's thick side and pulling down the warm teats. The cow always seems grateful, she lets out a sigh when she empties her. Other than that they are blank, boring animals who seem forever to be chewing. They look at her as she approaches them, every time, as if they've never seen her before in their lives. They remind her of the island women, who still will not give her much beyond a nod, an occasional, grudging inquiry into her comfort that is not meant to be answered.

A week later she is told about her sheep. A dozen of them, grazing in the neighbor's field, mentioned casually again, by Malachy as she chats with him at the salt house where she buys fish. Again, presented to her as if they've just been babysitting until she got around to collecting them. Then there are the hens and a rooster brought up a few at a time by the men who have been minding them since her uncle died the autumn before. She vaguely remembers the solicitor mentioning livestock, but after packing up and settling her life in Portland and making the journey she had forgotten it all.

"They'd have kept them for themselves," Emer explains. "Like anything else left behind. Only they're fond of you."

And so all the things that have supposedly been stolen from her are being handed back in spades. She takes it as a good omen.

Emer brings over a churn and teaches her to make butter the consistency of ice cream that she eats with a spoon. The eggs from her hens are exquisite. The bright orange yolks cling to the brown bread like golden gravy. She rediscovers the steel-cut porridge of her childhood after a delivery from the mainland, and simmers it overnight on the fire, dolloping it with the ice cream butter and shaking a brown sugar crust on top. She loves eating by herself, no one to answer in between each delicious mouthful. On foggy days—her favorite weather because of the shroud of stillness and mystery—she cannot see the sea or the other houses and she imagines she is the only one on the island. She chews and swallows in pure silence, listening to the old, familiar longing gurgling deep inside the well of her soul. The yearning to have someone growing inside her again, so she is no longer alone.

MOST OF THE TIME, she is not alone, though she does not invite the company. She is called in on every day by grinning men offering to help rebuild her house or tend to her growing herd of livestock, and the strange fosters of Emer and her little boy. Emer is both grumpy and eager, a girl desperate for a friend who pretends she can't be bothered. She looks like a twelve-year-old tomboy: tall as a woman but thin and underdeveloped. Her face is at times pinched and angled as a furious fairy, but when she thinks only Niall is watching, it softens. She is so uncomfortable in her body it's almost painful to watch her: she will yank at her clothing and scratch as if the material, or her very skin, is a constant torture. Brigid has already seen that no one touches this girl, no one but her son. The men, who already squeeze Brigid hard enough to pinch around her waist when she says something that amuses them, never put a hand on Emer. Her one eye is a sharp, angry blue, startling, gorgeous and lonely next to its shrouded mate. Her lips are so full and dark they look bee-stung and she gnaws at them, hungry for something she's never had.

Brigid remembers girls like this, so lonely, so miserably self-conscious they can't see that they're not as hideous as they imagine. She always had a weakness for those girls.

Emer finds a way to see Brigid daily, bringing her stolen goods or following her on a walk, her manner slightly put out, as though Brigid needs her company and she will oblige, when really, Brigid can tell, it is Emer who needs someone. The boy is lovely, an antidote to his mother's shadowed disposition, flitting about her like a firefly in the darkness. But he lives in another world. She's heard him talking to it. It is not necessary for him to seek out company. He could take or leave all of them, she gets the impression, aside from his mother. He is always coming back to her, to touch her hand, her skirt, to press his face to her side. Like he gains some comfort, some grounding from the contact. They whisper in Irish to each other, thinking Brigid won't understand them. *A chuisle mo chroí*. You are the pulse of my heart. It is an endearment, Brigid remembers with a chill, meant for lovers.

One day as she walks the cliffs she meets Emer and Niall and asks them about the stone huts, ten of them in varying stages of decay, the intact ones shaped like beehives, that sit empty and resolute, facing the onslaught of the open sea.

"Saint Brigid built them," Emer says in her quick, unfriendly voice. "For her postulants. She was the only woman ever ordained a bishop, because she rattled the priest by making fire come out of her hair. Usually it was only men who were given monasteries."

Niall, no longer afraid of the dog, is leaping around her, trying to get Rua to run with him and his pig. Rua, clearly unused to such play, sits next to Brigid, leaning against her leg, waiting for their walk to resume.

Emer tells Brigid about the abbey, how each clochán housed two women, each nun had an *anam cara*, a soul friend, who was their partner in everything. They copied the Gospels over and over in Latin and Irish, then illustrated them like the Book of Kells. They worked the land together, tended the animals, prayed together, slept on one pallet to absorb each other's heat. The women chose their partners and had a ceremony to celebrate the commitment. They were meant to spend their entire lives together.

"Like a marriage," Brigid mutters.

"Like all nuns, they were meant to be brides of Christ. But he wasn't much help with the cattle."

Brigid wonders if Emer even knows she can be funny.

"Pretty racy," Brigid says. "For nuns."

Emer blushes, glancing over at Niall.

"A lot of them came here for cures," Emer says. "Brigid was said to have healing in her hands."

"So I've heard," Brigid says. Emer blushes, hard.

"Sure it's all nonsense," Emer scoffs. "People still come here, like yourself, looking for holy remnants, looking for miracles. There's no miracles on this island that I've ever seen. Not Christian ones, anyway."

She's not a very good liar, Emer. She can't look at Brigid as she says this, and her voice is much more animated than she ever allows. Plus her son's open mouth is a dead giveaway.

"People believe a lot of things if they need to," Brigid says. Emer shrugs, opens her mouth to say more, then decides against it.

Instead she announces that it's time she and Niall were after the sheep, and they leave Brigid and her dog alone by the cliff's edge.

Brigid runs her hand over the low crown of a beehive hut. The clocháns are meticulously round, the stones angled gradually to form the roof, no mortar visible to hold them together. No windows, just a small arch to crawl inside. When Emer and Niall have disappeared down the hill, she sits inside the one still fully intact, which is thick-walled and perfect shelter from the abusive wind of the west side of the island. Rua crawls in after her, leaning warmth into her side. She isn't crying as much anymore, and her nightmares have eased. She tries not to beg, she tries very hard to be serene, to sit in the silence after a question waiting for an answer. The sea and wind sound far away and harmless inside this mound. Little caves of inspiration. Wombs of penance. She imagines small women inside, with only quills and pots of ink and piles of vellum, ripe and naked under brown cloaks, sure of their love and wanting for nothing.

IN THE SHED BEHIND her house, which Malachy has restocked with grain for the hens, the milking pails and stool, and various tools she will need to start a garden, she finds a collection of skulls. They are lined up in descending order of size—sheep, dog, rabbit, vole—on a shelf within the thick-layered stone wall. Behind the skulls, a pile of sun-bleached bones. She wonders if this was a child's collection Desmond couldn't part with or if that grown, lonely man wandered the island looking for death the way she looks for a miracle.

In the damp corner of the shed is a dirty tarp she pulls at, thinking it will be a temporary covering until the men can patch her roof. Underneath it she finds a diligently wrapped parcel, another waterproof tarp, then oilcloth, then softer, cleaner flannel, each layer closer to the object that waits underneath.

A cradle. Hand carved from driftwood soft and weathered by salt and wind, a pattern of limpet shells affixed around the edges and across the curved head. The bottom is carved like the hull of a boat, and it is darker there, water stained, as if it has spent time at sea. Brigid's mother once told her that this was how she got her to sleep as a baby, by laying her in the rowboat and tying it to the dock with a rope long enough to let it sway in the dark water. It was the way, she had said, that all babies in her family had been lulled, with the music of the sea as their lullaby.

Brigid brings the cradle inside and puts it next to her bed, and when she wakes in the night she reaches down to run her fingertips over the mountain range of limpet shells, like crenellations on the fortress of a royal child. She rocks it a little before she turns over, puts her arm around the warm dog and falls back to sleep.

It was wrapped so meticulously, hidden in that shed, as though someone had stored it with the intention that Brigid find it instead of the thieving neighbors. As if her uncle had known that it was the one thing in the house she might actually need.

CHAPTER 5

The Lightkeeper's Wife

1927–1933

There was a time, before it all went cross-eyed, that Brigid's mother was a soft pillow of flesh and a lilting voice that climbed into bed with her, pulled the covers over their heads and told fairy stories. She told them in Irish. It was a secret language, hardly anyone spoke it anymore, her mother said, not even in Ireland. Her stories were about heartless creatures who stole babies and lonely women for their own amusement. For Brigid, the more terrifying the story, the better. She liked a story that made her forget to breathe in the middle of it.

One of her favorites was about a mother who was stolen.

> *A woman was passing a fairy ring and stopped to listen*
> *to the music. She was pulled under the ground and an*
> *identical version of her, a changeling, was left in her place.*
> *Only her children could tell it wasn't her, and no one*
> *believed them.*
> *The new mother played cruel tricks on the children,*
> *starved them of their dinners, pinched them black-and-*
> *blue, laughed like a braying donkey when they cried that*

they missed her. The father preferred the fairy wife to the old one, whom he had often struck when he'd been drinking. This new wife spoiled him, giggled and flirted, kissed him shamelessly in the middle of the field, not caring who might see. It wasn't long before the mother was smugly round with a new baby.

But when a baby girl was born, the mother died. They lived on a remote island, far from any doctor or priest, and complications arose. The fairy may have just decided to abandon them, having had her fill of human life, but refused to return their real mother at the end.

The children did not grieve her; as far as they were concerned, their mother had been dead for over a year. But the father raged over the loss. He got viciously drunk and tried to drown the baby in the well. No matter how long he held it under, the baby just seemed to wait, her eyes wide open and shining up from the dark water, holding on to breath for as long as was needed, refusing to die.

The father ended up drowning himself, falling off the cliff and being battered against the rocks, though no one was sure if he took his own life out of grief and guilt or sloppy stupidity. The children were sent to the orphanage on the mainland. Only the oldest boy stayed; he was twelve and able to tend the farm. He wouldn't allow them to take the baby. He fed her milk from the cow and wore her tied to his chest with an old woolen shawl of his mother's.

She grew into a girl, half-fairy, half-human, who had the power to heal in her hands. She eased the pain of childbirth, lifted the fevers of children expected to die. Some of the islanders knew that she was the child of a changeling, others believed her power came from the holy well her father tried to drown her in. It was the same well the nuns had once used, saving the cauls of children born with the sac intact, filling them with holy water, to heal the barren wombs of women. No one cared much where it came from, pagan or Christian, as long as it was helping them.

When the girl was fourteen, there was a baby she could not save. She put her hands on it, but it had already died before it came into the world. The islanders who had called her a saint when she could help, called her a devil when she couldn't. They planned to punish her in the old ways, to burn her and see if she could heal herself. She was gone before they could try.

Her brother never revealed how she got away, no boats had come or gone on the island, she disappeared during a day when the sea raged them into seclusion. Some said she had thrown herself over the cliff, others that she had gone back under the ground to where she had come from. She was never seen, or heard from, on the island again.

"Where do you think she went?" Brigid would ask her mother breathlessly, whenever she finished this story.

"I think she swam," her mother would whisper in their little cave under the covers. "I think she swam until she couldn't swim anymore and found herself all the way across the sea."

So many of her mother's fairy stories ended badly. Brigid liked the ones where they got away.

BRIGID'S FATHER WAS A lighthouse keeper. The lighthouse was on an island, ten miles off the coast of Maine, two acres of layered gray rock, one side shorn down so steep it looked like it had been broken by something in anger. Stalwart pine trees grew between the cracks to form a miniature forest. On one corner perched the tower, painted white and splattered with yellow lichen, and set behind it, a white brick building with a red roof, two rooms meant for one lonely man. Instead it sheltered Brigid's small, painful family, three people shaped by isolation, shadowed between the dark sea and a constant, revolving warning of light.

Brigid and her mother were not supposed to be there. Such a light-house would normally be run on shifts, by men who returned to their families on the mainland for weeks at a time. But it was such an un-popular posting that when her father offered to take it on full time, so he could devote every spare minute to his painting, a hermit artist on an island out at sea, the state was eager to give it away. He was fed and supplied by boat, paid a salary he didn't spend, and left alone. Brigid was told never to show herself to the fishermen who passed by and greeted her father with three pulls of their bell.

"Am I a secret?" she asked him.

"A treasure." He winked.

Her father called her his deck hand, showed her how to polish the individual prisms of the Fresnel lens, layered together in a bee-hive of glass the size of a child, the light they were there to keep. A history of the lens was kept in a leather-bound book, each prism was numbered, every chip or discoloration recorded. There were multi-ple notebooks involved in his job, for logging boats, radio trans-missions, tides and weather. Brigid loved to climb up the perilous wrought-iron spiral of stairs, her father's enormous shoulders just behind her to break her fall. From the top of the tower you could see for miles, and the reflection of sea and sky and the angles of hon-eyed light trapped in the amber glass lens made Brigid feel, when they were up there, like they had climbed into another world. He painted her like this, a girl looking over the sea, her hair the same color as amber sunlight cupped in the deepest crevice of the lens.

By the time she was seven, she could tie any knot her father asked for, trim the wick with precision, knew the colors of his oil paints better than any art student he'd had. She could bait and set back a string of lobster traps, though he hauled them for her, since she was small enough to be crushed if they fell in the boat. She knew that a lobster was big enough to keep without the brass gauge, and could spot an egger before they opened the parlor.

"Always throw the mothers back," her father said. He taught her to punch their tails with the sharp end of the gauge, so the next lobsterman would recognize the breeders. "The ocean needs them more than we do."

These were her parents, Silas and Nuala: peculiar, intense, zealous. Their love was not consistent, it was as mercurial and varied as the color of the sea. It depended on the angle, which portion of the glass you looked through, whether they were tender or severe. They took turns with her, because when the two of them were in the same room, she, and everything else, tended to fade away.

It was like they set the room on fire. They were both struck by the same fever that flushed their cheeks and glazed their eyes. They touched whenever they could, her father often grabbed her mother in the middle of some chore, to kiss her neck, press her against the counter with a teasing growl. He would stand in the doorway to tell her he had fish for dinner, and she wouldn't appear to listen, instead she would reach out and put a hand on his forearm, as if she'd never seen it before. He would look at her hand, and lose his words. They closed themselves in the bedroom in the middle of the day, or her mother padded barefoot out to the lighthouse at night, and Brigid grew up with the sounds that accompanied these sessions; they were as familiar as the moaning of the wind and the sea.

They loved each other too much, Brigid thought, when she was old enough to analyze it. They couldn't see through the fog of it. It possessed them. "A chuisle," their mother often whispered to him, and she would hold his hand so his rough palm cupped her jaw and the soft spot at her neck. *You are my pulse.* They were in each other's veins.

SHE BEGAN TO HEAR something other than love at night, voices rising in pitch and intensity, like a harmless wind escalating to a concerning one. A thump that didn't belong, a clatter, a shocked silence, a sound that could have been a cry. She stood by the door, feet bare, nightgown billowing from the draft that came in underneath. The lines of light around the door edges encircled her, framing her inside a dark rectangle, her hand on the cold brass doorknob, gripping but not turning it. In the bedroom, within that illuminated rectangle, she was still safe, and what was happening outside it might not have been real. She would stand until her hand on the knob had fallen asleep, the fingers full of stabbing glass pins, then she would let go and get back into bed and will herself to sleep beneath the dark weight of the covers.

There would be detritus to further confuse her in the morning: a green bottle with a silver ship on the label, her father's evening drink, so potent it made Brigid's eyes water if she got too close to the open glass, half-full the night before, would be empty and lying sideways on the counter. Shards of shattered glass hastily gathered in the dustpan but not emptied into the wastebasket. Once, what appeared to be a small, jagged bone lying on the porcelain drain, which on closer inspection she decided was a tooth. Her mother too ill to get out of bed, something wrong with her that couldn't be named.

Blood, sometimes. On a dishtowel, a handkerchief. A dark painting of it on the seat of the outhouse. She asked her father only once, when her mother didn't emerge for three days and he brought her tea and took away armloads of darkened sheets to be scrubbed in boiled seawater. Some rags he didn't bother soaking but fed directly into the cast-iron stove.

"What's wrong with Mam?"

"She'll be all right," he said, but he wouldn't look at her.

Something had fallen out of her, Brigid thought. Something she had wanted to keep inside. Like the tooth, only worse. She didn't know what it was. She didn't want to know.

Once she heard her mother screaming, accusing him, weeping about a baby. There had never been a baby. She imagined this was how babies were made: by drinking fire and bleeding and lying in your bedroom until a new, dark being was formed out of it all. But a baby never came.

She helped her mother after she emerged from these bedroom sessions, though she much preferred her father's chores. Her mother showed her how to make dense boulders of brown bread. No matter how many times Brigid did it she could never remember the steps involved and could not make bread herself, she forgot key ingredients, the baking soda, the salt, or let the whole thing burn black in the stove. She knew her father's paint hues and the chips on the lens prisms by heart, but couldn't cook a simple meal. "Your memory is choosy enough," her mother said. She wasn't angry, she merely sighed and gave her something less complicated to do.

Sometimes she thought her mother's face looked a bit lopsided, one cheek puffed out as if she was storing food in it. Or she moved too stiffly, carefully, as though trying not to spill something hidden in the walls of her back. Once, Brigid walked into the bedroom just as her mother lifted her blouse above her head, and saw a livid green and purple thing on her back that looked more like something alive than a bruise. Later that night, when she was asleep, Brigid pulled the sheet back to look at it again. Her mother's slight, spaghetti-strapped nightgown was thin enough to see through, but even in the bright moonlit room she couldn't find the mark. It was gone.

SHE WAS NINE THE first time she saw him hit her. The yelling was loud that night, insistent, as if they'd forgotten their usual attempt to hide it. Later, when she thought about what finally made her open the door, she decided it was hearing her own name, her mother called it out, like a warning. She opened it in time to see her mother's flailing arms and wild hair, see her hurl a glass and watch it shatter by her father's head on the stone wall of the chimney. See the look of angry terror behind her father's dark beard, the huge, gulping steps he took toward her, his hand, the enormous stone of his fist, driving at her face, so decisive and blunt that Brigid thought for a moment he was trying to knock something out of her, whatever invisible thing that had possessed them both. But it wasn't that. It was merely this, her tender, powerful father hauling his arm back and punching her mother, on purpose, in the mouth. The crack it made, the sound of the bones in his hand meeting the flesh of her face, was a shameful sound, something private, that she should not have been allowed to hear.

"Fuck," he yelled, livid, guilty, frightened, like the time he dislodged three prisms from the lens and they shattered and he had to radio to ask for their expensive replacements. Furious at his own careless stupidity. As if he meant to caress her and misjudged the pressure of his hand. Then he saw Brigid, standing in the dark doorway. His shoulders dropped even lower, he could not meet her eyes. "Shit, shit, shit," he moaned, punching the wall this time, hard enough that Brigid heard something else crack. He left the house, tears carving thick pathways down into his beard.

Brigid padded over to her mother, who had slid down to sit against the wall, unable to move, her eyes closed, leaking tears. She squatted down and reached a hand out to the pulsing hot mess that was the lower half of her mother's face. She wanted to fix it. But her mother opened her eyes and shook her head. She let go of her own mouth to stay Brigid's hand. Her front teeth were dark and pressed in at an angle that was not right. Her lip was split so deeply it looked like a fish sliced down the middle and splayed in two.

"Don't," her mother slurred. "Leave it."

She would learn later why her mother left the bruises. She wanted to leave all the comforting to the one who was to blame.

"What's happened to Da?" Brigid whispered. He looked possessed, as if some dark beast had dragged him under the sharp rock and left behind a monster who used fists like he intended to break her mother in two.

"It's only the drink," she lisped through the blood and split flesh and fear. "It's all right."

"Oh," Brigid said. She was dumbfounded.

It made no sense. The silver ship drink that made her father glassy-eyed, heavy-lidded and sloppy also turned his fists into punishing stone?

Though Brigid had been angry at the idea that they were hiding something, once she found out what it was, she regretted ever being curious. It was no longer possible for her to go back to being the girl in the nightgown who listened to noises, but had not yet made the mistake of opening the door.

IT DIDN'T HAPPEN EVERY day. Or even every week. Months could go by where all that passed between her parents was the familiar foggy-eyed desire. Had it been constant it would have been easier to hate her father. As it was she both loved him and feared him, as though she had two fathers. Two fathers on shifts like lighthouse workers, appearing to relieve each other just at the moment the other reached a breaking point.

Her father apologized with paintings. In the lighthouse room that was his studio, there were stacks of her naked mother, lying down, looking out of the canvas with a dark, feverish happiness. After he hit her, he painted her wounds.

Brigid watched through a round, dirty glass window as her father used his brushes to heal what he had done. Eventually he put down his brushes and came over to her, he would cry and she would kiss his tears away, and that was when their bodies would come together, together in a way that Brigid through the thick dirty window couldn't fully understand, but she imagined it was something that grew between them and all they could do was hold on tightly, like they were being pulled by a current, until it let them go.

They both became something else. It was as alarming and as hopeful as if she had watched them transform into slick-skinned animals and flop into the sea.

Later, when her father was up in the tower, Brigid looked at what he had painted. He painted the bruises onto thick, ragged-edged paper he seemed to keep just for that purpose. There were heavy black folders full of renderings of wounds as they changed and healed and faded. He could capture the exact red of her blood, then the darkening to black as it crusted and healed. He painted scars with the detail of beautiful features. Just as he had a recording of every ship that passed, every barometer reading, the nightly position of the moon, every wounded prism, he had a painting of every injury he had ever given her. It was some sort of penance, the way he recorded it. Soon after he was finished apologizing, her bruises disappeared, as if his remorse was all they had been hanging around for.

BRIGID WAS TEN BY the time they found out about her hands. She was helping her father in the oil house, watching as he emptied hot oil into a drum, and a spill glugged over and grabbed him. Her father swore, clawing at his trousers, trying to rip the fabric away.

Brigid went to him, her hands reaching for the dark spot on his thigh. He tried, not gently, to avoid her and when this didn't work, to bat her away. "Nuala," he barked, her mother's name, then "you," as if he couldn't recall her name at all. Backing away from her he tripped on a toolbox and in the instant of backward sprawl he was helpless and before he could stop her it was over.

She put her hands on his thigh, spread them wide to try to cover the oil. For an instant, the pain he must have felt when it spilled racked her, but that was merely an entry, a trip over his pain into what happened next. There was a pulling sensation, heat rose up her arms and through her shoulders and into her head and then crashed down into the trunk of her body, like a wave on a rock. The oil on his thigh evaporated, the hole it ate through his trousers was still there, but the skin underneath was now tender and pink and hairless, like a sunburned child's. Either her father didn't feel the relief of pain yet, or it was merely his instinct, because he hit her. He knocked her off her feet just at the moment where the pleasure of removing the fire was at its peak. He thumped a hard hand to her chest and sent her reeling backward, where she banged the back of her head on the rough cement wall. For a while, until the opportunity occurred to do such a thing again, Brigid believed that the sickness that followed this—vomiting until nothing was left but her body heaved anyway, three days of a fever so high her parents fought openly about whether to radio the coast guard—was because her father had hit her, and not because she had healed him.

It had only ever been something she had done to herself, playing with matches in her cove by the woods, burning her fingers then drawing the burn away, the same way she played with adding twigs and shells to the fairy houses she built, an experiment of magic and nature. She pulled the burn away and it felt good and that was all she knew. She'd kept it a secret because of the feeling it brought. The loosening, building, mind-evaporating hum was something she didn't want either one of them to know about. It didn't make her ill, but if she did it too often, it did exhaust her. Her father's burn was the first real wound she had ever tried to heal.

While she was still recovering, she waited for an apology, some indication that he was grateful or full of remorse. But he never came in; it was her mother who tended to her when she was ill.

Her father came to find her in the woods when she was better. Since the time when she first saw him hit her mother, his eyes were always pointing somewhere else when he was talking to her, or unfocused, as if he was purposefully blinding himself to what was in front of him.

"Does your mother know?" Brigid shook her head. She liked to answer her father in gestures, because it forced him to flick his eyes in her direction.

"I think it best you don't tell her," he said.

"Why?" Brigid said.

"You know why," he said. Brigid shrugged again, forcing her father into eye contact. "She might think you're touched. She might want to do something with it. With you. Understand?"

"Yes," Brigid said. He was lying. Her mother knew more about these things than anyone. She told her stories of just this sort of magic. But though she felt a pull of guilt, Brigid liked having a secret with her father. Like the secret language with her mother, or the secret of the penance paintings.

Secrets meant you were loved.

FOR MONTHS AFTER SHE first healed him, her father avoided drinking from the ship bottle. He didn't want to cause an injury, Brigid thought, that his daughter might be obliged to heal. But then the violence seemed to build in him, as if there was a ceiling on the loving ways he could touch her mother, and when he reached that, he needed to do something else. He drank, he hit, he apologized.

One night she heard her name called out like a curse by her

father. As soon as Brigid came out, her father fell to his knees and started to cry.

"Help her," he said. "I went too far. Something is broken." Brigid laid her hands on her mother for the first time, but it didn't work.

The attempt came rushing back at her, like a deliberate slap in the face. Understanding, then revulsion followed. Her mother opened her eyes, challenging her to tell, but Brigid never did. She pretended to heal her mother's broken bone, but she didn't do a thing. Her mother healed herself. Nuala had the same secret inside her hands that Brigid did. Most of the time, Brigid realized, she chose not to use it. If she healed herself, her husband would have nothing to apologize for.

Brigid saw it now. Despite years of being battered, her nose broken, cheekbones and ribs cracked, wounds splayed open like mouths across her face, her mother didn't have a mark on her. She was as flawless and lovely as the young girl Silas had first painted, first captured into this violent spiral that neither of them seemed able to leave. She had healed all her scars, even as she stayed and asked for the wounds.

HER FATHER HAD ALWAYS spent his nights in the lighthouse, drinking large thermoses full of coffee, so he could continue the conversation of light between the tower and passing ships. Brigid still slept in the bed with her mother, where she had once listened to fairy stories of women stronger than any of the evils that threatened them. Her mother had less and less to tell her these days.

"Why do you let him?" Brigid said once, and her mother stiffened. "You're stronger than he is. Why do you let him hurt you? Why do we stay here?"

"You wouldn't understand."

Brigid said nothing, but her silence demanded more.

"I was a girl when he found me. I was in trouble. He saved me."

"What trouble?"

"It doesn't matter. He's a part of me. Like you are. You don't choose who you love."

Something resonated in Brigid then, she wanted to scream and rage and insist that this was rubbish. That she wouldn't fall for it. She would choose whom she loved, or she would not love at all.

"But he hurts you."

"Not in a way I can't bear."

"We could leave. We could swim away, like the stories."

"Just because I'm strong enough to leave, doesn't mean I want to."

"That doesn't make any sense."

"It could be worse. It could be a lot worse."

But Brigid doubted that.

"There are other ways to be hurt," her mother tried. "He only uses his hands." Her mother paused. "He *can't* hurt me. Don't you see? Any more than he can hurt you."

"But he has," Brigid said. "He does." Her mother stiffened, held her tighter, pretended she didn't hear.

She fell asleep before Brigid could ask the question she most wanted the answer to. She whispered it anyway.

"Are we real?"

She didn't know what was true anymore. The story they were trapped in or the ones her mother no longer told.

When she was ten, Brigid wanted a changeling baby. In her mother's stories, babies were stolen from their cradles, a fairy left in their place. Other babies were given to women who couldn't grow one themselves. Fairy children, lent to the world, had a foreign loveliness and fire in their eyes. On her mother's island in Ireland, there were places known as entrances to the fairy world, green roads, the ancient stump of a tree, a cave in a stone cliff by the sea. Places where children could hear music and laughter and a pull to something that would swallow them away. Where something else could be born.

Brigid set up sites on the island where fairies might hear her request. A circle of stones in the woods where she built fires and burned and healed herself while waiting. A cave down by the shoreline that was swallowed at high tide, but dark, wet, and promising at low. An old oak tree whose trunk she could not fit her arms around, which she surrounded with a colony of fairy houses made from bark and pine needles and shells and moss.

There was the chance, she knew, that she would be stolen instead. The instant she passed through bark or damp mossy ground or stayed in a cave until the sea swallowed her, she planned to gorge herself, eat and eat from whatever she was offered, drink goblets of fairy wine until it ran down her chin, eat beyond the point where she felt she might be sick, to make sure that there was not the slightest chance she could ever be returned.

Either way, stolen child or fairy gift, Brigid would no longer be alone.

HER MOTHER'S HANDS SHOOK her for a long time before Brigid relented and opened her eyes. The first thing she saw was the blood. Her mother had smeared it on the sheet and the doors and the walls. There was so much blood Brigid assumed it was coming from her, but she pulled her out of bed and outside, barefoot over ice and rock, murmuring "Hurry, hurry," even though they already were.

Inside, the studio was a mess. The fight was an epic one. Smashed glass, ripped canvas, they had broken and torn and shattered it all. More blood than Brigid had ever seen. Streams of it, puddles, smears, soakings, blood like spilled and wasted paint. Blood leading in an ungraceful sweep to her father, still and curled up in the corner, where he'd pulled himself then stopped. Brigid didn't want to go near him, she wanted to turn around and go back to bed. But her mother was still holding on.

"I hit back," she said, pulling Brigid along. "I hit him too hard." Brigid's bare feet warmed on the bloody floor. "I can't fix it."

The fire iron was still where she'd dropped it. His head was a mess, the blood as dark as his hair but glistening, weighing down his curls as if he'd just emerged from a deep and oily sea. It pooled beneath him black and so thick she could tell it was already cold.

"Right there," her mother said, pointing to an indentation in his skull, a broken pit behind his ear. There was something in there, in that pit, something besides bone and blood, something neither one of them was ever meant to see. An entrance, Brigid thought, an underworld.

It was not something Brigid could put her hands on. Her mother forced her, pulled her down to her knees in the blood and pressed her daughter's hands to the pit and begged her to close it. Nothing happened. There was no heat, no rush of pleasure, there was nothing inside him that she could get a grip on. He was gone.

"He's not in there," Brigid mumbled.

"No. Nonononono." Her mother paced the round room in her bare feet, leaving bloody footprints in a spiral, swearing and crying and mumbling to herself. When Brigid tried to talk to her, she looked as if she didn't know who she was, or what language she was speaking. She looked like something other than a mother, like the changeling that had replaced her who could not figure out how to leave.

PART OF BRIGID WAS relieved when nothing happened. When she put her hands to her father's head and found it empty. The relief opened a throat constricted with guilt. Though she would have saved him, though the reality of her father dead—the father who had once held her hand and shown her how to polish light—made her want to fall into darkness herself, not saving him meant that they were free. It meant that someone would come in a boat and take her away and it would be better than being with the fairies because she could escape and still live in the world. She thought her father dying would break open the trap that was the three of them.

But her mother decided to stay.

"They'll take you away," her mother explained. "I'll go to jail. Is that what you want?"

"I'll tell them," Brigid tried. "I'll tell them it was his fault."

"Look at us," her mother said. "There's not a mark on either one of us. No one will believe you."

Brigid stopped arguing. She was only a child. None of this had ever been her decision.

It wasn't hard for her mother to pretend. They left his body in a cave that was walled off by enormous boulders pushed in by the sea. The boat still delivered supplies and thought nothing of leaving the wooden boxes on the dock. They had never liked Silas, who was gruff and impatient with small talk, so they dropped things in a hurry to avoid him. Brigid knew how to run the lighthouse, how to log the boats and punch in the Morse code at the appropriate times. How to pull the enormous bell three times in greeting to a passing boat, each ring a bigger lie. Her mother burned stacks of sketches in the stove, annihilated images of her broken, bruised body, swallowing them with flame. She refused to listen when Brigid said they could be used as evidence. She alternated between periods of energetic destruction and collapse, taking to her bed and not leaving it for days, weeks at a time. She had hallucinations, open-eyed dreams where she grabbed Brigid's arms and tried to warn her of something.

"They'll burn me," she said. "They're waiting with the fire irons. They'll burn me and kill the baby."

"There is no baby," Brigid would insist, and then feel guilty that such pragmatism sent her mother into a fresh episode of tears.

Brigid ran the lighthouse by herself then, signaling the boats, manned by those who knew nothing about what was happening underneath the light. At some point it occurred to her with a rush that they could be here for years before anyone came. They could be here forever, two women who could barely meet eyes or speak, having murdered the only thing that bound them to the human world.

ONE SUMMER MORNING, BRIGID was swimming in the cove when she saw a sailboat. She was halfway to it before she even realized what she was trying to do. She swam so hard she forgot to pace herself, and the sailboat moved quickly out of her sight. She swallowed water, couldn't keep her head above the waves long enough to cough it out, swallowed more. She panicked, struggling. She felt something large and warm brush against her legs. Suddenly, she was not afraid. It was so easy to stop struggling. To believe that falling beneath the sea would save her. This is where the fairies have been all along, she thought, as she felt a small arm circle her neck, and heard a whisper that seemed to come up from the water. *Brigid*, the watery voice said in the secret language, *mo chuisle*. My pulse.

She woke on the shore, coughing and vomiting seawater in a violent gush. She lay for a long time, her bruised and scraped body heavily alive in the sand. When she felt strong enough, she walked back to the water. She lowered herself into a tide pool and watched the blood, sand and all the hopes she'd had for being stolen lift off and swirl away.

LATER THAT NIGHT, IN the bed they shared, Brigid's mother said simply, in Irish, "Don't ever try that nonsense again." When Brigid didn't answer, her mother put an arm around her waist, pulled her in tight.

"Don't give up on me," she said into Brigid's neck, moving her hair aside. "I don't know how to start over again. But we'll figure something out."

Her mother had been the one to rescue her. Not to save her, but to chain her there. Trapped in a story worse than any fairy tale she'd ever been told.

Brigid stopped wishing for a changeling. Once she imagined that her mother was the brave fairy girl who swam herself across the sea, now Brigid thought the story was about her. She knew exactly what it felt like to be that fairy girl, an accident born from the blasphemous joining of worlds. She couldn't escape this life any more than she could hurt herself.

It wasn't just happening to her or around her, all this darkness. It was part of her.

She couldn't bring a baby into all of this. She imagined it slipping away, like newborn seals that had to be nudged back up the rocks by their enormous, aggravated mothers.

It would have nothing to hold on to.

WHEN BRIGID WAS ELEVEN, the state decided to renegotiate with her father, and though her mother forged his signature on letters requesting an extension, it was denied. Three young coast guard sailors, eager to prove themselves, arrived on the island expecting to talk down a madman, but found instead two wild-eyed, emaciated women and the bones of the lighthouse keeper rattling around in a cave of sharp gray rock. Nothing magical saved them. The world that Brigid thought had forgotten them merely stumbled in.

In town, the police pulled a confession out of her mother as easily as a needle drawing blood. She was sent to St. Dymphna's

Asylum, from where, it was well known, no woman ever left. They weren't sure what to do with Brigid, who wouldn't say a word. She was as tall as a grown woman, with wild, fire-colored hair and a look on her face that made the adults required to help her extremely uncomfortable. In the end, Brigid was sent north to an institution that bore her name, St. Brigid's, run by a group of Irish nuns who had a reputation for reforming the most damaged and bold of wayward girls.

Her mother had told them her father had abused them both. That was why she had killed him, because he was hurting their child. Brigid didn't learn this until later. Somewhere in the shuffle of policemen and social workers and doctors, Brigid and her mother never said good-bye. Brigid was left to wonder alone, until she grew tired of wondering anymore, which one of them—the mother who had stolen from her, or the mother who had saved her—was the one she should remember. The fairy or the saint.

CHAPTER 6

Bonfire

June 1959

On June 21, the longest day of the year, the older children come home from secondary school for the summer and the whole island gathers to meet them at the quay. Five teenagers looking taller, filled out, and more interested in each other than they were the year before.

There are only eight families left on St. Brigid's Island. Someone is always leaving, uncles, cousins, classmates waving from the mail boat in their good coats, mothers keening after them as if at a funeral. They leave for jobs and wars, for marriage and school. For life. Only six men are capable of lifting the heavy boats and working the hard land of the island, and Rose and Emer are married to two of them. The rest are women or children under the age of twelve. When children turn twelve, they leave. They go to the mainland to attend secondary school and they only come home during the summer. By their first summer home, they are already different, already gone.

Rose and Emer are standing on the grass hill that looks down on the quay. Emer can't help fidgeting, she is eager to get up to Brigid's, where she spends most days, with the excuse of helping her fix up the house—but Rose and Emer never miss this.

"Seems like it was only last summer that was us," Rose whispers to Emer, squeezing her arm affectionately.

You mean you, Emer thinks, trying to pull away, but Rose is used to this and ignores it, threading her arm through Emer's elbow and holding tight. The side of her belly against Emer's arm feels obscene. Her bump has grown quicker than ever this time, and the men have been slagging Austin, saying it's probably quadruplets. Emer would find this mortifying, but Rose has never been embarrassed at her own body.

The teenagers, like the Yank, have to be handed down from the big boat into a currach; Austin and Patch row out to them. Emer can see Austin greeting the only boy with a shoulder slap and a whispered comment that flames his ears. The girls he hands down sweetly, with a wink, like they are his own. Patch keeps the boat steady, avoiding the greetings, he is known for fierce shyness around women and children. They angle the currach into the cove, timing between waves that could upend them, and at the slip they lift children up to where their mothers have been waiting months to get their hands on them.

"Look at the face on Oisin," Rose says to Emer.

Oisin is the pimple-faced son of Malachy and Kathleen. He is getting on so well that there is talk of him having the points to study medicine.

"What are you on about?" Emer says.

"Himself and Deirdre are trying so hard not to look at each other they're practically falling off the quay. Those two have been busy this winter."

"Don't be crass," Emer says, shifting uneasily as she does at any mention of romance or sex.

"I'm only observing." Rose smiles.

"Oisin can do better than Deirdre," Emer says. "She won't last long in the city."

"He'll come back here, so he will," Rose says. "To be the island doctor."

"And who will pay him for that?" Emer says.

The island isn't funded for a doctor, or a priest, a lighthouse or a new harbor, not even for electricity or a community telephone. The government would rather give them a new start. They want people off the islands, so instead of Inis Muruch, where they have relatives, they are offering a cul-de-sac of eight brand-new houses on the mainland. For reasons she cannot wrap her mind around, no one wants to go but Emer. You'd think the government was trying to burgle them rather than give them new houses when you hear Rose voice her opinion on it.

Rose makes her way to the quay, to hug and fuss over these children as if they are her own. Austin reaches out and pinches her rear, she laughs and slaps him away, delighted. He grabs her for a kiss. Emer looks away. Their public displays of affection have always sickened her.

"Howaya, Emer," a few of the teenagers say as they walk past, avoiding her eyes. She nods at them. Her husband walks up the road to their house without a glance at her.

Niall is already up at Brigid's house. He has no time for the return of the prodigals. He doesn't care about these teenagers any more than Emer does. But neither does he have her desire to feed off the feeling they bring home with them, the broad, fresh faces that are a little unfocused, a little absent, as if half of them has been left in another, better world. It fills Emer with jealous rage, but she can't help coming to see life rise off them like smoke, just the same.

EMER AND ROSE GREW up assuming they would leave, leave the island, leave Ireland, because that is what children did. Old women crossed themselves any time they passed the quay, remembering all the children the island had lost to the world. Emer looked forward to the day she would leave for secondary school the way she had once anticipated being stolen by fairies. It was the only hope she had of escaping the treeless three-mile stretch of bog and rock. Of escaping herself.

The summer before they were due to leave for secondary school, their mother had a stroke. She collapsed in the kitchen and when she woke, she couldn't move or speak, so the doctor was rowed over. Auntie Orla explained it to the girls when the doctor said she would need to go to the hospital. Rose broke down in the loud, dominating sobs that always required attention. Emer raised her voice above the noise to ask if it was a "fairy stroke," the illness said to affect those who were being stolen, still halfway between this world and the underground. She asked with such a gleam in her eyes that her auntie Orla crossed herself. "Stolen child," she muttered as she turned away. Emer didn't flinch. She'd been called this before. She still wished it were true.

Their mother came home with one half of her face frozen, a useless arm curled like a broken wing to her breast, and a deadened leg that seemed to weigh as much as the rest of her, the foot turned permanently inward. The way the paralysis pulled her mouth made it look like it was half-open and ready to scream.

This was one month before Emer and Rose were due to leave for school. There was no discussion. Their mother could not be left. Everyone on the island could barely feed their own families. There was no one to take them on the mainland, or in America, where some other widowed families went. Their mother's three brothers had all been killed fighting for England in the war. Even if they'd had a place to go, their mother declared, she would never leave the island. Not with her baby boy still in that water.

Rose and Emer were already used to the chores. They milked the cows, fed the calves, did the laundry and the cooking, and dug, alongside the other orphaned children, endless rows of potatoes in September. As girls they had ridden side by side on the donkey creels full of turf, now they led the donkeys themselves. They carried knives in their aprons, knit circular scarves to protect their heads when they went out to tend the animals. But after their mother's stroke, it was as if they became women, as hard and old as their mother in a few months. Emer, at least. Rose maintained some callow girlishness. She continued to go to the island school whenever she could. Emer announced loudly, whenever she set off, that she was wasting her time.

It wasn't long after this that Emer started her monthly bleeding. Her cramps were like water breaking onto rock, constant, unbearable. So much dark, clotted blood fell out of her that nothing could stanch it, not the thick flannel folded between her legs or the modern sanitary napkins, coveted and few from the mainland, that had to be tossed, like most rubbish, into the fire. Emer bled through them all. After one humiliating accident in the church pew, during a Christmas when the boys her age were home from school, she stayed near the house for the first week of every month. She had headaches that felt like bees swarming in her head, that made her vision vibrate and sunlight unbearable. She added these to the growing list of things that locked her away and let her sister get on without her.

Rose's blood, when it started the next year, was dainty and spare, a pink stain on a cloth that could be rinsed clean and forgotten, or thrown on a fire without threatening to smother it.

"Mind yourselves," their mother slurred. "A man can put a baby in ye now."

"Wouldn't that be the straw," Emer scoffed. But Rose smiled and winked at her.

TWO YEARS AFTER THEIR mother's stroke, the island teacher convinced Rose to go away to school after all. She never thought to make such a suggestion to Emer, who had stopped showing up altogether. One of them would have to stay on the island with their mother, and Emer was the obvious choice. When Rose tried to ask Emer what she thought about this, Emer acted so uninterested that Rose was hurt.

"I'll stay if you want," Rose said.

"Sure you will. Don't you always do what you're told?" Emer said.

Emer refused to speak to her for the rest of the summer, but Rose left anyway.

It was the longest winter of Emer's life. There was storm after storm where they couldn't leave the island for weeks at a time, and Rose couldn't come over to see them. She didn't even make it for Christmas, celebrating the holiday with the family she boarded with in town. Emer and her mother sat silently in front of the tough goose whose neck Emer had wrung with a pleasure that startled her. The few times that Rose was able to get over, that autumn and again in the springtime, Emer was barely civil to her, cruel, distant, angry to the point where she often imagined slapping her sister's face hard enough to leave an ugly mark and a betrayed expression. She had never wanted her hands to suck happiness out of someone as much as she wished they would out of Rose.

At Easter, when they were working in the kitchen together, peeling potatoes and making bread, Rose tried to reach across the floury table and grasp Emer's hand.

"I know how difficult it must be," she whispered, so their mother couldn't hear. Emer dropped her knife in her apron pocket, put her shawl and headscarf on and walked out into the fields, leaving her sister, who somehow managed to both be self-effacing and get everything she wanted, alone with the dinner half-prepared.

ROSE ONLY LASTED THAT one year. Her first summer home from school, the weather so fine that the bleak winter seemed like someone else's memory, she told Emer she wasn't going back. She'd fallen in love with Austin Keane, eighteen years old and finished with school in Galway. For years everyone assumed he would get the points to study medicine, but he refused to take the exams. He was moving back in with his mother and younger sisters, to fish and work the land like his father, who had drowned at the same time as theirs, before him. He and Rose both believed that staying on the island with their families was more important than any academic or worldly ambition.

"Got into your knickers then, did he?" Emer said when Rose told her this. Rose ignored that.

"You can go now, Emer," Rose said, her eyes so bright with possibility Emer found herself wanting to poke them. "Go to school on the mainland, if you want. Mammy can live with us."

Emer acted as though the suggestion were ludicrous. Rose was confused and spent a good deal of time trying to convince her. Telling her about Galway, and how much there was to do there and the bookshops and the train to Dublin. Emer lost her temper eventually, snapping at her sister's pretty face.

"Sure you're only disappointed for yourself," she said. "I won't go gallivanting about to make you feel better, or be made to pay for it later when you've ten children and no hope of getting away."

Rose went cold then. She would go cold, if Emer pushed her enough, she wasn't all sweetness and warmth, even if Emer was the only one who knew it.

"I'm sorry Austin prefers me, Emer." And just with one sentence, that was how Rose would do it. Emer could rage and insult her and whinge, but Rose, eventually, would cut her down with one retort. Because she knew, and had known all along, how Emer felt about Austin.

He had held her hand once. The summer she was thirteen, at the St. John's bonfire. Austin, just home for the summer from school, had fumbled in the dark for Rose's hand, but got Emer's instead. She was so shocked and delighted by this she forgot about what her hand did to everyone by then. Austin yelped, pulled his hand away and swore to himself in the darkness. Rose, standing to the side of Emer, giggled at the swearing, and that was when Austin realized his mistake. Emer felt him shudder to himself, shake it off and guzzle stout he'd nicked from the keg, as if he needed fortification against the cold dread that had seeped from her hand.

But for the breath-holding second before she ruined it, Emer lost herself. She let go in the wet darkness, buoyed by the flattering pressure of Austin's hand. In that instant it wasn't like watching Rose, it was like being Rose. As if she had stolen from her sister the assurance, dense and impenetrable, that she was wanted.

Emer didn't go. The subject of school on the mainland never came up again. She told herself she was staying to spite her sister. She remained out of a vague hope that was more like fear. Fear that, were she to leave, without her sister beside her, she would be as ugly and cruel and paralyzed as the mother who obliged them to stay behind. And that no one would dare to reach out for her hand ever again.

IN THE FIELD BEHIND Brigid's house, Niall is running circles with the pig and dog, whom he has taught to play keep away with a sun-bleached sheep femur he found in the garden.

"Seems like a big morning," Brigid says, gesturing to the quay. She is sitting outside her door on a kitchen chair, like an old island woman already. She looks tired, Emer thinks, and it occurs to her that Brigid's energy isn't as deep as it appears. It can run dry.

"It's just the children coming home," Emer says. "It puts them all in a tizzy."

"I can imagine."

"There'll be a ceili tonight at the bonfire," Niall says. He has run over panting, the pig standing to attention nearby, bone in his snout, grinning with victory. "For St. John's Eve. Will you come, Brigid?"

Brigid grows still. "Should I bother?" she says casually, but it sounds breathless.

The island men have checked on Brigid daily, but the women have barely spoken to her. They will be friendly tonight, Emer knows, forgiving, with the children home and the two barrels of porter they came with. It would be the right moment to be introduced, when they are feeling loose and grateful enough to give strangers their time. They won't give her the well, any more than Emer, even though Brigid seems to think the longer she stays the closer she gets to being told. The eager desperation Brigid barely holds in check rattles Emer, as if it is she, not what she knows, that Brigid is so taken with.

Emer shrugs and pretends the question barely interests her.

"If you care for that kind of thing," she says, turning her blind side to Brigid's questioning eyes.

Niall comes in when they're making bread to announce that Fiona and Eve are coming up the road. Emer's hands freeze in the mound of flour.

"Who are Fiona and Eve?" Brigid asks.

"My nieces," Emer says.

Brigid walks outside to meet the girls, who have had their Saturday baths and their red gold hair plaited and are wearing their best clothes for the bonfire. Fiona is carrying a plate of freshly baked scones.

"My mother wanted to welcome you and say she hopes to have a chat at the ceili tonight," Fiona says. "She couldn't get away as she's bathing the babies. The plate is yours as well." Fiona looks to Emer like she might jump out of her hair ribbons, she's so keen.

Emer hadn't asked Rose if she had any of the fuchsia pottery from Brigid's house, but the other women who begrudgingly handed over their pieces must have told her.

"Thank you," Brigid says. "Won't you come in, girls?"

She makes tea and puts out the plate of pink and blue sweeties she keeps ordering from town because they are Niall's favorites. Fiona looks around the cottage with such probing interest it borders on rudeness. She sits straight in her chair and accepts one of each color sweet and nibbles daintily at them. Eve, just as pretty but on the shy side and as a result, fiercely boring, takes a whole handful and gobbles them greedily the same way Niall always does. Then she looks like she regrets eating them so quickly, because she has nothing to do while her sister leads the conversation.

"Are you from New York?" Fiona asks Brigid.

"I'm afraid not," Brigid says. The men asked her this as well. *Everyone*, she has said to Emer, *wants me to be from New York.* "I'm from Maine."

"Oh," Fiona says, with no attempt to hide her disappointment. "I'm going to New York someday. I want to be an actress."

Emer gasps in amused disapproval. Fiona flicks a glare in her direction, and continues.

"I saw a film once at the cinema in Galway with your woman, Marilyn Monroe. She's brilliant. I do the recitations at the Christmas concert on Muruch and my teacher says I'm the best in the class."

Rose would be mortified. Though she is proud of Fiona, who has top marks, she wouldn't allow her to be so boastful, so bold. And she certainly wouldn't encourage any nonsense about New York. She's hoping Fiona will be the island teacher. For the most part, Fiona pretends to like her role as her mother's right hand, she cares for her siblings and takes on the endless chores without complaint. Only Emer noticed, when Rose announced the new twins at Easter, Fiona go pale and still, like she had just been told she was pregnant herself. She is the only one of Rose's children who has no fear of Emer. Emer suspects if she tried her hands on the girl, she would flick her right off like she does everything else.

"But, Fee, no one comes back to visit from New York," Niall says.

"You could come with me," Fiona dares, and Niall backs away from the table. He moves to stand next to Emer and puts his small hand in hers. Emer grasps it tightly and tries not to smile.

This is one thing she has that Rose does not. None of her girls is as devoted as Niall. They can't be. As soon as they are old enough to walk away from her they do it, without turning back to check if she is watching. There isn't enough of her for any of them to cling to.

"Will you go to New York too?" Brigid asks Eve politely, who looks at her blankly for a moment, then blushes and shrugs.

"She just wants to get married," Fiona scoffs.

As if that's not the only option available, to the both of them, Emer thinks.

"Are you married?" Fiona says, bold again.

"Not anymore," Brigid says. But she gets up and puts more water on before Fiona can ask what that means. Fiona looks so enthralled by this she nudges her sister, who glares at her, still angry at her slag.

"I might not get married," she whines. "I may take the vow."

"You're only saying that so Mammy will swoon over you," Fiona whispers. Eve tries to kick her, but Fiona dodges this at the same time she darts her hand out and pinches her sister hard.

"Girls," Emer warns.

Fiona catches Emer's one eye and looks quickly away.

Brigid comes back over with a fresh pot of tea.

"Tell your mother I look forward to meeting her," she says. Emer clenches her hands into fists. The girls leave as quickly as they can, they start giggling as soon as they are far enough down the green road to believe they are free to do so. They are carrying Brigid's

message, and with it Emer's dashed hopes, as heavy and easy to give
away as that plate full of scones.

ROSE MARRIED AUSTIN WHEN she was fifteen, with a three-day-
long party on Inis Muruch, and they moved into his mother's house
until he could build them their own. Emer was left alone again
with their mother. After their honeymoon to Dublin, Rose blushed
whenever her new husband was nearby. It wasn't embarrassment;
the blush was connected to some hot expectation. Emer could tell
Rose was always wanting to get him alone, and he her. They rarely
managed it. They lived with his mother and his three sisters all in
the one little house. Emer had seen the old women cluck and shake
their heads at the way they eyed one another, even in church.

"Will you mind the way you look at him," Emer said to her once
after Mass when they did it again in full view of the priest. "You're
making a holy show of yourself." Rose laughed at her.

"It's no sin to admire your own husband," she said.

Emer learned one day what these looks were all about. She
was walking to the cliffs to check the sheep and heard something
coming from the clochán. Someone was breathing quick, as if
they'd been running and were trying to catch it, but also broken,
as if they were afraid. For a moment, Emer though it was the fairy
woman. But then she heard another breath, deeper, with a rhythm,
like an animal that knew how to sing a song. She recognized Austin's admired voice even when it wasn't using words. Emer knew
that she should turn around and go back down the hill. These were
not noises that she knew, but she knew that they were private. Even
as this thought formed, she was crouching by the clochán, going
right for the small hole in the stone that she knew was there. She
peeked in, needing to see what it was that had so changed her sister's expression.

Emer watched them for a long time, until she had to slow her own heartbeat and breath, lest they should hear her through the stone, then she crawled away through the bracken, wet from the damp ground and the slick well she hadn't known was inside her.

Emer had never imagined that the chores of marriage, and of making babies (she knew the basics of it but hadn't realized there were such options), could be anything like what she witnessed that day. That you could be taken away by someone, snatched and filled up and adored, stolen by someone else's hands and mouth, without once losing yourself.

EMER MARRIED AUSTIN'S OLDER, less attractive brother the summer Patch came home from Dublin to help Austin fix up a ruined cottage into their new house, and Rose was swollen with her first set of twins. They were thrown together, Austin having written him at his sister's request, after Rose suggested how fitting it would be that they marry brothers and their children be closer than cousins. Patch was studying for the lighthouse service and about to get his first posting. It could mean, Rose assured Emer, living all over Ireland. Often wives and children were set up with houses in the nearest town, so the men didn't have to travel far on their weeks off.

Emer and Patch barely had to participate in a courtship before they were engaged. It happened around them, like weather, the swirling wind and rain of opinion, the insistence of others that they fall in love causing them to feel dizzily aroused.

"You're not as senseless as some girls," he said once, as though trying to convince them both. He only resembled his brother when he smiled, which wasn't very often. In that way he and Emer were a perfect match.

By the time she wondered at the wisdom of it, it was done already. There was no trip to Dublin, no weekend on Muruch, just a simple ceremony in the small island church that had no pews; women brought their milking stools, men stood around the edges. The priest hurried off immediately for fear of the weather turning. Their mother stayed the night with Rose to give them a honeymoon. Rose had done Emer's hair and makeup, taught her to shave her legs and armpits, lent her a nightgown. Even Emer had been surprised at how well she looked in the glass.

Patch barely glanced at her, blowing out the candle before quickly stripping his clothes off and climbing into the bed. He smelled strongly of soap, and she had a brief image of his mother scrubbing him clean in a kitchen tub for the occasion. There was the same grunting, and heavy breath, and a pain she hadn't expected, but that passed quickly. She waited to feel something like what she'd witnessed in her sister. There was nothing. Only a friction that quickly became unbearable, then a grunt from Patch and it was over. He was almost asleep when she spoke up.

"Would you not put your hands on me? Or your mouth?" She knew it was a mistake the moment she said it. The whole bed stiffened along with him.

"Are you hurt?" he said. She said that she wasn't. "Then what are you on about?" He looked as if he regretted the whole thing. She had been careful to keep her hands to herself, but still he looked a bit like someone who had just clasped her palm, and been pulled down into despair. He turned away from her and was soon asleep.

The first few times she tried to move underneath him, to think of Austin's voice and her sister's catching breath, but there was nothing, only that crowding friction, then wetness from him, then the feeling that she'd been emptied, and would never be full of what her sister had. And the look on Patch's face, as if it were something like revulsion that propelled his groaning release.

Then he left for his first appointment, Fastnet Rock, a lighthouse so desolate and remote there was no possibility of her going along. She was left alone with her harpy of a mother, calling out criticisms with grating persistence. It was as if she had never been married at all.

The first time Patch didn't come home when he was due, Austin had to travel to the mainland, drag him out of the pub and row him home. It wasn't the first time, it turned out, just the first time since their marriage. He'd lived away from the island so long, no one had known but Austin.

"You'd think Austin might have warned us," Rose said angrily when they were back. They stood in Emer's doorway watching Austin half carry him up the road. Rose had two babies strapped to her chest in a way that allowed her to nurse them and do the chores at the same time.

Emer went wordlessly inside. She was pregnant, the goal of marital fumbling successfully attained, and had already given up on the fantasy that she might feel anything more for her husband than she felt for anyone else.

PATCH WANTED TO NAME the baby Padraig, after himself and his father. Emer named him Niall, and allowed her husband to choose his second name, though grudgingly. The boy was born on the first of May at the hospital on the mainland, small and big-eyed and silent, with wrinkles like a worried old man lining his forehead. He wasn't able to eat. The first time she put her nipple in his mouth, it flopped right out, as if he hadn't the strength, or the interest really, to keep it in there. Her milk came in, her breasts swelled and burned, and though he rarely cried, he shrieked when she tried to feed him. He fought it, balling his little fists and twisting his neck, and her milk leaked like tears down his cheeks. The nurses tried to show her how to do it properly but each of them gave up when, after touching Emer, a rush of hopelessness overwhelmed them. The doctor was consulted, but he just seemed embarrassed by the whole thing. He suggested tins of baby formula, which was thick and beige and vile-smelling; Niall swallowed it only once before being sick and never opening his lips for it again.

There was a nurse who only came at night, an old woman with Connemara in her accent, who watched and waited through all the fuss. She came to Emer's room on the third night and, whispering in Irish, showed Emer how to pinch and knead just behind the nipple to get her milk out into a jar, then dribble it slowly into Niall's mouth. Once he'd tasted it, he started gulping, as if it had taken him three days to realize that he'd been hungry all along.

"My own mother was the midwife on Inishturk," the nurse said. "Don't be telling the doctor what I show you. They think the old ways are no better than witchcraft."

She pointed underneath Niall's tongue, where a little cord of glistening tendon held him so tight that even when he cried, it could not extend out of his mouth. She took a small scalpel from her white pocket and before Emer could say anything, she thrust it into his mouth and flicked, once, with a sound that made Emer lose her urine into the already bloody clothes on the bed. She hated herself in the next moment, for not even thinking to move her son away from a madwoman with a blade. But Niall didn't cry, just looked at them both and yawned, a small swirl of blood collecting in his mouth and staining his drool pink.

"That'll sort him," the nurse said, and Emer just held him closer, grateful that he didn't seem hurt, angry that it was no thanks to her. The next time she put him to her nipple he didn't scream. He didn't suck, but kept it in his mouth, and she kneaded like the nurse had shown her and he swallowed a few times, sweet, loud swallows that let rush a joy through her like nothing she'd ever felt. A lot of it ran off down his cheeks and into his neck. He grew tired and let his face fall away. She worked the rest of her milk into a bottle the nurse had placed close by, and poured the formula they thought she was giving him down the sink.

She brought him home to the island, fed the tins of formula to the calves, continued to express her own milk into a tiny porcelain jug with a fuchsia blossom painted on the side. Their best jug, the only delicate thing they owned. She fed him from the lip of this jug, decanting sips into his eager little mouth. He was like a man with a pint of stout, deep swallows with pauses for sighing.

At the end of his first week, during a night feeding, he turned his head away from the jar. Her breast was exposed from expressing the milk and he latched onto it with such force and precision she jumped a little at the shock, but he held on. He was suckling. She could tell the moment it happened that he had never done it properly before, the tug that went all the way up her breast and beyond, as if he were intent on swallowing her whole self, body and soul, into the gaping hole of his mouth and throat. She began to cry, heaving sobs that she tried to control because she was afraid it would distract him and he would forget what he was doing. Patch woke up because her crying shook the bed, rolled over and looked at her, puzzled and a little wary. He'd never once seen her cry, and she had never taken well to direct questions.

"Are you well, then?" he risked.

"The baby's eating," she said.

"That's grand so," he murmured, confused. Patch hadn't watched any of it, he'd looked away when any fuss around her breasts seemed to be going on, so he couldn't imagine why a baby eating would suddenly make her cry.

Emer spent the next week in bed, Niall nursing almost constantly night and day. Rose came by with toddlers trailing by her side, the next set of twins heavy and round beneath her apron. She baked them bread, milked Emer's cows, tidied the house, churned butter, swept the hearth and kept the fire up, left a plate for Patch for his tea and brought another plate to Emer's bed. Emer did nothing but watch the baby drink, as if he'd never get enough, and for once she was grateful for her sister, who asked nothing but seemed as proud of the sight as Emer did herself.

"Isn't he a dote," her sister would murmur, and Emer would hold the baby up to nuzzle his neck, hiding the flush of love that flamed over her face.

WHEN ROSE'S SECOND SET of twins was born, when Niall was six months old, Emer went to see her in the hospital. She asked for the nurse who had helped her, whose name was Bridie, because she wanted to show her what a strong mouth he had now. None of the nurses knew whom she meant. She asked every staff person who came into Rose's room, until Rose told her to stop. She was exhausted by the birth and had no energy for Emer's prodding anxiety. The secretary at the front desk looked through the books and told her there was no nurse named Bridie from Inishturk and there never had been.

Emer went home to the island with Niall tied tightly to her bosom, her neck swollen with dread. There were stories about babies who couldn't eat, whom fairies fed with their own milk and thus laid claim on them. "Some children the fairies save," her mother had said when she saw Emer expressing her milk. "But you're only let to have them seven years. Your brother was one. That's why he was took into the sea. His time was up."

"Ridiculous," Rose said later. "The old fool." Despite everything she'd seen, Rose seemed to maintain a naive, optimistic attitude toward anything that smacked of an underworld. As if it could be tidied away where it would no longer bother them. Most islanders pretended the same. It would never do to say you believed in such things out loud. It was asking for interference. Instead they gripped their rosary beads and called on saints and parceled out holy water and fire, as if this were any less foolish.

Emer had been too drugged by this new ecstasy, this swoon that happened every time Niall pulled milk from her, to care what her mother said. None of the fairy world had come near her since the age of ten. But six months later, thinking of the imaginary nurse and Niall's strange eyes—they had developed a ring that looked like burning turf in the middle of the stormy sea blue—Emer's old desire to be taken was replaced by a fear that part of her, the only part of her that had ever been lovely, had already been claimed.

Emer told Patch she would not have any more babies. She told him something had gone wrong during Niall's birth, something inside her would never heal (he looked away at that, the thought of anything inside her too much for him) and that if he came to her again and got her with child it would kill her. If it occurred to him not to believe her, he didn't say so. She thought he might be relieved. Emer knew what sex with her was like for him. Once she realized there would be no pleasure involved, she had stopped holding her hands back. When he entered her, and she pressed her palms lightly to his back, Patch was seized with a feeling that was similar to when he passed from happily drunk to miserably so. A weight bore down on him, a weight of misery he couldn't hope to escape, misery he could not stop from thrusting into until his release. The way he kept drinking past the point where it felt good anymore. Once she'd known she was with child he had willingly backed away. When his young wife sat him down and told him they would never again have relations, he agreed with a nod and went out to the fields. If she didn't know him she might have wondered if he had even heard her. He found what he needed elsewhere, off the island on his tears, she knew this. They never spoke of it.

This was how Emer assured that no other babies would force her to take her eyes off this first one. She couldn't afford to be distracted.

She'd seen how divided Rose was with multiple children. How early they wandered away from her, and Rose was often soothing the accident of a toddler while trying to nurse an infant. Emer couldn't risk this. Constant vigilance was required to hold on to Niall.

She never left the baby alone. If she was forced to go out to the cows or the well she tied him within her shawl or left the fire iron across his cradle like a prison bar. Until he was three, she dressed him like a girl and never cut his long dark curls, a tradition the islanders had abandoned, not remembering that the fairies preferred boy babies. She kept all the superstitions she once scoffed at or purposely broke during the time she wanted to be stolen herself. She buried a piece of burning turf in the ground in the hope that he would live, like the stories told, for seven hundred years. She brought him to Saint Brigid's well, the holy well that was kept secret by the islanders, said to cure illness and infertility and protect babies' souls. She didn't believe in the power of this well—if it were true she would have two eyes—but she did it anyway, just in case. She avoided the raths, didn't walk down the green road past Desmond's house but went around by the field instead, squirted the first release of the cows' udders into the dirt to appease the creatures under the ground. She crossed herself and glared blame at anyone who dared to admire him aloud. "Don't overlook a child," it was said on the island, for the compliment would render it vulnerable to snatching. Any time Niall was ill she didn't sleep, but sat up beside him drenched in her own terrified sweat, her neck pulled so tight she had to lean forward to manage each breath.

She let Rose put a woven Saint Brigid's cross over his cradle, and finger a trinity of holy water on his forehead. But Emer didn't trust Saint Brigid any more than she trusted the fairies. Her stories were so odd and warped with pagan magic and prediction—a druid prophesied that she would be born neither in the house nor out of it, and would bathe and suckle on the milk of a red-eared fairy cow—she almost seemed worse.

The fairies wanted Niall, she was sure of it. They had left something in her, she was tethered to them, like a debt, and Niall was the payment. His fiery eyes, the way he could hear things no one else could, he seemed half gone with the good people already. The memory of that fairy nurse, sliding her knife into his mouth and kneading Emer's milk, was enough to make her heart go crosswise. They could come after you in the most unlikely places.

For years Emer held out hope that Patch would take them off the island. Take them to another part of Ireland where there was a lighthouse and a town and the land held no memory of what she owed it. But Patch made a bollocks out of all that. Drank on duty and let the light snuff out, causing a fatal collision of vessel and rock.

It's the evacuation Emer has pinned all her hopes on now. Perhaps, if they all leave and give the island back, the fairies will let her go. Instead of using the land and the sea to reach out like a long arm and drag her back every time she almost gets away.

They've been preparing for the bonfire for weeks, all the island rubbish collected from where it has lain in their gardens for the last year and moved to the field next to the small church. Furniture broken or rotted with damp, cardboard and paper, plastic containers, building materials, fence posts, weeds and old fishing nets, an old rotted door with a ship's window at the center. Once, the fire was used as a religious ceremony for burning broken rosary beads and old scapulars, but in later years it has become the easiest way to rid themselves of modern rubbish.

Emer puts Niall down for a rest after tea and wakes him again at eleven. It is still dusk, gray-blue sky clinging to light that lasts for all but a few hours this time of year. They walk up the road and stop in to collect Brigid. When they pass Desmond's hay field, a piercing croaky cry rises out of the night silence. Brigid is startled.

"It's the corncrake!" Niall says, and starts calling back to it, imitating the repetitive raspy calls.

"I've been wondering what that was," Brigid says. Niall tells her, as if he's conducting a schoolroom, that it's a bird that only comes to the island in the summer, and croaks until it convinces a female to settle down underneath the nettles . . .

"It'll keep you up all night if it decides to nest there," Emer says. "We had one in our field last summer and I nearly went mad from the racket."

"It does sound like an alarm clock you can't shut off," Brigid says. "But I've always slept through mine."

"What's an alarm clock?" Niall asks. Brigid laughs and explains.

Emer can't stand the corncrakes. They cry all night, rhythmic sirens that pierce her brain, and she can still hear the echo long after dawn when it finally rests.

"Nana says they're the voices of fairies that have failed in their mischief," Niall says brightly. Brigid chuckles, but Emer crosses herself.

The men are coming across the fields with torches; Emer can see the fire moving at the level of their heads. The torchbearers, who have brought the fire from their own hearths, converge on the pile and light it all together, their individual fires rushing toward each other's with a whoosh of paraffin oil. The men gather around the barrel of porter they rowed over that morning from the mainland. They have brought their own pint glasses from home. They call out friendly greetings to Brigid, who smiles easily at them.

Brigid seems to make a decision then, looking at the women gathered together, handing out sandwiches by the fire. She walks over before asking Emer and sticks her big hand out to Rose, bold and Yank as she can be.

"Thank you for the scones," she says, and Rose beams as if they've been friends for ages.

"Brigid and Mary be with you," Rose says to Brigid, and then their mother is offering her working hand, and Kathleen and Nelly and Margaret and Geraldine, and their aunties and cousins and grandmothers, and the next thing Emer knows they are all smiling and laughing. They ask if she is sorted in the house, as if they haven't ignored her and begrudged the time their husbands have given her for the last seven weeks. Emer stands back from it all. The children are lighting sticks and throwing them into the air. The teenagers are gathered in a clump, devising plans to pinch drink when the men aren't watching. She could have told Brigid weeks ago that this reception was only a matter of time, that as soon as it was clear that she wouldn't give up after a week, all she needed to do was approach them in their own territory. Mass would have done. They were harder to reach than the men, and kept to themselves more, but they were polite enough once you knew them. She can see the look of approval flitting between the wives. Brigid is sound enough. Not a hint of the mad family she came from. They can put aside the stories and stop wondering if she means any harm. She will never become one of them, she will never be far from suspicion, but they will let her believe she is.

Emer had wanted Brigid to herself. With one handshake, she belongs to all of them, and Emer finds herself on the perimeter again, dropping there naturally, like a coal spat aside and burning apart from the fire.

Halfway through the first barrel of porter, Malachy takes out his fiddle, Seamus the squeezebox and Michael Joe the bodhran and the music starts up, jigs and reels and hornpipes, women and children dancing in the flickering light of the fire.

Then they start hooting and demanding that Austin sing. Emer backs away, sitting down on a wall away from the heat of the flames. She can't stand too close when Austin sings. He has a low, powerful voice that every generation of men in his family is known for. Emer hates her sister the most when she thinks of the moments Rose has that voice to herself, late at night in the darkness of their bed.

Patch's voice, when he chooses to use it, is high and grating, often so unbearable in the house that she fakes one of her headaches to get him to stop talking. He is happily drunk like the rest of them, but he will be the one to keep drinking when the others are done, keep drinking as long as he can still swallow. He will sleep outside, by the withering bonfire. He always does.

After twelve verses lamenting the Irish emigration to America, Austin asks Brigid to give them a song, and instead of blushing and waving them away, as Emer expects her to, she obliges.

> *A stór mo chroí, when you're far away*
> *From the home you will soon be leaving*
> *'Tis many a time by night and by day*
> *Your heart will be sorely grieving*
> *The stranger's land may be bright and fair*
> *And rich in its treasures golden*
> *You'll pine, I know, for the land long ago*
> *And the love that is never olden.*

This leaves Austin hooting and smiling as though he's poured her out of the keg himself. The women fall all over her again, praising her voice, which is tuneful, if rough. *Ah, go on, you're a great woman, altogether.*

A stór mo chroí. Treasure of my heart. One of the many endearments Emer shares with Niall that are meant for lovers. She wonders if Brigid even knows what it means.

The jigs and reels start up again, and the islanders take turns leaping over the edges of the fire. Brigid has a go, using her long legs to clear the flames with power. Emer has never jumped through, not even for luck before her wedding. Islanders say you can tell a couple's future by the way the flames leap. Austin and Rose made the thing blaze after them like a roar of approval before they were married. Emer imagines had she and Patch gone through it, the fire would have sputtered out in disappointment, or worse, lit her up like a dry stick, as the dolt of her fiancé stood by and watched her eaten up into the summer night's air.

Emer is so preoccupied with watching Rose and Austin and Brigid, she forgets about watching Niall. She sees the other children first, giggling and pointing at something on the other side of the fire.

Niall is walking toward the bonfire. Not to light a stick or jump over the edge, but as if he means to enter straight into the heart of it. His eyes are flashing, the same color as the flames that reach to fold him in. Emer is too far away to grab him herself, so she screams.

Everyone stops what they are doing and looks at her, when she meant for them to look at Niall. Only Brigid seems to know why she screamed. She steps up quickly to Niall and, knowing better than to touch him, just puts herself between his determined eyes and the fire and says his name softly. To Emer's surprise he stops, looks at her, his pupils pulsing as he tries to focus on something other than what he was seeing in the fire.

"May I have this dance?" Brigid says and Niall blushes, mumbles a no thank you and hurries to Emer's side. Now they are all looking at both of them, women tsking and men shaking their heads, and Niall presses his face into his mother's middle, trying to hide.

"I'm sorry, Mammy," he says. She squeezes him tight, not trusting her voice to sound kind. Emer would like to put her hands on everyone, to grip them all until they can feel what she feels, until they are pulled into the dread that rises to choke her every day. But she has to keep her hands soft to stroke the hair of her son.

As soon as Niall learned to talk, Emer quizzed him mercilessly, asking him if he heard the fairies, heard the music, saw the lights.

He was so eager to please her that he often said yes, he could hear music. When she appeared alarmed he said he hadn't heard a thing, and they would wind each other into a frenzy with Emer barking questions and Niall trying to answer what she wanted to hear. He'd end up in tears and Emer would feel like she was being choked by the grip of her fear.

She would have to stop herself then, from lashing out, from shaking him silly, so afraid he would be stolen from her that she was almost willing to hurt him if it made him understand.

Now that he is six, he knows the correct answers, or at least the ones that make her eyes stop spinning in her head. He knows the rules. Never take the food they offer. Don't be tempted to dance to fairy music, but run away, run as fast as you can in the other direction. Run to your mother.

"I will never go with them," he has said, so many times, a small hand placed into the tension of his mother's forehead. All he needs to do is put his hand there and the headaches that once plagued her for whole days vanish in an instant. Only he can make her smile, wiping the look of pure terror away from his mother's face. But he can't take away the fear she has every day, that it will be her last day with him.

After a time the ceili resumes. Austin, a bit worse for drink now, is dancing slowly and shamelessly with Rose, who smiles as she closes her eyes and rocks against him. The older women say a few prayers for the crops and drop in a headless statue of Brigid and a plastic rosary that burns blue. The men will spread the ash over the fields in the morning, and will sober up in time to do it, albeit without moving their heads too quickly. Except Patch, of course. He won't recover for days.

Brigid comes over to stand next to Emer and Niall.

"So, what do the women have to say for themselves?" Emer asks. Brigid's jaw tightens.

"I've been invited for tea," she sighs. They dodged her questions about the well, so.

As a consolation, and because she feels grateful for her quick reflexes with Niall, Emer tells Brigid to take some of the embers for her fire.

"When you move in or build a new house, you light the fire from a neighbor's or with the midsummer embers. Every fire on the island is said to come from Saint Brigid herself. We never let them go out. It brings luck to the house." Emer pauses, then adds dismissively, "So they say."

"Is it the superstition that bothers you, or the optimism?" Brigid says, but so quietly to Emer that it is like a secret between them, rather than ridicule.

Brigid takes a tin mug from one of the women. Emer sees what happens next, and though everyone else is standing there, she seems to be the only one who notices. Brigid scoops a serving of glowing embers out of the fire. She fumbles a bit with the mug, drops some coals and picks them up with her bare hand and puts them back in. Not quickly, like someone avoiding a burn. She grips her palm around bright orange coals and holds them like they are nothing. Then she starts, and looks up, as if she has forgotten herself and is worried someone has seen. She looks straight at Emer and freezes for a moment, waiting, to see if Emer will react.

Normally, at the hint of anything so otherworldly, Emer would snatch her child and run in the other direction. But the fear that usually grips her neck is not there. Instead there is a little thrill that blooms larger when she sees Brigid wipe her fingers on her skirt, and the fingers come away clean, rough from house and farm work but not even slightly burned.

They walk back together, a mug of glowing midsummer between them, Niall half-asleep and stumbling, resting his face against her hip. When they say good-bye, Emer, in an unaccustomed gesture, can't stand the suspense, so she reaches away from Niall to squeeze a good-bye into Brigid's free hand. It is the same temperature as her own, the fingers bony, the skin a bit looser from age, calluses on the edges and softness at the center, a hand just as disappointing as any other she has touched in her life.

Her neck tightens at the thought that she has been seeing things, inventing magic where it doesn't exist. That she and her son are alone in this, after all.

Then Brigid squeezes her fingers, and winks at her.

CHAPTER 7

Beehive

July 1959

Once the house is sorted, Brigid builds the hives. She asks Malachy in June, but by the time the timber and wire and tools arrive, July is half gone. She builds the hive herself, impressing the men with her easy wielding of hammer and saw. She's done this before. She sands and paints the outside, carves inverted handles into the sides. She takes a lot of care, the men say to her, building a useless box. She smiles and ignores them, and assembles frames around squares of wire netting. Ten of them fit snugly together into the box, sliding in on perfectly spaced, painstakingly sanded grooves.

She makes a special trip off the island to collect the bees. She doesn't trust the invisible handoff that brings her everything else, from tools to towels to soap to books, to ferry something so precious and alive. She imagines it being left on the pub counter for two weeks, which happened once to her bag of apples. It costs her a small fortune to be driven to an apiary outside Galway and spend the night in a hotel. The next day, she holds the buzzing cage wrapped in brown paper and string on her lap for the lift back and the currach over. Malachy and Michael Joe row her the entire nine miles back to the island. The dark waves out at sea toss them so high in the air that when they finally fall it is as if Brigid has lost half her body in the process, the middle of her hooked by the sky as the rest drops back down to the plank seat. She hugs the cage with one hand and the seat with the other, trying not to dwell on the image of it flying overboard, dark water gulping down her precious box of life.

When she walks to her house, the newly-painted yellow door beckoning all the way uphill, Brigid is not surprised to find Emer and Niall waiting for her. They come almost every day the weather allows it, so much that she often welcomes the torrential days where she can hear herself think again in her own house. It doesn't seem to occur to Emer that Brigid might crave solitude. Now that she has been to almost everyone's house for tea, Brigid knows there is no one on the entire island besides her who lives alone. People live with their children, their parents, their grandparents, their widowed sisters. Beds are flattened and full, siblings grow up sleeping to the rhythm of the others' breath. She has already deduced from Niall's comments that he and Emer sleep together, Patch banished to the hearth bed, a cushioned corner made up in every island house, for extra children and in-laws, right beside the fire.

Brigid still sleeps every night with the dog. Emer discovered this once while tidying the bedclothes.

"Ach, the dog's been in this," she said and Brigid made a crack about doing what she needed to keep warm. The look on Emer's face was as bad as if she'd said she was having sex with Rua. Niall was delighted and tried to sneak the pig into their bed the same night, which Emer tossed back outside with a squeal.

He has a way with animals, Niall does. The pig, which he has named Cabbage, half the size of the dog already, follows him everywhere. He can milk the most resentful cow, hypnotize sheep into submission when his father needs to shear them. While Brigid gets pecked gathering her breakfast each morning, her hens allow Niall to pick them up, and they nest in the crook of his arm, cooing softly while he strokes the retracted feathery mound of their necks. He pockets their small, warm eggs as if they are jewels. Fur-matted cats hopping with fleas follow hopefully behind him on the road. And Rua, who still distrusts every other islander, especially Emer whose disapproving eye sends her tail curling between her legs, will actually play with Niall, play with the clumsy abandon of a puppy who has not yet been kicked.

This affinity for animals goes along with Brigid's general impression of Niall, that he is otherworldly, not fully with them, one ear halfheartedly listening to people while the other is attending to a world no one else can see. He is more than dreamy and self-absorbed. For much of the time, Brigid feels coldness around him, an empty pocket of air, as if he is not there at all. As if the life inside him has gone somewhere, and what is left is only pretending to be a boy.

She wonders if Emer knows the cause of this, but hasn't yet tried to ask. It is clear that something about him distresses her. She is always calling Niall back to her side, as if too many minutes away from her risk him not returning at all. Niall hasn't reached the age yet where this will bother him; he is still happy to reassure her.

Brigid is already too fond of Niall, but Emer is more difficult to relax around. Though she is used to Emer's one-eyed scowl of disapproval, her greeting today borders on hostile.

"We didn't know you were going over," Emer says.

"I didn't know I needed to report my every move to you," Brigid says. She keeps her voice light and winks at the boy. Niall has knelt down to kiss the face of Rua, who met her at the quay, wiggling herself into a frenzy, but now looks beaten down by Emer's tone. Niall tries very hard to make up for his mother.

"You might give a person a bit of warning," Emer says. "That dog of yours followed Niall home and howled at the door to be let in."

"Did you let him?" Brigid looks at Niall. He grins. Emer grunts disgust. But she is deflating now, getting hold of herself. She backs off when she thinks she has gone too far. It's these moments that affect Brigid the most—watching this caustic girl try to make herself more likable.

Brigid goes inside and puts her precious parcel on the table. Emer comes next, then Niall behind her. Brigid notices again how the two of them are like Irish weather in a room, ominous clouds followed by unexpected sunshine.

The fire and the kettle are already on. No one knocks here, they just call and poke their heads in if the top half of the door is left open for air. If Brigid's not home, Emer will let herself in anyway.

Emer sets about making tea. The parcel on the table begins to vibrate and buzz, and Emer's face grows white and pinched, her one pupil swelling with fear.

"What in the name of Saint Brigid is that?" she says hoarsely.

"Bees," Brigid says, pouring fresh milk into her tea with a satisfying plop. "For my hive."

"That's what you went to town for? Were there not enough creepy crawlies here for you already?"

Emer is not letting the package out of her limited sight.

"I haven't seen any honeybees," Brigid says.

"There used to be," Niall says. He has been encouraging the dog to jump up and put her paws on his shoulders, so they can dance. Emer snaps her head around and glares at him.

"Who told you that?"

"Auntie Rose."

Emer makes the island gasp and silences herself with a large swallow of tea.

"Will you have honey, then?" Niall asks Brigid.

"That's why I got them," Brigid says. "Honey is the great cure-all. It'll save us from the winter colds."

"Doesn't seem worth the work," Emer says.

"Well, I have to keep busy, don't I?" Emer looks away. She has remained stubborn about the well, but Brigid still pushes, even when she isn't asking directly.

"May I help?" Niall says.

"You won't go anywhere near those bees," Emer says suddenly. "If you do, I'll tell Himself to take the belt to ye."

There is silence after this. Clearly this is not a threat she uses often by the betrayed look on Niall's face. Brigid is a little disoriented, hearing Emer refer to her husband with the same mocking, disrespectful title Brigid's mother once used for her father.

"It's safe enough," Brigid assures her. "There are ways of hypnotizing them, with smoke. I've never been stung and I've been doing it for years."

Emer stands suddenly, scraping her chair back. Brigid is sure she is going to leave, to storm away in a rage that will remain unexplained, dragging her disappointed but loyal son behind her. Good riddance, Brigid thinks. After a few days off she is wondering why she puts up with this snarled-up fist of a woman at all. As if she is fighting an invisible set of arms, Emer lurches forward, knocking into the table, then plops back down in her chair. Though she is clearly furious or, Brigid thinks, terrified, something inside her cannot leave. She reaches for her tea and drinks it down, one long swallow, for strength. Brigid and Niall stare at her, as if waiting to see what some invisible puppeteer will make her do next.

Brigid feels a pull of guilt, as if her own arms are yanking the strings. She came here intending to escape this sort of thing, this confluence that she doesn't invite but grows like a weed in the space that reaches between herself and other women. Emer needs something from her, something that Brigid is no longer willing or even able to provide. Not to another adult. She wants a baby, but instead she has these two misfits, hanging around and not telling her how to get it.

Niall comes over and puts his hand on Emer's forehead, swiping the palm across like he's wiping moisture from her brow. Then he leans in close, touching his forehead to hers. For the first time Brigid sees her smile. It fades quickly, it is not something meant for anyone else to see. But it is gorgeous, it transforms her, she looks more like her son than anything like herself. Something tugs on Brigid, low in her belly, and she has to look away to stop it from pulling her any more.

She pours more tea, and Emer nods slightly at the consolation.

AFTER TEA, BRIGID HEADS out to her handmade hive to release the bees. Niall, at the instruction of his mother, climbs up on the stone wall, so he can see what she's doing without getting too close. Emer keeps an eye on him from even farther away, leaning inside the back door, the bottom half of it shut tight.

Brigid sets the cage down on the ground. She has taken the paper wrapping off and can see the bees now, clustered in the corners of two mesh windows. She lifts the outer and inner cover off her hive. She takes three frames out to create a gap and lifts the travel cage, thrumming with what feels like fire, and begins to pry out with her knife the sugar can that plugs the opening. It moves up with difficulty, anchored by sticky wax. When she finally lifts the can, bees spill out the edges of the hole calmly, as if they can't even fly. She reaches her hand inside the writhing hole and pulls out the small wooden box, no bigger than a tin of tobacco, covered in a thick coating of bees, like it has been dipped in them.

"These are the queen's attendants," Brigid calls up to Niall, shaking them gently off into the hive. Now she can see the mesh circle and the queen bee inside. "Right here is a plug of candy that the bees will slowly eat through to let her out." She removes the wax on one end of the cage with her knife and uses it to secure the queen's box to the side of one of the frames. The bees are starting to wake up now, to fly and buzz and swarm around her. The majority of them are still clustered together, intimately swarmed, crawling all over each other in massive clumps of what has always looked to Brigid like love.

She turns the cage over and gives it a few sharp shakes, and bees shower in as cleanly as flour into a bowl. She hears Niall draw his breath in wonder. A few vertical turns and thumps to empty the inner corners, then she replaces the frames, swipes the edges free of stragglers before putting the inner cover on, then upends the sugar can on top of the escape hole. She explains to Niall that this will feed the bees until they have built their combs, until they are settled and the queen is laying eggs and the workers are divided and given their duties.

"There are three types of bee," she says to Niall. "The queen, the female workers and the male drones. The drones are only for fertilizing the queen. They don't do anything else. They can't even sting. It's the women who rule the bee world."

Niall nods, but it seems like he is not really listening to her. His eyes are unfocused, like he's turned them off. He is listening to the bees. She sets another wooden box on top of the sugar can, and then the outer cover, the top of which she has covered with shiny metal, to pull the sun. She walks away to let them settle in, a small cloud of anxious guards circling the box, painted in the same deep yellow she used to transform her door. Most of the bees have stayed inside, snuggling down into their new home. She thinks of one of her first nights on the island, curling up with the heavy cotton sheet and pillowcases that Emer returned. She had hung them on Brigid's clothesline, so that although they were slightly damp, they were infused with fresh sea air and sunshine.

One little rebel tries to sting her as she walks away. But it changes its mind because as it lands on her neck, it is overwhelmed by a feeling of dopey peace and forgets its intended attack. She brushes it gently away and it flies back to the hive. She wasn't completely honest with Emer, she still gets stung. But she has grown immune to it. It is a pinch, nothing more, the swelling and pain that follow for others hasn't happened to her since she was a girl.

While she explains to Niall how she will harvest the honey, Emer makes fresh bread at the table, with such violent arm movements the dog retreats outside to avoid her. She looks as if she's trying to calm herself down after witnessing some violation. Brigid watches Niall go over and put a hand on her arm, which helps her to calm her jerky movements and take a breath and let whatever is trapped inside her—anger and misery and fear—move to the edges, like the outer ring of disturbed bees, so that her core can get on with its work.

OVER THE NEXT WEEK, Niall finds ways to come alone to see the bees. It is not easy for him to get away from his mother, Brigid knows, she is the nervous, hovering type. He convinces her to let him bring his father and uncle their midday meal—bottles of tea wrapped in woolen socks, scones and thickly buttered brown bread, boiled eggs wrapped tightly together in a cloth parcel. There is too much work now, at the height of the summer, for the men to come home for lunch. He promises to sit and eat with them, but instead leaves the food and walks the wrong way to Brigid's house, while his mother is occupied with Rose and all his girl cousins. Brigid always has candy for him, and a lovely concoction of warmed milk and honey, so sweet it leaves a pleasant ache in his mouth.

She brings him to the hives and pulls out the frames, showing him how quickly the workers have established their hexagonal wax city, where they separate the jobs of tending to young from producing and storing food. Niall's effect on the bees is similar to her own—he soothes them into sleepiness. Neither of them needs smoke to hypnotize the bees into submission, even while taking honey. Brigid knew this already about Niall, that he would be safe and useful, and that Emer had no need to worry. Still, he makes her promise not to tell his mother. She does this easily. She has been accused before, because she is not a mother, of taking children too seriously. Of keeping their secrets, as though she were a child herself. It is not childishness, but longing that compels her. She can pretend they are hers, for as long as it takes to tell a secret. Just as she is distracting herself with this exercise in life—helping bees make a home so they can make more bees and flowers—Niall is a distraction from the urge she has to go back to crawling across the wet ground howling with need. Niall is a great help to her, another pair of hands for the tricky pulling apart and putting together of the intricate puzzle of the hive, and he calms her down. His mother, Brigid thinks, worries too much.

THEY HAVE THE HIVE open when Emer catches them. She runs all the way there, after Fiona reports that Niall is not where he is supposed to be. In fairness, Rua tries to warn them, but they don't stop to notice her slinking, whining performance, too entranced by the humming, sweetly fragrant bees. Amid them, it is impossible to hear the back door or the squelch of Emer's bare feet across the damp grass. Brigid notices the bees' reaction before she even sees Emer there.

They start to swarm. Lifting out of the hive in massive sheets, forming, by some complex communication of pheromones, a single-minded cloud. It hovers above them for a moment, awaiting instructions. Brigid thinks they are leaving, because the only time she ever sees this behavior is when the hive gets crowded and the older bees decide to move on to let the younger bees flourish. Niall looks up at the cloud with a distracted smile on his face, cocking his head as if trying to decipher something beneath what Brigid realizes, too late, is an angry thrum. The dog barks. Emer shrieks her son's name.

Then he is gone, swallowed whole by the swarm, which has morphed to resemble the shape of a boy. Emer is running to him.

For a beat, Brigid thinks he will be all right. She thinks they have covered him with the same sleepy silence that they sometimes cover her hands. Then Niall begins to scream.

Emer is trying to wipe the bees off him, like sluicing water from hair after a swim. Any part of him she uncovers is quickly swallowed up again. Brigid, knocking her aside, ducks and pushes her shoulder into his hips, bending him in half and lifting him off the ground. The bees are stinging her now. She runs for the well, a thick stream of water that runs over rocks and collects in a stone pool, before falling off a small cliff to the ocean. Not the well she's been hoping to find, but large enough to submerge a bee-covered boy. She lays him down in it and holds him under the flow by lying down on top of him, the icy water seeping through her shirt to assault her breasts and stomach. The bees rise again, what is left of them, making their way back to the hive. The rest, dead, a thousand of them, float in the water and cling to Niall's clothing like black and yellow moss.

When she pulls Niall from the water, he is already swollen, his neck huge, his lips deformed, his breath an inefficient desperate wheeze. Brigid lays him on dry rock, opens his mouth and clears it of the bees that have made their way inside.

"What's happening?" Emer says. The sound coming from Niall's throat is horrible.

"He's allergic," Brigid says and she shakes her head at her own stupidity. "Did you know he was allergic?"

Emer is beyond answering her, she is reaching for him and Brigid loses patience, knocking her away for the second time. Brigid spreads her large hands over Niall's throat.

It is painfully familiar, the pull that ransacks her, the distinctly sensual rupture she had sworn she would leave behind.

Then she is being sick quietly onto a cluster of bright yellow lichen, and Emer is holding Niall, wet and shaking with fear, his lips and throat and face back to a reasonable size. Niall holds his bare arm out and brushes stingers, which gather like wet stubble into clumps he flicks onto the grass.

"You said you wouldn't let any harm come to him," Emer says, when Brigid has stopped retching.

"I'm sorry," Brigid says. She looks up expecting daggers, but the way Emer is looking at her is not what she expected. Another thing she'd thought she'd left behind.

"Some touch," Niall says, smiling and pulling Brigid's gaze away from his mother's, inserting himself between them, clean as a knife.

The three of them sit for a while, until the bees that are left settle down, until Niall and Brigid begin to shiver from the wet weight of their clothing and Emer, no longer in a frenzy of buzzing fear she arrived with, suggests tartly that it is time they go inside.

BACK AT THE HOUSE, they won't leave. Brigid is spent, irritable, she wants to be alone. But they hover around her, Emer makes her a plate of smoked fish and brown bread and heats water for more tea. Niall rolls around on the floor with the dog. Brigid wishes briefly that the bees had attacked Emer—the one who angered them, she is sure of it—instead. And that she hadn't interfered.

Emer sits down across from her, watching her eat. She is deciding whether to say something. Brigid silently encourages her not to.

"They took my eye," she says.

"Who did?" Brigid doesn't want to know this, but she can't back away now.

"The bees," Niall says.

"No," Emer says. "The fairies."

"I'm sorry." Brigid doesn't know what she's supposed to say. She is not hungry now and she is suddenly so exhausted she wants to push her tea aside and put her head right down on the table.

With a quick, whispery argument, Emer sends Niall out to fetch water, reminding him to stay away from the bees. She watches him from the small window.

"That's what I have," Emer says. "What those bees tried to do. It's in my hands." Brigid doesn't want to talk about Emer's hands. She doesn't even want to look at them.

"It can't touch you," Emer says. "Same as with Niall."

Brigid feels hot, like something is rising out of her, it's all she can do to keep herself in her chair. Part of her wants to stand up and knock this girl over, the other part wants to clench her vicious hand and lead her into the other room, press her down on the bed. She never should have let them in.

"They say your grandmother was taken." Brigid refuses to look up, but she is listening. "By the fairies, like. Your mother was the child of that changeling. Her own father tried to drown her and she washed back up again, good as new. They called her a witch. The islanders said it, there was some test they had, and she passed. Or failed, depends on how you look at it. She left the island as a girl, got away from them and nobody saw how."

Brigid can't swallow anymore. There is something, large as life, lodged in her throat.

"They say she couldn't die," Emer says. "That's the story about her. That she was touched by the fairies and was immortal because of it." Brigid flinches thinking of the bruises and cuts on the flawless flesh of her mother. A lifetime of attempts that were healed, one by one.

"Oh, she died all right," Brigid says. "Eventually."

Emer comes back from the window, sitting down across from

Brigid. She puts her hands on the table between them. They both look at them. Work roughened, red and peeling, but still, underneath that, they are as young as a girl's. They don't have the loose skin of Brigid's, youth starting to let go its tight grip on bone. Brigid puts her hands in her lap, pressing her fists, an old habit, to the lowest, emptiest part of her belly.

"If you've the healing in your hands," Emer says. "What do you want Saint Brigid's well for?"

But Niall comes in and stops them from sharing any more.

BRIGID HAS A RECURRING dream. In the dream she stands in front of a mirror and sees in her reflection something she never sees while awake. An absence, a mildness, which smoothes her features and makes her young, younger than she's ever been because even as a child her face was burdened. In the dream her face has no fear, no regret, no desire. Absence and peace. Despite the warnings of her mother, and now Emer, Brigid believes that this island is where she will find her dream face, a peace that has eluded her for her whole life. That with enough tea and turf and walking in wind that screams in her ears, her face might settle into the one from her dream, where she is no longer torn apart by feelings of others, free from desire and all its disappointments. Where the slack failure of her belly might smooth away and leave her, where the memories of what she took for years, from countless women who trusted her and laid back while she pulled them inside out, will fade into the mild, blameless blue of ocean and sky. Where what she has been can disappear so the thing she wants has room to become. She crawls into the stone huts of nuns and thinks of their sacrifice, their letting go, those who lived with nothing and cherished it. She'd like to be empty. She'd like to be emptied of it all and feel as if she is full. She'd like to make room for what she wants to come next.

But now what came before is beginning all over again. Now the islanders will know what she can do and will expect it. Now there will be so much coming into her she will not be able to be empty and receive the only thing she truly wants. Now another damaged, deadened girl has felt a promising twinge in her presence and is looking at her hungrily, wanting Brigid to show her what it means. And Brigid won't be able to resist.

CHAPTER 8

St. Brigid's Home for Wayward Girls

1933–1936

Every one of the Sisters sounded like Brigid's mother. They had emigrated as an entity, an exodus of Brigidine nuns from Connemara who came to Maine to start a Home for Wayward Girls. The rumors about why they were there were thick, layered by years of speculation in the minds of their imaginative charges. That they had once been wayward girls themselves, that they'd all had babies, and if you lifted the dark folds of their skirts you would find the evidence, skin that had been stretched then vacated and left not quite the same. Once the evidence of their shame was taken away, they were given habits and made to care for the next crop of impregnated girls as penance. Some thought that the nuns *were* the babies—that they'd been born to unwed mothers in Ireland, raised by nuns and expatriated to do the same; shame, beat and leave hopeless a whole new generation of sinful girls.

This was suggested during a dorm room discussion, voices rising from the thin, squeaky cots. Every ten minutes the door would open, Sister Margaret would say "Whisht!" with the same vicious impatience as Brigid's mother once did. It only shut the girls up for a few seconds.

"If that was true," a girl named Mary said. "What happened to the boy babies?"

"Priests."

"Drowned."

"Eaten!" The voices came in quick succession out of the darkness.

"There weren't any boys," a girl said. "Everyone knows those babies are always girls. That's how God punishes you."

"Of course there were boys," a girl named Jeanne said, dismissively. She had a grainy, mannish voice. "The boys get adopted by rich folks in Boston. They go to Harvard. Then they knock up their girlfriends and send them back here." There was a silence as everyone digested this.

Jeanne had stringy brown hair, a bald patch worn above her forehead where she couldn't stop pulling it out. One eye and cheek were given over to a wine-stain birthmark, and the saturation of color changed with her mood. She smoked cigarettes and had fat, wormy scars on her arms from when, rumor had it, she had once tried to kill herself. She was the same age as Brigid, twelve, but seemed old before her time. Brigid hadn't had the nerve to talk to her yet, but Jeanne often caught her staring, which left Brigid hot, confused and mortified.

All the girls in this dorm were either too young or too lucky to be pregnant, they were here because they were orphaned or molested or abandoned. Not unwed mothers or adoptable babies, but unwanted and in-between.

"Why do the *boys* get adopted?" someone whined in the dark.

"What are you, some sort of retard?" Jeanne said, and Sister Margaret came in again, whisthing, and this time they settled down, not so much out of obedience or sleepiness but because they were too discouraged to continue the topic. In the silence, Brigid could still hear them all, a roomful of girls, turning fact and fiction over in their minds, the same way their lean, underdeveloped bodies flipped like fish between the stiff sheets.

BRIGID HAD NEVER GONE to school, never done a calisthenic or purposeful exercise, never ridden a bike or counted money. She'd never had a friend. Unlike the girls who had come from farms she had not handled horses or cleaned out stalls, and though on the island they'd once had hens, they refused to lay eggs for so long her father had just wrung their necks. Their milk, sour and smelling of urine, had come from a moody little goat that submitted to her mother's hands with a look of pure disgruntlement. Brigid was a terrible cook, she couldn't sew a stitch, and she had never seen a mop.

At the convent she was expected to work. Clean and scrub and wring until her hands were cracked and bleeding from the harsh soap and hot water. Overnight, alone in her bed, she ran healing fingers over the skin, until she realized that if the nuns saw you had smooth hands they made you do even more. So she let the raw cracked skin form into calluses that dirt could not escape from.

Before breakfast they worked, after breakfast they had school in their scrubbed-out classrooms. Brigid could read but had no concept of what to do with numbers, so she often ended up grouped with the six-year-olds. After school were exercises in the cold yard, jumping jacks and running in circles, tennis against a cement wall. Then more work. Dishes, laundry, toilets, floors. Cleaning was a never-ending process, much like the purification of their souls. They would never be pure, but they were expected to attack the tarnish daily. Prayer was an astringent, prayer and penance, like bleach and scalding water. Kneeling on stone for so long it felt as if your kneecaps had shattered under the pressure and you could barely limp back to your dorm. Lashings, given not so much as a punishment for rudeness or shirking but as a lesson in the graceful acceptance of pain, girls' backs ripped into ridges that would heal and form a shell they could bear their life upon.

Once a week, in the early hours before an interminably long Mass, the girls lined up in the pews of the chapel and went behind the altar to confess to Father Hanrahan. He came on Sundays only, up from Bangor, and seemed equally uninterested in the nuns and the girls. It was said he was only there for show, that every such place needed a priest to maintain the illusion that someone was in charge. He spent five minutes with each girl. He tried to glean something, anything, out of Brigid, she suspected at the prompting of Mother Superior, but she remained as monosyllabic as she'd been since arriving. "If you don't let it out, my child," he said once, "the sin will fester inside you. It will eat your soul away. Let it out so God can forgive you."

"Yes, Father," she said, but she didn't volunteer anything.

He eventually sighed and gave her handfuls of Our Fathers and Hail Marys, prayers she didn't know, and traded her for a more malleable girl, one who liked to try to shock him or another who burst into tears over her own unworthiness. Brigid kept her soul locked up tight.

MOST OF THE OTHER girls ignored her. She didn't try to get attention, wasn't vying for the roles of rebel or saint, hardest worker or cleverest student or basket case. She worked at being invisible, and they allowed it. Only Jeanne could not leave her alone.

"I heard your mother murdered your father," she would say when they were scrubbing in adjacent stalls in the bathroom. "How did she do it? Did you help?" The other girls stiffened with anticipation when they heard the cruel things Jeanne said to her. But

Brigid, who had grown up with parents who sometimes spat the worst things that came to their mind, ignored her. Jeanne was worshipped by most of them. She cursed readily and creatively. She was known for alarming sessions in deserted broom closets and bathrooms where she would wrench something violent and luscious out of another girl's body, something most girls, especially the young ones, had barely suspected was there, and leave them limp and wondering when she might do it again. Most of the girls, the ones of a certain age where something was happening that no one bothered to explain, watched Jeanne with breathless hunger, wondering when it would next be their turn for the few thrilling moments in a bathroom stall, trapped against the cold tile wall, Jeanne's hands working on them until they could barely stand up. The lucky ones were captured by her in an empty dorm, or in one of the offices with leather sofas. If you met up with Jeanne and there was an available surface, something you'd never even imagined would happen. She would lay you down and do something that later the girl could barely explain, something that left their faces fired with shame and revisited delight.

Brigid, when she heard these whispered rumors, late at night in her hard, exposed bunk, turned over and pressed the pillow around her ears, trying not to think about Jeanne's huge, chapped, angry mouth.

AT ST. BRIGID'S THERE WAS a separate floor for the pregnant girls. They came when their bellies were no longer easy to hide, and left after the baby was born and given away. They had their own schoolroom, which wasn't used very much, the idea being that if they could read and write there wasn't much use in bothering after that. The lucky ones would still get to finish school, or get married, but most of them would end up doing alternate versions of what they did now, laundry, scrubbing other people's waste off of toilets, boiling up tasteless, filling meals for large crowds. The younger girls rarely got to see them, because their sins were so garish and alive, bellies like enormous blisters underneath their frumpy uniforms. The littlest girls, before they were unceremoniously told how it all worked, thought there was something contagious about the swollen stomachs, that either you could become engorged yourself if you were touched by them, or that the broken morality that landed them there could seep into you, and eventually cause you to make the same life-ruining mistake.

What Brigid noticed most about these girls, when she glimpsed them move, not so gracefully, through the hallway past their classroom, was that they weren't girls anymore. They were not much older than she was, the youngest swollen belly belonged to a girl of thirteen, but the babies inside them transformed them into something else. The lewd jut of the belly, the small gestures that surrounded it, hands placed without thought on the top, or slid underneath like a ballast, showed that whatever child the girl had been before had been swallowed up by the new one growing inside.

They were supposed to be a warning, these girls, trapped by their sins, lonely for their families, not allowed to keep their babies. Brigid couldn't get enough of them. She volunteered for jobs that gave her glimpses, sweeping the hall near the room where they sewed, their enormous forms wedged between their chairs and the frantic sewing machines. She washed windows so she could watch their halting, unbalanced exercise in the yard. She lay in her cot at night, rolled up her itchy nightgown, and ran her rough palms over a child's flat chest and belly, closed her eyes and imagined a swelling, a growth, a body full of something else, something that was, mercifully, not her. Like the changeling she once begged for, not from the ground, but forged from the very soul that desired it.

When babies were ready to be born, the doctor's car came and stayed the night. The doctor often took the baby away with him, a basket in his passenger seat permanently there for this purpose. Only occasionally would a couple come to St. Brigid's, young, healthy, ridiculously happy people who took the baby and left behind a foul mood. No one liked such blunt happiness displayed in the corridors of St. Brigid's, least of all the nuns. It didn't belong, and left everyone fantasizing about things they'd sworn to leave behind.

Sometimes, the baby died. The nuns always said that this was a blessing.

JEANNE WAS THE FIRST girl Brigid healed. She was known for getting the worst of Sister Josephine's whippings, a masochistic nun who would stop only when a girl begged forgiveness, because pure stubbornness meant she passed out before ever giving in. She liked to pull up her nightgown and show her scars to new girls, just for the satisfaction she got from the release of their lip, the tremble, the tears when they realized, with a glimpse of her ugly back, what their life here would be like. She had tried it on Brigid when she'd first arrived and the other girls had gaped at how easily Brigid, who had barely spoken to anyone, laughed.

Jeanne paid her back for that laugh two weeks later. She and Brigid were cleaning the dormitory bathroom and Jeanne attacked with no warning, a punching, kicking, hair-pulling dervish. Brigid didn't hit back, but did what her mother used to, made herself as small as possible to minimize the damage, and waited for Jeanne to give up. By the time she did, the white tiled floor was brilliant with blood. A kick had made it through to her nose. Sister Josephine pulled Jeanne off her and dragged her to her office for a caning, and Sister Margaret, a gentle but ineffectual nun, gave Brigid a cloth for her bleeding nose and walked her to the infirmary. Sister Margaret cleaned the blood off Brigid's face with astringent and hot water, but found no wounds or bruises underneath. Since she wasn't injured, she sent Brigid along to be caned as well. When Brigid arrived at the sister's office, two other nuns were carrying the unconscious Jeanne to the infirmary.

Sister Josephine hit her twice, two hard, slicing blows, before Brigid said it was enough and that she was penitent. The nun was surprised, sure Brigid would be the stubborn one, let one more fly before sending her on her way.

She watched the corridor until Sister Margaret left the infirmary for afternoon prayers, then stepped in to find Jeanne lying on the cot behind a white screen. Jeanne was so occupied with stifling her convulsive sobs that she didn't hear Brigid come over to her. She was lying on her side in only her underwear, her back pulpy with scars and fresh lashings sliced through them. There was so much there, so many times she'd been hit or begged to be hit again, that Brigid realized, as she reached out to touch it, how hard Jeanne had worked to build up such armor. She was sorry that she had laughed at it. The whole time Jeanne had been hitting her, Brigid had been waiting for this part, the part that came later, the penance.

Jeanne turned her head at the first touch, but before she could react, throw her off, sit up and try to fight her again, Brigid put one hand on her back and the other she brought to Jeanne's mouth, crossing a finger over her lips that asked for promised silence. She spread her fingers out over the bloody gashes, closed her eyes and pulled. The heat came out pulsing, angry, and coarse, so different from the quality of her own wounds that at first Brigid thought something was wrong, and that she would not be able to do it. Jeanne's wounds lashed out at her, pulling the places in her body not in one long slow climax, but in quick wallops of pleasure, so that by the time she was done and the wounds were gone, Brigid felt not peaceful like she usually did, but unfinished. She used her hands, hot and full and still tingling, to turn Jeanne over onto her now painless back. Jeanne's body was caught in the middle of a meta-morphosis. Girl with woman half emerged, with lean, childish hips and hard, swollen lumps of breasts that poked up with the same angry defiance as her face. Footsteps in the hallway startled them both, Jeanne pulled the white sheet up to her neck and Brigid reeled back, overcome with nausea, and Sister Margaret came in to find her vomiting in the white sink.

THAT NIGHT BRIGID LAY awake, her heart bonging, waiting for something to happen. She saw Jeanne get up, slipping soundlessly through the shadows, and she counted to sixty before getting up to follow her. Jeanne went to the infirmary, and when Brigid arrived there she found the girl already lying naked in the same spot they'd been interrupted. She thought of her father and his studio and the apologies she never got, and reached a hand out to touch her. Jeanne's back arched, she closed her eyes. Brigid lifted her night-gown above her head and climbed onto the table and pressed into another girl all she had once wanted pressed into her. They opened their legs and mouths and hands, and what Brigid once imagined growing between her parents grew between them, for a terribly long time, something that cracked her open and never went away. Even after it was over and they were hastily dressing, worried about nuns patrolling the hall, it was still there, waiting impatiently for the slightest touch before it would swell again and take them over.

Later that night in her cot, when Jeanne came to slip under the covers with her, it was as if they had never let go, as if they had been pressed together for the hours in between, waiting for the right moment to begin to move.

In the summer, they worked outside. They sunburned until their skin peeled off in swaths, leaving a lighter imprint of freckles un-derneath. They planted seeds, watered, weeded and picked what grew from them. They milked cows, stole eggs from angry hens, and tended the bees: a whole city skyline of tall wooden hives with drawers so heavy that they needed two girls to pull them, heavy with the honey the nuns sold to the town market. They weren't meant to taste it, but they did, feeding each other fingerfuls when no one was looking. Brigid got used to the sound of bees behind everything she did, a dizzy buzz urging her through chores, toward the next moment she and Jeanne could steal alone.

They found each other every day, capturing slivers of privacy in a place where their every move was watched. Lying down in blueberry fields, standing against giant oak trees in the woods. Brigid loved to watch Jeanne's face, the way her birthmark darkened and the cruel mask fell away, as she lost herself to Brigid's hands. Jeanne called it making love. This name made sense to Brigid. She had waited for love but now knew it had to be made, sometimes by ripping something apart and sealing it back together again, or pulled out of someone the way they were learning to pull clay into the walls of a cup. You built it, with fire and clay and honey and skin. You made love. They hid this because they were supposed to, but not one bit of it felt wrong.

THE FIRST TIME SHE bled, a year after arriving, when she was thirteen, she was no longer naive enough to try to heal it. You couldn't live with twenty girls, half of whom had entered puberty, and not know that at some point blood would begin to drip under your dress. The nuns said it was a punishment for being a woman, but some of them, your first time, would let you lie down for the afternoon with a hot brick. Jeanne was shocked when she found out the holes in Brigid's reproductive knowledge. Though she had breasts now, Brigid, breasts that grew so quickly she needed a larger dress every month, breasts as soft and welcoming as Jeanne's were angry and hard, and her period, she had missed some important information somewhere. She believed that now that she was bleeding, Jeanne would be able to put a baby inside her. Jeanne felt almost bad about shattering the delusion, but not bad enough to be gentle about it.

"You moron," she said. "You need a boy for that."

It was a while before she learned that Jeanne didn't have all the facts either. But even when she knew it was from a boy, she still wanted it, wanted a baby growing inside her with the same longing that drove her to press her hands into wounds, or her mouth to Jeanne's chapped lips. The longing to be rescued. It seemed, in the short time she'd known about it, exactly what she was meant to do. She was dejected when Jeanne first told her. There was no part of her that desired to do with a boy the things she did with Jeanne. Other than the priest, Brigid hadn't seen a man since the doctor who dropped her off. There was another doctor, one who slipped in to deliver the babies, but they never saw him. Apparently she would need a boy, at some point, to get what she wanted. She hoped to find the kind that quickly disappeared, like the ones who had abandoned the girls at St. Brigid's, while their babies were still growing.

Jeanne thought she was crazy. No one except rich, married women with nothing better to do actually wanted to have a baby. It ruined you. It stretched your body and then ripped its way out, they'd all heard the screams. Sometimes the girls even died while it tried to get out. Even if they lived, no one was allowed to keep it. The babies were carted away and the girl was left leaking blood and milk and ruined for any sort of normal life where you could live happily ever after. Jeanne had heard of girls who had survived the birth, left St. Brigid's and had gone on to kill themselves after all.

Yes, there were those who did it on purpose to snag a particular boy. But often that backfired, like with Jeanne's cousin Myra who was awaiting her due date upstairs, and then you lost the boy, the baby and your life. It just wasn't something a normal girl would *want* to do. She was so vehement, Brigid stopped talking about it, but the fantasy continued in her mind. Her belly grown hard, full of blood and flesh that was not hers, but was more a part of her than anyone could have been. More a part of her than her parents, who had been too caught up in their dance of brutality and forgiveness to love her, more than this rough, desperate girl who seemed to want to be violated to match what was happening in her mind. More than any of them, a baby would be the closest Brigid could come to love. She imagined it like stealing, more of an abduction than a creation, but once you'd gotten the baby, there was no chance of another world taking it back. Not if you held on tight enough.

That she was a child herself, planning on having a child, never occurred to her. She hadn't felt like a child in a long time. She wasn't even sure she had ever been one.

JEANNE WAS TAKEN FROM her bed the night her cousin Myra went into labor. Something was wrong. They wouldn't have come for her, thought Brigid, awake and listening from her cot, if everything were going to plan. Jeanne hadn't even seen her cousin since the first day she'd arrived, when the Mother Superior had allowed them a brief reunion visit in her office. Jeanne told Brigid that Myra had talked the entire time about her boyfriend, who was going to come and get her as soon as he saved up enough money.

"She's an idiot," Jeanne summarized.

A few hours later, Brigid was woken again by Jeanne's familiar hands, and she could tell before she opened her eyes that someone was with her. The hands were tentative, tapping at her as if they'd never touched before. Brigid opened her eyes. Mother Superior was there. She instructed Brigid to put on a dressing gown and they went out to the corridor.

"I'm not sure why I'm allowing this," Mother Superior said. "But Jeanne seems to think you have an ability to help. Do you, Brigid?"

Brigid glared at Jeanne. She had promised not to tell anyone. She didn't want to do it anymore, now that she'd found other ways to share her body.

"Yes, Mother," she said, wishing, not for the first time, that she was just a normal child with no idea what to do except cry for help when encountering someone else's pain.

EVEN WHEN HER FATHER died, there hadn't been this much blood. It was everywhere, smeared across the floor by the panicked soles of the nuns, burying the doctor up to his elbows, christening foreheads like dried-up dabs of muddied ash. It came out of Myra like something being washed in from the sea, clotting into enormous sacs. Brigid imagined if you broke one apart, you'd find a baby hiding inside. But the baby was still in Myra. Stuck.

Brigid was led up to that space, the space between Myra's legs that was the center of so much panic, even the doctor, tired and out of ideas and fed some lie about Brigid's mother being a midwife, was stepping aside to let her in. Myra was in too much pain, screaming, thrashing, struggling to close her legs which were held open by two blood-spattered and terrified-looking nuns, to even know that Brigid was there. Someone poured something clear and stinging over Brigid's arms.

Somehow she knew what to do. She put her hands on Myra, first one and then the other, as easily as if she were sliding them into wet clay. Myra stopped screaming. She whimpered, like someone whose pain has backed off, but the memory of it is still spilling over. The blood stopped gushing out, though this was hard to tell because of all that was already there. The baby had ripped places that Brigid sealed even as she reached for it. She felt the small hard joints, an ankle, a knee, the heel bone of a miniature foot. The leg pulled away from her, curling in on itself like something afraid. The baby was hiding, no intention of coming out, holding on, willing to let her mother bleed to death before leaving the only place that was safe. Brigid held on to it, letting her healing hands soothe a baby that was not injured, only afraid. She slowly turned it around so she could cradle the head, fists clenched to its chin, and gently, with no pain for Myra and a silent promise to the reluctant baby, she pulled it, long and slimy and covered in a white, waxy crust that beaded away blood, out into the harsh white room. Instead of handing the baby to the doctor or one of the nuns, Brigid stepped forward, laying it on the bloody sheets draped on Myra's still massive belly. The baby curled back up again, like a rubber band snapped back into shape, and stopped crying, as if that was where it belonged. Before they pulled her away, while she sealed the last rip in Myra that her own hands had helped make, Brigid saw the look on Myra's face. The pain had been gone for a while, as had the fear of dying. As soon as Brigid had first touched her Myra knew she wouldn't die. But the way she looked at that baby, as if it were just as horrifying as the wobbly clots of blood that came before it, made Brigid want to snatch it back, hide it in her nightgown, run away. Apologize for exposing it to this in the first place. Myra closed her eyes and turned her head and let the nuns, once the doctor pulled Brigid away and cut the cord, remove the baby from its place on top of her, as if its weight meant nothing at all.

THE DOCTOR WAS NOT like she'd imagined him. Brigid had never seen him up close, only the form of his shoulders and hat as he was rushed in and out to deliver and remove these little lives. She had assumed he was like the priest, old and craggy-faced and revolting, without a hint of kindness, but his face was young, open and feminine, with the large, barely blinking, eyes of a deer. His lashes were long and wet and it was clear that he had not yet in his life needed to shave. He came and stood next to her while she washed her hands in the enormous sink, watching the blood fade to pink, form a whirlpool around the drain and swirl away. He held a hand up and she thought he was going to touch her shoulder, but when she cringed, he put it down on the edge of the sink.

"It's easier when they don't want to hold them," he said.

Brigid said nothing. She was looking at his hands, delicate, smooth, with long fingers and only the slightest thickness at the knuckle. They could have belonged to a woman, or a child.

"Can you take out your own eye as well?" he asked. "Then put it back, like your namesake?" She looked quickly at him, before she could stop herself. Then back at the sink, but she could feel a smile stretching.

"Of course not." She was blushing.

"I'm not one to question miracles," the doctor said. "So I won't ask how you did that." His voice was light and high, a voice she imagined, had she ever met any, might come from a boy.

"But I'm going to insist that you do it again."

She didn't have to answer him, because she started gagging and a nun led her quickly to a bathroom. She was allowed to sleep the morning away in the empty dorm, where Jeanne visited quickly before running off to mop the floors.

"He took the baby with him," Jeanne said.

"I know," Brigid said.

The doctor was wrong, Brigid thought. It wasn't that the girls didn't want to hold them. When something is stolen from you, it is sometimes easier to act like you never wanted it in the first place.

CHAPTER 9

Ink

August 1959

Emer can't stop thinking about Brigid's hands. The long fingers, slender except for prominent knuckles that move like stones beneath her skin. When she pulled that poison out of Niall, Emer could feel a loosening in her own neck. Normally a late sleeper, now she is up before dawn counting the hours until it will be proper to stop by, just to be near them again.

Emer catches Brigid by surprise, out back trying to move her stubborn cow. Seeing Emer without warning, combined with the frustration at the cow, makes her face go dark, it looks fed up for a moment before she can rearrange it into a welcome. Emer is used to this face. Her mother gets it, Patch, Austin, and even, though she tries to hide it, Rose. Emer is not greeted with joy by anyone but Niall. She makes people start, cringe, slink away. If they are unlucky enough to brush against her, she makes them wonder why they bother getting up in the morning at all. Even the people who are supposed to love her dread being alone with her. She is already worried about the day that Niall first looks at her this way. The Yank doing it hurts even more than she thought it would. With Brigid, Emer wishes she could be someone other than herself.

She helps Brigid with the cow, and Brigid asks her in for tea, the obligation that Emer relies upon. Now that she is friends with Rose and other island women she will have even less energy, Emer is sure, to put up with her alone. But she is already bound by the custom of offering tea.

This is new to Emer, trying to make a friend. She's not very good at it.

"Why aren't you married?" she says, cringing at how it comes out, like an accusation. She stirs milk into her tea and tries, if not to smile, to at least straighten her face into something neutral.

"I was," Brigid says quietly, not looking up.

"Did you run away from him?" Emer says. "Is that why you came here?"

"No, Emer," she says. "He died."

"Car crash?" Emer says. She has heard this is how loads of people die in America.

Brigid sighs, pressing two fingertips against her temple. "Cancer," she says.

Niall is trying to dance with the dog and the pig, encouraging them to stand on their back legs. Brigid allows his pig inside now because it is as well behaved as any of them, though it can't really manage to stand on two legs.

"Poor Brigid," Niall says. The dog and pig sit neatly, looking up at him for their next instruction. It is so much easier for her child to speak to people than it is for her. How little time he spends, no time at all really, thinking about what he is going to say. It is the sort of ease that she hates in other people, like her sister, or Austin, or Brigid herself.

"Could you not heal him?" Niall says. "With your hands, like?"

"Nope," Brigid says, a catch in her voice that she coughs her way through.

"Why not?" Niall says.

"Hush, Niall," Emer scolds him, even as she feels grateful for his nerve.

"Some things are too dangerous," Brigid says quietly, "to get my hands around."

Emer allows herself a quick glance at Brigid's hands, tightened to whiteness around their mug. And it happens again, the pull, so strong it is like being accosted, a longing that has flared up in her, ever since she saw what Brigid can do. A vicious need, so sinful and foreign and unthinkable that it makes her dizzy. She is not even sure that what she wants is something that women do. She imagines, over and over again, like the fantasies of Austin that once looped in her mind, Brigid laying those hands on her.

ROSE HAS BRIGID OVER fairly often now for tea, and though Emer is always invited along, she hates these afternoons; she suffers physically every time Brigid smiles at her sister. The islanders are all taken with Brigid now, they like her big American laugh and her quirky hobbies and her expressions of respect and gratitude. She is constantly complimenting them, praising them, as if what they do mindlessly every day is actually admirable. Emer thinks she lays it on too thick, and is amazed at how they all fall for it. Still, no one will tell her where the well is. No matter how fond they get, she will never be one of them.

Their mother is the only one Brigid hasn't charmed yet. Clodagh doesn't speak to her, just sits out of the circle in her rocker, crocheting with one hand and looking up every so often to glare her disapproval. Brigid smiles at her, and pours her tea.

Rose's girls, of course, adore Brigid. Clare and Cecelia sit on her lap and try to feed her their porridge and she makes them laugh by pretending to gobble up the offered spoon. Fiona and Eve mimic her accent, borrow her busily patterned scarves, bite their lips until they think their mouths are as red as Brigid's. Rose's girls have always steered clear of Emer, and everyone on the island knows better than to hand her a baby. This has always suited Emer just fine, but watching Rose's girls fight to sit next to Brigid makes her want to pinch every one of them off their chairs.

"What did you do in America?" six-year-old Bernie asks her. "Were you a film actress?"

"Certainly not." Brigid winks at Fiona.

"Are you somebody's mammy?" Teresa adds, and Brigid's smile stiffens.

"No. I was a midwife. My husband was a doctor. He took care of babies."

"Like Saint Brigid?" Fiona says.

"I thought she was the patron saint of midwives, not one herself. Nuns don't usually have babies."

"Do you not know the stories?" Rose asks her. Rose has an annoying loyalty to the saint, and prays to her with the same ignorant fervor, Emer thinks, as a woman fifty years her senior. She raises her girls on tales of Brigid's miracles: hanging her cloak on nothing but a sunbeam, blessing cows to give endless amounts of milk, offering her well to two lepers to bathe in, and, when the first cured won't help the next, cursing him ill again. Even the toddlers know how to pray over the fire at night, smooring it in her name.

"Saint Brigid leans over every cradle," Rose likes to say, whenever someone has a baby. Emer hates this expression. She believes that something else, something prayer has no power over, hovered over Niall's.

"Emer told me about the convent," Brigid says. She looks at Emer then, so intensely Emer has to look away. "She said nothing about babies."

"Well, first it was only the nuns, for the isolation, and the peace, to finish the scriptures, that sort of thing. She brought her postulants here and built those clocháns and lived on not much more than sea air."

Rose pours tea into Brigid's just-emptied mug and continues.

"They had a reputation, mind, for healing, even now Brigid is the patron saint of childbirth. Some say that girls came here, when they were in trouble, and had their babies. And Brigid let them stay."

"There's nowhere in Ireland you could do that now," Emer explains.

"True enough," Rose says. "A girl gets pregnant nowadays, they send her to the laundries and sell her baby to rich Americans."

"Little pitchers," Emer warns. The girls are listening, rapt. Rose dismisses her.

"Not that we'd do that here, not in donkey's years," she says. Their mother lets out a snort of laughter. Brigid looks over, but Rose and Emer ignore her.

"There's nothing shameful in being a mother, sure," Rose declares. "It's what God wants for us."

Emer looks quickly between her sister and Brigid, a vise grip on her neck.

"It's not God who makes those little whores open their . . ." their mother starts, and Rose interrupts her, loudly suggesting the children run outside to play. Brigid actually leans over, puts a hand out and pats the woman's arm. Their mother is shocked silent by this. Eve, pouting, ushers all the little ones out the door but Fiona stays.

"Some say it's how she found her soul friend," Rose says. "Darladuach was one of those girls; she and Brigid raised her baby together. Darla was so devoted to Brigid that when Brigid was on her deathbed, she lay down and asked to die along with her. They say she died a year later, on the same day, the first of February, of grief."

Emer had forgotten this part of the story. She remembers now how she felt the first time she learned it at Sunday school. The picture in their book was of a dark homely woman standing like a child at Brigid's side. It had reminded her of how she felt standing next to Rose.

"Why did they leave?" Brigid says.

"I expect they hadn't the strength to carry on after that. Some stayed, they say, and had sons who grew to be men and married the daughters and that is where the island families come from. The fire that Brigid kept, the eternal fire that the nuns guarded so it would never go out, is the same fire we have in our hearths today."

"And her well?" Brigid says. "Didn't she leave a healing well behind?"

"Wouldn't you like to know?" their mother taunts.

Rose is blushing, realizing she has gone too far. "Och, that was all a long time ago now."

Emer is holding her breath. She thought perhaps Rose would tell her where the well is. But, true to island tradition, she is keeping it to herself.

"Some say she wasn't a saint at all," Fiona pipes up. "Only a fairy queen disguising herself as a Christian when it suited her."

"That's enough of that talk," Rose scolds.

"Others say there wasn't any magic to her," Emer adds. "It's just a story of women who wanted to get away."

Brigid looks at her for so long that Emer feels heat rush from her face all the way down to her lap.

"I know the feeling," Brigid says.

BRIGID'S NEXT DELIVERY, HAPPILY lugged up the road by Malachy, who is so taken with her he is ridiculed by the other men, is art supplies. A wooden case of pastels with more colors than Emer has ever seen laid out like precious, edible things. Bottles of colored ink and long, delicate brushes so fine they look like they might prick like a pin. Rectangles of charcoal that leave smudged fingerprints on everything Brigid touches, as if she has dipped her hands in the ashes from the fire.

"Are you an artist?" Niall asks, excited, when he sees the tools spread out on the table. The sheets of paper are thick and soft and jagged at the edges, and there are sketchbooks that he flips through delightedly, each and every page identically blank and waiting.

"I like to draw," Brigid says. "Though I'm not very good at it."

But of course, she is good at it. She draws the dog first, smudges of charcoal, shadows and lines that seem random, until a recognizable figure emerges. She draws the pig, capturing in a few strokes the expression of the thing, though before she drew it Emer didn't realize it had an expression.

Other days her drawings are not realistic at all. She draws odd mutations, Niall's head on the pig's body, her own fiery curls on the dog's. She renders them quickly and adjusts them to make Niall laugh. Sometimes they do it together, she will sketch a face and Niall will finish it off, putting wings and a stinger on himself or trousers on the dog.

"You don't have to let him scribble and ruin things," Emer says, but Brigid laughs this off.

"We're only having fun," she says. Emer thinks, if she could draw like that, if she could use her hands to translate lines and smudges into life, she wouldn't want anyone to touch it.

Whenever she draws Niall she gives his eyes fiery concentric swirls that look like they are moving, turning in circles on a white page.

One day, Emer is fussing about Brigid's kitchen while Brigid is trying to draw.

"Oh, Emer, sit," she sighs. "Pose for me."

"I wouldn't know how," Emer protests. Her heart is hammering so hard she's afraid it is audible.

"There's not much to it other than holding still," Brigid says. "And you're driving me batty moving around so much."

So Emer sighs and shrugs, hiding the thrill that courses through her at the thought of Brigid's hands drawing her. She imagines Brigid taking the charcoal and smudging it across her skin, like smothering a fire, dousing the hot anticipation that crawls all over her. Desire so strong it has lipped over into pain.

It's backward, having someone look at her so intently. So purposefully. Instead of what usually happens, eyes glancing at her and running away. Niall comes in and out with the dog and pig, checks Brigid's sketchbooks and nods, serious as a man.

She does not see any of Brigid's drawings until the end. What she had imagined, during the hours that Brigid's eyes studied her, was ugliness; bad posture, awkward limbs, a puckered pocket of skin where there was once an eye. She thought the drawings would be as disappointing as looking at herself in the mirror. When she finally sees them, she is suspicious at how pretty she looks. In the charcoal sketches, her torso is long and graceful, her neck and clavicle look like they belong to some other woman. Her face is absent of the clenching she sees in the mirror, not smiling but looking at least as if it eventually might. Her dark hair covers her patch so it looks like merely a shadow, her good eye is lovely, the lashes longer than she knew.

The ink drawings are stranger. In them her figure is recognizable, but instead of shadows and cross-hatching she is composed of furious swirls, swirls of what look like fire, then water, then air, some of them bumping into one another in the junctures of her body and creating a storm. In her middle, curled like an infant but taking up more space, is a version of Niall. He is half-boy, half-pig, a frightening deformed creature except for his face, which is beautiful. In the storm that swirls about her body his eyes are the only fixed and steady spot, the only place in the drawing where you can comfortably look. He stretches from her groin to her neck. There are whorls of dark water in her neck and her hands. But in her middle, where Niall is, the blue lightens to silver, like the color of sun on the sea.

"What is that supposed to be," she scoffs.

"What do you think?" Brigid says.

"Queer enough," Emer says, and Brigid laughs. Emer feels suddenly cold, like she's been wrapped in something that was ripped away.

"It's like you're drawing inside me," she says quietly.

"Yes," Brigid says, and Emer wonders if she understands. She doesn't mean that Brigid is interpreting her. What she means is that Brigid's pens, her ink, her coal-smudged fingers, seem to be reaching down inside Emer herself, reaching for something as deep and as secret as what she has spied on, what she had stopped wishing to find. And that something inside her is rising up, begging to meet Brigid's hands.

ON A CALM DAY, they take a picnic to the cliffs, spread a blanket on the grass between the clochán. Emer and Brigid eat scones and drink tea while Niall and the dog and the pig chase after birds. Emer hasn't spent this much time outside since she was a girl and has lighter streaks in her dull hair and a color to her face that her sister has told her is handsome. It's not just the color, her expression is a bit softer. Not so chiseled. Once, as she walked by Malachy in the fields, he said, "If I didn't know better I'd say Emer was smiling." This of course made her scowl, but she couldn't bring herself to hate him for it. Because Brigid winked at her.

They are like this since she started posing. Easier. Brigid smiles when she sees her coming up the road, instead of sighing and reaching for the kettle. Occasionally Emer cracks a joke and makes Brigid laugh and those moments are so satisfying, Emer wants to grab at the air between them and swallow it, so that she can feel this friendly, this loose, this enjoyed, all the time.

It is as though the drawing has softened Emer, as though a new version has been inked on top of the old. Right onto her skin. She has even posed nude for her—Emer, who can't undress in front of her own sister without turning away. She lay naked on Brigid's bed and felt drunk with the cheek of it. Looking at the drawings afterward, she is mortified at the jolt of longing she feels from the curve of her own breasts.

Even Emer's mother notices the change in her, and says, if she catches Emer smiling to herself, "Aren't you making a holy show."

Lying in the grass, listening to the wind rise and fall and the birds' wings flapping against it, Brigid's pen scratching at paper, and Niall laughing at the animals, Emer almost falls asleep. Then something yanks her, as if she is falling and instead of hitting the ground she is caught by a rope, and suspended, jarred and bouncing in midair. Anxiety surges at her neck and she leaps up, looks for Niall, barks at him not to get too close to the edge.

"He's all right," Brigid says. Not dismissive, she is reassuring. "I'm watching him."

Emer flushes, embarrassed and awkward again. She can't think of a graceful way to sit back down, so she stands, letting the wind whip her hair loose from its place behind her ears. She can see that Brigid has been drawing her again, drawing a peaceful, pretty woman stretched out in a bed of grass.

"What is it you're so worried about?" Brigid says.

Emer considers not really answering, as Brigid brushes her off when she asks too much about her life before or why she is here.

"Boys are prone to scrapes," Emer tries.

"He's pretty careful," Brigid says. "You're not worried in the moment, though. You're worried all the time." She flips back in her sketchbook to a quick ink drawing of Emer's face, eye closed. Though at first glance she just looks to be sleeping, Brigid has done something with her eye, with her mouth, that give off flashes of pure anguish, which then fade away, as if the picture itself is moving in and out of a bad dream. Emer looks at this drawing for a long time.

"When he was born he wasn't able to eat," she says quickly, afraid she will lose her nerve. "A woman helped me teach him and she wasn't, well she wasn't real. Wasn't human." She glances quickly at Brigid, but she doesn't look like Rose does when she tries to talk of this, ready to placate her. She just looks like she's listening, really listening, with no contradictions lining up behind her eyes.

"I think she means to come back for him. They'll try to steal him, the way they took me, but they didn't want me. They try all the time, they tease, pull him partway. If I get him off this rock, if I get everyone off, before he's seven, I think maybe they'll leave us alone."

"Why seven?"

"Seven years is how long they give you. Before they take them back."

"You think he's a changeling."

"He's mine. But a part of him belongs elsewhere. It does not live in this world. They want the rest."

"That's why you want the evacuation," Brigid says. "Because you think Niall will be taken?"

"You can see it, I know you can."

Brigid is quiet. She is thinking.

"Why do you have to get everyone off?"

Emer shrugs. "I can't see any other way."

"You could leave. If you wanted to."

"Please," Emer says. "I'm not you."

Brigid seems like she's going to argue with her, but then stops. She knows Emer is right. Brigid is a woman with no ties, with money of her own, with the American notion that running away is always possible. The box of who she is wasn't already lidded and sealed long ago.

"I don't think they'll take him, Emer," she says. Emer notes, even as she opens her mouth to argue, that Brigid doesn't bother to say they don't exist.

"You don't know. You haven't been here long. Some say they drove Saint Brigid away. That they took some of her girls, and she, the most powerful saint in Ireland, couldn't do a thing about it. When you cross them, there is no mercy. You'd be better off if you took them seriously yourself."

"It doesn't help anything. All this fear."

"What would you know about it?" Emer can't hold it back, the crying, and her voice is bending around it. "You don't know how I am afraid. It's not like fear for yourself. Not at all. You've no children, so you can't know."

"I'm no stranger to the kind of fear that strangles you, Emer."

Emer can't stand that, she turns away, tries to stifle a sob as it rises, as loud and inevitable as the wind.

Emer is facing the cliff, the drop her mother wanted her to take, the drop into sea air and wind that she wanted too, until she had Niall, when she no longer wanted it, though often she feared she would end up like her mother and throw them both off. She misses it, that blasphemous desire, that promise she kept to herself that she could take everything away, that she could destroy something completely, instead of a little bit at a time with the misery that comes from her hands. She doesn't have that anymore, that out. Now that she has Niall she is no longer alone with herself in the darkness. His light is insistent and it never wanes. He is like Rose on that wet hill, screaming at her daily not to go. She has no hold on the earth without him.

Brigid comes up behind her. She has never touched Emer before, but she moves in until her front is pressed against Emer's back, her strong arms have slipped underneath Emer's crossed ones, and she is hugging her. Emer leans back into her, feeling like the wind might knock them both over, wanting it to, wanting to fall and have this woman, every strange and promising inch of her, press Emer into the ground.

Emer is breathing too fast, and Brigid holds her tight and tries to calm it down.

"You're his mother, Emer," she whispers, her breath a welcome relief at Emer's tight neck. "You're a horrible crank to everyone else," she laughs, "but you're everything to him. He's not going anywhere."

Though Emer fears she might be pushed away she can't stop herself. She turns around, rotates within the cave of Brigid's arms, so she is facing her, so their hips are pressed together, their breasts, their arms wrapped so tightly you can no longer tell who is holding on to whom. They are exactly the same height. Brigid's mouth is right there and though in one minute Emer will think she imagined it, there is a pause, a lingering of Brigid's eyes on her lips that makes Emer's mind flare with the image of kissing her, open, wet, endless kissing of the kind she has never tried, until it falls back into the realm of impossibly wrong.

Brigid gives her one last, fortifying squeeze, turning this into something else, like the patting hand of someone who is already walking away. She steps back and the wind rushes in between them again. Niall comes running into view, laughing and being chased by the animals, just in time to miss it all. Emer sees Brigid looking at him, she tries to smile casually, hiding her real expression underneath. The way she looks at all children. Smiling as if she'd rather be crying because they are not her own.

"Can you help us?" Emer whispers. Brigid looks angry for an instant and Emer takes a step backward, thinking she has gone too far. But then the anger fades to weariness and Brigid smiles, looking at her but not really meeting her eye. There is something in this gesture that makes Emer go cold and still inside. The avoidance, coupled with the look of burden, it is the thing she puts in everyone, but she isn't trying now. She wants to find a way to reach Brigid. She is tired of pushing people away and still being surprised when they recoil.

But then Brigid nods. "Perhaps we can help each other," she says.

Her smile is a miracle. A genuine smile, directed at Emer.

Emer is too grateful, and too worried that she'll take it back, to disagree. The dog comes running up then, jumping on Brigid, and Niall flies into Emer for a hug. The pig squeals and bonks against their legs. And even as Emer squeezes Niall as tightly as she can, a part of her wishes that he'd stayed away for five more minutes, so that Brigid would not have been required to let go.

CHAPTER 10

Kidnapped

1936

After that first birth, Brigid was no longer just a girl to them. They were Irish nuns, their order named for a saint who colluded with fairies, and they knew magic when confronted with it. On the outside Brigid remained the same: a thirteen-year-old girl pulled without much kindness through long days of chores. To the nuns, whose lives were not much brighter, she became the promise of something. Proof that what they did was real. They came to her now, when she was sitting in class or sweeping a hallway, and wanted her to put her hand on their arms. Though she had never tried to heal any wound that wasn't physical, none of them believed her. They came away from Brigid's hand imagining a salve had been applied to their soul.

Matthew, the young doctor, who felt no need to argue with useful magic, requested that Brigid be fetched for every birth, even those that promised to be routine. He didn't believe in drugging the mothers because the drugs, even though they stifled the screams, made the process more difficult. He needed them to push, not pass out. He had seen too many babies' heads crushed by forceps, and had radical views of the natural process of childbirth. The nuns, being from rural Ireland, didn't mind these views, which was why he'd ended up with the job in the first place. He had observed Myra when Brigid turned the baby and he wanted every girl he delivered to be given the same balm. Some pain in childbirth was necessary, so a routine developed between them that moved quietly through the delivery room over the long tedious hours that bled into each other at night. If Brigid comforted too much, the natural contractions would slow down, or stop. The girl giving birth either lay on the cot, seizing up with each surge of pain, or walked around, squatting and grunting and making younger nuns blush. The rhythms of it, the build and release, and often the moaning, reminded her so much of what she pulled from Jeanne that Brigid sometimes grew embarrassed, rearranging her posture in the chair where she was supposed to wait until she was needed. When the pains grew closer together and they had no chance to recover in between, Brigid would be called over to touch their writhing bellies. Matthew wouldn't let her ease it too much. They needed the tight bands of fire to push out the baby. Without it, the body, he explained to her, would not know what to do.

These breaks also eased Brigid's own illness, gave her a handle on it, so that, during routine labors, she could push through a vague feeling of fighting the flu. Other labors, she barely managed to hold it in until she returned to her dorm, where she collapsed with chills and vomiting, or a headache that temporarily blinded her.

She did most of her healing in the last moments, when the baby's head was warping the mother's groin beyond recognition, when the space between her hips and the open folds of her vulva looked deformed, studded with poking bones.

Often, at the moment the baby's head finally broke out, Brigid would feel not triumph but something deep and cold and more like failure. As if she'd assisted in some sort of death. There was grief once the baby was out. Even the girls who held their babies and cried and kissed them didn't get to do so for long. The babies pushed their way out only to be ripped away. Brigid often went back to her cot and, spurred on by fever or cramping, cried silently, thinking of the worst of the pain, the pain she could not ease, that came the moment that girl and baby, meant to be together, were pulled apart.

Brigid liked to imagine the hospital where Matthew worked, where the process of giving birth was actually a positive one, where there were smiles and presents and congratulations rather than silence and pinched faces and the sneaking around of doctors who brought no relief in their heavy bags. Where babies were the long-awaited reward instead of the last part of the punishment.

Sometimes, after the mother had been taken away to the infirmary to recover, Matthew was packing up, and the nuns were stripping the bloody linens, Brigid would hold the newly bathed and swaddled baby. They were so warm, as warm as the inside of the womb they'd come from. She whispered endearments to them in Irish. My heart, my light, my pulse. She kissed their impossibly soft feet.

She never saw the mothers again. Soon after the babies were out of them, the nuns had them dressed and packed, rags stuffed into their bras to soak up the weeping from their breasts. A car would arrive to take them away—a guilty-looking boyfriend, a stern social worker or pale, stony-faced parents. They went back to their homes, their high schools, their jobs. Brigid imagined them afterward, going about their lives, pretending nothing had happened as grief doubled them over like a surge of labor, as their bodies keened from every orifice, blood, milk and tears pouring out of them with no consolation in sight. Nothing could stanch such grief; it would be there, inside both the mothers and the babies, the rest of their lives.

The nuns said the babies were better off. They were being given to parents who could love them. But Brigid had her hands inside these girls, inside their wombs. It was not for lack of love that babies were being stolen.

SOMETIMES WHILE SHE WAITED through a labor, Brigid looked at diagrams in Matthew's medical textbook. Wrinkled wombs, flowery fallopian tubes, smooth, serious-looking ovaries. She read that eggs lived inside these sacs. It wasn't a man who made the babies, like she'd thought, but a man and a woman together, the tiny sperm unlocking something in the woman's egg, so it could grow and change and swell until it could no longer be hidden from the outside. Brigid imagined, on those nights when she thought back to the diagrams and Matthew's eager, boyish voice, that her eggs had been there all along. On the island with her parents, in the lighthouse where she failed to pull her father's life back, in the orphanage where Jeanne's hands could make her forget herself, all that time, she had been incubating this possibility. This hope.

The need for a man was a technicality. Her baby was already waiting inside her.

BRIGID WAITED FOR THE right time, knowing that to rush it was to risk everything. Matthew thought she was only a girl. They developed a rhythm where he no longer had to call for the time for Brigid to step forward, she already knew. They grew to work seamlessly with one another, one encouraging the girl to push through pain, the other alleviating it. Matthew usually stepped aside when Brigid touched them, or averted his eyes. Despite everything he'd seen, he treated these girls' bodies with a modest deference that made a few of them, not to mention a handful of the nuns, want to love him. But they never got a chance to see him and after what amounted to days of pain and relief and blood and defecation and vomit, they usually forgot by the end of it all that they had thought him attractive. They were never to see him again, any more than they were allowed to see the babies he pulled out of them. Only Brigid saw

him repeatedly, was greeted by his shy, eager smile, which he gave
when the nuns weren't watching and which always jolted her a bit,
in a similar but sweeter way to the throb inside her whenever she
and Jeanne saw the chance to be alone.

Once he forgot to give Brigid space, during a labor that was going
along fine and started to tilt at the last minute. While Brigid was laying
her hands to ease a contraction she felt a jolt of something going hor-
ribly wrong. She panicked, stepped back and he saw it, walking up
behind her quickly, putting his stethoscope to the girl's belly, that was
shifting, large mounds of flesh pushing their way across and diving
down again. Like whales coming up out of the sea.

"It's the cord," he said quickly. He put his arms on Brigid's, the
first time he'd ever touched her, too intent on a solution to be shy or
modest about it. He held her arms from behind, told her to quickly,
quickly, his breath hot and urgent in her ear, slip her fingers beneath the cord and loosen it from the baby's neck. As she eased the
tight band, her hands inside gave the mother another moment of
pleasurable relief, and Matthew, still holding her forearms, felt it.
She felt the jolt of longing ricochet back to him, so shocking him
that he let go and backed away, but not before she felt something
grow between his hips and her back, the possibility she had been
waiting for. After the birth was over, he packed up quickly, not allowing Brigid time to sing and softly rock the newborn. She barely
got it cleaned up and swaddled before, avoiding her eyes, he took it
roughly and left with curt instructions to the nuns.

It was three weeks before he returned again. Three weeks where
Brigid continued to make love with Jeanne but could no longer
lose herself in it. A memory infected her pleasure. She would watch
Jeanne's mouth twist and smile, and have to look away, remembering the moment Matthew had glanced at her with a longing that
resembled fear.

WHEN A NUN FINALLY woke her in the night and brought her to the infirmary, her stomach was knotted at the thought of how he might greet her. Or not greet her. He didn't look up when she came in, he was taking the girl's blood pressure, but as she washed her hands and arms and put on the nurse's gown he always had her wear, she could feel him watching her, and when it was time to go over and touch the girl who was yelping, as if alarmed by her own pain, she stood next to him. He turned to look in her eyes and it was a shock how he didn't try to hide it at all, but let her see everything, the desire and the shame. Shame, his eyes hinted, that wasn't going to stop him.

It was all they could do to get through that birth, mercifully straightforward and short, only two hours of rapid, biting labor that Brigid barely needed to help. The baby was expelled out with such force, in one great wave of painful joy, Brigid almost dropped him. After the baby and mother were cleaned up, the nun brought the baby downstairs to the new parents who couldn't bear to wait the few more hours it would take Matthew to deliver their child to them. Matthew said something low to the remaining nun and rather than lead her back to the dorm, the nun retired, leaving Matthew with the keys. If Mother Superior had been there it never would have been allowed, but most of the other nuns deferred to the doctor as if he were as infallible as the priest. So they shuffled off and Brigid wondered later if they knew and envied her the soft click of the lock on the door.

He was driven by something that was not gentle, but he was still Matthew, shy and too kind to abuse her, so she had to put her lips to his first, ease him down into a chair, lift her gown and lead his trembling hands. He kissed her cautiously and whispered the words she had waited to hear as a girl.

"I'm sorry."

It lasted longer than it ever had with Jeanne, longer than a nighttime of labor, longer than her father had mouthed apologies into her mother's bruised and battered skin. It lasted longer than her life so far and still it wasn't over.

She knew what Matthew was feeling. She had felt it inside of Jeanne.

Eventually he let out a regretful moan, shuddered, holding her with a desperate grip, then grew still. What they'd created continued to move through her, new waves breaking just as the last one retreated.

He kissed her for a long time, filling her mouth with gratitude, kissed her with such serious and gentle intent, she felt it reaching below the ocean inside her, deep down to meet the place where something, she was sure, something akin to love had just been made.

SHE LOST THE FIRST pregnancy quickly, only a few weeks in. Just as she could feel a pop inside her body when her egg was released and began its way down, she felt the moment where the jumble of cells that was her baby let go, loosened its grip, almost playfully, like a child swinging and dropping from a tree limb. It happened when she had her hands on another baby, the one trying to stay inside Kathleen McKenna, and she was giving it the gentlest of tugs to encourage it out. Just at the moment where the baby gave in and Kathleen groaned in relief as Brigid's hands dissolved her pain, Brigid felt her own child slip, fall away, and the corresponding seize of her womb, as if it were trying to grab on to it, a sob of protest that came too late. By the time she got back to her dorm, she had started bleeding, and spent two days examining but finding nothing recognizable in the brown clots she rinsed from her monthly rags.

The next pregnancy was harder to arrange, since Matthew, after the first time, remembered to take precautions. At first he pulled away just at the crucial moment, and it was all she could do not to cry in disappointment. Then there was the time that she managed to hold him down, he was a small man and she was tall and big-boned for fourteen, and when he realized her intention he started to sit up, but came inside her anyway, and was furious afterward. She told him that it didn't matter, that she'd not yet begun to bleed, but he wasn't convinced and the next time brought rubber sheaths that left her smelling medicinal between her legs. A darning needle prick to each of the sheaths in his stash was enough to guarantee that her body started swelling up again. This one lasted longer, a lot longer, and it was months between laboring girls, months where she only saw Matthew twice, when he came by to help with an-other girl's miscarriage, and that time the nuns didn't leave them alone, so he couldn't see how taut her stomach had become, tight and stretched like a drum.

She was breaking Jeanne's heart, she knew this, and tried to ease it a bit, by continuing to touch her, keeping their encounters so dangerous and brief that it was natural that she didn't get a turn. It wasn't long before Jeanne demanded to know why she cringed if she tried to touch back.

"I'm bleeding," she said. Since they all had their periods at the same time, Jeanne knew she was lying.

Brigid's body ached to be touched but she was afraid for the baby, that Jeanne's rough hands might make it let go.

And then, before she could move away, Jeanne, sliding her hands down, felt the swell of Brigid's lower belly and lifted her dress to look at it.

"I guess you got what you wanted," she said, and walked away. She stopped trying after that, stopped coming to her in the night or cornering her in the bathroom or leaving notes about meet-ing by the boiler. One day, when Brigid ran to the bathroom to throw up, she found Jeanne there with another girl, a new girl who looked as frightened as she was thrilled by Jeanne's hands venturing under her smock. She tried to push Jeanne away, pointing at Brigid, but Jeanne just closed the stall door and kept at it, and even while Brigid vomited next to them, she could hear the impatient breath she recognized from when Jeanne reached inside her for the first time.

BY THE TIME MATTHEW came again to deliver another baby, Brigid was no longer vomiting and she had traded her dress for a wider version in the laundry room. Matthew tried not to look directly at her when she walked into the delivery room, not wanting the nuns to see the relief and desire flushing their faces. They moved side by side throughout the night, easing the girl's contractions, wiping away blood and feces and vomit, mostly waiting in the heavily warped time that occupied a birthing room. When the girl's pelvis was distorted with the final drop, Matthew, listening with the stethoscope, gestured to Brigid to hurry and release the cord strangling the little neck. Brigid reached in but it was harder than usual to find; the baby's head was so large she couldn't get her hands past it to reach its neck. She had to rip the girl a bit, masking the pain, and pull the cord over like a shirt too small for a child's head. Just as she felt it free up, and the baby's head and bruised neck emerged, she felt a fissure inside her, not a letting go this time but a vicious, deliberate cleave. She doubled over with a sudden surge of pain and Matthew stepped forward to catch the pulpy rush of baby and blood and mucus and cord. In the business of spanking for a cry, cutting the cord, and toweling to find healthy pink skin, no one noticed that Brigid had lowered herself to the floor and crawled away, as if it were all about gravity, and the lower she was to the ground the less likely she was to lose what was inside her. She was a virgin to the type of pain attacking her, and yet it was perfectly familiar the way it rose and peaked and released only to come again harder the next time. It was only when Matthew needed her to stop the hemorrhaging from a placenta that would not detach that he noticed her. There was a lot of confusion as he left his patient and tried to get Brigid to rise, and he saw that she too, on the back of her orphan's nightgown, was bleeding. Somehow, Matthew, whispering in his sweet, confident voice, got Brigid to stand up and walk over to his patient, release her placenta and stanch the gushing blood, searing the vessels with the fire of her hands. By the time the girl on the table was all right, Brigid was passed out from her own blood loss, and wouldn't know until later the panic that ensued and the secrets Matthew revealed with his reactions. He sobbed when the half-formed child was expelled from her. It never took a breath. Brigid remembered only the moment when she stopped her own hemorrhaging. She could smell the odor, like new wood being burned, that accompanied the application of her fiery hands. She healed herself, but could not save what grew inside her.

BY THE TIME BRIGID woke up, in one of the rooms they gave to girls to recover from the birth, Matthew was gone. The Mother Superior was the one who told her. Given what had fallen out of an innocent girl with no access to men, from now on no doctor would be needed at St. Brigid's Home for Wayward Girls. Tears poured silently down Brigid's face.

"He's lucky," Mother Superior said. "I could have reported him to the police, had his license revoked. But he agreed to never return here if I let him disappear." Brigid held herself still, not wanting the Mother to see that her words were like blows.

"I think you know enough now," she went on, "to be our midwife. There is no reason we need anyone from the outside. When you are old enough you can take your vows."

"I'm not staying here," Brigid said quietly. Mother Superior gri-
maced.

"You're already ruined for anything else."

A MONTH LATER, JEANNE and Molly found Brigid in a bathroom
stall slashing at her wrists, trying to cut quicker than the slices
could heal themselves. They led her back to the dorm and laid
her on the bed. Both of them, first Jeanne whose body she knew
by heart, then Molly, the new girl, softer, pudgy, with a smell as
promising as rising bread dough, climbed in beside her, sand-
wiching her body between theirs, absorbing her convulsions and
sobs with the same silent thoughtless mercy that she used to seal
open wounds. When Jeanne tried to kiss her, Brigid pressed her
lips still, realizing too late that what she was grieving for was not
only the child that had come out of her, but the man who had put
it inside.

SHE WENT BACK TO her life of cleaning and studying and sealing
up pain, with less hope than she'd ever functioned with before.
Brigid was thin enough to appear breakable, and her only desire
seemed to be to find ways to go back to her bed and sleep, sleep that
never refreshed her but that she clung to like a life rope, not wanting
to come fully to the surface of anything.

It was Jeanne who gave Matthew back to her. Through a complicated series of communications involving arriving and departing
pregnant girls, she arranged it all. She and Molly woke Brigid in the
night, which took some time because she slept as if she were holding
on to her dreams for dear life. Jeanne hadn't included Brigid in the
plan, in case it didn't work, so when Molly told Brigid they had a

surprise, Brigid began to cry, lying back down as if the promise had drained her.

They sat her up, Jeanne bracing from one side while Molly wrestled socks and shoes on her like she was a toddler. They draped her arms over their shoulders, and pulled her across the silent dorm into the dark hallway. Brigid's feet began to move, and the more they moved the more she wanted them to, and the next thing she knew they were running, holding hands, Molly and Jeanne laughing softly, delirious with possibility. It didn't matter if the nuns heard, Brigid thought, in that moment, they were three girls flying down polished halls, they were untouchable.

They ran down the stairs and ducked into a classroom, the same one Jeanne and Brigid used to escape from because of the disguised broken lock on one window. The panels of glass Molly pushed went outward, like a doorway. It was so dark, Brigid couldn't even make out a shadow of what she was dropping into. Jean helped her onto the sill, took the last second to sear a quick, angry kiss to her lips. Brigid was so numb from months of grief, and confused by the darkness and the plan, that she remembered later that she should have kissed back, thanked her, said good-bye. They held her arms and dangled her over a dark abyss, the window frame pressing pain into her wrists. Then they let go and she dropped, only a few feet but it felt like it might go on and on, into waiting arms. She knew it was Matthew by the way he caught her, confident and shy at the same time, and the smell of him, antiseptic hands and sweet breath, and though she was perfectly capable of walking now, she held on to his neck and let him carry her, whispering apologies into her hair, letting him tell her that she would never again, after her cruel parents and cold nuns and girls just as broken as she was, never in her lifetime would she have to be alone.

They drove quickly through the night, Matthew's car packed with what he had salvaged of his life. Over the next few days, as she realized what he had given up by stealing her, his practice, his license, his family, she would have instants where she lost breath and thought and word. She would feel, simultaneously, like pain blooming into pleasure, pure relief that he had taken her right alongside the terrible thought that he could just as easily have let her go.

CHAPTER 11

The Well

August 1959

Brigid doesn't try to seduce Emer. She tries to stop it. But even as she tells herself that it will end just like all the others—with gossip and shame and another quick move, a packing up of her life to escape the rage of men she steals women from—she sees herself doing it. Sees how she is pulling Emer in, stroking her, tempting her, long before she even lays a hand on her. She thought this might be a problem the moment they first clasped hands on that quay. She always knows, she can recognize the women who will desire her, tell them apart from the ones it would never even occur to.

It wasn't until she healed Niall that Emer started looking at her that way. Something was switched on then, and though she clearly has no experience with women, her want is there, raw and demanding regardless. It makes her clumsier, self-conscious, and awkward, but also more attractive. The flush, the bright eye, the way she looks at Brigid's hands, her breasts, her mouth. She is like no one Brigid has ever met, and yet, in Emer's desire, she sees all of them. Matthew, too feminine to be attractive to most women, who never quite recovered from the guilt of the crimes he committed, and made love to her with a combination of deference and violence that took her breath away. Jeanne, that scarred, hardened girl, awkward and rough on the outside, gorgeous underneath the carapace. All the women since, the women Matthew ignored and forgave because of what he thought he'd done to her, women who felt burdened, lost or unattractive, who did not believe it when men told them they were beautiful. Most of them had never imagined that this was what they wanted, another woman running her hands over every flaw of their body, until they were cured of the idea of their ugliness that had burdened them for so long. Brigid made lonely women lovely, with the same hands she used to mend their open wounds.

At first, she keeps Emer at a distance, pretends she doesn't even know what the girl wants. This seems to make her even more desperate. Her loneliness is so acute Brigid can practically hear it, like a keen that runs just under that sarcastic, vicious monologue delivered in an enchanting brogue.

Then there is the picnic on the cliff where Emer opens up and tells Brigid what she is afraid of. Brigid comes so close to kissing her, to soothing Emer the one way she knows will work, by validating her desire, that the effort not to leaves her dizzy and slightly nauseated.

It occurs to her that she could seduce Emer into revealing the well. But she doesn't want any more casualties from love affairs. She just wants a baby.

She is grateful for Emer's awkward inexperience. Were she bold enough to make the first move, Brigid would be doomed.

After the picnic, they go back to Brigid's cottage and Emer shows her the picture of the council house she keeps in her apron pocket, folded and unfolded so many times it has faded to nothing at the creases. It's an architect's drawing of a modern Irish bungalow, ugly and squat, made of concrete and slate and pavement instead of grass in the yard.

"These houses aren't any better, Emer," Brigid says, though even as she says it she knows they are not speaking of the same things.

The houses will have heat, electricity and running water. They are luxurious if you don't notice they have no soul.

"If you want to leave so badly, why don't you do it? You don't need the whole island to go with you. Why doesn't Patch get a posting on the mainland?"

And Emer tells her why, quietly, simply, like a child telling a dirty secret for the first time, of her husband's last posting, where he drank so much he let the light die out and caused an accident on the rocks. He was fired, lost his pension and would never leave the island for work again.

Brigid says nothing for a while. She wants to give a speech rallying Emer, telling her she is not at the mercy of her husband, but she knows better. Just because Brigid had a husband who wasn't a trap doesn't mean she hasn't known plenty of women who have been tied up and suffocated within a man's mistakes.

"I understand," she says finally. "I do. But I don't see it happening. They can't make people leave the only home they've ever known. Not even for central heating."

What happened to this girl, Brigid wonders, to make her so vicious? Because that's what she is, a tightly wound ball of ferocity, lashing out at anyone who approaches her with those nasty fingers. At some point she decided that if she was going to be unhappy, she would pull everyone else down with her.

"It will happen eventually," Brigid says. "You'll find another way, if it's what you really want."

Emer looks quickly at Brigid, and Brigid can feel that eye linger on her mouth, and on her hands tightening around the mug of tea. Brigid has seen this many times before, watched as a girl's body opens the possibility in her mind. Where the unfathomable turns into a necessity.

Emer can't even imagine saying out loud what it is that she wants now.

SKETCHING EMER STARTS AS a way to avoid repeating all of this. She sees Emer's raw need and thinks she can heal her another way, without complicating it all by touching her. But then she gets caught up. She translates Emer's body into smudges of charcoal and suddenly, despite her promise to remain alone, sexless, an uncomplicated vessel whose only relationship is with a dog, she can't stop thinking about it. She feels doomed. Their course is as inevitable as the sea rising up in a storm. What she wants to do with Emer will feel like healing, like teaching, but she knows that it is more like theft. She won't be able to help but steal every sensation she thrusts upon Emer. She will steal her from her husband and her son and her plans for a better life, and Emer doesn't even know it yet. She will think she is being saved.

Even remembering all the guilt and complication and lying and fear, she can't help but savor the familiar beginnings. It feels so good to have someone want her again that she forgets, for long ascending moments, that this has never, not once in her life, ended any other way than badly.

AFTER MATTHEW STOLE HER from St. Brigid's, they drove north through the night to Canada, where they pretended they were married until she was old enough that they could be. Though charges were never filed, Matthew couldn't go home; his reputation was gone, his family disgraced. The first few months were dark and miserable ones for the both of them. Matthew often ended lovemaking with tearful apologies. He begged for her forgiveness.

"Stop saying you're sorry," Brigid would say, crying that he still refused to believe her, the only person she had ever fully believed in herself. "You've done nothing wrong. You didn't kidnap me. I came with you."

They had to move often. In the beginning they kept moving

whenever anyone grew suspicious of her age, they were often asked if Matthew was Brigid's father. Later they moved when the rumors grew thick about the things Brigid did with the women who came to them for help.

They continued to deliver babies. Sometimes for married women who wanted to deliver at home, but more and more, as the war came, for women who were left alone, discovering they were pregnant after their boyfriends had already been shipped to Europe. Women and girls just as scared and abandoned as the ones they had known at St. Brigid's. The difference was, with Matthew and Brigid, they were not expected to hand their babies over at the end.

In every town they moved to, they filled their extra bedrooms with pregnant girls, new mothers and babies. Brigid had never forgotten the pain of those girls severed from their children, so she and Matthew gave unwed mothers time to bond with their babies, nurse them and decide for themselves. If they chose to keep the baby, Matthew and Brigid helped them find jobs and homes and daycare; if they chose to give them up, which some still did, they helped arrange adoptions with couples who agreed to keep in contact, and send the mothers photographs and letters about their children. For twenty years they moved around, first in Canada, later in New England when the memories of their crimes had faded, and ushered women and babies through the first few fragile months of their lives together.

In every place they lived, Brigid got pregnant and miscarried. Sometimes it would happen in such rapid succession—pregnant, miscarriage, pregnant again—that she felt continuously with child, but never allowed to give birth, never reaching the part where she felt the flutter of life inside her, before it was pulled away too soon to survive. It seemed that healing the girls brought it on, but by the time she tried to keep her hands to herself, something inside her was already broken. More than once Matthew found her curled up amid the blood-soaked bedclothes, her hands pressed so tight between her thighs that she could barely feel them when he pried them away.

"Why can I help them and not myself?" she asked Matthew. "They don't even want their babies." But she knew that wasn't true. They didn't want to be pregnant, but they did want their babies. Wanting them and keeping them were often two very different things.

"Maybe it's me," said Matthew, who felt each miscarriage almost as deeply as she did. "Maybe this is the punishment for what I did to you."

Matthew was not a religious man, neither of them bothered with that. But he had been raised Catholic, and he couldn't quite escape the idea that he had sinned by falling in love with a broken girl with magic in her hands.

"Don't be daft," Brigid said harshly, sounding like her mother or one of those nuns, women with no patience for whining self-pity. "It's not *your* fault."

But she wondered if it might be.

She went to a specialist who told her that, by the looks of things, her womb and cervix were never meant to hold children. They were incompetent.

"How can I fix that?" Brigid said. The doctor looked at Matthew, then back to Brigid.

"We can't fix it," he said. "It's not an injury. It's just the way you were made." He told them to stop trying, that eventually it could kill her.

"Doctors don't know everything," she said to Matthew, but he made her get a cervical cap and refused to make love without it.

"We have each other," he said. She didn't tell him it would never be enough.

BRIGID WANTED TO REMAIN faithful to Matthew, tried to resist the temptation of the girls who lived in their home. But sometimes, after a miscarriage, this resolve would bleed away, and she would fill the empty space left by another baby with the swollen bodies of these women, many of whom had no idea what their hands and mouths were capable of until Brigid came to their rooms, closed the door and taught them in the darkness. She only chose women who looked at her a certain way, whose eyes lingered on her mouth, who exuded sexual tension even when they couldn't recognize it. These women hadn't had anyone to teach them about such pleasure. It was another form of healing, Brigid told herself, overwriting the memories of unsatisfying, sometimes violent encounters with men. But the truth was, she was the one who needed healing.

Every once in a while a girl would confess to her priest or her parents, or her crippled boyfriend back from the war, what had occurred with Brigid in the fevered months of her confinement. That's when they would move, find a new place where no one knew them, and start all over again. Matthew forgave her every time.

Matthew suggested that they adopt one of the babies the women decided to leave behind, but Brigid refused. He didn't understand. He had not reached deeply into their wombs and felt the familiar rip in their souls as they birthed a child they could not keep. It tore the same places as having them born too soon sliced in her. Brigid found loving mothers for the babies they gave up, but she would never be one of them. She couldn't pretend. She couldn't be part of the cleaving and then raise the child as her own. She would remember, every time she held it, that it was not.

WHEN BRIGID WAS THIRTY-FIVE and Matthew fifty, he fell ill. Brigid could sense it in him way before the doctors found it. He had headaches that blinded him for hours at a time, and when she tried to heal them, she felt a dark space, like a wet, nasty hole that she could not see the bottom of and didn't want to put her hand into.

It was a tumor in his brain. Though the prognosis was dire, the oncologist was continually amazed by his patient's refusal to die. The mass was inoperable and grew rapidly, except it kept shrinking, despite Matthew's refusal of treatment. It never went away, but got small and then grew again, like a child playing with a balloon.

Nothing had ever made Brigid as ill as reaching her hands toward that tumor. Each time she shrunk it, she ended up in her bed for days with high fevers, body aches, vomiting, dehydration. She lost too much weight, her hair fell out leaving whorls like birds' nests in her brush. Matthew tended to her; she had no energy left to heal herself. He would lie next to her on the bed and wipe her face with cool cloths, put straws to her lips, murmur his love and apologies as she thrashed and moaned and forgot whole days. When ill, she was trapped in her childhood again, on that island, with people she could not trust not to murder each other.

The last time she was ever pregnant (darning needles work on rubber cervical caps too), she made it halfway through, the longest her body had ever managed to hold on. Matthew was in the hospital, declining rapidly since he would not let her heal him. If there were even a chance that it might harm the baby, he wouldn't risk it. She could have done it anyway, when he was sleeping, but she waited, crouched around her own middle and terrified. Terrified of losing the first baby that had grown big enough for her to feel moving, and of letting go the only person who had ever loved her without limits. She told herself she could hold on long enough that she could have both of them.

He died the night the nurses convinced her to go home and get a decent night's rest in her own bed. When the phone rang at four a.m., she knew before lifting the receiver. Four a.m. was a time they saw together a lot. Babies tended to come then, in that timeless space between night and morning, in those moments where even the weariest body got a rush of adrenaline to spur them on. It was also a common time for people to die because they needed that extra surge of energy to finally let go.

After she hung up the phone, she felt something sever inside her, and a pain worse than anything she had ever felt drove her to her knees. It took only minutes. She delivered a miniature boy on the floor of her bedroom, saw him breathe once, an inhalation that lifted his entire torso, as if he could hold on to it, and defy nature. Then he died. She woke in her own hospital bed, after one of the pregnant girls discovered her unconscious and hemorrhaging, the elfin child in a vise grip in her arms. A doctor she'd never met before, who was younger than she was and so awkward she almost felt sorry for him, told her she'd had an emergency hysterectomy. She would never be pregnant again.

The next year of her life was as unbearable as any that had come before it. She wanted to die but felt already dead. She kept remembering herself as a child, and all the hope she'd had that when she grew up she would be happy. Her life's work had given her glimpses of this, but without Matthew her heart was no longer in it. It didn't seem any better, somehow, being a woman. The world still stole from her the same as when she was a helpless girl.

She sealed herself up just enough to go through the motions. She had occasional affairs with women, but never with men. She painted, she walked the promenade and looked at the sea, sometimes while holding the hand of a frightened girl in early labor. She resigned herself, even as her heart still raged, that it would never be her.

Then she got the letter from Desmond's solicitor about the island and the house. Her mother's stories started coming back to her, of holy wells that gave babies to barren women, and fairies that lent their dark gifts in exchange for the chance to live in the world. Her mother had died years before, in a fire in St. Dymphna's Asylum. She was no longer there to warn Brigid of the cost of such magic, or to remind her of how badly all her stories ended.

THE WEATHER STOPS CHANGING; for the entire month of August there is rarely a cloud in the endless blue sky. The sun is much stronger than Brigid expected—no trees means no shade—and it remains in the position of high noon for hours. Rua wearies more quickly, seeks out the shore more than the fields, flops her belly down in the frigid ocean for relief. Brigid takes off her shoes and walks in the same water, watching Niall and his cousins splashing between the seaweed-covered rocks. The weather has made all the islanders giddy, it is not just the children who are bright red with sunburn, their eyes manic from the overdose of sunshine. No one wants to be inside. The women bring their teacups and their dinner plates outside and lay out picnics on the meticulous stone walls. They bring their chairs out and knit and peel potatoes and darn clothing, moving their spots around the house with the circle of the sun.

After three weeks of unrelenting heat, the well closest to Brigid's house dries up, and the one further up the hill ceases to flow soon after that. Malachy brings her water in large ceramic jugs on the back of the poor, overheated donkey. He says the weather is good for the hay, which they are cutting all over the island to store for the cattle in the winter. Malachy and Austin cut her field down for her, and when they have gone, the hay collected in clochán-shaped piles in the field, she finds a bird's nest, whorled out of hay into the ground, eggshells cracked and abandoned. Niall tells her it's the corncrake's.

"They might have left a spot around the nest," he says, shaking his head. "Now she will have moved on." Brigid worries until she hears the male again that night. She knows it is the same corncrake. She can now distinguish the corncrakes in their separate fields. Their voices are as varied as people's.

"Has the island ever had a drought before?" she asks Emer the next day. Niall is running circles around the dog and pig, mocking them with a sheep's thighbone he found in a field. He runs too close to Emer, almost knocking into her.

"Would you mind yourself," Emer snaps. Emer gets irritable with Niall now, she is so caught up in her longing for Brigid. Niall drops his arm, dejected, and Rua yanks the bone from his hand. Emer pulls Niall in for a quick hug of apology.

"Every so often we get a summer like this," Emer says. "The last one was when I was a girl."

"Will the island run out of fresh water?" Brigid asks.

"Saint Brigid's well never runs dry," Niall announces. "It isn't meant to. It's holy."

Emer glares a warning at him, then flicks her gaze back toward Brigid. Brigid is holding her breath.

"We may have to visit that one soon enough," Emer mumbles and lets, as she does often now, a smile creep into her one eye, burning blue and relentless, like the summer sky.

THREE DAYS LATER EMER volunteers Niall to help his uncle and father mend a currach, and asks Brigid if she wants to go on a walk. She's pulling at the collar of her blouse, a nervous gesture Brigid has noticed—Emer hates to have fabric touching the hollow of her throat. Brigid excuses herself quickly and goes into her bedroom to fetch the pouch she keeps under the mattress, just in case.

They walk up the green road, a road that was formed by the tedious work of nuns, with a wall of piled slate on one side, ditches to divert flood, and a dense, level carpet of mossy grass. The road is littered with pellets of sheep dung, some glistening black, most faded to the color of hard dust. They walk all the way around to the cliffs, which are quiet today, the normal scream of wind tamed by the heat to a breeze.

Emer gets far too close to the edge. Brigid reaches for her arm, thinking Emer's faulty peripheral vision is to blame. But Emer boldly links her fingers into Brigid's and pulls her along.

A hidden path, no wider than a sheep's hooves, steps down into the abyss of the cliff. For an instant it seems they will step off into the gliding sea birds, but then Brigid sees it, how it winds around and down into a hidden cave, a small room carved into the side of the sheer cliff. After a balancing act that leaves her dizzy and wobbling over the drop, they are inside a sanctuary almost half the size of her living room. Carpeted in moss, a natural hearth in the stone-layered earth, at its center a stream of water pours into a deep well. It is damp in here, cooler than the weather has been in weeks; the sun hasn't passed its peak and fallen west, so the room has been in shadow since yesterday. The sound of fresh water seems louder than the salt waves crashing below. Emer settles herself onto mossy ground and reaches for the tin mug left in a natural shelf in the wall of the cliff. She dips it into darkness and lifts it again, taking a long drink and turning to offer it to Brigid. Lust, which seems to grow stronger every time they are together, rises off Emer like steam. She isn't bothering to hide it now, she lets her hand linger a bit too long when handing over the mug. Brigid sees that Emer brought her here because she hopes that this will be the place they can finally grab hold of one another, far from anyone who might stop them. She takes the cup offered to her and tips it to her lips. The water is delicious, so cold it hurts her teeth. She empties the cup. It is the kind of water that makes you realize just how thirsty you have always been.

She kneels down, waiting for a sign, waiting for the warmth in her middle that tells her it has worked. But there is nothing. Only more thirst and the burden of what Emer expects next.

"You've heard the stories, then," Emer says.

"Some of them."

"Saint Brigid left it. They say the water never ceases to flow, same as her fire. The nuns were meant to watch over it, but once they left, the islanders didn't see many miracles. They used it to bless babies, and soak the blue cloth that is said to be from her cloak, that sort of thing.

"In my grandmother's time, they say a woman came all the way from America with her blind son. Saint Brigid was known for blind cures, you know, because of the time she plucked her own eye out to avoid getting married.

"She laid the boy down and let the water run over his face. They say he sat up, rubbed his eyes and said, 'Mammy, look at the sea.'"

Brigid is quiet for a while. "That's not the story my mother told me," she says.

Emer shrugs. "There are others. Every family has one. Barren wombs filled up, dying children saved, curses of fairies reversed. They say the islanders got worried because every time they let some blow-in use the well it failed them for a while. Some thought we weren't meant to share it. That Brigid herself wanted it only for those committed to staying here. We keep it hidden now. Took the cross away."

"Why did you bring me?"

Emer shrugs and looks down. "It hasn't worked in donkey's years. I don't see the harm."

"Emer," Brigid says quietly. She is sitting as far away as she can, the font of water between them, but Emer twitches, as if Brigid has just grabbed her.

"Isn't this what you want?" Emer says.

"Yes," she says.

"I want to give it to you." Emer is trying to hide her hands beneath her thighs to stop them shaking.

"Thank you," Brigid says, carefully. "I'm grateful to you, Emer."

Emer shrugs, but she is blushing.

"What do you want it for?" she says. The silence is long, all Brigid can hear is water, beckoning, and Emer attempting to regulate her breath.

"I want to have a baby."

Emer snorts. "Did no one let on you need a man for that?"

"I need a miracle first. I don't have a womb."

Emer makes that quick, dismissive noise in her throat. "That's a tall order," she says. She gestures to the water, and says, softer now, "Go on and see, then."

Brigid takes the pouch from the pocket of her sweater, pulls the stained handkerchief out from within it, and opens the precious package on the smooth slate ledge that surrounds the pool of water. In all her years of midwifery, it wasn't until the end that she delivered a child born with the caul, which promises, depending on who you ask, good fortune, second sight, a lifetime's safety from drowning. The mother had no interest in such superstition, and had let Brigid keep it. Brigid herself, her mother once told her, had been born this way, entirely encased in a membrane that she had to puncture and peel off to pull Brigid, blue and tightly curled, into the world.

The caul is webbed and delicate, so old and dry that when she picks it up and lowers her palm beneath the water, it fills up for an instant, grows and stretches like the memory of a small skull, then breaks up and is absorbed so quickly it is as if it was never there at all. She barely has time to whisper her wish, swallow what she can, and feels suddenly foolish, heavy, burdened by hope she should have let wash away long ago.

"Were you born beneath the veil?" Emer says. For a moment, Brigid is confused, and thinks of the nuns of her girlhood, black curtains of cloth instead of hair. Then she realizes that Emer means the caul. She nods.

"Niall was as well," Emer says. "Patch and Austin keep it in the currach. It's meant to protect them at sea."

"It isn't mine," Brigid says.

"It's in your family, though. Your mother had it. Was she the one who told you to bring it here?" Brigid wants Emer to stop talking. As if her voice, like her hands, might drive away the promise swirling in the water.

"Don't be thinking the caul comes from the saints. It's the work of the good people. It's like asking a priest the way to the brothel."

A laugh bursts out of Brigid, loud and out of place in the still room. "I'm not fussy," she says, "about where my miracles come from."

"Some good it did me," Emer sneers, as awkward and cruel as she gets. "My sister tried to heal me with this water after my eye went. Miracles don't work for some of us."

Emer looks miserable, so caught between her two selves, the one who hurts and the one who gets hurt, that Brigid flares at the sight of it. There is something about this cursed, awkward girl that her hands throb to fix. Like a wound gushing blood that she must stop before she thinks of what will happen afterward. She is suddenly, furiously, aroused. And so her wariness and secrets drowned out, she crawls her way across the moss, and kneels in front of Emer. She kisses her, straight on the mouth, gently until Emer's lips open up, then relentlessly, pushing the grateful girl onto her back and pressing her into the soft ground. Her abandon is instantaneous, the clenched, furious, terrified Emer is gone, and every inch of her is reaching out like hungry flames, begging for the salve of Brigid's hands.

After a while, Brigid reaches up to flick open the leather patch above her eye and Emer freezes. Brigid feels her switch from helpless to dangerous in an instant. Feels the surge of wretchedness that tries to draw her in. She deflects it with her own hand, threading their fingers and pulling Emer's palm, trapping it between their breasts.

"It's all right," she whispers. The skin beneath the patch is bumpy and purple, a keloid scar raised up and obliterating what were once eyelids, which the doctors in town ignorantly sewed shut. In a better hospital, they would have fitted her for a glass eye. Brigid kisses the horrible spot gently, like a mother pretending to ease the wound of a child. Emer pulls her hand free and reaches for her, arching her hips and pulling her face down and kissing her hard, with teeth, with anger, with everything she tries to blame on everyone else.

Brigid gives her what she wants. She does everything that Emer has been imagining with slow, thorough reverence. She takes breaks to fill her mouth with the painfully cold well water and then let it flow from her lips into every place where Emer thirsts. They make furious love by the ancient drip of water, and Emer surprises her by turning it around, without asking for permission, as so many women have before. She dips her hand in the same water, and reaches inside Brigid, who grabs on, trapping Emer's wrist in her hands so she will not pull away. She watches Emer's face as the pleasure moves through her for so long it is almost painful, like water so cold you can barely swallow it, watches Emer's eye widen in recognition as Brigid's insides seize upon her hand.

Later she will tell herself she felt it, felt the instant life flared inside her, but really she is too lost in what she has started to notice what the water begins.

CHAPTER 12

Anam Cara

September 1959

"Where are you off to now?" Emer's mother chides. "Not to that Yank's again."

"She needs help with the sheep," Emer replies.

"Would you not have a mind to help your own sister?"

"Rose doesn't need my help." Her mother huffs at this.

"That woman's turned you cross-eyed. You've no sense at all."

"I don't know what you're on about."

"Don't you, now?"

"Would you not leave me be?" Emer mutters. She wants to scream it, to rage like a child pushed to her limit, but it would give her mother too much satisfaction.

She wishes they would all leave her alone. Rose, Austin, Patch, even Niall, or the fretting over him anyway. She misses the days when she could put the fire iron across his cradle, or wind him to her front with a long strip of flannel. When he is out of her sight, with his father, or at Rose's house with the girls, Emer's neck tightens with anxiety, fear rising and swarming in her throat like the memory of those bees. The moment she lays eyes on him, it breaks away. The possibility of it returning is always there, it crouches, ready to flare again when he runs outside of her limited vision.

Now she wants him to go somewhere else. Just for an afternoon, for a guaranteed hour instead of the few minutes that stretch into one, to wander off and know exactly how long he will be gone, so she can have this possibility, this promise of Brigid's hands reaching for her again.

She hadn't dared imagined that all the time she had wanted her, Brigid had felt the same. The thrill of it, that moment when Brigid moved into the pained space that separated them. It was like being handed the option to become someone else altogether.

WHEN ROSE AND EMER were eleven, there was a young teacher in the island school who taught them about the druid Brigid alongside the traditional lessons about the saint. The druids believed that souls radiated around bodies, and when a person found their *anam cara*, soul friend, it meant that both their spirits began to flow together, like two streams meeting to fill a well. The teacher used this metaphor to partner the children up for studying their sums and spelling. Having a soul friend challenged you, she explained, awakened you to yourself so you could accomplish things you wouldn't have been able to do on your own. They could remove what was weighing you down, like the peeling off of drenched clothes. Saint Brigid had Darla, and her postulants paired off together, because Brigid was not only a Christian saint. She carried with her stories that were more ancient than Jesus.

The girls in the school fell in love with this idea. During their dinner break they gathered behind the stone wall and reenacted the druid ceremony of friendship. Girls paired off, wound their shawls high around their necks, clasped hands and recited, with the utmost solemnity, "I honor your path, I drink from your well, I bring an unprotected heart to our meeting place." They took water from the school's well and sprinkled it on each other's hair and pressed their lips together with the fervor they imagined they would one day kiss boys. Everyone wanted to be Rose's *anam cara*, but since no one wanted to be Emer's—they wouldn't dare hold her hand and they shuddered at the thought of her chapped, angry mouth—Rose always chose her sister out of loyalty. They didn't kiss or bring much enthusiasm when it was their turn, but there were only eight girls in the school, and Rose couldn't afford to insult any of them by not playing along. The lads, who were the ones they were practicing for, played football in the field and paid them little mind.

The priest, who only got over to St. Brigid's once a month if the weather allowed, sent that teacher packing when word of her irreverent lessons reached him. He was used to island superstition, and thought it harmless; he was Irish, after all. But it was one thing to hold on to whispered, fireside references to the good people, it was quite another to have a schoolteacher confusing the Christian saint with a pagan goddess.

Rose and Emer were both relieved when he put a stop to it. Rose because the whole business had seemed a bit sinful all along, and Emer because watching her classmates tilt toward each other's lips made heat rise so furiously in her throat she imagined that, if anyone dared to kiss her, she would spew fire into their mouths. She despised the lot of them, and she resented that none of them wanted to be her partner; they all wanted Rose, and they blamed her even more for keeping Rose away from them.

She thinks of this the first time Brigid kisses her, pushing her back onto the ground beside the well and letting the holy water pass into her mouth. She had wanted one of those girls to kiss her, hard enough that it would push away the clog left inside her throat by the fairies. Later, when she watched Rose in the clochán with Austin, when she saw what followed kissing, she wanted that as well.

Now she wonders if Saint Brigid and her nuns were devout at all. She imagines them in the clocháns, not only praying and transcribing but also lifting off their habits and pressing against each other, letting themselves drop away into another woman's mouth.

Worship has an entirely different meaning now.

ROSE INVITES BRIGID OVER for the Saturday evening meal. The weather is still hot and cloudless, the drought has left the islanders sunburned and with an unquenchable thirst they are not accustomed to. Such merciless sun usually bothers Emer's eye, but it now seems fitting. The island is as ablaze and longing for release as she is.

Brigid has been to everyone's house now, for tea or a meal or both, she knows every islander's name and can't walk the road without stopping to talk to a dozen people on the way. They all know she was a midwife and have started coming to her with small ailments. She stitches up Malachy's hand after he slices it gutting fish, she sits and listens to women who have unexplained pain, or abnormally heavy bleeding, or urine infections. It seems just having tea with her makes most of the women feel better immediately.

"Are you healing them too, now?" Emer asks, but Brigid denies it.

"Sometimes just listening is enough."

When Rose complains of a line of fiery pain shooting from her buttock to her calf, Brigid gives her a bottle of fragrant oil and tells her to have Austin massage a spot on her lower back.

"It will be fun for the both of you," she says, and Rose, though she blushes, smiles knowingly in that way that used to make Emer furious. Now Emer finds herself, at odd moments, thinking of Brigid and smiling the same way.

The only one who won't take help from her is Emer's mother.

Brigid suggests that daily exercise, shuffling around with her cane, would do a lot for her aches and, possibly, her mood.

"We're the same age," Brigid says. "We have a lot of life left." Clodagh scorns this.

"Mind your business," she spits. "No one invited you into mine."

Instead of showing offense, Brigid treats Clodagh with extra veneration, and whenever she is over, she repeats Clodagh's caustic comments as if they are useful and she's dying to hear more. Their mother eventually goes silent, as she doesn't enjoy hearing herself repeated.

Dinner that evening lingers on, normal bedtimes blurred by the two bottles of red wine Brigid brings as a gift. Emer is grateful that her husband is getting drunk on the mainland instead of here—he would drink more than the rest of them, more than the two glasses that make her edges go soft. She can't imagine him managing to say a word to Brigid. Austin slags Brigid a bit about the usual things, but is mostly quiet while she and Rose jabber on about Saint Brigid.

"There wasn't a man on the island then. Brigid wouldn't allow it. Only the boys that were born to those unwed mothers. They say she wasn't too fond of them, either. But once they were here, well, it wasn't easy to go."

"Why not?" Brigid asks.

"She burned all the currachs," Rose says. "The original boats she came with, she and Darla set them alight in the cove so they wouldn't be able to leave. They had to wait for a boat to come to them."

"That's either serious devotion," Brigid says, "or madness."

"It's a lovely spot to be marooned, I've always said," Rose says.

"I agree." Brigid smiles.

"That's not what you say in a storm," Emer quips, but neither woman seems to hear her. Only Clodagh looks her over with that permanent scowl.

Brigid helps Rose put the children to bed while Emer does the washing up. Austin sits with his dirty socks up on the table, right in Emer's way.

"I don't think she's the full shilling," Clodagh says, when Brigid carries a sleeping toddler into the bedroom.

"Oh, give it a rest, Mammy," Emer says.

"You can't say a word against Brigid," Austin laughs. "Not to Emer, anyways. She's besotted." Emer whacks at his feet with the dishcloth, then turns to hide her blush. Austin chuckles and moves over to the fire to light his pipe.

Brigid stays late and by the time she is ready to leave, Niall has fallen asleep with the older girls in the loft bed.

"Leave the child here, Emer," Rose says. "He's too big to carry anymore."

Emer stiffens and hopes that Brigid, across the room, is pausing her breath in the same anticipation.

"Would you walk Brigid home?" Rose says. "I'm knackered as it is. Go and help her with the chores we stole her from."

Austin looks up at Emer for a second, with something other than his usual polite sweep of eyes. He knows, she thinks, he can sense what she and Brigid are about to do. But then his eyes pass over her and fix onto his wife and that familiar grin creeps up. He has plans of his own. Funny that his smiles still hurt her, even though she is looking forward to someone else's mouth.

Emer and Brigid leave together. It is September and the sun goes down earlier every day. Soon enough the darkness will be far longer than the light. But the breeze is mild, and the stars and moon are unclothed and the road to Brigid's house appears lit up from within. Emer imagines she can hear within their footsteps an echo of anticipation, the thud and shuffle of lust. This is how Austin and Rose once felt, back when they had to walk to secret places where they could touch each other. Emer recognizes the feeling though she is still alarmed at whom it is attached to.

"IT'S ALL RIGHT," BRIGID croons, when Emer starts to tremble, overwhelmed by the ache that grows fathomless as Brigid slowly removes her clothes.

It is all too much this time. Her mouth is so large, her kisses huge and wet and gaping, as if they want to swallow her, her hands are hot and skidding off Emer in their eagerness, gripping occasionally as if they are grabbing her back from a fall.

"I've not done this," Emer says softly, when they are fully naked for the first time, side by side on the hearth bed, bodies glowing and soft and mirrored, one an older version, just beginning to release itself in places, by the light of the turf fire.

"Not with anyone else. No one touches me. Even when they do . . . It's difficult to explain."

"You don't need to," Brigid says, rolling on top of her. Emer can barely keep up with what is happening. It's like a new body being born under Brigid's demanding hands.

After it is finished and the fired-up patches that Brigid ignited slowly throb and go out, she grows cold and searches for the blanket by their feet.

"I thought you were married," Emer says suddenly.

Brigid laughs. "I was."

"But you've done this before."

"Yes, Emer."

"With women, I mean."

"I loved my husband. But I had this with women as well. A long time ago."

"It's a sin, sure," Emer says.

"So they tell me."

"Will you leave us now?" Emer says, letting this new fear rush forward, fear that swells with the same urgency as her desire. "Now that I've shown you the well?"

"I'm not going anywhere."

"Which man will you get?" Emer whispers. "To give you the baby?"

And Brigid kisses her in a way that feels almost angry, but Emer wants this so much that she can't stop to question what emotion is behind it. This time, Emer pushes Brigid onto her back. She does not pause and wonder what to do, she has spent enough time imagining it. She is astonished at Brigid's reactions. Delighted that her hands, her mouth and her body can be so skillful, can pull such violent pleasure out of someone else. Pleasure instead of disgust.

She stays too long; dawn has already come and gone by the time she half hurries away from Brigid's house. She goes the high road, avoiding the quay and the men readying the currachs for Mass. But then she comes across Austin and his dog driving a group of sheep to a virgin field. Before she can help it, she blushes so quick and hard it seems audible, like a gasp in the still, mist-thick air. Austin has the same blue eyes as Niall, and he locks them on her now. He glances quickly down, raking his eyes over her, then back to her face. Emer thinks he can see everything she just did, and his gaze feels both like a violation and a compliment.

"Out for a stroll, Emer?" Austin cocks his head and winks at her.

She walks the rest of the way home burning with anger and embarrassment, furious at being seen, at being ridiculed, but mostly bewildered that Austin's eyes have the power to undo her still.

THE NEXT WEEK, EMER allows Niall to start school. She had planned to keep him home another year, though at six he is a year older than most in the infants' class. His cousins walk him there in the morning and Emer picks him up in time for dinner. It is the longest she has ever been without him. She walks straight up the road and pulls Brigid's curtains in the middle of mild September mornings.

Sometimes she even leaves in the nighttime, when Patch is off on the mainland, Niall sleeping sweetly in her bed. It is like tearing something as she leaves him there, runs over the brackish grass and stone and arrives, breathless, only to have Brigid take her breath even more. Brigid is always happy to see her, and after they make love her gaze cools into gratitude, something that never happened with Patch, who, back when they had relations, finished with a grunt and a shudder as if he'd just done something distasteful. Even with Brigid, though, there is a catch that reminds her who she is. There is an element of torture in it all, an arm thrown over her face, a twisted expression, a clenching of the mouth and eyes that so reminds her of when she inserts pain and doubt into people that sometimes she wonders if it is all a form of the same thing. If pain and pleasure are so closely linked that just the slightest turning can change it. There is violence in love, more than she'd imagined there would be.

She runs home on these nights, terror in her throat, ripping through the damp air as if it is trying to stop her, barging into the house to fall next to Niall and hold him close, kissing his face, pausing at his lips to make certain he is still breathing. Still himself. To see that she has not abandoned everything just to feel something that, to be honest, by the time she arrives home, has faded into disbelief.

There are moments with Brigid—not having to do with lust but afterward, lying in the bracken watching the clouds move, or walking without touching along the cliff edge, Niall and the pig and Brigid's dog bounding ahead of them—where Emer has a foreign feeling. Cupfuls of time where she feels no anxiety or anger or ugliness or regret. Where nothing swarms or seizes within her and all she is aware of is a still, liquid feeling of joy. It is not the same as the joy Niall lends to her, which allows her to forget herself and delight in him; this happiness originates inside her. The first time it happens she is jolted, as though from an invisible hand, then smiles as wide as the sky before them.

"Will you look at that," Emer murmurs, and Niall squints at her suspiciously. His mother is not prone to admiring nature.

Everything looks sharper now, the changing colors of moss and heather, the deep, autumn sun that feels warmer because of the chill in the air, and she imagines this is how the island looks to Brigid, looks to anyone who feels this way, like a paradise.

This new bliss of Emer's is so dense she manages to keep it for whole minutes, long dark nights, entire soft days, before she feels the sharp intrusion of fear, the coiling premonition of regret. Such elation, she thinks, must be what other people feel—her sister, her son, Brigid, a group of married nuns—they must grow accustomed to it, and she imagines it is just as easy to be stolen by joy as by misery.

She takes Brigid's hand on impulse; usually they try not to touch in front of Niall. Brigid stops walking and turns to face her, pulling her hand in to hide it behind the flap of her jacket, and pressing it promisingly against her warm thigh. Since their mouths can't meet, they lock eyes. Emer thinks she can see Brigid's pupil pulse in the exact rhythm of her own aroused heart.

"*Anam cara*," Emer whispers, before she can stop herself.

And though Brigid smiles, and squeezes her palm, something trips in her gaze, the pupil misses a beat, and she looks away, toward Niall and the pets. Emer convinces herself that it is only prudence that makes Brigid not echo this name.

CHAPTER 13

Fairy Music

September 1959

There is a fair amount of back and forth, but in the end, they all decide to go over to Mass without Emer. When she wakes to bright weather, Emer is so sure she is going that the consequences don't register when she feels the heat on Niall's forehead. His face is flushed, and when he opens his eyes they are wet and foggy.

"Oh," she says, confused. "Are you ill?" Niall looks at her without much interest.

"I'm only tired," he says and turns around and falls back to sleep.

She is so disappointed at the realization—he will have to stay in bed, she will have to stay with him, she will not be going over for a day of music and food and summer visitors—that she forgets to be worried about him being ill. She doesn't even think of it for the next while, during all the debate of who will go and who will stay. Her mother is determined to go and see her cousins back from Liverpool staying at the hotel, and so struggles into her black dress and shawl and sits stubbornly by the door with her cane, refusing to discuss any other option. Patch has an appointment with a man from the mainland about the sheep and does not suggest changing it. Rose, of course, offers to stay. Emer gets irritable then.

"Do you think I can't take care of the one child?" she snaps at her sister, who is all dressed for Mass but has come down to check on her.

"I do, of course," Rose says, tidying the table rather than holding the blade of Emer's gaze. "I thought you'd want the company."

"Fierce company you'll be," Emer scoffs, "with those two hanging off you and your face falling over missing your trip to the shops."

"You're in a bad twist today," Rose says casually, though Emer can tell she is hurt.

"Go on, then, and stop the fuss. I'm grand as I am. Bring us a packet of crisps."

Emer turns around, blinking away the burning in her eyes. This is Brigid's first trip to Muruch. Rose and the other wives convinced her to go. Now Emer will miss it.

Of course as soon as Rose leaves, insulted but keeping her smile up, Emer wishes she had stayed. Now her beautiful sister will be with Brigid instead of her.

She watches from the front stoop as they load the currachs. The whole island is going, it is one of those days where no one fears the water. Brigid is at the quay, well turned-out in a colorful skirt and blouse. Emer watches Patch lower her, then Rose and the girls, down into the boat. She has a brief, fierce hope that Brigid will ask Patch where she is, and decide to stay behind. But Rose says something that makes Brigid throw her head back and laugh, and Emer turns into her house, closing the door on them all.

It isn't until the day is half gone that she realizes Austin is still there. She goes out the back door to dump the dishwater and sees him walking the fields to the southeast. He holds a spade up in greeting, then stoops to the weeds. Just the sight of his long body and that shock of hair, dark as bottled ink and down to his collar, is enough to fluster her and she forgets what she meant to do next and goes to check on Niall instead. He is feeling better and able to sit up in bed for toast and tea.

When she goes out to hang the washing, the sky has darkened, and she can feel the wind picking up. The sea between the two islands is choppy now, gray and menacing when this morning it was as blue and smooth as the sky. It has happened before, going over to Mass in calm waters and having to stay with their cousins overnight when the weather turns. As a child, Emer loved those emergency holidays, all the girls jumbled together in the hearth bed, pretending to sleep while they snuck glimpses of the adults' smiling faces by the light of the fire. It was completely the opposite of being stuck on their island; there they were stranded in civilization. Once they stayed for five whole days and Emer cried the morning they'd woken to sun and agreeable sea.

By the time Austin calls in to her, the rain is lashing sideways, the wind so loud in the hedges that she can't tell the difference between the battered branches and the roar of the sea.

"Howaya keeping, Austin," Emer says, not looking at him, stepping aside for him to duck in through the door. He smells of rain and wind and sheep, of wet clothing and work, he smells so like her own husband that if she doesn't look straight at him, she won't know the difference. Except when he speaks.

"That wind would skin a fairy," he says happily, and Emer almost laughs. He removes his hat and shakes the water from his collar. "They won't be back tonight, sure. The sea's walled them over."

"You'll be wanting your tea, then," Emer says, moving around the room without looking at him. She sees out of the corner of her eye, teeth flash; he's smiling at her.

"I can feed myself, Emer," he says. "I only came to check on you. How's himself?"

"I expect he'll be well over it tomorrow," Emer says.

"Grand, so," Austin says, still standing, beginning to turn awkward as even easygoing people do around Emer.

"You might as well eat," Emer says. "If you're going to stand there all evening." Austin pauses, he would clearly prefer to leave. As if Rose is behind him whispering a request, he takes off his woolen jacket, hangs it on his brother's hook and sits in his brother's chair.

They eat potatoes with butter and cabbage and mackerel and wash it all down with milky tea. Emer sneaks a few looks at Austin as he hunches over his plate, his cheeks are smooth from a recent shave, which means he planned to go over to Mass and changed his mind.

"Rose asked you to stay behind," she realizes aloud.

"It's no bother." Austin smiles. She looks away. He is handsome enough with a straight face but when he smiles it is something else altogether. His smile is like a boy's, nothing held back, quick and full and mischievous and it still does something terrible to Emer.

"You'll miss the session," she says, clearing the plates to avoid another smile. Austin is usually asked to sing after Mass, he often comes back hoarse on a Sunday night from granting all the requests. Everyone on Muruch loves his singing, and often he'll sing with his father, who has the same deep voice. Every summer there is some visitor from Dublin or Canada who wants to arrange a tour, but it never happens. Emer knows from Rose that Austin never follows through on contacting them.

"Sure Rose is expecting the album any day now," Emer jokes.

"Don't be holding your breath," Austin says. "I'm only a fisherman."

"'Tis better than being a fisherman's wife," Emer scoffs.

Austin snaps to attention. "Do you not think Rose is happy enough?"

"I'd say Rose is delighted," Emer says. Austin actually blushes.

"Arrah. Pardon," he says, realizing.

"Not a bother," she says. She pours more tea.

"Patch," he begins, then he runs out.

"Patch is Patch," Emer says. "We'll leave it, so." Austin nods.

Silence stretches between them. She puts the kettle on for tea.

"Niall's a comfort to you, sure," Austin says.

"He is."

"It's a pity," he starts. She stops him.

"That's enough of that now. I'll not be pitied about being unable for more. I'm not Rose, I don't want a houseful. I like a bit of quiet to think."

Austin looks at her oddly. This is the longest string of sentences she has ever said to him.

"This island's not quiet enough for you?" he says.

Niall comes stumbling into the kitchen, hair tufted up in the back, rubbing his eyes.

"Howaya, Austin," he says pleasantly, then climbs straight into his mother's lap without request or invitation. He still does this; Rose usually puts a stop to children in her lap after the next set is born. Emer had hoped he would always do it, but she's realized lately that he has to hunch to fit in the space between her lap and chin. Soon enough it will be like having a man in her lap. She didn't realize how soon she would miss it, the smallness of him.

"Bad dose, eh, Niall?" Austin says.

"Aye," Niall sighs, snuggling closer to Emer.

"I've the cure outside," Austin winks. He goes to the door, opens it and picks up a jug of poitín he has left on the stoop. He struggles to close the door again on the wind.

"You're a terrible man altogether," Emer says. Niall smiles.

"A little scailtin and you'll be in the fields come morning."

"May I, Mammy?" Niall wiggles around on her lap, excited.

"If you must," she says. She's never given Niall the spirit-laden punch that children are fed for colds and flu. She has an idea, which contradicts everyone else's, that the alcohol is not good for him. But she doesn't want Austin to leave, so she heats a bit of milk on the coals, pours a little of the strong, clear liquid into it, dabs a spoonful of butter and stirs the sugar in. A squeeze from the last of the lemon she has on the dresser, wondering if Rose will be able to get her another.

"Make the old ones a spot as well," Austin says. She pours hot water into two mugs of poitín, adds sugar to hers and slices the left-over lemon rind with her knife into two slivers. Austin makes a fuss out of clinking his mug against the boy's, as if they are in the pub. Niall's eyes widen at his first sip.

When Niall asks him, Austin takes a tin whistle out of his pocket and plays a few tunes, one thigh knocking his chair with the beat. Niall gets up for a brief dance, tapping in the old style, but also spinning and laughing. Emer, who never dances, stays stiffly in her chair. In the lamplight, she thinks she can see the fiery ring in Niall's eyes grow larger, and that look of remove, and so she pulls him back onto her lap and feeds him the rest of the mug.

Emer can feel the poitín working on him as he drinks it down, with each sip Niall grows heavy in her lap. When he's done, half-asleep against her, Austin stops playing, takes the mug from his hand and lifts him, walking into the bedroom. Emer doesn't like Austin carrying Niall at all, she thought she would as he leaned over, that there would be a moment where she imagined that they were married and Niall was his, but it's not like that. It's the same as when anyone pats Niall's head or squeezes his shoulder or asks for a kiss from him. She needs to squeeze her fists to keep from dragging him back. When he was a baby she always made up a reason not to let people hold him. If an auntie grabbed him regardless, Emer would have to sit on her hands, her milk letting down in protest. Those were the moments he was most likely to be stolen: right in front of her, when she let her vigilance be compromised by manners.

Austin closes the door to the bedroom, comes over to the fire, and makes them two more drinks. The rain lashes against the panes, the wind screams and Emer thinks of Brigid and Rose in her cousin's house, bright-eyed and laughing and enjoying themselves. Trapped on the better side. Austin empties his drink in two swallows and makes himself a third, reusing the lemon rind.

"The dog," Emer says suddenly, standing up. "Brigid won't be back to let Rua in." Austin laughs at this.

"That dog is well able to sleep out in the rain," he says. "She pays far too much mind to that creature. Just like a Yank." Emer sits back down. She can't help wincing at the thought of Rua's narrow face, and the way it looks back at Brigid when they are walking on the green road, its amber eyes wet with loyalty.

"Fair play to her, though," Austin says. "She's able enough." Emer hides her blush in her steaming mug.

"Sure, she won't make it through the winter," he adds. And though Emer once said the same thing, the bitter taste of lemon regurgitates into her throat.

"She may surprise you," she says. Austin looks at her strangely again. She has no poise while taking about Brigid. She almost wants to rip her collar open to let out the heat that even thinking of her stirs up.

"Sure, with you and Malachy waiting on her all the time she has both a husband and a wife."

"Stop acting the maggot," Emer says. Women are meant to respond with disgust at such unnatural suggestions. It wasn't until she was with Brigid that she discovered how often men made them. It is like a game between them, how crude they can be about women and their intimacy.

"Will yer man in the government give her a house as well?" Austin says. "Or will you just let her share yours?"

When she was a girl she thought Austin was sweeter than the rest of them. Now he has the same cruel eyebrows and mocking voice as the boys from her childhood.

"You should sign on," Emer says, avoiding his eyes. "You'll get the best house with all those babbies."

"Rose would never agree to it," Austin says. "We're just after building the house here."

It's as if Emer has been struck.

"Would you go?" she says incredulously. "Would you leave the island?" Austin won't look at her straight.

"You've to pay for all those modern conveniences. And the land is desperate. Full of rock." He seems to get taller suddenly, in his chair. "But would I live in a place where my every move didn't depend on the swell of the sea? I'm no fool, Emer."

"Have you told Rose?" Emer says. Austin glares at her, contemptuous.

"Rose. She wouldn't take a castle in Dublin over this place. She'd live here on her own, like some manky nun in a clochán, if I let her."

Emer remembers the stories Rose once told her about the year she was boarding for secondary school. The teenagers stayed all week in a rooming house in Galway and snuck porter into their rooms and had quiet parties late into the night. The boys would sneak into the girls' rooms and take turns snogging each of them in the darkness.

Rose and Austin would end up in a corner together long after the others had tired of the game and moved on to something else. She'd lost her virginity one of those nights, as easily, she'd told Emer, as she'd first let his tongue between her lips. *I'll not regret it*, she said, even though she gave up secondary school and he gave up university and all those offers from music agents for that first set of twins. For the first time, despite the way he looks at his wife, Emer wonders if Austin regrets it. Or if Rose even asks him.

Austin has stopped talking now, both of them struck silent by what he's dared to say so far. She is not sure why this realization—that Austin is something other than completely devoted to her sister—makes her heart beat so quickly, with occasional interruption, a skip that feels like both anticipation and dread.

Emer takes a long swallow of her drink. Austin refills her mug with straight poitín now, buoyed by her familiar silence. They drink quietly and, Emer thinks later, with purpose. Until it begins to take effect.

The drink does the same thing to her as an hour with Brigid. She sinks into her body, her limbs loosen, she sits back and crosses her legs, her neck grows long, she runs her hands through her hair. The clenched ball she normally is lets go, unravels and stretches happily, like a waking cat. She is suddenly aware of the wet of her mouth, the heat in her cheeks, the way her chest rises and falls—nothing about her body feels awkward. She smiles, and her smile is not the normal clenched grimace.

Austin likes her like this, she can see it. He has stopped looking at her warily, and started joking with her, slagging Brigid and her early antics with the livestock. When she begins to smile, he imitates Brigid and Rose talking about literature over dinner. Emer actually giggles when he exaggerates Brigid's American accent, making her sound like an old, haughty intellectual. Still, he seems to remember what books they were talking about. She forgets that Austin used to be scholarly. Now he's just a farmer and a fisherman, like the rest of them. He pours them each another drink. The jug appears to be bottomless.

Whenever she laughs, Austin widens his eyes, encouraged, expectant. His irises reflect the candles with little jumps of yellow flame.

"Look at you," Austin says. "Smiling like a basket of chips. You've changed altogether. Rose said as much. Has Patch finally copped on between the sheets?" Emer giggles and suddenly they are both laughing so loud and long she is afraid Niall will wake up. But he doesn't, not then.

Another drink—Austin has two to her every one—and she's asking for a song. He obliges, closing his eyes, allowing her to watch

his face in the hearth light, without once having to look away. He
sings another verse of the song Brigid gave them at the bonfire.

> *A stór mo chroí, when the evening mist*
> *Over mountain and sea is falling*
> *Oh turn around and when you list*
> *Then maybe you'll hear me calling*
> *The sound of my voice you might hear*
> *Which calls for your speedy returning*
> *A rún, a rún, won't you come back soon*
> *To the one who will always love you?*

Austin's voice is like a hand reaching deep inside her. She can't stop
herself from looking at him when he finishes the song and opens his
eyes. He looks back, really looks at her, she imagines, for the first time in
his life. She catches his stare, holds it, pushes it back. Something flashes
in there, deep in his eyes. He sees the person only Brigid has seen.

She wants to laugh out loud, at how much she wants him to do
this, how inevitable it feels, even though it's the most inappropriate
thing in the world, her sister's husband looking at her with lust.
She's not shocked, and it doesn't even occur to her to pretend to be.

So when he moves into the dying firelight and mutters *give us a
little kiss*, she smiles along with him, like they're children playing at
a harmless game. She can see the ring in his eyes now, like a small
fiery circle, but tells herself it is a trick of the firelight. She does
not hesitate, she does not want to pause and think perhaps they
shouldn't. This is what she has always wanted and the drink and the
storm and her sister's absence, and her new confidence from Brigid,
make it the easiest thing she has ever done. She won't stop to ponder
what it is inside her, inside his eyes and that room and the drink,
that makes this vile behavior as easy and natural as letting Niall
climb into her lap.

She barely feels the first few kisses, still reeling at the thought of them, then she starts to kiss back, and his lips are as luscious and foreign as his voice. She had expected, with the drink and the pipe and the memories of Patch, that he would taste like a man—ruined—but his breath is as sweet as a child's. Austin cups her face with his rough hands, the fingers, like Patch's, cracked with work and embedded in soil, and she opens her mouth. She knows now from being with Brigid how to step into him, how to press, how to arch her back and show she is willing for more. He grabs her waist and grunts gratefully. She thinks briefly that perhaps he, too, has been waiting for this moment all along. For the time it takes to start it, she believes wholeheartedly that Austin is kissing her for the same reasons she is letting him. *A rún.* My love.

Then it gets rougher. Slightly, like abandonment to passion, then more so, becoming something else entirely. His tongue thrusts deeper than is comfortable. She feels the drink glug up from her stomach. She pulls away to keep from burping in his mouth, and to break the pressure that has quickly moved from tender to rude and demanding, and mostly because she has a brief image of her sister actually seeing them at it, the same way Emer once watched Rose and Austin through a hole in the stone.

"Austin," she says. "That's enough, so."

He coaxes, that voice swooning whispers just at the side of her face.

"Rose wouldn't mind," he insists. "She never minded in the boardinghouse. She shared me with her friends, so she did. Surely she'd share with her sister as well."

As ludicrous as this is, somehow during his whispering he has half walked, half pushed her to the hearth bed, which is deep and soft and warmer than any bed in the house. He pushes her down and lies straight on top of her, kissing her into the softness, and her throat clogs in fear. Lying down was not the right thing to do, she can see that, but she isn't sure how she will arrange getting up again. When she tries to sit up, the look in Austin's eyes so unnerves her—for an instant there is no blue left in them, or even darkness, it is like looking into the orange heart of a fire. Though it fades when he turns his head away from the light, the scowl he gives her so reminds her of the way he has always looked at her that she can't bear it, so she kisses him again. Each kiss takes her farther away, like she's caught in a current and it's clear she can't make it back and that she never should have gone swimming in the first place. She's doing this all wrong. She started bold and now she wants to take it back.

She tries to use her hands. She puts them flat to his chest, willing whatever misery is in them to stop this. It doesn't work. Her hands on him are not the horror they usually are to Patch, nor do they stir up the bliss she elicits from Brigid. Something else rises to her touch. She tries to put her hands beneath her instead, but he pulls at one, pressing it to where he is hard and demanding. She wonders briefly if it is her hands making him do this or something else, something that was in him all along, but it hardly matters. She can see now how impossible it will be to stop, whatever it is.

He pushes her blouse aside and dives at her breast, taking her nipple into his mouth. She inhales sharply, and he takes this for encouragement, and sucks harder. With Brigid this had felt good. With Austin it is horrid.

"No, Austin," she manages and he looks up at her, his mouth circled in saliva, loose, lecherous, grinning. As if they have some secret language, as if no is the most welcoming word he can hear. He fumbles quickly, freeing himself from his trousers. He grabs up her skirt and yanks down her drawers.

"No," she says again, but it only eggs him on. He moves up toward her face and presses his mouth to hers again, hard, not a kiss, more like a gag.

"Hush," he says. "You'll wake himself." She goes cold at this, silent, realizing all of a sudden exactly what she has put at risk.

"Austin," she pleads in a whisper. "In all fairness. Stop now."

He gets a look then that does more than disappoint her.

"Sure isn't this what you wanted," he says. "Isn't this what you planned?" He is slurring. She realizes, with a drop in her stomach, that he is very drunk, as drunk as Patch after days on the tear. Why did she not wonder, before now, what was in that jug?

"I planned nothing," she says. She's not sure what he means. Hadn't he come over here?

"Aren't you the one Rose came back here for?" he says between clenched teeth. She is not sure she has heard him right.

She can feel him on her thigh, nothing between them, a hot threat. Like he is holding a weapon there. She doesn't want to move for fear it will puncture her. He moves a hand down and pushes her legs apart. She is shaking now, the muscles in her legs are useless to defend her.

"Austin," she tries again. "Don't. Think of Rose."

That's when he puts the hand to her neck. His hand is broad enough that it fits across the front, the callused space between his thumb and first finger resting just on the hollow spot that always tightens when she is afraid. He doesn't grip, just holds it ready, and looks her straight in the eye. His eyes are burning now, they are dark pits of fire, there is nothing left that she recognizes. His face is moving in and out of shadow and for a brief, horrifying instant he looks like someone else, something pinch-faced and slightly feminine, and she hears, though the mouth in that face does not move, a shrill voice chanting, *go on, go on, go on*.

The decision is left to her. If she moves, or gets up, because suddenly she wonders why hasn't she just gotten up before now, walked to the door, and told him to leave, the hand will tighten. She knows it as sure as she knows what his other hand is doing as he positions himself between her legs. Whatever is inside him now, whatever she let in here with the drink and the music and her blasphemous desire, has no intention of letting her go.

Later she will remember making a choice, firmly, completely, like the shutting of a door. But in the moment it happens without her consideration. She opens her legs, and lets him, surprised at how easily he slides inside, with none of the discomfort or resistance she remembers with Patch. It used to feel sometimes that her husband was forcing himself into places that weren't meant to open, tight bony places that bruised and chafed and were sore all the next day. Something is bigger inside her now, or gone, and it barely hurts, not even at the back when he thrusts. It seems she is deep enough to absorb it all, whether she wants it or not.

"Ah, you're well ready for me," Austin mutters and she cringes but doesn't argue with him. This is no longer a body she recognizes. The only familiar thing is the vise around her neck, the threat that a movement or word or swallow will crush her. She could care less at this point what happens below, with the threat of that hand focusing everything in her throat. That hand has been there her whole life; the only difference now is that it's attached to something.

It takes ages. Much longer than Patch ever took. She closes her eye and tries to go somewhere else. While Austin is thrusting, driven by something within him, but also outside of them both, unable to be stopped, she yearns to be carried away, like when she was a child, when she could turn her head and see something, a curtain, a cliff's edge, an invitation to another world.

She opens her eye and she sees Niall. He is standing quietly in the center of the almost dark room. The tears that are running down her face into the bedclothes are also falling on Niall's flushed face. She can't shake her head without Austin noticing, so she widens her eye in warning. Niall sees it, turns around and walks quietly from the room. Austin seizes on top of her then, gripping her neck to the point of pain, then falls down next to her. He leaves one arm draped across her neck and keeps it there for a long time.

There is a terrible moment later on, where she tries kissing him again. Partly she does it to stop looking at him; the face, next to her in the bed, otherworldly, the eyes not yet returned to blue, partly like asking for an apology she won't get, mostly because she wants to turn it all back to the beginning, when it could still have been just a curious kiss. They're too far gone for that. Austin turns his mouth away. He doesn't want to kiss her anymore.

THE NEXT DAY THE weather hasn't cleared and Niall sleeps later than usual with no sun to pierce through the curtains and rouse him. Emer moves carefully around the kitchen trying not to strain. She goes to the privy and wipes away viscous, rank liquid with a cloth until she feels scraped raw. She is fiercely itchy and longs for a bath. Though she expected Austin to slink away once Niall wakes, he stays with them the whole day, mends a few things Patch hadn't gotten around to—the hearthstone where it broke away, a wobbly table leg, shows Niall how to bait hook with baby eel wrapped in leaves and mummified with a wrap of string, leaving the hooks on the windowsill until the fishing weather returns. He jokes with the boy, and Niall, showing no loyalty whatsoever, smiles and follows instructions willingly. At one point, while she is tidying up the hearth bed, stripping the linens off to put in a hot wash, one of the poitín mugs rolls out from underneath and falls onto the stone floor and cracks into two thick pieces. She almost starts to cry, the reality of last night coming at her like the pottery has been thrown in her face. Niall and Austin look up at her.

"Mammy," Niall scolds. "You broke it." Austin whistles, mocking his boldness.

The accusation catches her throat and she wants to scream

something at him. She picks up the pieces while Niall leans into his uncle and learns a hitch knot.

She cannot tell how much her son remembers about last night or even if he understands it. She wants to ask him, and when Austin goes out to milk the cows she says "Niall?" Her voice comes out strange and angrier than she means it to and he pretends not to hear her. She doesn't have the energy to say it twice.

She makes breakfast for the three of them, then dinner, then evening tea, Austin showing no sign of leaving, like the weather that refuses to lift. It is as though he remembers nothing from the night before, or he has turned it into something else, and believes she actually wants him here. It's like they are pretending that she and Niall belong to him now. She is too afraid of him, of herself, of what still lurks around them in the house, to say otherwise.

She thinks of her sister over on Muruch, past the excitement of staying now, anxious to get her children home, to be crowded in her own house rather than someone else's. Missing her husband. She wonders if they'll pull at each other's clothes as soon as they can, hungry for each other the way that has never seemed to wane, and if she will smell something different on him, some guilt, some remnant of her sister's wet fear.

She wonders also if Brigid will smell it on her, the next time she puts her face between her legs. Whether there will be evidence of betrayal, of that invited assault.

They spend another night alone, sitting at the fire like an old married couple while Niall falls asleep in her arms. There is no more drink, between them they finished the jug the night before. Austin smokes a pipe and minds the turf fire and cleans up the dishes from their tea. Niall's breathing is clear now, his chest has lost the wheeze it had yesterday, his nose crusted rather than runny. She holds him against her, asleep he seems not much heavier than when he was a toddler. No words pass between them for a long time.

For an instant, she thinks Austin is chuckling over some thought in his head, but realizes, horrified, that his shoulders are shaking and the broken, eruptive noise is him weeping. He is crying and trying not to. She looks at him, narrowing her eyes.

"What are you on about," she hisses, angry and bitter and fully herself again.

"What have we done?" he says. "This will break her heart."

Emer almost can't speak over what rises in her throat. "Neither of us will be telling Rose," she whispers. "Have you gone mad?"

"I don't know," Austin blubbers. "It won't happen again," he promises.

Emer looks away. She is not sure what combination of man and changeling was in her bed last night, but Austin is himself again. He is no longer attractive to her, and she is newly afraid of him, but still, there is a stab of disappointment that he will give her up that easily, with relief really, and that perhaps none of it had been about any desire for her at all. And this, after all, almost seems the worst of it. The way she fooled herself.

"There's something vile in you," he says in that deep, bruising voice. In a moment he will go away, out into the rain and wind, leaving her alone with the echo of what they have done.

"It wasn't me did that all by myself," she retorts. But she is no longer sure.

IN THE MORNING THEY all come back, the men worse for two days of drink and dancing, the women smiling and full of news and tea and packages wrapped from the shop. Austin pulls Rose out of the currach onto the slip, after she hands him the two toddlers that he turns and passes to Emer. He swings her around in a hug, hiding the look on his face in her neck, and she laughs and pounds his arm, embarrassed but delighted. Really, she's delighted by anything and everything he does and always has been, Emer can see this now. She wouldn't believe anything dark in him, even if it were her own sister who swore it. Brigid, though she hasn't seen Emer in days, slips away in the commotion and by the time Emer looks for her she is halfway up the road with the dog. No hello, no handshake, no hint that later she will make this better, make the last two days go away as easily as a bee sting. Emer is left to follow her family home.

Niall tells Patch, at teatime that evening while Patch is telling her how much he got for the sheep.

"Mammy was taken," he says suddenly, and Emer stops chewing, the potato growing cold on her tongue.

"What's that?" Patch says distractedly, annoyed at the interruption.

"Mammy was taken. She broke the mug. Austin showed me the hitch. And we made up the eels."

"Are you ill?" he says to Emer. She shakes her head. Mumbles something about turning her ankle and dropping the mug.

"Show me the eels, so," he says to Niall. Niall reveals the wilted, reeking pile behind the curtain. Patch promises they will fish with them in the morning.

When she puts Niall to bed that night, he asks her to lie down with him, and he curls with his back to her belly so they fit together like wooden spoons.

"Did he steal you?" he whispers. Emer shakes her head against his hair.

"I'm all right," she says. "You mustn't speak of it. I'll be angry if you do." This is the biggest threat she can think of. He hates for her to be angry, and will do anything if there is the slightest chance of it.

"I won't," he says. "Don't use the angry voice, Mammy. Use your other voice."

"All right, *a chuisle*," she says. She sings to him softly, he smiles and wiggles around contentedly. He never stops moving, not even in bed, some part of him is always twitching, wiggling, reaching out. She holds him so tight for a moment he complains and she loosens her grip.

"Settle down," she murmurs. He tries. His wiggling slows to a minimum. He's almost gone.

"Was that even Austin on you, Mammy?" he asks, just before he falls asleep.

Faces rush at her, first Patch then Brigid, one looking like he wants to die, the other aroused, inviting, but still, underneath it, a well of regret. She thinks of Austin's eyes, lit from behind by a consuming fire that was all too familiar. She sees now that there is little difference between the times she has lain with Patch, the secret sessions with Brigid, and this, this violation that isn't one, this cruelty that she asked for, that she invited to penetrate her as surely as she asked for the abuse of those bees.

The fairies came in. She let them in, with the drinking, the music, the flirtation, she left the door wide open. It must have been fairies, or her own cruel hands. It couldn't be Austin, the boy Rose married, who had done such a thing. Could it?

In sleep her son is perfectly, frighteningly still, like his spirited self is gone and left a husk in its place. Niall falls away before she can say she isn't at all sure who it was—a cruel man or a changeling. Or which of them—Austin or herself—was to blame.

PART TWO

The Stolen Child

The host is riding from Knocknarea
And over the grave of Clooth-na-bare;
Caoilte tossing his burning hair,
And Niamh calling Away, come away:
Empty your heart of its mortal dream.
The winds awaken, the leaves whirl round,
Our cheeks are pale, our hair is unbound,
Our breasts are heaving, our eyes are agleam,
Our arms are waving, our lips are apart;
And if any gaze on our rushing band,
We come between him and the deed of his hand,
We come between him and the hope of his heart.
The host is rushing 'twixt night and day,
And where is there hope or deed as fair?
Caoilte tossing his burning hair,
And Niamh calling Away, come away.

"The Hosting of the Sidhe," William Butler Yeats

CHAPTER 14

Corncrake

October 1959

Even before Emer tells her about Austin, on the days where their only opportunities to touch are snatched, breathless moments, Brigid spends the nights afraid of what she has risked. She imagines Emer remembering the Catholic girl she is and confessing to her husband or her sister. Brigid was a fool to gamble this way, on an island where they can take the hope from her in the blink of an eye. She can hear her mother's voice warning her not to underestimate them. *The islanders called her a saint when she could help and a devil when she couldn't.*

She will avoid Emer then, engaging Niall, tending the hives, gathering honey or sketching together, so that he won't leave them alone. She watches Emer move from annoyed, to frightened, to dejected, her eye welling up at the possibility that what she came for will not be offered again. Longing rises off her—Brigid feels it because the same thing is rising out of herself—as furious and lustful as a swarm of ravenous bees.

Her desire for Emer surprises her. She hasn't felt like this in a long time. This willing to lose herself, to feel like you have no choice but to surrender to their hands. No matter how hard she tries to keep Emer at a distance, Brigid always gives in, and makes love to her with a violent abandon that frightens her afterward. As though despite Emer's inexperience, her deep, almost childish need, Brigid is actually the young one, so desperate and manic in love that she is unable to see past the next encounter.

Brigid can see what happened on Emer's throat even before Emer gathers the courage to tell her. Not a bruise exactly, or a wound, but the suggestion of one, a memory, cowering at the hollow in her neck. Something with a mind of its own that waits, deliberating its next move. It has been there since the day they came back from Muruch, after three days trapped on the wrong island, where Brigid was queasy and claustrophobic and yearning for her small cottage, her loyal dog. Regretting what she started with this girl who is a snarled and twisted bramble of longing and bitterness, who can still drag love across Brigid's body in spite of herself.

"While you were away something happened. I did . . ." Emer changes course. "Austin took . . . em, we had relations. Austin and myself."

Brigid's limbs are filling with a heaviness that seems more than physical, and she wants to lie down, go outside and sink into a rough cushion of heather and fall asleep in the sun. But she forces herself to look at Emer instead. There is a long beat where she has no idea what she will say next. She has a cruel instinct to get angry with her. To use it as an excuse to end this affair that has become too much for the both of them.

"What happened?" Brigid says. It all comes out of Emer in a jumbled rush, she skips from end to beginning, from shame to accusation and back again, a story where the motivation, and the instigation, is never fully clear. The truth escapes her, just as she thinks she has grabbed hold of it.

"I didn't intend it," Emer says. She is fighting tears, her face red from holding her breath, her one eye widened, expanding the socket as if by doing so she can keep the tears from falling out. The first tear will be like a plug, a stone at the mouth of a well, and she will not be able to stanch the flow once it begins.

"It's not always intention that ignites these things," Brigid says. Emer shakes her head.

"That's not what I mean. I've fancied it for as long as I can remember. But something else happened. I was willing enough. I intended to kiss him. But then something turned and I tried to stop but it was too late."

"Tried to stop him?"

"Tried to stop . . ." Emer can't decide which pronoun to insert. The story will continue to warp and change in her mind, as she inserts variations, myself, it, them, us. It will go round and round in her, and she will not be able to halt it by blurting out only one.

"Emer," Brigid says carefully, because Emer is trapped inside something that requires care. It's like coming slowly upon an injured animal and trying to help it before it bolts. "What do you mean?"

"I told him not to do it. I told him we should stop. I told him to think of Rose."

"You told him no?" She sees Emer searching her mind, shaking it, trying to find the clean memory through the thick fog of recollection.

"I did. More than once."

"He forced you."

"Not exactly," she says. Emer sits forward, she wants to shorten the space between them so her words won't blow away, so her explanation can be caught and understood. "Something came over him. Like a fairy stroke. I might have been the one to put it in there."

"I doubt that," Brigid bites. "It's called rape. What a bastard." But she stops when she sees Emer's shoulders drop even more, and the shaking of the hand she raises to her neck.

How many girls has she seen like this, bent over themselves, as if they can fold in half like a cloth spotted with blood, fold away all the horror and shame and tuck into a drawer within their minds this thing their bodies will never forget. How many times has she tried to have men punished, only to see the girl they violated penalized even more? She is not a fool, she will not suggest that Emer tell anyone, not Rose, or the priest, or the guards, a nine-mile row and a twelve-mile car ride away. She would need Patch, or Austin, or one of his cousins, to row her there in the first place.

Sometimes there were men, men with souls like Matthew but minds and bodies hardened into a carapace that could summon violence, who took care of these things. Who enforced a justice that did nothing to erase the crime. It had its own purpose, this revenge, it gave a grim satisfaction. But Brigid is an outsider here, and does not know the men well enough to even imagine whom she would ask of such a thing.

Emer is pulling at her collar, warping the wool of her jumper away from the invisible weight at her neck.

"I'm sorry, Emer," Brigid says. She can see that her angry thoughts will only increase the pressure. Emer's throat is perched on the edge, all it will take is a word, a breath, a thin sliver of skin to bring the weight of a lifetime down to crush it.

"I'm so sorry," because there is nothing else to say. All the other words will have to be thrown into the fire and forgotten.

It is not until she touches her, until she slides from her chair and kneels by Emer's, and takes the girl's clenched, furious face between her hands, and kisses her eyelid, closed so tight against what she no longer wants to see, that Emer is able to cry. Ugly, thundering sobs that wrack her body like a series of blows, crying that is too violent to completely succumb to.

"What have I done?" Emer says, when the sobbing subsides, and Brigid shushes her.

"Stop that, Emer. It was done to you."

"It couldn't have been him alone," Emer says.

"Why not?"

"It's Austin. He's married to my sister."

"It happens all the time," Brigid says. "It's not your fault."

"There's something ugly in me," Emer says. Her head is resting on Brigid's shoulder. Brigid puts her hand to Emer's hair and strokes it, pulling it between her fingers, like separating sections to braid the hair of a child.

"Why can't I stop from calling it up?" Emer says, her voice hushed with terror, as if to even ask such a thing aloud is to set something unstoppable, like a flame touched to an island bonfire, used to burn a mountain of discarded life.

"I don't know," Brigid says. This is not the right answer. She feels Emer stiffen, the angry coiled center of her getting ready to spring out again. Emer sits up, kisses her, tries to reach beneath Brigid's blouse with her angry, desperate hands. Deep inside Brigid an ache blossoms that feels so like lust, she opens her mouth, and leads Emer to the bedroom. In an attempt to heal, or at least overwrite the memories of Austin, she brings the girl to a whimpering conclusion, but when Emer tries to do the same, Brigid realizes that the feeling is not desire, but revulsion, like something deep inside the place where she longs to be sated is screaming at her to stop.

"Shhh," Brigid says to Emer, gently deflecting her hands. "We're both tired. Just let me hold you, and we'll rest."

THE UNMASKING OF AUSTIN does not surprise Brigid. There was a moment with him that told her, that lifted the curtain away and showed what skulked underneath.

It was after the Lughnasa bonfire, the festival on the first of August that marked the end of the summer and the onset of the harvest, Rose sent Austin to walk Brigid home. He'd lunged at her drunkenly by her front door, trying for a kiss, and she had pushed him firmly away.

He covered his sneer of anger quite deftly with a smile.

"Would you rather one of the women walked you home, then?" he said.

She did not let her gaze drop from the ugly implication in this.

"Good evening, so," he muttered, after a beat, when he realized that she had no intention of answering.

Before he left he spat, a purposeful, ridiculous gesture, meant to stand, she supposed, for some sort of dismissal, or warning.

Men, she thinks, can be as foolish as boys; too bad they have the power to twist that foolishness into danger, as easily as the turning of a rock in the sand. It doesn't help that these women encourage it, that grown men on this island are treated with the same dismissive, devoted impatience they bestow on unruly boys. It's humiliating, Brigid thinks, for the lot of them.

She does not think much more about it until Emer tells her story. She doesn't think a fairy possessed Austin. But she can imagine what Emer's hands might do to a man already poised for violence. She has seen it, saw what Austin was capable of in the gleam and shadows that were created when he turned his head away and spat into the dark ground.

She puts a hand to Emer's neck that day, and pulls just enough of the damage away for Emer to breathe, to hold her head up, to forge ahead, as grumpy and unpleasant and as normally as she can. There is a minimum, Brigid has learned, to what she can heal without getting ill herself. A psychological salve, as long as she doesn't go too long, is safe enough. It will make her tired, but nothing else. She couldn't grab hold of every wound in Emer even if she wanted to. She cannot twist herself so deeply in the coils of Emer and Austin and the fire they have started. She has something much more fragile to hold on to.

AFTER EMER LEAVES TO collect Niall from school, Brigid goes back into her bedroom, too heavy to remain upright. She has been pregnant so many times before that she adjusts to the signs of it before she remembers that it shouldn't be possible. The queasiness that creeps in, so subtle it is a while before you realize it has been there all day. The disconnect in her throat when she breaks open an egg, the subtle turning of the smells of her home from a comfort to an assault. The band of tightness that stretches above her pubic bone, as if a stone has lodged just under the soft mound of her belly. She reaches her fingers below her waistband to see if she can ease the feeling, but it's permanent, it's not going to budge. She feels like this, as if her body has already expanded to make room for something that barely has substance yet, for days before she allows herself to hope for what it means. Aside from generous waist pinches and Austin's sloppy lunge, no man has even touched her since she arrived.

The well has done what her mother promised. It has given her not merely a womb, but the baby as well. She hopes that what is growing inside her is not a fantasy, or a dangerous pact with the darkness that lurks in Emer. She will call it a blessing from the saint, though she has no evidence to distinguish the gift of a saint from the bargain of something that lives beneath the world.

She lies in bed next to Rua and pulls her soft ear through her fingers, making her sigh and stretch and put her thin face on Brigid's belly.

"Shall we have a baby, Rua?"

The dog thumps her tail, willing to agree to anything, as long as she's allowed to lie beside Brigid, her adoration is simple and boundless, unmatched by the damaged humans who surround them.

The corncrake shrieks mercilessly in the field behind her house, repeating his endless warning, frantic that no one will translate the message.

Be careful, Brigid imagines him screaming. *Everything they give you, they can also take away.*

But by now Brigid has her own warning system. The child growing inside her already tells her when it has had enough.

CHAPTER 15

Cursing Stone

October 1959

Emer is adrift. Inside her is a great swell, it has rent her down the middle and now the two halves are moving apart like a body dragged by the current from an overturned boat. Her neck feels pressed for most of each day, her diaphragm is rigid, she has to stop and lean over and pull with all her might to get air deep into her lungs. Most of the time this fails, her breathing refuses to delve below the shallow, and she fears the space will shrink a little more each time, until she stops breathing altogether.

In the days after Rose returned, Emer was wound tight as a spring, jumping at everything Patch and Niall said as if she'd forgotten they were in the room. She spent those days inside, though the weather was fine, because the thought of meeting Rose or Austin in the field, of watching them approach her, was too much to bear. The knock she was expecting on the door never came.

Things do not improve even after it is clear that Austin has not told. Emer tells Brigid because she thinks if she lets it out her breathing will ease a bit. Brigid doesn't seem shocked, or even that interested, beyond an interrogation of blame and a simple "I'm sorry." She lays a hand on Emer's neck just long enough for her to breathe for a hour, but when she leaves the weight comes straight back in, like the sea air greeting her as she steps out the door.

HER DESIRE FOR BRIGID does not wane, if anything, it grows, but now it's a desperate, angry desire. Brigid avoids her, then denies it. If Emer comes up behind her, in the field, in the house, Brigid deflects her hands. She makes excuses, Niall will see, or Austin, whom she claims already suspects.

"Let's lay low for a while," Brigid says. "We don't want anyone to find out."

"I don't care if they know."

"Believe me, Emer, you do."

"Is it because of Austin? Because I let him touch me? Is that why you don't want me anymore?"

"Of course not."

"Then what is it?"

"I'm just being careful. It's not about you."

Even before this, every time Brigid reached for her was a relief. The last time they made love before the night with Austin, Emer had been asking about Brigid's husband, jealousy making her tactless, and, as if to prove her loyalty, Brigid seduced her rather than answer.

"Come here," she'd whispered, and Emer leaped out of her seat and into Brigid's hands driven by a lust tinged with fear.

They did not bother with the bedroom, but dropped right to the floor; the fire beside them burned as hot as the sparks they ignited in each other. At one point, Brigid called out her name, with a yearning that filled Emer to the brim. Emer imagined holding tight and rolling over, rolling them both into the fire with the same abandon as she once fell into a cavern of bees. The fire, rather than burning them, would just make it all last longer. They would never reach the point where they redid their clothes and Emer started to doubt it all, reading too much into Brigid's lack of eye contact. The point when they were two people again instead of the one glowing brand of lust that bound them. She wanted to reduce them both to ash, in the moment when they cried out with the glorious pain of it, at exactly the same time.

This is her fear: that Brigid has discovered that Emer disgusts her after all, that what Emer has learned to depend on—Brigid's hands—will be taken from her, with the same cruel disregard as a fairy withdrawing its promise.

IN OCTOBER, ALL THE old things come back to frighten her. She fears for Niall and keeps him home from school for a week after the teacher mentions that he often spends lessons gazing out the window and mouthing one half of a conversation no one else can hear.

"What were you doing?" she asks him.

"Listening to the music," he says, so casually that she feels a surge of vomit in her throat. "I think Austin was playing his whistle in the field," Niall says. But the men have been at sea all week, pulling the lobster pots.

In the house, Niall is clumsy and distracted. He spills milk all over the new bread, leaves the bottom half of the door open so the pig comes snuffling in. Emer keeps barking at him, and though she apologizes she does it again immediately, which makes him look at her with wide eyes and become even more forgetful. Finally, hating the havoc they wreak on one another, she sends him back to school. She regrets it almost immediately. Without him there is nothing in her small, damp, ugly house but herself and what she has done.

When it is her turn to care for her mother, the woman seems livelier than usual and peppers Emer with cryptic comments about

Emer's appearance, or Brigid, whom she still disapproves of, or Niall's seeming a little slow, until Emer imagines strangling her with the kitchen cloth or plunging the thinning blade of her knife into the woman's limp mouth.

Seeing Austin is like being accosted. He won't look at her directly, but still she feels his eyes following behind her, watching to see if she will dare tell. Rose is behaving strangely and Emer is paranoid, every short response or look of weary burden makes her sure Austin has finally confessed it all, and blamed her for it, telling her sister that she is a heartless whore. She worries that Rose won't even bother to ask her side. What if Austin declared Emer a liar and told Rose never to speak to her again, and Rose actually listened to him?

Emer's headaches return with a vengeance, and she spends entire days blind beneath a wet cloth in her bedroom, insisting that Niall stay in the house but also remain silent, which is so impossible for him to do she ends up scolding him, and just that rise in her voice causes her to vomit until she is sure the inside of her head is as empty as her stomach.

"Would you ever untwist yourself?" Patch says one evening, when every mention of Rose or the girls or his brother causes her to knock over a jug or drop her fork with a clang on her plate. Her mother looks at her with a knowing grimace. Niall looks away, preferring to focus on what no one else can see. And Emer realizes how impossible that will be, to ever uncoil the fairy threat from the human mistake, to ever untwist what has been done to her from what she has done herself.

BRIGID IS ILL. THE freckles on her nose leach away, leaving only their outlines, the skin beneath has a tinge of green. She doesn't want to touch Emer, or kiss her, or even talk to her, she wants to lie down in bed with the curtains pulled and eat only dry toast and read poetry and cuddle with the foul-smelling dog. She waves away Emer's offers of help, of company, and grows weary at her insistence.

"I just need to be left alone," she says. She can't see that Emer can barely breathe. She won't even look at her. "Just for a day or two, Emer, would you find something else to do?"

But Emer cannot stop coming over. When Niall is at school she has nowhere else to go. She sits in the outer room, keeps the kettle boiling in case Brigid wants tea, and listens to her being sick quietly, without explanation, into a waiting bowl.

EMER SEES IT ONE day, when Brigid moves in front of the fire and the light shines through her oversized blouse. The soft pouch of her belly is tight now, stretched and ready as a drum.

Emer goes cold with dread.

"Is that a child in there?" she says. Brigid turns away but not before Emer sees her smile.

"It is," she says.

"Did the well heal you, so?"

"I believe it did."

"But who was it put it in you?" She thinks of Austin making Brigid laugh, Malachy bringing back her stolen cow across the sodden fields. The priest, who'd come to her for tea once.

"I haven't been with a man, Emer. Perhaps it was an immaculate conception. Only not so immaculate."

"That's not funny. Who was it, really?"

"The saint," Brigid says. "Or a fairy. It doesn't matter."

"Jesus wept," Emer says, and the hair on her neck rises. There are so many things wrong with this she can't even begin.

"What will you tell the women?" she asks.

"Why do I have to tell them anything?"

"You must be joking."

"Fine. I'll tell them it was that Australian I flirted with on Muruch. He's the perfect alibi. Gone already."

"You flirted with an Australian? Was it him, so?"

"No. It was nobody."

"They won't like it, you not being married."

"This is what I want, Emer. There is no one to say I can't have it."

I wouldn't be so sure of that, Emer thinks, but she doesn't say it out loud.

"Are you not afraid?"

"Of whom?" Brigid looks defensive.

"Of what that baby might be."

"I've seen enough darkness to know it's not inside me, Emer. This baby is a gift."

"They don't give things for free, the fairies. I know."

"Saints do. Anyway, I'm not afraid."

There is a silence where Emer digests this. She rewinds to the well, she can't remember anything other than the glorious relief of Brigid's body, the way they used the water to satisfy their yearning. What had they put inside her?

"Is that why you won't touch me anymore?"

"Emer . . ."

"You got what you wanted and good riddance to me?"

"I care about you and Niall both."

"Is that how you get everything you want?"

"Emer," she almost whispers. "That's enough."

But Emer can't stop now. She wants it to hurt.

"What happened to the other baby?" she says.

"What baby?" Brigid stiffens.

"Your belly had a baby in it before. Who'd you use to get that one?" Brigid reaches down with the fingers of one hand and presses there, just above the pubic bone, remembering. Her wide shoulders square up. She directs toward Emer such a look of fury, Emer's legs go weak just at the eye contact.

"Be careful, Emer," she says. Then she turns around and goes back to the fire.

"I'm sorry," Emer says. She doesn't want this, this fury she is so familiar with, she doesn't want to feel for Brigid the same hatred she feels for everyone else.

"I miss you," Emer murmurs. "When can I have you back?" Brigid pretends she doesn't hear. Emer thinks she sees something in her profile, a pained look, a cringe of regret. But what is the pain? Is it from being with Emer, or being without her?

"I'm tired," Brigid says, raking the coals to prepare to bury them with ash for the night. "I'll see you tomorrow, all right?"

She won't even kiss her good-bye, but turns her head so Emer's mouth bumps her cheek. Emer walks home through the autumn darkness, her heart banging with a new dread she cannot name.

"WE SAW AUSTIN ON the road," Niall announces one day, entering the house with his father.

"What?" Emer barks. "Why, what's wrong?" Patch just looks at her, annoyed.

"Don't have a cow," he says. "We're off to town when the tide is high. He asked that you stay with Rose for the night, in case she needs anything."

Because Rose, Emer thinks, is the one we are all worried about.

"I will, of course," she says.

After he leaves for the quay, Emer packs up a little fish and the morning's bread in her basket, Niall's nightshirt and her own on top, and pulls her cowl over her shoulders. They walk slowly up the road to Rose's house, a ruin renovated by Austin and Patch, white-washed stone with two bedrooms and a loft in the generous roof.

Austin had wanted to put on a new slate roof, but Rose had insisted they keep the thatch. Austin humored her, though it meant more work for him.

"I like the way the birds nest in it, and the softness of the rain," Rose said at the time.

"Sure it's easy enough to refuse modern conveniences when you're lucky enough to have them offered to you," was Emer's two cents.

Rose is heavily pregnant now, and not as radiant as she usually is. Her face is swollen and carries a sheen of effort. She catches her breath a lot, twitching with the discomfort of being kicked from within. When these latest babies are born, Emer will have to be over here all the time, feeding Austin and the girls, doing the laundry, milking Rose's cows while she nurses the infants in the damp prison of her room. Other women will help, they always do, but for reasons no one can fathom, Rose, after childbirth, relies on Emer the most. How can Emer do it now, when every glance at her sister makes her think of Austin's hand laid like a gentle threat on her neck? How can she look her in the eye when she knows that she asked for it, that she stole him from her sister like a heartless fairy?

At Rose's pine table, Emer cracks an egg into a bowl and sees a deformed, bloody embryo clinging to the yolk. She heaves, so quick and hard there isn't even the time to know it is coming, or aim, so she is sick directly into the bowl beneath her hands, ruining the egg. She clings to the table with terror, and when she dares to look up, Rose is staring at her, a gleam of amusement in her eye.

"Well," she clucks. "Something you've been wanting to tell me?"

Emer thinks she will faint. Rose cops on and comes around the table, takes her arm and leads her to a chair.

"Oh no, no no no no no," Emer chants, thinking she does so in her head, but Rose shushes her.

"It's all right, pet," she says, and she sends one of the girls to the well to fetch a fresh glass of water. Niall stands like a statue halfway across the room, the same hot fear she feels in her throat throbbing in his eyes.

"Every baby is a blessing," Rose whispers. "You'll see."

"OH," BRIGID SAYS WHEN Emer tells her. "Well, then." She is unable to hide her surprise, or, Emer thinks, her annoyance.

"I need your help," Emer says. Brigid goes pale.

"No," she says.

"You only have to pull it out of me," Emer says. She is pacing the floor, Brigid is sitting by the hearth. "You pull things out all the time."

"It's not a bruise, Emer."

"It's more a bruise than anything else."

"I don't do that," Brigid says. Emer blinks, as if she is out of focus as well as not making sense. "What I mean to say is, I can't," she continues. "I'm sorry."

Brigid is quiet for a while. Emer can't understand why she looks so worried. Not sympathetic worry, but nagging fear.

"It wouldn't be the worst thing in the world to have it," Brigid says gently. "No one will know it's not Patch's. It would give Niall someone. The way you have Rose."

"I never wanted Rose."

"You don't mean that."

"I do, sure."

"It could be someone for you too, Emer, when Niall is gone."

"Gone? Gone where?!" She has left Niall with Patch at the house but he's no better than useless at the vigilance.

"To school."

Emer plops onto the chair across from Brigid and drops her forehead in her hands.

"You don't understand."

"I do understand. I understand what Austin did. I can't undo it. But you're not alone."

"Have you no notion of what this child might be? I can't risk it. I can't. It could be the fairies, found a way to finally get inside me. To take Niall."

"It's not a fairy, Emer, it's a baby." Emer shakes her head.

"Sometimes it's possible to turn things," Brigid says. "Sometimes you decide what you will allow to be taken from you."

"That's how it works for you," Emer says. "Not for the likes of me."

Brigid nods and sits back again. Emer thinks suddenly that she doesn't want Brigid to give up. She wants her to take her hands, keep arguing, keep saying those three words she has never believed before: *You're not alone.* She wants to rewind to the part where Brigid was still hoping to reach her. She wants her to say: *You have me.*

"Will you not leave the island with us?" Emer says, in a breathless flash of boldness. "We'll go somewhere, to America even, say we are widowed sisters, raise the babies together."

Brigid looks at her with such compassion, Emer imagines for an instant that she will smile, relieved, and say yes.

Instead she says this: "I want to stay here. I need to take care of myself now, Emer. And so do you."

Emer feels like the very floor has dropped beneath her feet. She is overcome with vertigo, and holds her breath until the urge to be sick passes.

"I can't have it. I can't."

"All right, Emer," Brigid says. "If that's how you feel, if you don't want another baby, I think we both know who can do something about it."

Brigid stands and walks to the table, picks up her knife and begins to peel a small, dirty potato. Emer can see she is angry with her. Emer wonders why she isn't angry with Austin, or Rose, or this wretched island that imprisons them.

Why is Brigid the one who's angry? she thinks. Isn't she the one who offered Emer something else, then snatched it away?

I thought we'd take care of each other, Emer wants to say. But she doesn't want to hear the answer to that.

"I can't hurt myself," Emer says. "It doesn't work that way."

"It's not you, though," Brigid says. "Is it?"

SHE LEAVES BRIGID'S PULLING at the collar of her blouse until she hears a few stitches rip. The sun is setting in her field of vision like a fire she can't look at. She stumbles blindly up the hill. She wants the screaming in her head to be swallowed in the wind of the cliffs.

She thinks of Austin's cocky grin, and Rose's graceful beauty, and Brigid's lustful confidence, and the girls she went to school with, with their talents and their plans and their pretty skin or hair or figures and how they knew what was lovely about themselves and made the best of it. She thinks of the ones who got away, who can't afford, or perhaps can't be bothered, to come home again. She thinks of the women who stayed, and how they keep having children, all of them, one after another because they can't stop it, nor do they seem to want to. Their lives appear to make them as happy as Emer's drags her down. She thinks of her mother and how cold and finished she was by the time Emer was old enough to recognize her, finished even while she had children she needed to stay alive for. She thinks of when she still wanted the fairies to rescue her, before she became afraid of them robbing her of what she loves the most. She thinks of the few times she went to Galway, before Niall was born and she was still a girl, when she stood still on the busy street and let person after person pass her by, with their clothes and their looks and their plans and their senses of humor, and a destination, all of them, and how she always thought, if I stand here, stand here very still, something or someone will scoop me up and steal me away and surprise me with a life. And no one ever had. The only one who had come close was Brigid. But she didn't give her a life. She gave her a dirty secret, even more useless and repulsive than what Emer had alone.

She thinks lastly of Niall, who before this barely saw her hate, who, with those eyes fogged by visions, refused to look past her adoration of him. He saw her splayed beneath Austin, saw the ugly rutting, and someday he will know what it means. This baby will be like a nail in the coffin of all that. It will put Niall at a distance, it will make him see something, something of what is really her, and eventually he will either avoid her or glide past her like the rest of them. Even if the fairies never take him back, he will be stolen away from her. He will be like all the teenage boys who leave the island for school or work, he will come home wearing the closed face and distant eyes of an Irish man. He will be able to see, after he learns about the world, the way she is, the way she makes people feel when she cradles their hand. She pulls their happiness away. It is really the only remarkable thing she has ever been able to do.

She passes the nuns' clocháns and stumbles along the cliff edge and climbs down to Saint Brigid's well. On one wall, she heaves aside a large slab of slate, revealing an opening that has been worried into the cliff wall, and inside this a basin, which holds one heavy round rock. *An clocha breacha*. The cursing stone. Some islanders say the fairies put it here, as a dark objection to Saint Brigid's healing. Others say it was left by Brigid herself, who had a dark side, a temper, a tendency to hurt and humiliate if she was pushed. Like the poor man she sent stumbling away by ripping out her eye. Or the leper she cured and then infected again when she saw he wasn't worthy. Most islanders don't believe in it anymore, but still tell their children never to touch it. The curse can be turned back on you, they say, if it is not just.

Emer has never used it before. She's not even sure how the thing works. But now she wants something big, something that can break open and release what's inside her, so she turns the stone, iridescent with moss, clockwise in its shallow rock bowl, pulling apart the lichen that has grown to hold it there, like roots that when they rip release a foul, stagnant smell. All the faces of the people who are happier than she is, the faces that look up at her with drained patience because they find her such a burden to be around, revolve over and over in her mind and it is not until she has turned the stone three times and stopped that she remembers what she wanted to do in the first place.

Later she will know what she has done. She will remember how she turned an ancient, evil stone to ask it to clear her womb, and what she asks for instead, and is granted, is the power to destroy everything.

CHAPTER 16

Coffins

October 1959

Islanders call them storms that are born in the sea. No warning from the sky, no darkness or wind shift to make the men pull up their gear and head for home. The sky is bright blue and favorable for as far as they can see, and then it is upon them, the wind and the rain and the chaos seem to rise up from the ocean, just like the swells. In storms like this one, in the past, men have told of clinging to their boats and seeing, when they look up, the other side of the maelstrom: beyond the cluster that swallows them the sky remains as clear and uninvolved as the divide between two worlds.

This time, there is no one left alive to describe it.

BRIGID WATCHES IT FROM her field. Watches the fog descend and the sea rise, in one spot, like the great watery hand of some creature reaching from beneath. They are so close, six men in a single currach, coming home from a few pints on Muruch. She feels like she could walk out herself and pull them in. Rua keeps running forward and back, barking at her to do something. Then the rain and fog hit them and she doesn't see anymore. They must be all right:

They were not very far from shore, and Niall doesn't come to tell her otherwise. Rua whimpers and paces in the house all night, though there is no thunder to disturb her.

It isn't until the morning, when the weather clears and she sees all the boats anchored out from the quay, that she knows how bad it was. She has never seen so many people come to the island at once.

It is a stranger, a man from the other island she has never met before, who tells her the sea took it all, the boat, the bodies, the heads of families, the last six young men on the island that needs young men to keep it alive. Like the sea itself knew what to take and chose to swallow what would leave the most damage. Patch and Austin Keane, twenty-nine and twenty-seven years of age; their cousins, Seamus and Peter O'Halloran, twenty-four and twenty-one; Michael Joe Cullen, thirty-two, their lifelong friend; and owner of the vessel, Malachy Moran, thirty-nine. Six wives, twenty-eight children left behind.

"Stole any hope of remaining here, so it did," the man mutters.

Brigid walks away from him in the middle of this prediction, up the road to the women who need her.

THEY START TALK OF the evacuation almost at once. During the search for any buriable and comforting piece of them, through the suffocating cloud of grief and despair that grips the whole island, as thick and untenable as fog, they begin to mumble about it, just one more inevitable thing that will be thrust upon them.

They'll not let us remain now.

Sure, how will we, with no men?

Are you not inclined to pack it in altogether?

'Tis better for the children to be raised on solid ground.

They talk of it at the wakes, in six tiny houses, where off-island men set their glasses on the lids of empty caskets.

Will they not take them on Muruch?

Sure they barely have room for themselves.

The shame will be in leaving this land. The land on the other side is all rock.

The sea is hard here, all the same.

Only one body is recovered, Malachy's, to put inside the pine. The priest suggests carefully to the widows that they find something, anything, to put inside the caskets. Preferably something light, something that will not roll or knock inappropriately around. Since they all died in the thick jumpers knitted with patterns to identify them, the widows have to find other pieces of clothing, a cap, a nice jacket worn only to Mass, a photograph of the children, a figure carved out of soapstone wrapped in a woolen scarf.

Niall offers to be the thing inside his father's casket. He says it aloud, at Rose's house, amid a group of women, islanders and visitors from away, who are all so aggrieved they are having trouble remembering whom to comfort.

"I'll be very still," he says, looking around at them eagerly, a little excited to have thought up such a creative solution. Emer, who has been tending the kettle, puts it down and walks quickly across the room, scooping him up in her arms, holding him tight as if she can smother what everyone has heard.

What is he on about?

He's a queer one, is he not?

Niall looks around at them, Brigid sees him realize that what he said was terribly wrong. He starts to cry and Emer has to take him outside, past the women she looks at like she might burn them to a crisp.

Children shouldn't be mollycoddled, they end up quare as their mothers before them.

His mother was touched, as a girl, I remember well the stories.

God knows how they made it this long.

'Tis a grave, this place, a watery grave.

THE FUNERAL PROCESSION IS attended by Muruch men, who carry the almost weightless coffins from home to church to the graveyard that sits above the quay. During the walk the women wail together, a rhythmic incantation somewhere between a scream and a song.

"What are they singing?" Brigid whispers to the Muruch man next to her.

"Keening," he says. "Legend says the druid Brigit was the first to do it, when her son was killed in a battle. It a horrible sound." He shudders.

"Yes," Brigid agrees. "But beautiful too."

Mostly it is familiar. When her father died, her babies, Matthew, every time a baby was ripped from a mother's arms. It was the sound she heard in her heart.

They say things about Brigid in the Irish they believe she will not understand.

The Yank is a comfort, sure.

She's no stranger to grief, you can see that.

Brigid takes it all in stride, she moves among them with the confidence of someone who has been faced with senseless death before. No hesitation, no simpering questions, no "Is there anything I can do?" As if people in the grips of sudden death can ever take the time to think of what others might be able to do.

She cleans their houses, keeps their fires up, washes the faces and does up the buttons of their children. Brings their eggs in, their milk, their washing forgotten on the line. She brings them enormous jars of dark, thick honey, like something you might spread on a wound. She says very little, as if knowing that her accent might be too sharp, an insult in a cocoon of grief that only someone from this island can understand. She moves through their houses, sweeping and pressing and wiping, and every once in a while, when a contraction of vivid pain rises up in a wife at the thought of her husband or a mother at the thought of her boy, Brigid will put her wide, calloused hand on their back or their shoulder and clear a little space in the midst of the pain, just enough for them to inhale past it. She can do this much without harming herself or the baby. She doesn't take the pain away, she merely shifts it, just at those moments when it seems too enormous to bear. Coaxes it away from its relentless clenching of their hearts.

She doesn't touch Emer, as much as she wants to. She would like to ease her grief, to apologize for how she ended things, but when she goes to see her, something has changed. Emer spends the days after the funeral in Rose's bed. The children are told to let her be, and move through the house in hushed, tearstained pairs.

"She lost the baby, poor pet," Rose confides in Brigid. "First the lads, now this. She's wrecked with grief."

"Emer?" Brigid whispers when she goes into the darkened bedroom. Emer, lying in the bed, turns her head as if it weighs more than the rest of her. Her face is so pale it looks skeletal, her one eye blazing with what looks like a fever, or derangement.

"Was it my fault?" she whispers hoarsely.

Poor Emer, Brigid thinks. The girl is grieving, only not in the way her sister believes.

"Of course not," Brigid says, and she moves toward her, with the intention of sitting by her side.

But her belly seizes up, the baby lashes so violently she feels like it could bruise her from the inside. *Don't* is the word that comes into her head. *Don't.* As if her own child is wailing, but no one else can hear it.

"You'll be all right," she says uselessly, and she hurries out of the room, out of the house to breathe the air and calm the maelstrom inside her. Instead, she ends up vomiting violently by the stone wall. The baby has given her messages before, of when to stop using her hands, just like her sickness used to, sickness that varied depending on the wound.

But she has never felt anything like the fear that grips her at the thought of touching Emer. Just a few days ago she could still touch her, though sex was out of the question. Now, the baby won't stand for it. The darkness in Emer's hands, the power that never affected Brigid, which Brigid could once transform into pleasure, is stronger now, or she has lost her ability to deflect it.

THE CHILDREN CAN'T GET enough of her. They follow her around, dirty hands in her skirts, and if she manages to sit down they swarm onto her lap, squeezing to make room for their siblings and cousins. She does not need to hold back for them. She places her large palms on the crowns of their heads and washes the whole of it away, silencing the keening of their mothers, which they hear like an echo that will never fade.

Niall takes to sitting in Brigid's lap, or holding her hand as she walks across the field to gather forgotten cows. Being with Brigid makes his crying subside, where the arms of his mother make it swell up all over again. He is frightened of what losing the men means for his mother, Auntie Rose, his cousins. Niall doesn't want to leave the island, but he has never told his mother this.

"Mammy is ill," Niall says to Brigid. "It's like she's gone away."

"She'll come back," Brigid says.

"Ah, I know. She wouldn't ever leave me."

"Of course not," Brigid says quietly, not wanting to give a turn to the guileless faith of this child.

THEY HAVE THE MEETING in the school, and old Jimmy Moran, the one man left, stands at the back, out of tradition, though he is so wobbly Brigid makes him sit down at one of the small desks. The only other island men are boys, all under the age of twelve, trying to stand taller than they are. The priest from Inis Muruch is here, and a small, tidy, nervous man from the Galway County Council. He passes around the same picture Emer has of the bungalows on the mainland. Mortared walls, bedrooms on either end. Water taps in the kitchen. Toilets and proper bathtubs. Electric lights, gas cookers, radios. All on a lovely stretch of beach that looks out over the island on a clear day. To remind them, Brigid thinks, of what they have given up. Confirmation of their failure topped off with a water view. They are naming the new village Cois Cuain, which means safe haven.

The children, excited by the promise of dances at the hall and a real football pitch, want to go. So do the old women, who are tired and afraid of dying without a priest there to give them last rites. Jimmy Moran calls out that he will die in the house where he was born, and the women roll their eyes and shush him. Emer sits perched upon her little chair as if someone is about to hand her the keys any minute. Though Brigid has helped them, eased them through grief with her capable hands, she feels some of them cringe a bit when she speaks up, as if silently saying that she has very little right to do so.

"Why can't we have those things here? The other island has a telephone."

"Muruch has three hundred and fifty residents," the councilman says. "The county won't allow a phone on an island with less than one hundred."

"What do you do here, then," Brigid asks, "in an emergency? In a storm, or if someone is ill."

"We build a fire," Rose answers her. "A bonfire, on the hill. And hope that someone sees it and sends help."

"That's pathetic," Brigid says, glaring at the blushing man from the Council.

"Aye," an old woman says behind her. "That it is."

"What about a harbor?" Brigid continues. The council official, who had expected this to be tied up quickly, is starting to sweat, and wipes at his fogged glasses with his handkerchief.

"Wouldn't a proper harbor solve this? A place for larger boats to dock, emergency boats, in a storm, the way they do everywhere else?"

"It's not the government's problem that this island has no harbor. It would cost far more to build a harbor than it would to build these people a whole new village where they will be safe from the whim of the sea."

There are a few island gasps at this, then uncomfortable silence. Of course, most of them know this fact, have discussed it among themselves. Nonetheless they are surprised, insulted and a little inspired by the rudeness of saying it out loud. By the cheek of it, speaking about them as if they are livestock.

None of them is quite sure afterward what turns it, that little mistake of the councilman, or Brigid's Yankee confidence, or just the raw grief and weariness of the thought of packing it all up and abandoning their lives. Leaving the sea, which holds within it the bodies of their men that were never found. Somehow it is agreed that nothing will change just yet, they will press on, that they will see another winter of storm and isolation and abandonment through, see how it goes, as if without the men, it will not go a lot worse than it has in other years. They'll leave it so, and talk it over again in the springtime. Men will come over from Muruch to help them finish the harvest, store the hay, slaughter the pigs. They have the money from the sheep, the sale of cattle, the charity of the neighboring island.

"I can lift a boat as well as any man," Brigid says at one point, and a couple of women smile at that, including Rose, as if they think they might be able to as well. The councilman shakes his head to show he thinks them ridiculous.

Brigid requests a distress radio, normally reserved for islands with a lighthouse. And, after a whisper from Jimmy Moran, an iron winch to assist them in pulling the boats up. The man says he will see what he can do.

"Lip service," Jimmy says, loud enough for him to hear.

After the meeting, Brigid watches them file out of the school. Rua has been waiting outside and watches with her, her warm torso pressing encouragement into Brigid's knee. The women's faces are bruised under their eyes from weeks of mourning, the children look like startled rabbits, something inside them is frozen, waiting for the next threat to appear. Rose looks at Brigid with such gratitude, she is momentarily guilty. She is not sure this is the right thing for them. It is what she wants, and she cannot do it alone.

Emer looks as if she wants to spit at all of them, to spit and scream at the mild optimism on their faces, and at her sister, smiling as if this is some sort of victory. Brigid knows her well enough to feel what she is thinking. She thinks that these women are naive, so easily persuaded they have forgotten, because of a sunny day and an optimistic Yankee, that living here is like being slowly drowned, held down on a rock and left for the tide to come in.

She won't commiserate with Emer. She can't risk the feeling she has now. She has the energy of three women, flashes of pure, expectant joy she has to hide in deference to the newly widowed. She imagines the baby's life coursing in her veins, and knows that she could do anything, that she could run this island like an abbess, embrace a commune of devout women dedicated to their children and to each other, spread the cloak of her healing to include the sea. She wants to stay here, raise her baby amid these women she has come to admire, on this island she now loves.

"I'm sorry," she whispers in her mind, whenever Emer looks at her with that one eye, anger and fear and yearning jostling to be first, but Brigid turns away before she allows her remorse to be seen. She won't let Emer's desire to destroy herself get in the way. No matter how guilty she feels.

She has little doubt that this baby will make it. It has carved out a spot and wedged itself in there and will keep it tight and solid as a beehive stone hut until the very end. It will hold on through heavy lifting and work and the small amounts of fire she lets out of her hands to heal. For so many years it was her womb that failed her. Now her womb is out of the equation. This child shrouds itself. It warns her of danger long before she can fall into it. She has already decided that she doesn't care, doesn't care in the slightest, where it came from.

CHAPTER 17

Knife Box

October, November 1959

At the evacuation meeting, Emer barely hears anything, as if she is half-deaf as well as half-blind. She is permeated by liquid fear; it has risen past her neck and filled her ears, wavered into her remaining eye. Everything people say is muffled, like she is under the water and they are still calling from the surface. She is accosted by the realization of what she has done in the eyes of every single person who dares to look at her.

She is still bleeding, the remains of that night with Austin continue to fall from her womb. It is not the relief she expected. She started something by twisting that stone and now it is too late to turn it backward.

Brigid moves in and out of her periphery, Emer sees her laying her hands on the women, on the children, and the jealousy that seizes Emer is enough to make her forget to reign in her own. She is so careless one morning, helping braid her niece's hair, that she makes Teresa throw up. Fiona, fearless as Brigid, yanks the brush from her hand.

Emer hopes that, at least, the tragedy will bring on the evacuation. But by some dangerous concoction of magic and determination, Brigid convinces them all to stay. Only a month before, Emer would have been thrilled at the thought of Brigid hanging around this long, and watching her embarrass the men at the school meeting would have made her proud. Now she wants to wring the necks of all the women who praise her.

They will build the houses anyway, the priest assures Emer after the meeting. For when they change their minds. No one expects them to last. Emer is too paralyzed by the weight of what she has done to respond to this. She is being offered what she always wanted, but she can't drag her mind away from the casualties she accrued by asking for it.

"I WASN'T A GOOD wife to him," Rose says one evening, late, when the other women have gone home, but Brigid and Emer remain. All the children are asleep, snoring through noses clogged by weeping.

"Don't do this to yourself, Rose," Brigid says. She puts an arm around Rose's shoulders.

"I haven't shown him the bright side of my face in a while. This pregnancy . . . well, I haven't been in good form. He's been acting queer lately, giving out to the girls, barely taking the time to look at me, never mind kiss me. That was never a problem for us, you know. We've always been mad for each other."

Brigid tries to shush her, but Rose won't stop now.

"We had a row. An ugly one. He said things and I, I'm ashamed to repeat them. There was a time he got like that with drink, angry and cruel as his father before him. But he never, sure not since we were at school, did he ever let that get the better of him. He frightened the girls, this time, he grabbed my arm, I thought he was going to strike me.

"He said he wanted a better life. He said that to me. Austin. Can you imagine it?

"That was the night before he went off with the lads for a drink, and I wouldn't even meet his eye for the time between. I'll not know what he thought of me then. It will never be over, that row, it will stay in my mind the rest of my days. I will never stop wondering what he thought of his life when the water pulled him under the last time."

Brigid holds Rose's hands through this entire speech, patting, stroking, not shushing, just waiting for her to let all of it out. Emer stands away from them, still as death, keeping her mouth shut tight for fear she will spew out everything.

"Perhaps we should have left like you wanted, Emer," Rose blubbers. "If we had done, they'd be alive now. I never imagined living anywhere else. But that was selfish, I see that, because now we're cursed to live here without them."

She runs her hands over her massive belly, cupping the underside of it. "He'd have liked a boy." Emer almost gags, but she swallows it just in time.

"Do you think he was happy, Emer?" Rose asks, her face streaming and raw, and Brigid shoots a look of warning at her. *Don't you dare*, Emer can hear her as if she'd said it out loud. Something grows hot in her then, seeing the fierce look in Brigid's eyes, as if even she, like the rest of them, will do anything to protect Rose.

"Go away out of that," Emer says. "Wasn't he as happy as the next fool?"

And though Brigid squeezes her eyes shut and shakes her head, Rose lets out a brief, bitter laugh.

"Leave it to Emer," she says, swabbing the stream of tears and snot from her face. "You'll not let us wallow, now, will you, love?"

THERE'S NO SCHOOL ON the island for weeks, because every hand is needed for the work of getting ready for winter. The children have their jobs—the hens, the eggs, feeding calves and pigs, and, on Saturdays, bathing themselves and the wee ones, and knife sharpening.

This has always been the job of children, the sharpening of knives and polishing of cutlery, and Emer can remember that Rose started it very young, at the age of five, when the knives needed to be kept away from their mother. Niall and Fiona show this to Brigid proudly, taking the knife box, a long wooden board with a cubby of sand, down from its spot by the hearth. They drag their mother's knives against a layer of grit, and their grandmother's, worn thinner than the rest. They offer to do Brigid's and she praises them too much.

"They'll have their own sooner than I'd like," Rose murmurs and no one insults this with an argument.

When Niall isn't working, he stays close to Fiona and Eve. They were forced together even more than usual when Emer sent him to school, and then during the long keening days after the wake and funerals when she hid in Rose's bedroom, getting up only to change the rags of clotted blood between her legs. Emer was grateful for the distraction then, but now Niall's interest in the girls offends her. Rather than that look of pure relief he usually has when she comes to rescue him from mandatory time with his cousins, Niall looks annoyed when she suggests that it is time to go home.

"I don't want to go," he whines, stomping his foot and scowling. He has never behaved this way. Rose's girls have tantrums, tearful rages that subside quickly because their mother refuses to pay attention until they calm down. Niall, Rose likes to say, is a perfect angel compared to her girls. Emer has defined him from this phrase, and herself, often enough.

"Why can't we live here?" Niall says one day. "You can sleep with Rose and I'll sleep with the girls."

He is not the first to suggest it. It makes perfect sense—bonding together in the ruins, widowed sisters have done it before. Rose seemed surprised after the first week that Emer went home at all.

Emer hustles him outside, angry, embarrassed, avoiding Rose's eyes that follow after them. On the walk Niall grows meek again, apologetic, taking her hand.

"What are you lot playing all the time?" she says, trying to sound neutral, but it comes out like an accusation.

"We play house," Niall says. "I'm the father as I'm the only boy."

"What does the father do?" Emer remembers, vaguely, playing something similar with Rose. With dolls and wildflowers and broken crockery. She was always the one forced to be the man.

"I eat breakfast," Niall says. "Then I go off so I can die. After I die they wash me and put me in a box and cry and we start all over again."

Emer grows cold with it, the thought of them playing at their own lives.

"Sometimes one of them murders me," Niall says. "That's the fun part. Then we get to have a hanging."

It takes Emer a minute to remember to inhale.

"I don't want to move to the mainland," Niall says as if this is a natural segue in conversation.

"Why not?" Emer says huskily. Her throat burns.

"If we stay here, I'll marry Eve. If we move, she'll have lots of lads to choose from at school. I don't want to go to school, and Eve doesn't either. We want to stay here forever, like you and Auntie Rose."

"Brilliant," Emer says.

THE WORK THEY HAVE, now that the men are gone, is the back-breaking sort, and it never ends. In addition to everything they already do all day long, in and around the house, now they have the fields, the sheep, the sea. The teenagers come home from school on the mainland to assist their mothers, and the teachers give them

lessons to do at night, which they fall asleep over next to the paraffin lamp. Only one of these is a boy, Oisin, as slight and sensitive
and fragile-looking as Matthew.

Brigid organizes them. Like some aged, kindly nun, she finds out
what needs to be done and rallies them all into doing it. They dig
the turf in one frenzied week, the sun still shining like it's summertime, but dipping sooner in the sky. Women and children slicing,
tossing, arranging it in rows to dry. There is Reeking Day, which
takes three days instead of one, where they exhaust the poor donkey
moving all the hay the men cut in August and storing it in sheds or
in fields under oilskin tarps. Every last potato, cabbage and turnip
are ripped from the ground. The weather holds, warm and mild, as
if giving them a chance to figure it all out before it imprisons them
again.

"Who will pull the pots?" Rose asks, and Brigid smiles.

"I'm from Maine," she says. "I know what to do with lobster traps."

On calm days the fishermen from Muruch give them rowing
lessons, their faces twisted in disapproval. Brigid's arms are as long
and muscular as a man's. She learns quickly which women are the
best candidates: Kathleen, Malachy's widow, with broad shoulders
and a willingness to push through pain, Margaret, small but wiry,
toughened by years of lugging around the overly large baby boys
she had by Michael Joe, and Maeve, Kathleen's seventeen-year-old
daughter, tall and awkward and thick-necked as an adolescent boy.
Oisin, Brigid can tell, is relieved when she doesn't ask him to sign
on for his manly responsibility. Within a month, the four women
can get a small currach in and out of the water, timing it with the
waves, and pull the heavy oars in harmony the mile to Muruch and
back again. Brigid decides they will practice this distance and try
the mainland, nine miles away, in the spring. Until then, the men
from Muruch will bring them whatever supplies they can. They also

sell the lobsters for them, after Brigid teaches the women how to bait and set as many traps as they can manage.

All the island women are aching, callused, sunburned, muscles and eyes on fire, sweat-soaked and ripe as their husbands once were. Brigid, while beside them, pulling and slicing and rowing and digging, puts her hand out every once in a while to ease the aches. Just enough to make them think they can go on a while longer. She needs to take care with Maeve, who responds to Brigid's touch with such a vicious surge of lust, it often leaves her too confused and ashamed to get anything done.

In November, the time comes to slaughter the pigs. Of the six that came in the springtime, only Niall's is left, one slaughtered in October by Austin, the others traded to the mainland for necessities. Normally, the pigs are killed and shared among the families, one at a time. Niall's pig will be enough for all of them.

Emer does not want them to do it. Cabbage, though not as eager to play, or able, as he was in the summertime, still follows her son on the road.

"Why didn't you sell that one, then, when you negotiated for the others?" Emer argues with Rose.

"Sure, didn't we hand over the pigs we could find," Rose says. She is irritable most of the time now, with a mug that rivals her sister's, their mother says. "That creature runs wild."

"You can't slaughter the thing in front of him," Emer says to Brigid. Brigid opens her mouth, looking like she's about to agree.

"Are you wanting to protect him from the sorrows of the world, so?" their mother says. "It's a bit late for that."

"She's right," Rose says.

Brigid and Emer look at her, as if an impostor dressed up like Rose has spoken instead.

"I don't mind," Niall says. They turn to see him peering over the lip of the half-door. "I knew he would have to go. I want to be there when you do it."

Brigid looks at him hard, and she can see he is trying to stand tall, and not flinch. She nods.

A man from Muruch explains how to stun it with a hammer, but Brigid merely smiles and ignores his instructions. She has Niall help her instead. He calms the animals, he always has, with his hands.

Rose is too enormously pregnant to be useful. Emer is there, grudgingly, and Kathleen and Margaret. Niall leads Cabbage into the barn, whispering, scratching behind his ears, the pig stumbling with pleasure and trust. Niall gets it to lie down in the earth and put his enormous head in his lap. He strokes the thing until it falls into a sort of coma, dropping heavily away from Niall's hands. He looks up at Brigid and her knife with tears in his eyes.

"All right?" she says.

"Go on," he says, moving aside, pretending to be brave.

Brigid drives her knife in at the top of the breastbone, then cuts up to the middle of the neck and twists the way the man showed her. Three women hold the head up so the blood can rush, steaming and thin into a metal tub. They will use this for the blood pudding. Emer holds the tub steady, looking like she might be sick and ruin it all. Brigid is feeling queasy herself, the stench is overpowering, but she breathes through her mouth and shakes it off. She resists the urge to place her hand over the wound she has just made, and reverse the waterfall of life pouring out.

It takes them all day to bleed, scald, scrape and gut the pig, another day to cut away at joints and pack pound after pound of salt into its flesh. They throw the useless bits to the dogs, except Rua, who paces outside and growls her disapproval. The pig's head is shoved into a canvas bag, just like the one the piglets arrived in, and boiled for days in an enormous pot outside. The whole island has fresh pork for a week; they hang the salted meat in Emer's shed, a gruesome reminder of his pet swinging at Niall's head every time he enters.

BRIGID COMES TO SUNDAY dinner at Rose's house after the slaughter. She watches Niall pause before he takes his first bite of pork. He closes his eyes, shoves it in, and chews. In that moment he seems more like a child than he usually does. Though still not a typical one.

Emer eats quickly and without small talk. Clodagh's table manners are similar, though her bad arm keeps her from eating quickly. The pork is overcooked, tough, both strong and bland. It tastes like the blood smelled. Brigid feels suddenly close and nauseated in this kitchen, full of turf smoke and pig fat so thick it has settled onto every surface, including their skin. She holds a hand to her lower belly, the swelling of which she is still hiding under oversized shirts, and breathes through her mouth.

"Are the bees all gone?" Fiona asks. "The hives are so quiet." Clodagh makes a disapproving gasp. She rarely says a word to Brigid directly, and refuses to be eased by her hands. All Brigid's attempts have been flung off silently, like she might push her way out of an uninvited embrace. She is a woman who prefers her pain. She has shared, loudly, how mortified she is at having Brigid's dog inside the house. Rua stays by the door, waiting for her to be done.

"They're hibernating," Brigid says. "They sent the drones out to die and the women will stay hunkered down till spring." She says this before she thinks about how it will sound.

Clodagh erupts then, with an ugly laugh.

"Sound familiar?" she says. Emer looks at her like she'd like to slit her throat. This is how she looks at almost everyone but Niall, so her mother doesn't even bother to turn her head to deflect it.

"Have you had your fill, Mammy?" Rose says, standing quickly and whisking away her plate. "I know I have." Her expression is mild, but her voice holds a warning, and their mother darkens with a blush and says no more.

CHAPTER 18

Midwife

November 1959

Rose is supposed to go to the hospital a full month before the babies are due, but she keeps delaying it. She says she doesn't want to leave the children, that she has so much more to do with Austin gone, though Brigid has silently taken care of most of it. Whenever she makes plans to go, the weather turns.

"Mind you don't wait until it's too late, Rose," their mother says. The older women, the ones who still have time to sit down for tea, dip their biscuits and suck at their teeth in agreement.

"You don't want to be having the babies here, in the middle of a storm, no doctor and nothing to ease your pain."

Rose dislikes the hospital, Emer knows. She hates being put to sleep and not seeing the babies come out. The last time, she had checked in a week early, and said nothing to the nurses once she was in labor. She hid it for so long that by the time it came to push the young doctor was flustered and confused and forgot all about putting her under. She pushed them out so fast they shot into his trembling hands. Rose believes she can have this set all by herself and still have dinner on the table.

"Foolishness," the other women say, whishting and dunking biscuits with disapproving vigor.

"Island women used to have their babies here," Rose says.

"Aye. And haven't we stones in the graveyard to thank for it?" The women cross themselves, biscuits in hand, crumbs springing about.

"We'd a midwife then," Austin's mother says. "And little choice. It's pure foolishness for someone to choose to have her baby here now. You'd never forgive yourself if something went wrong."

"Brigid's a midwife," Rose announces. Emer whips her head around like an animal ready to bite.

A midwife, is she? From America as well.

Surely she trained in one of those posh hospitals.

Ah you're in good form, so.

The women are muttering as one now, slurping the last dregs of their tea, and Rose warms the pot up for them and smiles at Emer. Emer doesn't even try to smile back this time. She can't decide which thing she is most annoyed about. The fact that Rose seems to know everything about Brigid now, or the thoughtless confidence of her sister, who even after such tragedy, still assumes that what she wants will necessarily go as planned.

A STORM HITS THEM the last week of November. Not a day that any man would dare get in a boat, let alone a woman enormous with her fourth set of twins. When her labor starts, Rose is alarmingly chipper, moving about the house with purpose, stopping occasionally to breathe long and slow, and bend, in a way that makes all the girls stop what they are doing, bend and breathe with her. Then she straightens up again, smiles and winks at them and says, "That wasn't such a bad one, was it now?" and proceeds with her chores.

This goes on all day, Rose's enthusiasm waning a bit as the contractions wear on but don't seem to get either closer or stronger. They are consistent and draining but useless, like a fire that flares and then dies, refusing to light. "I don't understand," she whispers once to Emer, sweat beading on her upper lip. "It's been eight hours. I should be well finished and having a nap." Emer mutters something dismissive. Her labor with Niall had gone on for two whole days. How like Rose to question when anything is the slightest bit different from what she desires.

Brigid calls in and takes Rose into the bedroom to check her progress, while Emer eavesdrops at the doorway. Brigid says, "Every labor is different," and Rose says, "Not for me." Brigid leaves her resting and comes to tell Emer that it may be a long time. Emer brings the girls over to her house, leaving them with her mother and Niall, and comes back to Rose's to wait out the labor along with the storm.

In the small house, with the wind howling and rain lashing on the windows, Rose paces and groans and begins to lose herself.

"Something's wrong," she says, and the next pain stops her in her tracks. She seems to forget for a minute her ritual of deep rhythmic breath and instead gulps clumsily and without success until the siege subsides.

"It's not like the others. Something's not right."

"Emer," she says, after the next one. She only has time to say one thing between each pain. "Get the cloth."

It's a tradition she hasn't bothered with since the first pair, the blue cloth blessed in Saint Brigid's well, said to be the way Brigid herself eased the labor of the women who escaped to her: with pieces of her cloak. Emer gets it from a drawer in Rose's chest, soaking it from the bottle of holy water Rose keeps on a high shelf in the press. She binds it with ribbon to her sister's writhing belly, and Rose uses one of her fleeting breaks to smile her thanks.

It goes on, and Rose stops trying to speak, or smile. She walks, she stoops, she leans on Brigid. Brigid holds her up, rubs her lower back, murmurs words of encouragement and wisdom. None of it seems to help. A pain tears through Rose while Brigid is holding her, so massive and loud that Brigid is thrown back and away with the invisible force. Rose screams. And for the first time since she's known her, Brigid looks to Emer as if she's not quite sure what she is doing.

"What's wrong?" Emer asks in a whisper, as Rose gives up pacing and tries to escape the pain by lying in a fetal position with the covers over her head.

"I don't know," Brigid says.

"Will you not ease her pain?" Emer says. "She's had enough."

"Stop asking me questions," Brigid barks.

She tells Emer to sit behind Rose and prop her up.

"Rose," she says loudly. "I need to put my hands inside and feel the baby."

"No," Rose says, trying to close her legs, but Brigid is too strong for her. "No, don't. I can't stand it."

"I have to, Rose, I have to check something. You need to let me in."

Rose screams louder than ever as Brigid pushes her hands up inside, feeling around for an answer.

"Something's wrong," Rose says. "What's wrong?"

"Shush, Rose," Brigid says, as harshly as if she were talking to Emer. "You're all right. You need to push now."

"I can't. It's not time."

"It is time, Rose. Push."

Emer expects a baby to shoot out after a few good grunting countdowns, but nothing comes. A hairy globe of scalp appears and retreats, over and over with each contraction, never making any progress. The pushing goes on so long that Emer can't keep track of the time anymore. The storm rages on, so thick with clouds and rain that there is barely a difference between the black of night and the gray of morning. It takes them a long time to notice the dawn.

"I can't, Emer," Rose says at one point, caught in the limbo of this child who is no longer in but will not come out. "I'm going to die."

"Stop it," Emer says. "You're nearly there."

Finally, Brigid pulls out an enormous baby, face up, its features squashed, ugly and covered in what looks like wax. Brigid seems barely interested in this baby, who starts screeching and turns bright red, dumping it onto Rose's stomach, where Emer has to grab a leg to keep it from sliding away onto the bedclothes.

"Keep pushing, Rose," Brigid says.

"Can't I have a wee rest?" Rose murmurs, trying to look at the baby, so close to her face she can't really focus on it.

"Not now, push. Quickly, love."

Emer holds the slippery infant on top of her sister as Rose pushes and roars.

Another one comes out, a smaller one, the color of heather buds, purple blue and not moving and wrong. Not a baby at all, is what Emer comes close to saying out loud.

There are a lot of commands and confusion, and Emer almost loses her grip on the first baby trying to follow Brigid's orders. She wants her to hold the thing for an instant while she quickly binds and cuts the cord, then she takes it away, closer to the fire with garbled instructions on how Emer is supposed to care for her sister's womb. Something about massaging it for the afterbirth. Emer does nothing but watch what happens next, completely ignoring her sister and her womb and the first baby, whose cord has not even been cut.

She thinks at first that Brigid is going to put it in the fire. Set it on the hearth like a changeling to see if it's real. It is not even half the size of the first one, with brittle, wrinkled arms and legs and a blue that her sister must not, Emer thinks, be let to see. "Where is it, Emer," Rose whispers, exhausted and unable to focus her eyes in the dim room. "Where's the other baby?"

"Whisht," Emer hisses, as if silence might stop the horrible outcome from entering the room.

Brigid grabs a shawl from a nearby chair and lays it on the hearth, putting the baby down gently in front of the glowing heat of a turf fire that is never allowed to die. She wipes at the thing with a cloth, massaging its limbs, its tiny chest, clears the mucus from its eyes, nose and mouth with her pinky finger. Then she leans down and almost takes the thing in her mouth, covering its entire face with open lips, and blows, blows, then presses the chest with two fingers, like she is testing risen dough. She waits, blows, presses again. Just at the moment where it is surely too late comes a weak, protesting little cough. Then a thin cry.

Rose lets out a wail in response. Brigid settles the now pink baby in the waiting space in Rose's other arm. She tends to Rose and the afterbirth, all with quick, confident hands, no sign of the panic and impotence that pulled at her face only minutes before.

Once the babies are cleaned and swaddled and introduced to their mother's breasts, Rose can see how starkly different they are. Girls, like the rest of Rose's babies, everyone assumed they would be, it was something of a joke how Rose's body could make nothing but girls. One of them is plump and pretty and serene like every other baby of Rose's, the other wizened, scowling, not quite sure what to do with her hands, her mouth, her mother's breast. She seems to look directly at her sister latched onto a nipple and opens her little mouth to let out a wail of righteous anger. Her fists are clenched with what already seems like a lifetime of frustration.

"Oh, this one's like you, Emer," Rose laughs.

What Emer was thinking was that it looked not like a baby at all, but like the wizened, possessed fairy she had grown to expect as a child. As if any moment it might open its mouth and speak in the voice of the underworld.

Rose nuzzles it and pulls it closer, monster or no.

"Will it die?" Emer says to Brigid, as she washes her hands and arms at the bucket.

"It was close, but I don't think so," Brigid says. She lathers between her fingers. "She's little, but strong."

"Did you heal it?"

"That wasn't magic, Emer. That was medicine."

"Is it part of the curse?" It's out of Emer's mouth before she can stop it, and once out, she does not want to take it back. She wants Brigid to know. She wants to be forgiven.

"What curse?" Brigid says, tired, annoyed.

"The curse I set with the fairy's stone."

Brigid looks at her, eyes widening. "What stone?"

"It's next to the well," Emer says. "I . . ."

Brigid sucks her breath in with an island gasp. "You *didn't*, Emer."

"I was only trying to clear my womb," Emer whispers. "I think I drowned the lads as well."

Brigid looks like she is battling something ugly in her mind, fighting something that Emer hopes will never win. She shakes her head.

"It's only a baby," she says. "Not a curse." But she won't look Emer in the eye. "It has nothing to do with you."

The way she says it, cold, final, removed. Like she's shutting a door. When she reaches for the dishcloth to dry her hands, they are trembling.

THERE IS A MOMENT in every labor where, no matter how many times a woman has done it before, she thinks she will die. Without this moment, Brigid knows, the baby would never be born. It is as necessary as pushing a bucket beneath the surface of a well. Darkness doesn't do its job if you believe, when you are inside of it, that it will ever let you go. It is not something any of them is allowed to remember. Brigid suspects even she will forget it, when her time comes.

For the first five days after the babies are born, Brigid doesn't leave them once. The weather is desperate, the seas raging, wind so loud she can't remember not being aware of it. "The sort of wind what leaves you deaf for a week," Clodagh says. Brigid sleeps on the hearth bed, when she can catch a few minutes, but mostly she holds on to one baby while Rose tends to the other.

Brigid tries not to think too much about Emer's sideways confession, she can't. The baby inside her reacted when Emer said it, with jolting kicks that felt like panicked alarm. Whatever Emer has done, Brigid needs to stay away from it. From her.

Brigid wants to hold the smaller baby more than the other one. This wizened, cranky thing that tried to betray them. She told Emer the truth, she didn't heal it. The first baby came out facing the sky instead of the earth, the second with the cord wrapped round her neck. Brigid used only medical knowledge she had from Matthew, and waited for the babies to emerge. She breathed into the second twin, felt the thing shudder and resist. As if it wasn't a baby at all, but a furious changeling with no intention of giving in. She half expected it to open its eyes and speak to her. But then it cried and became merely a newborn who survived a close call.

Brigid can soothe it better than her own mother can. She knows exactly how to cradle the more precarious lives in her hands. Brigid's baby grows quiet and content when she holds this one to her stomach, reassuring them both.

ROSE NAMES THE LITTLE one after her sister, and the fat one after Brigid. They call her Bridie. There is no natural nickname for Emer, so Rose calls her Wee Emer, and somehow, given to this peeling, wrinkled baby, the name that once sounded harsh and unmusical to Brigid now feels lovely to croon. She is the first of Rose's girls not named for a saint, which Clodagh points out with a complacency that drives Rose to shush her crossly.

Emer is doing all the outdoor chores she can manage in such weather, avoiding Rose, though she follows Brigid with her reproachful eye. She won't hold either baby. Brigid doesn't want to think too much about Emer right now. She feels like someone Brigid knew a long time ago, whom she is wary of, but she can't remember why.

Wee Emer can't eat. Whenever Rose puts her nipple in the baby's mouth, the girl fusses and won't latch on. Brigid checks when the baby wails—this one cries a fair amount, enough that Brigid has no doubt she will be OK—and sees that underneath, her tongue is pulled so tight she can't extend it out of her mouth. She disinfects her pocketknife and uses it to clip the tethered membrane, which makes the grown Emer cross herself. Wee Emer stops crying instantly, as if relieved. Brigid shows Rose how to express her milk; there seems to be no end to it, it flows from her whether a baby is suckling or not. "I'm the Lake of Milk," Rose jokes, telling her what happened the time Saint Brigid blessed the cows. Brigid feeds the baby with a soaked corner of a cloth until she learns to use her tongue.

Rose tells her the story of Saint Brigid's birth while she nurses the strong baby in bed.

"Saint Brigid's father was a chieftain, and her mother, Broisech, was his slave and mistress. A druid foretold that the child in her belly would be born at sunrise, neither in the house nor out of it, that it would belong to both worlds, and that it would be greater than any child born in Ireland. The chieftain's wife was so jealous that she sold Broisech away to another castle. In that house a queen labored in the night but the baby was born dead. At sunrise, Broisech bore her child in the doorway, with one foot inside the house and the other outside it. This baby was brought to the Queen, offered as a replacement, but when Brigid was laid down next to the Queen's baby she breathed it back to life. That was Brigid's first miracle."

"And you're our saint," Rose says, reaching out a hand to squeeze Brigid's.

"That wasn't a miracle," Brigid says. "It happens all the time. Some babies take a minute to breathe."

"Still, I'm grateful to you. And every baby is a miracle."

"You're more of a saint than I am," Brigid laughs, and Rose gives her an intoxicated smile.

THIS WAS ALWAYS BRIGID'S favorite time when she and Matthew had the maternity home. All the women were encouraged to stay with their babies, even if they eventually decided to give them away. The first few hours and days stretched to an unfathomable length. They would remember it, Brigid knew, every one of them, as occupying a larger portion of their lives than certain decades. The hushed wonder of the newborn, the warmth, the insubstantial weight, the flaking skin and tiny fingernails, the butterfly flare of nostrils, the pursed buds of their mouths. The way they spring back, after they are stretched out to be cleaned, into the tightly curled form they took in the womb. The sigh that emerges when you swaddle them tight, their relief at that familiar cramp. Those first few days after birth are a limbo, a tributary between pregnancy and motherhood, between waiting for life and living it; right in the middle you can step onto a stone where they are the same.

Even Emer and Clodagh can't stain the bliss that soaks the cottage the first few days. They try, with their gasps and their scathing comments, but they are outside it, harpies who cannot penetrate Brigid and Rose's enraptured cocoon.

Brigid and Rose coo at the little feet and earlobes and fingers, and run a soft flannel soaked in warm water into the fat creases of one and the hollows of another, they lie down with them, skin to skin, naked babies wrapped inside their blouses, letting the warmth they produced when they were inside seep back in from above. When Rose notices her swollen belly, Brigid admits she is expecting too, and holds her breath. But Rose is delighted.

"Was it the Australian, then?" she says. Brigid merely smiles. "I don't know that we can find him."

"It doesn't matter," Brigid says.

"No," Rose sighs. "I suppose not. We're only women now."

When everyone else is asleep, in the timeless deep night, they lie next to one another in the bed, a baby on each of them, and look at the thing reflected in the other's eyes. The slow recognition of what they are holding on to, these tiny bodies that are entirely infused with trust. This is why Brigid could not stay away from birth all those years, even when it sliced her with regret. She covets this time. When they are first born, before things get more complicated, you can press your skin to theirs and absorb that faith, as though you, as well, are being held by something that will never let you go.

THE DOCTOR, WHEN THE weather finally allows him through, six days after Rose's labor, is furious at the lot of them. He stomps with angry purpose from the quay up to Rose's house. It is the same doctor, Rose tells Brigid, who was there when Emer lost her eye. This, Brigid feels, is enough of a warning.

The doctor hands his coat and hat to Emer without looking at her.

He asks Rose how she is feeling while he polishes his spectacles.

"If I was any better I'd be unbearable." Rose beams at him. His frown remains.

"Where is this Yank everyone's on about?" he demands. Brigid steps forward, and with her hair loose and her men's trousers, in an old flannel three-buttoned tunic that once belonged to Austin, she can see how she looks to him, bold, with an arrogance not familiar on the island, or in Ireland, an arrogance that is particularly American. She will milk this now, however they dislike it.

"What sort of medical training have you?" he says. Brigid tells him that she trained as a nurse midwife in the States, adds that she has attended hundreds of births.

The doctor makes a dismissive noise at this information. "Were there any complications?"

Brigid tells him of the long labor and Wee Emer getting stuck up behind the other, cord round her neck, needing mouth to mouth and chest massage to breathe.

"How long before the baby began breathing?" he asks.

"Less than a minute, I'd say," Brigid answers.

"Did you do the Apgar?"

"Yes. A two after birth, a nine five minutes later."

"Hunh," the doctor mutters, as if he doesn't believe her.

He examines Rose, then the babies, one at a time, unwrapping them and prodding until they are both screeching at his cold, rough fingers.

"There's not much to this one," the doctor says. "Is she nursing?"

Rose can express milk into a jug from one breast while feeding a baby on the other. Not a bother on her, the island women say.

"She is," Rose and Brigid say together, and he glances up suspiciously. He finishes examining baby Emer and walks away, leaving her frail, angry, yellow-tinged body flailing uncovered on the table. Brigid re-covers her quickly, swaddling her tight in the wool the doctor has cast aside.

He packs up his bag, letting out occasional disapproving gusts of breath, like an angry horse. Every time he does it, Emer jumps.

"Your babies," he says to Rose, "not to mention yourself, might have died. There's talk this Yank has persuaded you people to stay here. You, madam"—he waves at Brigid dismissively—"are taking lives you have no claim to out of God's hands."

He wrestles with his coat, and makes one last biting remark.

"She'll likely end up touched, that one," he mutters, gesturing to Emer in the cradle. Then in the same breath, he remarks how sorry he is to hear about the passing of their husbands. He looks at Emer oddly on his way out, as if he is trying to place her.

Brigid shuts the door hard behind him, as though she means to catch his generous backside on the way out. After the last comment, she expects morose faces, maybe tears, but she looks at Rose and all at once they are laughing. They can barely speak, holding their sides and breathless with it, but Rose manages to get out a few imitations of the doctor's high-pitched, nagging voice—*You, madam*—which just sends them off again. They wail with laughter and look at each other, mouths open in silent hilarity, gazes focused on the other's wet and dancing eyes.

Emer is furious, Brigid can tell, but it can't touch them, she is as helpless as the men who, were there any left, would be made to stand outside while the women got on with things.

CHAPTER 19

Feet Water

December 1959

There is almost nothing that makes Emer lonelier than the sight of other women laughing. It's like a fracture, somewhere inside her, watching Brigid and Rose laugh together. She thinks they look like sisters. Or wives. Or some other conglomeration—similar to the fantasies Emer had when she was with Brigid—a different kind of family where every adult member is female. Like the ancient society of women who loved each other before them.

She had this once, this affinity with Brigid. It was the first time she understood what it was like to be Rose, or Austin, with their lascivious looks and whispers. But the woman who adored her (she did, didn't she?) now won't look her in the eye. If she comes upon Emer unexpectedly she will flinch, step back, like every other islander. Emer once took grim satisfaction in people's fear of her, but she doesn't want to be dreaded anymore.

It is as though someone took Brigid aside and reminded her which sister was the better one, and now she has chosen Rose. All Emer can do is stand apart and watch them laugh. It wouldn't be any worse, she believes, to see their tongues reaching into each other's mouths.

The children go back to school now that the autumn work has subsided, and Emer, avoiding Rose and Brigid, is often alone. One afternoon when she goes to collect Niall at school, she sees that all the children have been let out to play. The air is full of the sort of shrieking that accompanies unsupervised children in a school playground. It takes Emer a while to distinguish Niall's scream from the others. It is not playful, but a panicked wail that sounds so like the cries he let out when he was an infant and couldn't eat, she feels her breasts grow heavy with memory. She quickens her pace on the bright green path and tries to distinguish him in the crowd. Niall is off on his own, ten yards from the rest of them, he is howling and throwing stones. The other children are laughing, or shouting back, and Fiona is trying to speak to him softly, but it doesn't seem to matter what any of them are doing, not to Niall who cries and rages at the whole lot, nor to Emer, who can see nothing but her child with his face twisted in pain. When she gets to him he looks at her without recognition, no blue left in his eyes, and raises his fist as if he means to pound her in the face.

"Niall!" she hisses, stopping his hand and squeezing a warning into it. "Niall?" Then his eyes focus and he knows it is her and his face falls into childish tears and she gathers him up. There is a half-assed explanation of a childish game gone wrong, and a lecture from the teacher about how little he minds her, and a claim from Eve that he'd gone off in a fit for no reason, but through it all, all Emer can think of is the look in his eyes when he'd almost hit her, how he'd not even known who she was, how he'd been gone, gone somewhere far away.

She has always worried about music, fairy forts, the lull of dripping honey. She sees now how he can be stolen from her, in the bright of day, even while she holds him in her arms. This is what she should have been afraid of all along.

It is subtle, the ways he is taken. For moments, the boy she has always known will vanish. She'll be speaking to him and look up and see that his eyes have gone together in a squint, and he is not listening to her but to something no one else can hear. "Niall," she'll bark, and it won't reach him, she'll have to practically scream it and grab his shoulder before his eyes will go straight again and then he'll look startled, hurt at her tone, not at all concerned by his own absence.

"I was speaking to you."

Then he'll get annoyed, as if she is bothering him about trifles.

"Would you never leave me my life?" he says once, his voice as deep and dangerous as a changeling who speaks from the cradle with the wizened voice of an old man.

It happens again in the currach on the way home from Mass. Kathleen, Maeve, Brigid and Margaret are rowing. The wind is strong enough that no one else could have heard it, she can only hear words spoken against the soft space of her ear. She is holding him and he turns his face up to say it, and the voice that comes out of him is not his own, or the fairy's, it is Austin's.

"It should have been you who was drowned." She stiffens and wonders if he can feel how her heart seems to stumble over itself, to stop beating in shock and then rush to catch up. When they get home he holds her hand up the path, smiling and chatting as if nothing has happened, and spends the evening drawing little animals for her and wrapping them in paper and twine like gifts.

"*A chuisle mo chroí*," he mimics, just before going to sleep. *You are the pulse of my heart.* She lies watching him for hours, her neck crushing inward, watching his still, blank face as the light fades with the shrinking candle, looking for some evidence of the thing that is lurking inside him.

SHE TRIES TO TELL Rose that he is being taken, slowly but surely stolen from her. But Rose dismisses it.

"He's only a lad, Emer. He's after losing his father. The same thing is happening to the girls."

"It's not the same," Emer says. There is something between her and Niall that Rose doesn't have with her girls.

"Did you think he'd be that way always, so?" Rose scoffs. "Your pet? They grow away, Emer. They're meant to."

"That's not it," Emer says.

"He's your only one, so this is the first time you're seeing it, but that's all it is."

"They tried to take me," Emer insists. "They're after him now."

"Those are only stories. You were stung by bees."

"I was touched."

"You weren't, so. It's just who you are. Nothing more."

She says it as if Emer's evil power, the way she can leave people drowning in their own minds, can be chalked up to moodiness or a disagreeable disposition. Rose has seen the same things as Emer, but she seems to believe that her will to dismiss them is stronger than the fairies themselves.

IT'S NOT EASY TO get Brigid on her own. If she manages to come up behind her in the field or back garden, Brigid will start, put her hands to her belly and say, "Jesus, Emer. Don't sneak up on me like that."

She used to love it when Emer embraced her from behind, she used to lean back and guide Emer's hands to where she needed them.

"Will you help . . ." she gets out once, but then Fiona interrupts and Emer can't say any more.

Brigid looks relieved, Fiona smug. Before Emer knows it, they are walking back to the house together, she is alone.

ON ONE OF THE darkest nights of the year, when the sun is gone by the middle of the afternoon, the husband Emer murdered comes home. She is steeping the tea in the pot when the door bangs open with the wind and he is there, massive and dark and wet, taking off his coat and cap and hanging them on the hook, dropping a load of turf into the hearth box. He stumbles around, sniffling from the cold that runs his nose, making noises somewhere between animal and man. Emer is petrified. Frozen in her chair, waiting for the moment where he sees her and remembers what she has done and forces her to her knees with the blame of it. She thinks of what his body must be like after two months beneath the water, white and swollen and eaten away, and knows she will have to touch it, because surely the punishment for killing him will be to resume having sex with him, and this thought starts her screaming. She screams and she screams and it is not until she sees that the hands holding her wrists are small and soft and belong to her son that she stops screaming. It is Niall's face in front of her.

"When did you come in?" she says.

"I'm here all along," he says. "I brought in the turf. Didn't you watch me walk in the door?" Emer shakes her head.

"Have you taken leave of your senses?" Niall says. He is so young still, how could she think he'd gotten bigger, he looks as small as when she still carried him in her arms. He goes to wash his feet in the bowl that waits by the fire for this purpose. His feet are the same shape as they were the day he was born, squat, ugly toes with nails soft enough to bend. When he was a newborn, they were as clean and smooth as the rest of him. Now the nails are caked with earth, the cracked soles stained brown by the bog. No matter how he scrubs they will never be that clean again.

He takes the basin and brings it to the door, flinging out the dirty water, in the island tradition: It's bad luck to keep the feet water in the house overnight. There was an island girl, the story goes, who forgot to do this and the fairies carried her off the same night. She was gone with them for seven years before she was let home. She was returned the same age as when she'd left, still a girl, still in her nightgown, but she had no toes. She had danced them off.

"Come here," Emer says to Niall, and he obliges. She holds on to him, too tight, he squirms and tries to get away.

"I'm only just in from the cows," Niall says. "Not off to America." She doesn't laugh as he means her to, but clutches him tighter and pretends to believe it, even as she knows, inhaling—she has known for a while now—that the smell of him is all wrong.

"WHEN IS YOUR BABY due?" Rose asks.

"In May," Brigid says.

"I hope you'll stay on," Rose says. "You've come to mean so much to Emer." Brigid looks away.

"Oh, it's not easy to tell, but I see it. She never had a friend before you," Rose says. "Folk steer clear of Emer, because of what is in her hands. She's able to rid herself of it, I believe. I'm not sure why she doesn't want to."

Because she's like my mother, Brigid wants to say. *And yours. Sometimes people get pounded so much by life they choose to burn back at the pain rather than douse it.*

"Aren't you afraid of her?" Brigid asks instead.

"Oh, Emer isn't able to harm me," Rose says. "And even if she were, she wouldn't. Any more than she'd hurt Niall, or you, for that matter."

Brigid can't bring herself to say it. Can't look into that lovely face and tell it: *Don't be so sure.*

"I must say," Rose adds, "I'm glad you're here all the time. You've eased the whole business for all of us, so you have."

Clodagh, who has been pretending to doze in her rocker, rises to this opportunity.

"Are you not going to ask her who the father is?" she says.

"It hardly matters," Rose winks at Brigid. "I don't see him here."

Brigid isn't attracted to Rose, though she can feel Emer's jealousy, as palpable as winter damp in the room. She pities Emer, greedy and vicious and alone, but even if it were not dangerous, she tells herself she is no longer interested in romantic love, or sex. Her baby grows so quickly she feels fuller, more complete, every hour of the day. She has left so many babies behind, the ones she birthed as well as the ones she lost. She does not have to leave this time, after the babies are born. She will stay on and help Rose feed and bathe and dress them, she will be the midwife to the next woman who needs her, she will birth her own baby into this island of women and girls. She will stay here because there is a space she can fill perfectly and without suspicion, because on this island women dance with each other, walk the roads holding on to each other's waists, curl up together on the same beds to sleep, and it never occurs to them to be ashamed. This island was settled by women who lived together, they had ceremonies where they were essentially married, where they bound their souls, and their bodies, for life. Brigid doesn't need a ceremony, and her body is occupied. She would like to be the woman who convinces them to stay.

When she pulled that crushed, wizened, barely human form out of the forgotten crevice in Rose's body, and had to lay it by the fire and breathe life, not magic, inside, she decided she was done with something. Done with the manipulation of women's most tender parts, and the way she used them to fill something that had never been there. The way her father once pretended to apologize to and caress her mother, the way it appeared to be generous and guilty and really all he was doing was consuming her alive. Feeding her pleasure so he could suck it back into himself. Brigid is tired of pleasuring women, and of teaching them how to wring pleasure out of her. She wants that part to be over, had wanted it over when she moved here, but forgot for an instant, tripped a little, when presented with Emer's raw and awkward need.

She is surprised at how cruel she begins to sound when Rose mentions Emer. Dismissive, unforgiving, done. As if rejecting Emer has earned her a film of Emer's disposition, a trail of unease like something left on a stone by a snail.

"I might call in and see if she needs anything," Rose will say and Brigid will convince her, without even saying it aloud, not to.

She knows that the longer Rose leaves her, the further away Emer will slip. Brigid's want of this life, this island, is enough to make her cruel. Though she once promised to help Emer, and had wanted to heal her, now she sees that Emer is not something to heal but something to stay away from. Emer could ruin it all. She destroyed her own family, she'll stop at nothing to get what she wants. If it suited Emer, she would reach in and yank Brigid's hope right alongside the bloody limbs of her half-formed child. Brigid will do whatever is necessary—she will turn her sister and her son against her if she has to—to avoid losing this one last best chance she has ever been given at life.

"Leave her be," she says to Rose, over and over again, and Rose listens, because, Brigid knows, there is a part of her so tired of missing her husband and a lifetime of being Emer's better twin that it would like to have someone else carry away the burden of her sister.

"WHEN SHALL WE TELL the others?" Brigid asks Rose. It has become difficult to hide her growing middle, even behind the yellow waterproof she wears most of the time now. She is nervous about the reaction. Though they have accepted and welcomed her, she has seen before how quickly even women can turn when you dare to betray their ideas of decency.

"I'd be inclined to tell the lot of them at once," Rose says. "Keep the lips from flapping, if you know how I mean."

So they do. On a wet day when the women are gathered at Rose's, their hands roughened with new calluses, from rope and oars rather than knives and churns. Kathleen, Nellie, Margaret, their mothers and mothers-in-law, the grandmothers and teenagers left at home to tend the smaller children.

"We're expecting a wee Australian in May," Rose says cheerily, while refilling the teapot. "I told Brigid we'd all pitch in, of course. I don't want her lifting that boat any longer."

There is a heavy silence that goes on long enough to set dread thronging inside Brigid. The women look at one another, at her, at Rose, and seem to come to a collective decision.

It's not as if we weren't in the same position ourselves once. Quite a few of us, if you remember.

Don't mind the talk. She's one of us now and we take care of our own.

That's a blessing, so it is. Babbies born after forty are touched with luck.

Won't it be a stunner, that one? With your complexion, and that Australian was an eyeful.

Sure, aren't we an island of women and children now.

They reassure her, congratulate her, ask her what she'll name a girl, a boy. Later, when Brigid is washing up, she overhears the older ones whispering in Irish.

Same thing happened to her mother, don't you know.

That was another time.

How do we know it was the Australian? Kathleen always wondered if Malachy fancied her.

Whisht. It won't help any of us, that talk.

What about the stories? What her family had in them?

They're only stories, sure. She has no more black magic in her than I do.

We wouldn't be here still without her help.

I'm not certain that's for the best.

Rose is. Rose is sure of her and that's enough for me.

She's too fond of Emer for my liking.

Yes, well, she wasn't told any different. She's copped on now, I suspect.

Brigid can't decide if they believe in magic or not. On the one hand they are superstitious, never walking past places where fairies might cause mischief, crossing themselves multiple times a day. On the other they seem pragmatic and dismiss notions of fairies when it suits them. Rose will talk of Emer as if she is cursed and then act as if she is just regrettably sour. They seem to respect some parallel world at the same time as they brush the very idea of it away.

Brigid keeps a few things to herself. Only Emer and Niall know about the healing. The diffusing of grief she does so subtly no one suspects her hands are behind it. If someone cuts themselves or bleeds through blisters she doesn't mend it. As far as they're concerned her hands are just like their own, work roughened and compassionate. She suspects Rose knows, has guessed, but she is too loyal to say so.

She doesn't tell any of them she understands their Irish. Not even Emer knows that. All these years later, it still seems wise to Brigid to have a secret language. *You never know*, says her mother's voice, still as close to her ear as if she lies on the same pillow, *when you might need it.*

DECEMBER STORMS STRAND THEM for two more weeks. School is canceled, boats tied down to cement blocks on the grass, women can't even walk the road without hanging on to fence posts and digging the toes of their shoes into boggy ground. It's all Brigid can do to milk the cows, everything else is left to the rain. She wears Desmond's wellies, the toes stuffed with extra socks, and lines them up next to Austin's at Rose's front door. She stays most nights with Rose, teaches drawing techniques to her girls, learns to knit herself a postulant's tube scarf. They watch the stores of flour and sugar and tea sift away, portion by portion, no hope of replenishment in sight. It begins to look as if there will be no Christmas packages, something Rose's girls fear every year, with good reason. Half the time, they explain, Father Christmas does not come. He arrives in January, with a note of apology tied up with the oranges and apples and chocolates that come over on the boat.

Brigid goes ten straight days without a glimpse of Emer, though Niall comes over daily for a visit. On an afternoon where the wind and rain clear to a frosty fog, she tells Rose she will go back to Desmond's house and get the rest of her flour and tea. She walks the road, a brighter green in fog than it is in sunlight, unable to see more than two feet in front of her. Emer is not far behind.

Emer knocks on the door, announcing herself with the desperate pound of her fist. Brigid doesn't open it; she leans on the other side of the door, barely breathing, willing her to go away. Emer once walked in without invitation, but she has reversed to a formality with Brigid, an odd one considering the intimacies that occurred once she let her in. Brigid can imagine Emer on the other side of the wood, as the plans that propelled her up the path grow cold and her face heats up with humiliation. She hopes Emer can't hear her jagged breath, or the inner voice that, despite her resolve, still calls her name out with something like ardor—*Emer, Emer*—even as it begs her away. Emer lingers for a long time, longer than she should, hoping that Brigid will change her mind, then turns and stumbles her way back down the hill.

CHAPTER 20

Christmas Tree

When Festy manages to get across from the mainland and bring provisions for Christmas, Niall comes to tell Emer the men from Muruch are pulling into the quay. They have brought a pine tree for Brigid. She asked Festy to get her one to decorate for Christmas. When Emer goes down to the quay Brigid and Rose are together, smiling and laughing with the men, and the girls are all taking turns putting their faces in the branches and inhaling the smell of pine. The blasted dog is moving circles around them, jumping and filthying skirts with her paws. No one minds her anymore.

"Brigid got us a Christmas tree, Emer," Rose says. "Just like in a storybook. We'll have it inside the house with candles and sweets hidden in the branches. Why don't you and Niall come for tea and help us decorate it?"

"It'll burn the house down," Emer says bitterly.

Niall is running around on the quay rocks and she needs to bark at him to get some sense, and that's when Rose gasps her disapproval. Rose never has to tell the girls to mind their own bodies. They just do it.

"Ach, Emer," Rose says. "Try not to ruin Christmas for the lot of us, would you now." Fiona and Eve snicker, like women already, squinting at Emer with cruel glee. Brigid is busy directing women on how to hold the trunk of the tree without damaging the needles. Niall becomes interested in carrying it, but doesn't listen to instructions so just manages to poke himself in the eye. He is comforted by Eve and doesn't even look for his mother. And so they all fuss and carry on and walk away from Emer, so enraged by it all that she can't move, her face screwed up and ugly against the wind and sea spray, left on the abandoned quay. Not even the dog, normally compelled to keep the herd together, checks behind them.

ON CHRISTMAS EVE AT Rose's house, where everything they do emphasizes the absence of husbands and fathers, where Niall is the only male in a throng of optimistic but weary-eyed women, Emer has too much to drink and accosts Brigid in the bedroom.

The girls have their father's instruments out and are screeching out simple tunes on the fiddle and the concertina while the toddlers wallop the bodhran. Rose has been cheerful and kind to her all night, to make up for the scene at the quay, but Emer can tell she is thinking of Austin. It doesn't help that Brigid notices it too, and keeps touching her, touching her with those hands, which Emer knows from experience ease the worst of it, the worst of you, like shifting something inside just enough to let you breathe all the way. Emer keeps refilling her wine—another surprise Brigid had brought over on the boat—so she can swallow the rude thoughts she'd like to spew at the both of them. When Brigid goes to get some presents from the back bedroom, Emer follows. The musical cacophony is enough to cover their voices, and Rose, nursing two babies at once, will not be standing up anytime soon.

She had only planned to talk to her, to tell her about Niall and her visions, but she is so drunk and Brigid's body so familiar that she barely thinks as she reaches her hands to her waist. She wants to press into her, to feel again the only good thing she has felt in years coursing through her body. Even if it's only once more, and is taken away again at the end.

But Brigid deflects her hands, slaps them away like they are meant to hurt. She moves quickly, as far away as she can get in the tiny dark room. Her breathing is quick, her stomach under the pretty blouse is swollen, growing larger by the day.

"Don't, Emer," she hisses, sounding shocked, as if it hadn't happened countless times. As if it's wrong, Emer's mistake, instead of something she taught her to do.

"Just this once," Emer says. She hears the pathetic begging in her voice.

"It's not going to happen. I'm sorry, Emer. That's done now."

It's like being kicked in the stomach, the truth, even when you suspect it. Like her skin being ripped away.

"I'm sorry," Brigid adds, but she has to force it. The way she is looking at Emer is not sorry. There is no pity there. Only avoidance mixed with an undercurrent of disgust.

Emer's real voice escapes with a barking hiss, she almost spits it.

"Sure you wouldn't mind if it was Rose?" Emer says quickly. "I'm not much of a prize next to Rose."

"Jesus, Emer," Brigid says, "I'm not having sex with your sister."

"Only because she won't," Emer says. She sees how this hurts, a quick sting like catching skin with a sharp nail.

"Must you be like this?" Brigid says, and she turns away, so quickly and easily giving Emer her back that the swivel of it forces Emer's breath away.

"You said you'd help me," Emer says.

"Has there ever been anything in your mind but what you want?" Brigid says.

"And what do you mean by that?" Emer says.

Brigid lets out a little gasp of disapproval, like an old island woman. Her voice has a lilt to it now. It follows the same rhythm as every voice that has dismissed Emer her whole life.

"You'll not spare anyone, will you?" Brigid says. "Not a soul is safe that stands in your way."

"That's grand, coming from you," Emer says.

When Brigid tries to walk by her, Emer lashes out, like some animal inside her has been released. She clamps onto the woman's wrist, the same wrist she held prisoner against the mattress while she teased with the mouth she's just recently learned how to use. She holds it now, prepared to press all the ugliness she has inside it.

"You won't do that to me, Emer," Brigid says. "You can't." But she looks terrified.

Emer can't do it. Something holds her back. She is not sure that it is Brigid anymore.

"It's not me you should be afraid of, so," Emer says. "They'll swallow you whole, the lot of them. Rose too. When they find out what you are. They'll spit out your bones. They're hateful."

"No, Emer. That's you. I thought I could take it out of you. But it's too deep."

You could have, Emer wants to say. *You did*. But she sees that Brigid is gone. Whatever was there between them is now as cold and unwanted as the relations she has had with men before. She had thought there was something different, with a woman. But it turns out to be the same humiliating, violating, dismissive thing in the end.

Emer doesn't know the answer, any more than the rest of them do, Rose or Patch or her mother or even, now, her own son, to why she can't be loved. This is a rejection she expected, but somehow that makes it even worse. To have such low expectations and then to watch, time and time again, as they are realized.

SHE TRIES TO TAKE Niall with her. Something burst inside that bedroom and now her good eye has a blind spot, a smudge at the edge of her vision where there is nothing, as if the fabric of the world is beginning to peel away. All she wants is to go home and be with her son. In the middle of the tree trimming, the gaiety, the music, the first time she's seen him truly laugh since his father drowned, she tries to drag him away. Even as she sees how unfair it is, she can't stop herself. She can't stand to watch him so enchanted by the same people intent on making her miserable.

"We'll go now, Niall." His face falls, sure as if she's hit him with the words.

"The tree's not finished," he whines.

"You can't go, Emer," Rose dismisses her, not even bothering to glance in her direction. "Your supper's not eaten."

"We won't be staying for supper," Emer says. This is such a ridiculous statement, it's not as if there is anyplace to go, any real reason to leave except that Emer can't stand to be there.

"Don't be cross," Rose says. "Give the children a hand with the tree."

"I'm not one of the children," Emer spits. "And I've no intention of fussing over that bloomin' tree." She can feel the room changing, she is changing it, like the calm that comes before a storm on the sea, a stillness that is more about dread than peace, followed by onslaught. Her nieces' fidgeting gaiety has gone still at her language; they refuse to look at her. Niall is looking at her too hard.

Clodagh looks almost delighted. "You'd easier get a smile off a stone," she says.

"I'll make tea," Rose says, looking quickly from Emer to Brigid and back again, hoping for some explanation. Brigid's face is pale, clenched, revealing nothing. Emer feels like her own face is about to collapse, that if she says too much it will let loose and slide right off her, features broken and ugly and lost in tears. She wants to hold on to it, press her own cruel hands to her face and attempt to keep it on. If she cries she will let loose something terrible. She feels a sudden, sharp slice of pain behind her eye, and then a throbbing, like an echo.

"Niall, get your coat. Now." Niall looks at her for one more disbelieving instant and then he transforms into a small, angry man.

"No," he says. "You leave me be."

Emer grabs his arm and drags him to the door and tries to force him, thrashing and screaming, into his jacket.

"Let me alone!" he screams. "Don't touch me!" She hasn't had to put his arms in clothing since he was small and she is surprised at how strongly he can resist her, and this angers her more, that his body is big enough to dismiss her. She is furious, but his wailing insults stab her ears so she alternates between wrestling him and pushing him roughly away.

"You're horrid," he howls, and his hurt fuels her. She feels it coming before she does it, her hands on him changing into the ones that are not his mother's. She presses all her embarrassment, rejection and fury into the small arm of her boy.

"I hate you!" he screams. His face breaks, the anger crumples in on itself and the wail he lets out is pure, though it grates on her nerves as if it is put on. She cannot tell if her hands have hurt him, or if he is merely mourning the fact that she actually tried.

She tries not to look at anyone in the room, all of them frozen and staring, but cannot help a glance at Brigid. Because now she's regretting herself and wants to take it back, and Brigid is the only one who has ever let her do this, or at least the only one who hasn't had to, the only one, besides Rose, who waits long enough for Emer to say something good. She wants to lie down on the bed and have Brigid bind up whatever it is that is breaking up inside her mind and sliding away. But all Brigid gives her is one pitiless shake of her head.

Her vision swims in and out, one second she can see them, blurred as if under the water, the next there is nothing.

"Emer," Rose begins, but Brigid stops her from being saved.

"Let her go, if that's what she wants," Brigid says, and Rose's eyes widen at the boldness of it.

"Oh, how the mighty have fallen," their mother sings.

And though Emer could be convinced now, one kind word from Rose and the storm will subside, and she'll accept tea and make herself small and, if not agreeable, at least not insufferable, Rose stops, eyes glistening at the thrill of it, then shrugs and turns around.

"Let the boy stay, so," she says. "No need to drag him down with you."

Niall, quiet now, looking slightly ashamed, wiggles out of her grip and goes to stand between Fiona and Eve, who each put an arm around him and glare at her with the same pretty, disappointed eyes as Rose. This is such a shock, he has never not gone with her, has always chosen her, when pressed, over everyone else, for a moment she does not know what to do next. She considers picking him up and carrying him home. But she can barely see, and the stabs in her head are converging into an intolerable wave. She thinks she might be ill, seasick from her own pain. She can barely stand straight with the strain of it; she won't be able to carry him now. This is what she has been dreading all along, this moment where her son recognizes what everyone else has always known. When he is repulsed by her. How can she blame him? How can she force him? She does not even want to go with herself.

But she does go, slamming the door behind her, trudging through pellets of hail that mix with the rain, and in the five minutes it takes to walk to her house, she is soaked through and shivering and completely, cruelly alone, all the way down to her bones.

When she gets inside it is all she can do to remove her wet things and crawl into bed. As soon as her head touches the pillow, a dam lets loose the pain and she screams.

She knows what it is people feel when she takes their hand. Their insides cleave, not just for a moment, but all the way through the future of their lives, as if with one touch she can steal away every joy they once dared to promise themselves.

NIALL COMES FOR HER, sneaking in quietly sometime the next afternoon to convince her to come for the lamb dinner. She stays in her bed, where she has lain since she left, up only to change the rags of clotted blood between her legs. She doesn't budge, doesn't turn to him, doesn't even open her eyes when he puts a sweet, loyal, frightened hand on her forehead. If he speaks, she thinks to herself, if she hears his voice she will be able to open her eyes, and rise out of the darkness and smile and love him again. But he gives up just a beat too soon, and later she wonders if he knows this, that his voice will wake her, and if he withholds it, because he is finding out that things are a bit easier all around without her there. He says nothing, and she pretends she is asleep, and they both let their lies be believed. He leaves to go back to Rose's house, and she stays alone, letting it all pass by without her, with no ability to break the ugliness she has begun, and not enough courage to ask someone, her son, her sister, her lover, to help pull her out from underneath the terrible weight of herself.

She has been so afraid of this day for so long, the day her child turns away from her, that she is surprised at how easy it is to release her grip, and let him go.

CHAPTER 21

Brigid's Day

January, February 1960

In January the storms return. Days turn into weeks turn into a month where no one leaves the island and nothing comes to them. They are drowned and forgotten in the middle of an angry sea. They were never given the distress radio Brigid asked for. (They were given the winch, an old, rusty wheel that broke the first time they tried to haul a boat up with it.) If Emer were still speaking to her, Brigid knows she would say: *Do you see now?* But Brigid doesn't mind the isolation in Rose's house. Her belly grows bigger as Rose's babies fatten up and stay awake for longer stretches, turning their heads to follow the movement of the other children. The older girls and Niall play endless games of domestic imagination, twittering like birds in their laughter, distracting them all from the leaden weather. The sun still abandons them every day before five o'clock.

Emer has taken to her bed. For all of January she lies in the feathered box and Rose is the only one who tends to her.

"I don't know what is wrong with her, poor pet," Rose confides in Brigid. "Perhaps it's the grief catching up to her? She can't even bear for me to open the curtains. Says the light hurts."

Brigid says little in response to this, but she offers to take up all the chores except the ones that lead to bringing food over to Emer's and coaxing her to eat. She leaves that to Rose, who she can see will never abandon her sister, even while a part of her would like to be free.

Niall still spends nights with Emer, crawling into the ripened bedclothes. He comes to Rose's every morning, looking like something in him has been snuffed out, needing the laughter and lightness of his cousins to pull him out of the misery of his mother.

"Why won't she speak to me?" Brigid hears him ask Rose. Rose pulls him in for an embrace and whispers encouragement into his ear. "You must be brave for her," she says. "She will come back to you."

"I wish you could help," Rose laments to Brigid.

"I will if you like," Brigid concedes. But Rose gasps and shakes her head.

"She's adamant. Doesn't want to see you. I don't know what she's on about but we'd best not cross her now."

And Brigid lets her breath out as quietly as she can, and says yes, that would be the wisest thing, all around.

ON THE EVE OF St. Brigid's Day, the weather lifts a bit, not enough for a boat, but enough so the girls can have their parade without the threat of being blown into the sea. They have made a Brídeog, a life-size doll version of the saint, and carry it in front of them like a masthead, skipping the road and giggling, Niall blowing on a dissonant horn. Rose and Brigid walk behind them, infants tied tightly to each of their bosoms.

At each house, the girls knock at the doors and call out together: "Brigid is coming!" They must call this out three times before the woman opens the door and says, "She is welcome, she is welcome." They are let inside to dance a bit, Eve playing her father's tin whistle, the scarecrow saint propped by the hearth as a witness. The widows give them sweets.

Rose tries to steer them clear of Emer's house, but Niall is insistent. They knock, they call out, once, twice, three times.

"Go on your knees and open your eyes and let Blessed Brigid enter." But no one comes to the door. There is no lamp lit inside, no candle left in the window, no flutter of curtain to indicate that Emer even cares they are there. It is as quiet as one of the abandoned houses they marched by on their way up the road.

"Come along, children," Rose claps, "there is pudding waiting at my house."

She puts an arm around the dejected Niall. "You're grand, ladeen. She's resting, is all."

"It's horrible luck not to let the Brídeog in," Niall says.

Rose has told Brigid that the tradition started as a way of guarding the house against misfortune, particularly death, in the coming year. But now she reassures her nephew.

"Sure, Niall, you're old enough to know, it's only a game meant to entertain children."

When they return to Rose's house, the children stay up late teaching Brigid how to weave the saint's cross from green rushes. They bend the stiff stalks and weave them into a knot at the center, then out into four arms and tie off the ends. They make a small one for Brigid's baby, to hang over the cradle, and another for her door. One for each of their beds, and the front door of Rose's house. In the morning they will hang them, tossing last year's version, thick with spiderwebs and all that has happened since Brigid arrived, into the fire.

THE NEXT MORNING IS the first of February, Brigid's fortieth birthday and the feast day of the saint, and the weather releases its grip on them. The women who man the boat walk to the quay, put the currach in and head off to meet the anchored trawler, to collect their post, flour, sugar and tea. Brigid sits beside Rose on a chair outside in the sunshine, enormous now with her miracle child.

They gather together at midmorning and file into the church, carrying their milking stools, greeted by the priest who hasn't made it over from Muruch since October. The priest says the Mass quickly, blesses the wafers and places them on tongues, occasionally glancing at the windows to check the weather. He is not keen on being stuck here again. He has brought a box of white tapers for Candlemas, which he blesses and gives to each family to bring home, for protection against storms and evil in the coming year. After Mass he hands out treats to the children, crisps and chocolate from the shop, and they spend a good deal of time trading and trying bites of each other's treasures.

Emer is there, out of bed for the first time in a month, her dress hanging off her shoulders like there is nothing inside of it, a face on her that makes even the priest take a wide berth.

"How're you keeping, Emer?" the women mutter, but don't stop or meet her eye. They move on to talk to Rose and Brigid, one showing off her babies, the other glowing in pregnancy. Emer watches while women reach out and press palms to Brigid's belly, uninvited, and Brigid lets them, these same women who were so cold to her when she arrived, she allows them to coo and praise and molest her as if she is related to them. It is a disgusting display, Emer thinks, watching Brigid reveal her huge white teeth and call each of them by name, pronouncing them correctly now. She seems quite pleased with herself. She has no idea how quickly these people could turn against her. They barely need a reason; one slip and they'll turn their backs all over again.

Niall was happy when she emerged and walked to the church holding her hand, but now he is running around and screeching with Rose's girls and has forgotten her again. The priest tries to slide past Emer with a nod, but she snags him.

"How are they above, Father?" she says, and he looks none too happy to stop.

"Well, Emer, well enough. Isn't it lovely to see the sun," he mutters.

"It'll be lashing again by evening," Emer says.

"Sure, we'll enjoy it while we're able."

"At least you're *able* to leave," Emer says.

"How is the Yank getting along?" the priest deflects. "It's good of your sister to take her in. Widows helping each other."

"Is that what they told you, Father?"

"Poor woman, losing her husband while with child."

"Her husband died five years ago," Emer says. "You do the sums and see what sort of woman she is."

The priest crosses himself quickly and mutters some excuse to get away.

"What did you say to the poor man, Emer?" Rose says, coming up behind her.

"Nothing I'll regret," Emer says, and walks away from her sister, looking for Niall, pleased to see the sky darkening ominously in the distance. She'd like the day to be ruined for everyone. She has forgotten her candles, but doesn't bother going back for them.

She finds Niall sitting by himself, white as a sheet in the green field.

"What ails you?" she says. He opens his mouth to answer but instead he is sick, spewing crisps and chocolate and Cidona onto her shoes.

"Brilliant," she mutters, but still she wipes his tears away and holds his hand all the way home. Just as they get there the wind and rain return, knocking the door on its hinges and drowning out the sound of Niall, retching again in the ditch by their gate.

HOW KIND AND GOOD Emer becomes when her child is ill. How gently she is able to smooth his brow and know just where to press the cloth, to cluck and sing and shush him. Her hands are a balm, her voice is comforting, not a shrill invasion to the head, a songbird rather than a corncrake.

"It's all right, *a chuisle*," she croons. She almost welcomes it, the feeling of a fever on his brow, because now she remembers who she can be. She can realize how silly she has been, and get over her temper, and think again of them moving to the mainland, starting all over in a house where they can both forget all that has happened and who she has been.

She lies vigilant by his side, watches him flip around like a snagged fish, in the bed she washed and made up freshly when she decided to rise from bed and seek her revenge.

HE IS SICK EVERY half an hour until there's nothing left but foul froth. Every time, the pause between the heaving, where his face flames and he cannot breathe or make any sound, and the release seems to last a little longer. Each time she holds her breath, rigid with terror, waiting for the moment it releases him and he comes back to her. Afraid it will be the last, that he will be seized and his body will not be able to purge it again. He will be stolen away just at the point where he cannot even call out for help.

When Emer was sick as a child, it was Rose who tended to her. Her mother was useless when they were ill, she only got angry, as if the sickness were some personal affront. Emer can see this in herself now. By 4 a.m. she wants to hold him upside down and shake him, to slap him in the face and demand that he stop. She sees now, how much sense it makes to be angry with your child. Angry with them for making you so powerless.

By dawn, so much has come out of him he can't even manage

tears anymore. The storm has descended fully and she can barely tell when the sun rises, the black fading to a gray so pathetic it seems a waste. His head is so hot to the touch it shocks her, he is writhing with what he calls a fire in his side. When he opens his mouth to moan or be sick she can almost hear the angry venomous thrum of those long-resentful bees. When Rose comes in, Emer throws herself, grateful and desperate, into her sister's arms.

"Get Brigid," she says. "They're trying to take him."

THERE IS AN OLD island story that Emer has told Niall, about a mother who was taken away by the fairies, leaving behind her young son. One night, years later, he woke up and saw that she was back, looking like his mother but not quite the same, sitting by a table full of food and drink, a fire dancing in the hearth. She invited him to eat from it. But the boy had been raised to recognize fairy tricks so he refused, and his mother, or what was left of her, went away again.

When Niall first heard this story, he was puzzled. He knows that if fairies offer him food to steal him away, he should refuse.

But what if his mother is the fairy? Shouldn't he gorge himself then? Shouldn't he do whatever is necessary to keep her beside him, even if it is the one thing she has told him all his life never to do?

CHAPTER 22

Fairy Stroke

"It's only the virus that's been going around," Brigid says when Rose rushes into the house, her hair uncovered and shining with rain.

"It's more," Rose whispers and her face makes Brigid go for her waterproof.

One look at Niall, white and writhing in the bedclothes, and Brigid moves quickly to him, pressing one hand to his head and the other low on his abdomen. She looks up to Rose and Emer.

"Has the priest gone?" she asks.

"He went yesterday."

"What about that trawler?"

"Have you looked at the sea?"

"Tell Maeve to get the boat out. He needs a hospital."

Rose is growing colder and calmer the more Emer paces beside her. She speaks slowly.

"With those swells the boats will smash them to death before they can leave the quay."

"How do you get the doctor here in an emergency?" Brigid says. "How do you call him?"

"We don't," Rose says.

"What do you mean, you don't?"

"Have you not been living here all this time?" Emer shrieks. "We told you. In this weather we're trapped."

"What do you do, Rose?" Brigid repeats. "When it's a real emergency? A life-or-death emergency?" Rose widens her eyes and shakes her head in a subtle but unambiguous movement.

"Could you not just put your hands on him?" Rose whispers.

So, she does know, Brigid thinks. Emer is breathing fast and loud, as though the air in the house is leaking away.

"I can't fix this." It's too much, she thinks, and something dark yanks at the walls of her womb, as if the baby itself is clenching with fear. "It's appendicitis. He needs surgery."

"Saints alive," Rose says. "Austin's uncle had the appendicitis. Two winters ago."

"What did you do then?"

"We lit a fire," Rose says. "On the hill above the port. Next to the children's graveyard."

Brigid looks between them, narrowing her brow in anger. She turns away. They wait ages for her to speak. "Well light one, then," she says. "Light a big one."

Rose goes out the door quickly, the wind screaming inside for the moment it is open, then muffled with a slap when it closes again.

Brigid leans over Niall, lifts his shirt to press her hands gently to his side. He moans and curls in on himself like a snail shrinking into its shell. She dips the cloth in the pail of water by the bed and wipes his neck, his forehead, his bright, burning cheeks.

"It will be all right, Emer," she says kindly, and she reaches a hand out to pull her down to kneel by the bed. She knows Emer has been waiting for a kind gesture from her for a while, but she hasn't dared. Even now, she does it with difficulty, without looking her in the eye.

"They didn't come," Emer says, her voice barely audible in the whistle of wind against stone.

"What's that?" Brigid says, dipping the hot cloth back into cool water. She turns toward Niall again.

"When we lit the fire for Austin's uncle," Emer says. Her voice is a hot whisper of dread at Brigid's neck. "They didn't come."

Brigid presses Niall's head again with the cloth, hoping that Emer does not see the tremor of her hand.

"Whisht," she says, like an island mother. "They'll come this time."

SHE CAN'T HEAL THIS. Just being near him makes the child inside her writhe and dig painfully, as if clawing its way somewhere deeper inside her.

Don't, that voice whispers to her. *You can't save him. If you try, they'll take me too.*

She remembers stories of the fairy stroke, illness that couldn't be cured by magic because it was driven by magic itself. She remembers Matthew's tumor, how at the core of it was a dark well she could never reach. Niall feels like this now, as if he is being held away from them all, under deep water, and if she tries to reach him, she will drown.

She shakes off these thoughts, like a buzzing insect. He has an infection, that is all. She will wait for the fire, for the boats, for a doctor. Every once in a while, it was Matthew who had the answer, not her hands.

In the meantime she does what little she can. She uses a cherished blue cloth and cold water to give him an instant of relief, before it boils up in him again.

"I'LL LEAVE YOU ALONE," Emer is bargaining. Brigid hushes her, but Emer can't hear anything but herself.

"You can have Rose. I'll leave the island. I'll never bother you again. I'll not ask for anything else. I'll tell them to stop the evacuation. Please. Don't let this go on. Pull it out of him. Bring him back."

"Emer," Brigid says. "I'm doing all I can. The fire will work. They'll send a doctor."

"You can do it. I know you can. Why won't you try?"

And though Brigid gestures to Rose to take Emer away, to give her a cup of tea, to give her a break from the begging and pleading, she shudders at Emer's words.

She is the boy's only hope. Something won't let her save him. She is not entirely sure it isn't herself.

Don't, the voice in her head is her mother's now, her mother's voice that she hears so often these days, coming out of her own mouth. *Don't be a fool.*

BRIGID WATCHES THE FIRE from Emer's window. It is as big as the midsummer bonfire, big enough to push against the wind and swallow the rain before it can be doused. It is a signal, and they will keep it burning all night long. She thinks of her father winding the clockworks in the light, feeding the oil, polishing the lenses and the brass work, telling her that each lighthouse has its own particular sequence, its own voice, foghorns as distinct as dialects calling to blinded ships.

She wishes the island itself could make a noise, scream like a corncrake, drone like bees, call out with the desolate keening that comes from every mother who has lost a child. That the magic left in its ground and water, both holy and blasphemous, could rise together in a great cacophonous howl. A noise strong enough to carry Niall on its back across the sea.

She thinks of her mother, lying with their heads on the same pillow, whispering her worst choices as if they are only a fairy tale.

> *A woman lies on the edge of a cliff,*
> *holding the hands of two children*
> *as they dangle beneath her.*
> *One is her own, the other a changeling.*
> *She cannot tell between them.*
> *She needs both hands to save only one.*
> *Which hand does she let go?*

CHAPTER 23

Bargain

The women pile broken furniture, wreckage collected from the shore, an old currach that their husbands never repaired. All the rubbish that has collected since the summer goes into the pile. They douse the thing with paraffin to get it to light in the lashing rain. The wind is so strong the fire leans sideways, reaching out in a desperate plea. Oisin, who since the drowning has gone from a boy to a man before he is ready, minds the fire all night, while the women and children search desperately, going from house to house, shed to shed, looking for something, anything, to burn. By morning they are breaking apart their beds with axes, emptying cupboards and wardrobes and lopping the legs off tables brought to the island for their weddings. They burn the last of the great planks that were washed ashore from the submarine bombed during the war, the roof beams of cottages that were abandoned for America. They burn it all, as though, if they give up every precious last bit of wood they own, if they build the fire high enough, feed it until it sets alight and burns the sky, it might be answered by a miracle.

THOUGH ROSE TRIES TO ply her with tea and empty reassurances, Emer crawls into bed with Niall and holds on to him, imagining she can draw the fever into her own body, wishing that she had the same ability to pull badness out as she does to put it in. She prays to every good and evil being she can imagine. She does not care where the salvation comes from.

She lowers herself to her knees by his bedside and begs for forgiveness from a god she barely believes in. She wants to cut her own veins, burn sods of penance into her arms. She wants to turn her body inside out and let every bit of ugliness pour away until there is nothing left.

She would put him back inside her. Cleave in two and grow herself back together in a carapace. Never let him come out, eyes wide, hair dark as ink, thick as a man's, glossy and standing like a shock out of his head. The day he was born, he looked at everyone who entered that room as if he had something vital to tell them.

She knows now that all her searching was stupid and pointless, that she inserted pain into people while looking for something she'd had all along. The yearning for Brigid that still consumed her is gone now, as insubstantial as ash lying dead in the fire. Everything she ever wanted was given to her with this child and she never should have tried to have anything else.

They bring holy water, the women do, from Saint Brigid's well. She bathes him in it, pours it over him without thought to what dribbles down, sloshes it in desperate clumsy spurts, and gestures, without looking up because she cannot bear the resigned pity in their eyes, for them to bring more.

She calls to the same fairies she has scorned and blamed. They can even have him, she promises, if it means he will not die.

She remembers a tale where a woman gave birth to an unearthly beautiful girl. A fairy came to her when the baby was still in the cradle, and told her the child had been chosen to be the bride of a fairy prince.

"Take the glowing log out of the fire and bury it in the garden and your child will live as long as it continues to burn in the ground." So the mother did as she was told and her daughter lived for seven hundred years, married seven fairy kings, until a priest overheard the story, dug up the log and doused it, and she fell away to dust.

Emer holds on to her boy, hot as a glowing log himself, and addresses the darkest seeds left inside her. She will take back every cruel and selfish and hopeful thing she has ever done. Every kiss she gave to Brigid, the invitation she gave to Austin, the turning of the cursing stone that failed to put right her mistakes.

Tell me what to bury, what to burn, what to drown. Tell me what to do and I will do it. I will do anything.

Then she listens, desperate for a whispered musical answer under the screaming disagreement of the wind.

"Mammy," Niall says. "Tell them to stop that music."

EMER LEAVES ROSE AND Brigid tending Niall's fever and goes out into the storm. She climbs up the cliffs, almost crawling at times when the wind pushes against her, and down into the cave of Brigid's well. Niall has already been bathed in this water, and encouraged to drink it through the same small pitcher she once used to feed him breast milk. It made no difference, but she has come here anyway, to beg.

> *No fire, no moon, no sun, shall burn me,*
> *No lake, no water, no sea shall drown me,*
> *No arrow of fairy nor dart of fury shall wound me.*
> *Blessed Brigid, have mercy on me,*
> *Blessed Brigid, wrap me in your mantle,*
> *Blessed Brigid, mend my bones and save my soul.*

At each repetition the wind grows louder, the rain lashes cold icy bullets into the sanctuary, and Emer continues to pray. To saints and virgin mothers and forgiving sons, pressing the beads of her childhood rosary so tightly she thinks they might pop and turn to dust in her hands. When she can't feel her fingers anymore, she lies on the soft ground and lets herself have a moment of shelter from wind and ice and terror. She almost falls asleep there, until she hears Niall's voice, as clear as if he is lying on her pillow.

"Mammy?" he says softly, and then again, shocked, fearful. "Mammy, get out of there!" She runs home, dropping the futile rosary on the way. She is fooling herself. The only power she has is the cruel kind. God and the women who obey him are of no use to her.

NIALL HAS TAKEN A turn for the worse; any of them can see that. They've burned half the island and no one has come. It is only an hour or so before dawn, but the sky shows no signs of letting up. When Emer returns, Brigid isn't even there, Rose kneels in the bedroom with Niall, thumbing her rosary and praying like a madwoman. The women who are now the island's men stand in the main room, shifting awkwardly in their wellies, their shoulders still wet from the storm.

"Where is Brigid?" Emer demands.

"She's gone back to her house, Emer. She needed the rest."

"Wrecked from all that she's brought upon us, is she?"

"What are you on about?" says Kathleen.

"Only she's a changeling, is all," Emer says. "She has you all under her spell, otherwise you'd know it. She's put a stroke on my boy. The fairy stroke. Sure the same as her family did years ago."

"She's done nothing but good for us, Emer," Margaret says.

"Because it suits her. She has the healing in her hands, did you know? What else do you think she can do, if she's a mind to? Do you not remember the family she comes from?"

Emer's mother, quiet in the corner until now, raps her cane on the floor so they will look at her.

"That was a bad family, sure it was," she says. "Her mother was born of a bargain with the fairies. She was a whore, she lay down with any man who asked. She killed a newborn child, she did, strangled the poor thing as it was coming out of its mother."

The women stare at Clodagh as if she has just risen from the dead in the corner. "No one asked me," she quips, answering the question in their eyes. "You were all so taken with her."

Who knew, Emer thinks, that her mother could be so helpful?

"Do you know where Brigid got that baby?" Emer continues. Her heart is thudding with every word she utters, with the power of them, she can feel their minds pausing, looking back, tripping up, doubting their better instincts.

"Sure it's from that Australian," says Kathleen.

"Are you certain of that?" Emer spits. "Certain it wasn't Austin, or one of your husbands? She came here wanting a baby. She was pregnant long before she met that Australian. She told me herself."

The women shift uneasily at this, and Rose glares at them. Kathleen has gone white, thinking of how much time Malachy wasted bringing trifles to Brigid. Of the jokes the men made whenever they saw her, and the way his face flared up in response.

"Why do you think she drowned the lads?" Emer says.

"Jesus, Mary and Brigid." Margaret crosses herself.

"Didn't I see her," Emer says, "see her go to the cursing stone, turning and turning, and then there was that storm."

"That's quite the accusation, Emer." Kathleen steps forward. "Why would she do such a thing?"

"Ask her yourself," Emer says. "Ask her why she got rid of Rose's husband where she's so happily taken his place now. It's not natural.

She may have been married, but she has relations with women. She could help Niall if she wanted to. She has the healing in her hands. I've seen it. She could pull it out of him. But she won't and it's because she put that badness into him. Because I wouldn't let her do sinful things to me. That is the truth."

"Saints alive," her mother mutters, crossing herself. Her paralyzed mouth is twisted into a version of a smile.

She doesn't even need her hands. She sets in into the air, the darkness that seeps into their minds, that threatens to drown them, that is so familiar they do not realize it comes from Emer at all. They believe it is something that came from them, and not something Emer inserted like a blade. They can't see it, every loss or rejection or fear Emer has ever felt, gushing out of her in a torrent. She has let it all out at once, all that hatred and misery, as huge as a fabric that expands to capture what it needs.

They take it from her and carry it along. They are buzzing with it, whispering, spitting accusations out like flames. They are enchanted by the same darkness that drives Emer to destroy things. Their eyes grow shadowed, like storm clouds swallowing the sky.

Her grandfather lay down with a fairy woman and Nuala was their child.

They tried to see was she a witch.

They burned her, they drowned her. But she wouldn't die.

They say she swam all the way to the mainland.

We never should have let her child back here.

She bewitched the men first, isn't that always the way?

The women gather themselves in a knot. This is how Emer knows it is serious. It used to be the men who dealt with such things. Men and priests. But they no longer have either.

Who's to say that women can't be as violent and merciless as men? Or fairies. Or God himself.

CHAPTER 24

Fairy Tale

Brigid needs to leave. Since she can't go anywhere until the storm recedes—she is as much a prisoner as the rest of them—she concentrates on packing. She regrets bringing so many things to begin with. She has worn the same three pieces of clothing over and over again because it's all that fits over her growing belly. All the items the islanders brought back to her, the copper teapot, the fuchsia pottery hand-sponged by nuns in Connemara, and the things she had the men bring over from the mainland, the sheets and towels, the bright bottles of ink and thick ragged-edged paper, the bees, all of it she will leave behind. She will run away with the turf still glowing in the fire. Emer would say that islanders will steal it all, but Brigid likes to imagine it folding in on itself, walls and pictures and furniture and the skin she has shed into dust for the last eight months, swallowed whole into the earth, the way the bog swallows a tree and then petrifies it. Perhaps it will end up that her house is flipped to the other side, an underworld, where another kind of being altogether will sift through her things with delight.

She packs only clean knickers, her drawing journal, one bottle of ink, the few wee things she has knitted for the baby. A picture of Matthew, the address book with the numbers of people back in America she had thought she would never see again. Her passport, warped from damp that seeped into the drawer she'd stashed it in. Rua lies by the door, curled up, watching her every move, ready to follow.

She can see now how precarious it was, everything she built here, how it could all come to nothing in one violent winter storm. All that matters is saving what grows inside her. The sight of Niall's feverish, doomed face and that useless, continuously fed fire makes her know why this place is Emer's prison. Those summer days that barely got dark, where sea air and sunshine were as nutritious as her daily meals, seem very far away. For months she thought the child within her lived off this island. Now she is afraid it will die if she stays. As sure as she is that the pathetic fire in the graveyard will save no one.

She can't save Niall. And if she doesn't, Emer will never allow her to leave.

Emer bangs open the door without knocking, and Rua skitters away from it. For a moment, seeing her there with wet hair plastered over a purplish, desperate face, Brigid thinks Niall is already gone. But then Emer looks behind her, closes the door and paces around in a frenetic way, which means she's still in the throes of hoping she can turn it all around.

"They're coming now," she says. "I'm only a moment or two ahead of them."

For a second Brigid thinks she means the doctor, the rescue they are hoping for from the mainland. But she wouldn't be here if it was that.

Rua barks at her. She doesn't stop after one or two, but keeps on, relentless, barks over and over until Brigid must lead her into the bedroom and close the door. In there she stops barking, but whimpers, paces and scratches at the bottom of the door instead.

"Who's coming?" Brigid says.

"Your women," Emer sneers.

"Come to see if I'm a witch?" Emer avoids her eyes.

"My mother said some things to them."

"I imagine she did."

"If you heal Niall they'll not harm you. I'll convince them to let you go."

"I can't, Emer. He needs a surgeon."

"You're lying about not being able for it and I don't know why. I know you hate me but you love him. Why won't you pull it out?"

"I don't hate you, Emer. I've tried. I can't heal him."

"You're afraid it'll kill the baby."

Brigid says nothing.

"That's how you lost the others, isn't it?" Emer says. "I won't allow you to give up Niall for yours."

"I can't do it, Emer. I can't. You wouldn't, either."

"Well you'll try. Or you'll regret it, so. I can't stop them now. You don't know what they can be like. You would if you'd seen what they did to your mother."

"I know," Brigid says. A flash then, a girl moving across the room, in between them, like a frightened animal. She is only a vision, but to Brigid she seems as real as this girl who threatens her.

"You don't know all of it," Emer says. "Unless you help, they'll do the same to you. I can make them."

Brigid remembers meeting Emer for the first time, how she had tried to put this into her from the start, and Brigid had deflected it, but Emer is just coming back with a bigger hand now.

"What did they do to you, Emer, that ever made you so cruel?"

"Am I more cruel than you? You who'd let a child die."

They stand against each other, neither of them blinks, neither of them gives. They are Brigid and Darla, saint and changeling, lovers and enemies. Neither one will ever back down. This is about more than their hands, or themselves. It's about their children.

A polite knock at the door. No harder than the rain. As if they've only come for tea.

"Don't do this, Emer," Brigid begs. "I loved you."

"You used me," Emer says, her voice wavering.

"Just let me go."

"I can't," Emer says. "I have no choices left."

They file in, a dripping mass of them, too many for such a small room. Kathleen, Margaret, Nelly, Geraldine, young Maeve. They look like men, massive in their husbands' wellies and the oilskins Brigid had ordered from Dublin, and reeking of fire and the sea. The skin on their faces has grown so coarse from working outdoors it looks like it wouldn't bleed if you sliced it. And their hands: hands that were never pretty, after a lifetime of housework, hands that held their own knives and cut with them until the blades were worn slim as needles. Their hands are monstrous now.

Not one of them, though each of them has laughed with her, let her hand bleed comfort into their shoulder, looks Brigid in the eye.

"Will you leave us, Emer," Kathleen says.

There is hesitation in Emer now, as if she sees something she hadn't expected. She who expects the worst.

"Sure this is about my own child," Emer says.

Kathleen sighs, turning to Brigid. "Can you help the lad?"

"I can't," Brigid says. "He needs surgery."

"Emer says it's you what put it in him."

"Emer's upset," Brigid says calmly. "And not a little confused."

"There's been talk," Margaret says.

"About?"

"The baby, for one. Who really put it in you?"

"The baby is mine alone," Brigid says boldly. They mutter angrily to one another. Maeve looks her rudely up and down, as if disappointed by the news that she has no man to blame.

"Did you take our men? Was it you brought that storm?"

"I'd ask Emer about that."

"Emer," Kathleen sneers. "She's dodgy enough but she'd not drown her own husband."

"What reason would I have?"

"Maybe you wanted Austin gone. Wanted Rose to yourself," Kathleen says. "That's the other talk we've heard."

Brigid rolls her eyes at that, but Emer can see how frightened she is. Her normally proud shoulders are bent, curved in like the arms that hold on to her belly.

"What are you, some sort of lesbian?" Maeve asks. Two or three gasps from behind, at the concept or merely Maeve's knowledge of such a word, Emer can't be sure.

Brigid doesn't say anything at first, just looks right at Maeve, who flushes. Emer sees it again. How similar they are, the moments before violence and sex. How easily one could be mistaken for another.

"Wouldn't you like to know?" Brigid says then, bold as anything. She looks at Kathleen's hands. She is holding iron fireplace tongs by her side. Kathleen steps forward.

"Stop," Emer says. No one is more surprised than herself. They hold their breath, waiting for dispensation.

"I'll do it," she says. Kathleen gives her the tongs and walks back to the huddle of women.

Emer puts the tip into the depth of the fire, grasping a nugget of turf, an orange as deep and fierce as the only color left in her son's eyes. Brigid looks at her, curious, cold, with just a trace of how she once looked at her flickering at the edges of her mouth.

"I won't hurt you," Emer whispers into her ear, the fiery whorls of hair tickling her face. Amazing that in the middle of such terror she can feel that quiver, that weakening, of lust. "Just go to Niall now and I won't let them hurt you either."

"Emer," Brigid sighs, and Emer thinks of the ways Brigid has said her name, with breathless excitement, with humor, with tenderness. With love. Now, her name, two rigid syllables, is said with the same sickened resignation she has heard from everyone else.

"You can't hurt me," she adds quietly. But still, her hand reaches into her apron pocket to grip the island woman's knife.

That's when Emer puts the fire against her, the very same fire that has burned on that island for centuries, not to insert pain, but to give her something else. A story she was told over and over again, but never really heard.

THEY'RE COMING UP THE road, her brother says.

What will they do? Will they make me leave?

I don't know, Nuala.

Don't let them hurt me, Desi.

What happened? Why couldn't you save the baby?

I tried. The baby was already dead.

Desi looks at Nuala's hard, round belly and then turns back to the window.

Jesus, Desi says. *There's a lot of them.*

THE GIRL, NUALA, NEVER knew her mothers, fairy or human, or her father, or her orphaned siblings. All she ever had was her brother, Desmond, a boy who was also a man, because he needed to be, for her. They said he was simple. He couldn't read or write, had avoided school altogether, though he could do sums in his head that wool buyers double-checked on paper in disbelief. He loved the island, his dogs, the sea. He suffered people only when he had to, and then, when he was required to be around them, he looked like he was in physical pain. Women, especially, left him twitchy and mute. He couldn't look them in the eye. Men were willing to communicate in minimal grunts and grumbles over weather or the stubborn nature of sheep. He could stand in a field of men all day and never have to say a word. Women asked questions, demanded answers. Only his sister could talk to him, chatter on about whatever came into her head, because she didn't expect him to respond. Her voice was not the same violating noise in his ears. She belonged in his head, just like the wind and the sea.

When she was a baby he had carried her everywhere, strapped to his chest in an old flannel shawl of their mother's. She could remember snatches of this, how the weather, the rain and damp air and wind, couldn't penetrate. She could press her face against the fragrant wool at his chest and none of it could touch her. She was safer than she would ever be again in her life.

GO INTO THE BEDROOM, her brother says.

Don't answer it, Nuala says, stupidly. As if there is any way to bar an entrance with no lock.

They pound on the door, thuds that sound more like boots than fists. He shoves her toward the bedroom and she goes in without a lamp or candle, and stands within the rectangle of firelight that shines around the edges of the doorframe.

When no one answers their knock, the men throw the front door open and heave into the room, massive in their layers of wool, clumsy, like seals flopping themselves across the threshold.

Where's the girl, Des?

Leave her be. She's none of your concern.

I'd say she's my concern. That's my grandchild what she killed tonight.

She killed no one. She's only a girl herself.

She's a changeling is what she is.

You didn't mind who she was when it suited you so, says Desi, sounding like a man who talks back to bullies every day, instead of the brother who is afraid to ask for sugar in the shop.

Hold him, lads.

Desi's dog starts snarling then, and there is a scuffle and a canine yelp of pain and a man swearing and then the door is shut and Nuala knows the dog is outside, throwing itself against the door, with nothing to sink his teeth into. The baby flips inside her, painfully, as if it's trying to send a message. *Go,* it kicks, *before it is too late.*

HEALING THEM HAD BEEN the way she could make them not afraid of her. Her brother never understood why she bothered, the islanders had been suspicious of them since their mother's death and he was happy to leave it that way. He didn't have the same need as his sister; she needed their love. So she gave them her hands.

She'd always been able to heal her own childish scrapes and bruises, the broken limb of a dog, the burns on her brother from careless splatters of hot pitch while tarring the currach. When she started doing it for the other children, and then for the mothers in labor, she thought she could get love out of them. She felt it, whenever she pulled pain or fever away, along with it, like a gift, their love, clutching her for a moment before it released with the pain into the air. Her brother wanted no part of their neighbors' emotions, their anger and bitter gossip, their romances and feuds, their loyalty and love. Nuala wanted all of it. She gathered it like spilled sweets into the pockets of herself. She touched people not only to heal them but to feel for a moment all that life pulsing through them, love, hate, fear, regret, bliss.

She touched boys, then men. In the hay fields, at the shore, in the empty clocháns. She put her hands right where their want and anger and misery and hope gathered together and begged to be released. She pulled everything they had ever felt out of them, often thought she might shatter from the intensity of it gushing through her. With the men it required more, she had to lie down and let them push themselves inside her as deep as they could get, until they reached a place where she forgot everything except inviting them deeper. It wasn't forced or cruel or ugly, not to her, but what they wanted from her and what she was intending to give were two different things. The men knew it was wrong, even as she didn't. They had not been raised to believe that a girl should invite, or enjoy, such violation. They hated themselves, they confessed through a dark wood lattice to the priest, but went back to her willing hands again and again.

When she told her brother she was expecting a child, Desi didn't ask who it was from, which was a relief. It could have been any one of them, or all of them. He only asked if she'd been forced. When she said no, blushing, he asked nothing else. He got the family cradle out from the shed, the cradle that was said to have come from Saint Brigid herself, hand carved from the last of the island's oak, to soothe the babies of the women who ran to her, shamed, violated and alone. He polished it up and replaced the missing limpet shells, and she knew he would accept the baby with the same simple devotion he had shown to her. She couldn't wait to hold it. She felt as though she had fashioned it herself, this child, made it out of all the times her hands had grasped at love.

NUALA! DESI SCREAMS WHEN they have their hands on him.

She has a notion to climb out the tiny window, but is fumbling at the latch and thinking there is no way she will fit through it, when one of them enters the bedroom and pulls her roughly out by the arm.

Put your man in there. Keep him quiet.

How am I to do that?

You there, lad, go with him.

Two men drag her struggling brother into the bedroom and kick the door closed.

The men have taken over in the small room; the combined breath of them is making the air thick, fogging the windows. Men of every age, men she has lain down with and others who would never consider it. Boys, expected to be men even though their bodies and hearts have not caught up yet. Some of them can't look at her, others are looking at her way too hard.

What did you do to that baby?

It wasn't my doing, she says. Her voice is shaking, it sounds, even to her, like a desperate lie. *The child came out already dead. There was nothing I could heal.* This was only partly true. She hadn't tried. The child inside her had seized with such terror that she only pretended to use her hands. She couldn't sacrifice her own child.

Your woman says otherwise, the man says. She looks at him. She has seen this man's face warp in a way no one else but his wife has.

I wouldn't let a baby die.

We don't know what you are.

I'm no different than any of ye.

One of them is stirring the fire, breaking up the gray and orange logs, sinking the fire iron deep inside it to heat up. This fire never goes out, they bury it and revive it each morning, and have for as long as the house has been standing. Even their mother, the possessed, impostor mother, had never dared to douse the saint's fire.

Hold the iron against her.

If she heals it, she's the changeling and lying about the baby.
If she can't, she's nothing but a whore.

Neither of these options sounds reasonable or even bearable. There is a pause then, where she thinks perhaps one of them will laugh heartily and dismiss the entire business. She can hear the men in the bedroom with her brother, the sound it makes every time they knock his body back to the floor.

The first one to hold her down is a boy she once tugged at with her hands in a cave by the water until he cried relief into her hair. Now he cannot look her in the eyes. She pulls her mother's knife out of her pocket and slashes at him with it, but he grips and twists her wrist until she cries out and lets it go. He holds her arms behind her, driving his knees into the backs of hers to get her to drop to the floor. She can feel his terror, a slim hard threat pushed against her thigh.

Please, she says. *Please don't hurt my baby.*

Another man kneels down hard on her hair, jerking her neck back to stop that plea. They hold her on her side, her belly too big for her to lie on, and use her knife to rip at her dress back, splitting it easily down the seam. She can feel the fire coming off the hearth and off them for a whole lifetime before they actually bring the heated iron to her skin.

The first few times they burn her, Nuala can't stop herself from healing it. The men watch the skin rise up and knit itself back together, the welt of angry burn sinking into her back as if slipping into cool water. Once they see the wounds heal themselves, the fear of it is enough to make them want to burn her more. The boy continues to hold her down, and the way he holds her feels both like an embrace and an affront. Once he brushes a callused, nail-bitten hand across her breast and Nuala lets out a sob and calls to her brother and two men have to look away. It is more intimate, this scene of torture, than any act of lust or abandon they've participated in.

Desi howls through it all, held prisoner in the bedroom, sounding not much older than a child himself, crying her name and the name of their saint to have mercy on them.

The burning is meant to tell them something. But no one is clear about what to do with the answer so they just keep doing it, over and over again, until the burns no longer heal and her skin begins to act like it should.

You can't hurt me, Nuala says. *You can't hurt me, you can't hurt me. Not a one of you can hurt me.*

She stops healing herself. She turns inward, encasing her child with all the magic she has left, and lets them do it, lets them sear her with all the fear and doubt and misplaced lust they've ever had. This confuses them, they stop, there is a discussion about what to do. Keep going until they kill her? Apparently they've lost the stomach for that. They will wait instead, for the priest to advise them, an authority who can punish or banish her with the blessings of God himself. By the time they skulk away she is unconscious and her back is burned so deeply that in some places the bone shines through the blackened flesh. The last of them leaves with the morning, they do not have the courage to stay around and see if she will really die.

NUALA. IT'S ALL RIGHT, love. *They've gone now.*

   They didn't hurt me, Desi. They couldn't.

   Jesus, Nuala. Your back.

   It doesn't matter. The baby is safe.

   Her brother holds on to her as she closes the last of their wounds.

THE NEXT DAY NUALA is gone. Her brother never reveals how she got away, no boats had come or gone on the island, she disappeared during a day when the sea raged them into seclusion. Though there is talk of sending Desmond off as well, in the end they leave him alone. He has none of the power they fear and he keeps to himself. Some say Nuala threw herself over the cliff, others that she went back under the ground to where the fairy impostor came from.

She is never seen, or heard from, on the island again.

BRIGID DOUBLES OVER WITH the weight of this story, this fairy tale that Emer inserts with fire under her skin. The very same fire.

You were here before, it whispers. *Your mother was born in the doorway between two worlds. You began here, you belong to us. We will not allow you to get away.*

The air in the cottage is filled with the odor of what she has seen, the smell of fear and turf and blistered skin. It takes her a moment to realize that it is the wound on her back, where Emer has held the nugget of turf, that smells. It doesn't hurt yet. The women have not moved toward Brigid. They are muttering to one another in Irish.

We should have known. She's her mother all over again.

Hold the fire against her. 'Tis the only way to know.

Let Emer do it.

If Emer were any use, she'd have it finished by now.

Emer's right. She stole that child. Stole our men. She'd let the boy die.

Brigid knows what to do. It's an effort to fight it, to refuse to heal herself, but Emer, by giving her that story, has just shown her how to protect the baby. She had the ability all along. She takes what is in her hands and turns it inward, folds it like blessed fabric around her child. She does not keep any of it for herself.

"You can't hurt me," Brigid says to them all, without thinking, in Irish. This doesn't help her. They look angry at the very cheek of it, this impostor using their language. They move in, swarming her, pulling at her apron, her hair, their hands are pleas and punishment, raking her for answers. Maeve, who has imagined more than once a woman's hands beneath her clothes, is the first to reach for the tongs from Emer, intending to press fire into her back. She uses them to knock the knife out of Brigid's hand.

None of them has noticed the brightening.

When Rose bursts into the cottage to tell them the sky has lifted and they are no longer prisoners, they reel away from their tight circle. Maeve drops her hold on Brigid like a guilty boy with a stone. Brigid is left lying like a child by the hearth.

"What have you done?" Rose hisses. They don't know themselves.

"The boats are here," Rose says. "They've come to take Niall to hospital." All the women but Emer slip away out the door, her grip on their minds gone now, looking as horrified by the appearance of dawn light as they are at what they were about to do. Rose looks at Emer then, as if she might be able to explain it. Emer looks back at her sister, wide-eyed and pleading as a child, for another answer.

"Rose?" Emer says. "Why did you leave him alone?"

"Shame on you," Rose says cruelly. And she pushes Emer, who is left with the cooling fire iron, out of the way.

Rose kneels on the floor and gathers Brigid into her arms. She rocks her back and forth and whispers that she need not be afraid as Brigid sobs.

The dog has keened through it all, locked in the bedroom, she howls like a newborn left wet and alone. A cry that is relentless and piercing, with no intention of letting up until it is given what it wants.

Emer backs away, her lack of peripheral vision causing her to knock down one of the kitchen chairs. Her head sings with unbearable noise. She does not belong here. Not with these women, her sister, her lover, not in this house. Not in this world. She should be with Niall. She was distracted by the thought that someone else could save him. She is the only one who knows how. She never should have let go of her life's only vigilance for the time it took to wonder if it was enough.

Emer pulls herself out the door and hurries toward the place where they have already stolen her child.

CHAPTER 25

Ceili

Niall is on an island.

It isn't his island, or Brigid's or Rose's or his mother's island, though it is similar. It is a place where every road has two lanes, one trampled by people and sheep and cattle and children, and the other by something else. It is raining here, but at the same time it is sunny, you can feel the warmth dry the drops on your face even as they fall. There is always a rainbow. It doesn't look like something you would want to wish upon.

He thinks there is no one here, but then he sees they are all gathered together, having a ceili around a bonfire. They have lit it on the promontory over the port, the place known as the children's graveyard. As if the celebration itself is an emergency.

Everyone he knows is there, even the men who went on ahead of them into the storm. Austin is playing music and he looks terrible, he hasn't shaved and his eyes are rimmed with red and he can barely get a breath in between all the blowing. He tries to take the whistle away and say something, but nothing comes out. He goes back to the instrument. He has no voice. He looks, Niall thinks, like something else is making him play that whistle. The party has been going on too long.

His cousins are dancing. The little ones cry out about how their feet hurt, but Fiona and Eve cannot stop to help. Niall's dead father comes up to him, soaked to the skin, his trousers dripping puddles into the squelchy ground. "The arms are hanging off me after that row," he says. "Would you put a pint on for your father?"

"I would, of course," Niall says, but he's not sure how to do this. Everyone seems to be drinking, but the source of it is not clear. When he turns back to ask his father, he sees the man fumbling with his sleeve. He's having trouble with his arm. It seems to be falling off. Niall turns away.

Brigid is there. She is holding his newest cousins, the babies, the fat one and the little elf, and they are nursing from her, latched tight to her breasts. He stares too long at the enormous, dark curve over her nipples and feels his face growing hot with shame. It seems like he's remembering something and looking forward to something at the same time. She lets go of the babies, using both of her hands to receive an overflowing drink from someone. The babies stay put, hanging on by their mouths.

Rose is dancing, spinning, laughing, her hair loose and lifting into the air like something trying to fly away. She has a knife in her hand. She is slicing some enormous fruit, he can't tell what, and feeding it straight into people's lips. She twirls over to her husband and straddles him, laughing and riding him like a child playing at horses. Austin cannot stop whistling long enough to receive the dripping piece she offers.

The good people are everywhere, but they are not the strangers he expected. They are his neighbors, his cousins, his auntie and his grandmother. There are no small fairies leading them maniacally around by a leash. There is no one here, except for Brigid, whom he has not known for his entire life.

He cannot find his mother. There was a time when he truly be-lieved that they were one person, tethered by an invisible but un-breakable twine, a band that led from her neck, that pulled him back if he wandered even an inch too far. If her head ached, he knew it, if her neck tightened, he pulled at his own collar. If she took someone's hand and poisoned them he felt as if he had just emptied himself. When that thing that looked like Austin was on top of her, he knew it was inside her as well. He had felt it, it punctured be-tween his legs and pried, splitting them both in two.

But now he cannot find her, and it is worse than what has been happening lately, where he turns and sees her and she looks like someone he can't remember, not the woman whose love he has always been sure of, but someone he is wary of approaching at all.

The fire is massive; they are burning the whole island in it. Fur-niture, clothing, doors, cradles, carts, the plow, anything that might ignite has been thrown into the pyre. The islanders are ripping the clothing off their backs and cheering when it is caught up and con-sumed.

He sees the women who row the boat carrying lighted torches and climbing down the pathway to the slip. They untie the currachs and touch fire to them, launching them to burn on top of the sea. Saint Brigid did that, long ago, once she was settled there, sent all the boats away, set them on fire so no one would ever be able to leave. He will tell his mother this, when he finds her. She will not be amused.

He moves through the spinning bodies of islanders and every once in a while they catch his arm and turn him around, cheering when he gives in to the instinctive tap and shuffle of his feet. He doesn't want to dance, or swallow the dripping fruit that is being passed around, or kiss in the way they all seem to be, opening their mouths like they are feeding on each other. All he wants is to find his mother; he won't accept a morsel until she tells him he can have it. He wants to be small enough to fit in her lap again, and drink from the very heart of her, milk that, if he closes his eyes and remembers, he can still taste. Warmer and sweeter than the tea that replaced it.

He spins through the crowd and something starts to change, the sky grows dark, the fire climbs, the faces around him seep with shadows that look like spilled ink. Their features warp and twist from familiar to vicious and unrecognizable. Their voices are all wrong, high pitched, frantic, like impatient birds. The women are naked and have babies, half-formed and horrible, growing out of them, a head between two breasts, a foot protruding from an abdomen, a tiny, wizened hand reaching out of someone's neck. He tries to scream, break free of the whirling crowd, but he has no voice. It's because he can't find his mother, she is holding his voice hostage, it's why she always puts her hand there, to her throat, as if she is checking on something she has swallowed and is not about to let it come back up. His mother has stolen his voice, his heart, his feet. He cannot join in anything until she gives it all back.

Then he sees her, she is on the other side of the fire. She looks so miserable, so lonely, so much like she has always looked, no matter how hard he tries to pull it away. He knows, he has known for a while now, that no matter how many times he kisses or hugs her or pulls a palm across the screwed-up skin of her forehead, it will never be enough. She's too vigilant, she always has been, she will never let go of the fear of losing him long enough to actually take him in her arms.

He fights his way through the mob of dancing creatures, trying not to look as they grow more and more deformed. Brigid moves in front of him. She no longer has Rose's babies attached, she is moaning, she grabs his arm, lowers herself to a squat. Her colossal belly is transparent, and inside, coiled and writhing, is an atrocious pig.

Niall pulls his arm away and stumbles backward, right through the corner of the fire. He gets within the range of his mother's limited vision, coming upon her from the right so she will be able to see him with her only eye.

She spots him and for an instant she looks delighted, he has never seen her look so overjoyed, and he reaches out a hand to clasp the one she is raising to pull him in. She is holding something in front of her.

She is offering him something to drink.

CHAPTER 26

Stones

When Emer gets there, his breath has just gone.

The doctor leans over him, listening at his mouth, pounding his chest, then putting his loose, foul lips over the sweet mouth of her child and blowing so hard his chest rises.

She tries to go to him, to knock the doctor back, the doctor who appears to be devouring her son's face, but someone stops her with a clawed hand on her arm.

"'Tis the breath of life, sure," her mother reassures her. Emer remembers that doctor's breath, so sharp it's like he's breathing petrol.

"Why are you doing that?" Emer says. "Aren't you taking him to hospital?" The doctor doesn't even look at her but puts his cheek down, gentle as a mother, onto the warm pillow of Niall's chest. Listening. Emer and Niall do this in her bed, taking turns, she listening for Niall's heart, he listening for hers. *Mo chroí*, they whisper, my heart. It is one of their games.

The house is filled with people, island women, men from Muruch and the mainland, every one of them has at one time felt the bitterness that rises up from Emer's heart and pools like sweat in the palms of her hands. Everyone goes still, hushes, as if their silence will create the sound the doctor is hoping for. Not a breath comes to them for one beat, two beats, three. The doctor's head rises, lowers, pauses, and then gives up and lifts again. He shakes his head. A collective island gasp and click of the palate, a sound that means surprise, anger, remorse and disapproval all in one. They all gasp and Emer begins to scream.

She tries it herself, before they pull her away. Puts her hands on him, her cruel hands that have only ever touched him with love, presses his heart, kisses his mouth, keens into the warm dirty hollow of his ear. She puts a hand under his nightshirt, to feel the familiar warmth of his back. Only his back is not warm. Not cold exactly, but no temperature at all. She is shaking his body, insisting he answer her, and then she is pulled away, her grip pried off, familiar voices speaking nonsense about collecting herself. The priest comes in with his vial of oil to administer the last rites.

"He's not in there," she says to them, lashing out with the hands they cower away from even as they try to hold her down.

"That's not my son. They've taken him."

LATER, AFTER A TABLET and the pit of sleep where she can hear everything but say nothing, Rose is with her again, looking as if nothing has happened.

"Where's Niall?" Emer says, and Rose winces.

"Where's Brigid, then?"

"She's with the doctor."

"She has to come for Niall. Put her hands on him."

"She did, Emer."

"She didn't. I've been waiting."

"I watched her do it myself. It didn't do any good."

"Where is my boy?" she asks again, and this time Rose answers her.

"He's laid out on the table, Emer."

"We'll sit up tonight, Rose. We'll wait for him to come in and we'll snatch him back. He knows better than to eat with them. They won't be able to hold on. We'll wait here and he'll come. He will."

"Emer, love," Rose says. She has to look away from Rose's face. There is too much in there, she wants to slash at it. But she needs her sister to wait with her.

"You'll stay and watch over him with me?" Emer says.

Rose gives her another tablet, and Emer takes it because sleep seems more welcome than life ever has to her.

"You'll wake me with the moon, won't you, Rose?"

"I will, Emer. Hush now."

"Don't leave him alone. We don't want them stealing the body as well."

"I won't, Emer. I won't leave you alone."

IN THE MIDDLE OF the night, Emer gets up and sits by the table where they have laid out the small, still body of her son. His face has been leached of color, like someone has made a mold of him and left the outer layer unpainted. In the candlelight she can deceive herself into seeing rosy cheeks and a red mouth still moist with breathing and she can almost imagine she is waiting for him to wake up. That she is stealing the few, sweet moments she gets watching him sleep. How still he is in sleep, often it is a relief to her, after a long wet day alone in the house, to feel the moment he switches, from a twitchy, talkative boy to a gently breathing pile upon the bedclothes. She regrets that now. That wanting of stillness. She would slash herself to the bone for the chance to never watch him sleep again.

Rose sits with her for a while, the older girls left with the babies, but she keeps leaking milk and fussing around and asking if Emer needs anything and finally Emer sends her away. She prefers to be alone in the moment he comes back through the door.

The story that is going around in her head is this:

A woman died in childbirth, but a fairy told her husband she was only snatched, and if he waited up by her body in the moonlight he could take her back. So he waited, his wife's body laid out on one side of him, the cradle with the newborn baby and a set of tongs across the rim on the other. In the night, her spirit came in the door, and moved to peek in the cradle. When she did, he threw some holy water at her and grabbed her by the wrists and held on and wouldn't let go, the baby shrieking like a storm the whole time. She fell back into her body then, the spell broken, and sat up to soothe the baby at her leaking breasts.

Emer waits for her son to come through the door, so she can grab onto him so tight she can squeeze away death, and never, for the rest of her days, let go of him again.

"EMER, COME TO BED."

"I'm waiting, Rose."

"You're asleep on your feet, pet."

"I'll wait for him to come back to me."

"Emer, you'll be waiting a lifetime. He's gone, love."

"I'll wait regardless."

NOTHING THE FIRST NIGHT. During the day the islanders file in to weep and speak in low tones and kiss him until she wants to chase them all out with the broom. A second night of waiting. Her body has never done anything so precisely determined in her life. She waits with every cell and fiber of her flesh. She waits, burning up with it, slowly consumed by every moment he doesn't come, like a sod of turf eaten by fire. By the end there is nothing left of her. You could blow at her and she'd scatter, like the ash of a fire let to go out.

ON THE THIRD MORNING there is a row over whether to bury him. The priest has come over for it, bringing a small coffin from the mainland, and Emer bars the door with a cupboard. The men have to break through, knocking over the press she pinned against the door, all the delph crashing into shards on the stone floor. They grab on to her, screaming and writhing and electrified with pure sorrow. A few of the men who take turns holding her end up getting sick outside. No man or woman who touches Emer that day will ever forget the vileness that emerges, wave after wave of it, like a hive of evil broken open and raging with revenge.

In the end, the doctor has to give her a shot and she is not there when they bury her child.

ROSE CANNOT WATCH AS they say their prayers and begin to shovel wet earth onto the absurdly small coffin. She turns and walks away to soothe Wee Emer, who is squawking in her arms. This is the fussiest child she has ever had; she wants to be held twenty-four hours a day. The baby's cries and the wind almost drown out the vicious sound of wet earth on wood. The graveyard stands just above the quay, on the jutting circle of land where they burn their signal bonfires. Mostly it's children who are here, jagged purplish stone marking the graves of babies and toddlers from a time when women had so many and lost most of them. They say children never died when Saint Brigid was here, but when she was gone, the families that were left lost them, one after the other, to typhoid, tetanus, smallpox.

Siblings who never met nestled together under rough gray stone. Children don't die as often nowadays. Rose can't imagine that even when it was common, it was any less of a blasphemy. The first thing you see when you row a boat to this island is all the children who have already gone.

CHAPTER 27

Currach

Brigid sits very still, holding the mound of her belly as the doctor listens to it with a stethoscope.

"What's all this talk now, of burning and witches?"

"Just Emer panicking. She was out of her senses with the boy ill." Dying, she corrects herself, he was dying. She mustn't think of it. She must keep this from splitting her apart at the seams. The only way she can help Niall now is to leave.

"I heard the women called up to you."

"Not at all."

The doctor raises a weedy eyebrow and looks around. The floor is still a wreck of muddy treads, and the place reeks of something burned, meat that has gone off but is cooked nonetheless.

Brigid's back has healed. It smoothed itself as soon as Emer turned away. Emer is too grief-stricken to hurt her anymore. But she is going anyway.

"They burned your mother, they say. They're a superstitious lot."

"I'd like to go back to the mainland," Brigid says. "I'll get a lift to Galway from there."

"We can call in to the guards. Have charges brought against them. There's a smell of burned flesh in here that would sicken you."

"They did nothing. I want to have my baby in the hospital, is all. I'm afraid of what might happen out here."

"And you the midwife. Didn't you insist I wasn't needed?"

"I've changed my mind."

"After all your talk of staying you'll go as soon as it suits you."

"I didn't know," Brigid says.

"Didn't know that a boy could die with nothing but a fire calling for help? It's pathetic."

"What's pathetic," Brigid says, "is that they weren't given a telephone. Or a radio."

"So they could send a distress signal and still wait for the sea to swallow their boats? Don't be daft, woman. They should take the land being offered to them and be done with this rock. The government isn't to blame. The sea will do what it likes. It always has. At least they've a choice. Not like some."

He stops when he sees that Brigid is shaking so hard her pretty white teeth are rattling in her head.

"I'll take you across," he says. "Are you sure you don't want to stop at the guards in town?"

"Positive."

"I'll have some of the lads up to carry your things."

"There's no need," Brigid says, her voice quavering. She sounds more like an islander than ever. "I'm leaving it to the birds."

SHE CONSIDERS BRINGING THE cradle. Whether it was hand-carved by a saint or an ancestor doesn't matter; it was where her mother and grandmother were laid, where Brigid herself would have slept if her mother had been let to stay.

The man who held on to them both in that lighthouse was not

her father after all. He was just a man her mother asked to save her, whom she couldn't leave. Brigid can see why now. Nuala confused violence with love. She thought she only had magic enough for one life-changing swim across the sea. And she didn't want to run anymore.

She leaves the cradle behind, in plain sight in the bedroom for whoever dares to steal it. She won't need it. This baby will sleep in her arms.

ROSE COMES ONCE MORE, to the house, leaving Emer asleep and the body of Niall, bathed by island women, in the newly turned ground.

"How is she?" Brigid asks. Rose can't even say it, holds a hand to her mouth to keep from spitting out a wail.

"I'm so sorry," Brigid says. They are silent for a while, while Rose makes tea. Nothing is so unbearable that they won't stop to make tea.

"When I think of what they did to you," Rose says when the tea is poured, "it makes me sick it does."

"They were afraid."

"Did you heal yourself? The way your mother could?"

"Something like that."

"You couldn't heal Niall."

Some part of Brigid feels like she is not even there. She is standing on the edge of the cliffs, screaming all her terror and remorse into the wind. She has been there too many times before.

"No."

"Does it make you a witch, then?"

"It's only what I am. Same as Emer. Doesn't amount to much in the end."

"Where will you have the baby?"

"I don't know. Somewhere safe."

"Where's that?"

"I'm wondering myself."

"We won't stay here, anyways. Emer was right about that. Sure it won't be much comfort to her now."

"You'll miss it."

"Every day of my life, I suspect. Not as much ..." but she doesn't finish, though they both say the words in their minds.

Not as much as you'd miss a child.

Rose pours the tea into the two stained mugs Brigid has always thought of as hers and Emer's.

"She's nothing without him," Rose says.

"She'll have to be. You'll keep an eye on her."

"I will. I will, of course."

THEY LEAVE IN THE early morning, the sun still crawling its way above the mountains on the mainland. Brigid stops at the grave-yard, finds the disturbed spot, lets the wet of it seep into her knees, staining them the color of bog.

The doctor has summoned Muruch men to come collect them, the women with whom she learned to row will not be there to see her off.

"I'm bringing the dog with me," Brigid says to the doctor at the quay.

"Have you taken leave of your senses, woman?"

"I can't leave her behind."

"You can't take a dog like that off the island. It'll be chasing cars and get itself killed."

"I won't go without her."

"Jesus, you Yanks. The notion. You're after being persecuted and all you care about is that bleeding animal. It's yourself and that baby you should be thinking of now."

"I can think of more than one thing at a time."

He cocks his head, lets air gust through his teeth.

"Fair enough," he sighs. "Put a rope on the thing at least."

At the quay the dog hesitates, pulling away from her.

"Rua?" she says. The dog sits obediently and looks up. She puts the rope over her neck and pulls on it, but she doesn't budge. It's as if the rope or the future has frozen her in place. Brigid yanks harder and says "come," trying to sound firm. Rua looks penitent, but still won't budge. Something opens up in Brigid, something she imagines could swallow her whole.

"Rua," she says softly, trying not to cry. She feels as close to feral, incessant tears as a girl. A girl who hasn't learned to deter them yet. She crouches down, and whispers, begs, to something more than just the dog.

"If you want to be with us, you need to get in the boat." There is a pause where she thinks Rua will deny her and she won't have an idea what to do next. She does not know if she will ever be let back here to retrieve her. Then the dog sighs, stands up and walks to the lip of the quay, where she allows herself, with as much dignity as she can muster, to be lifted and placed kindly into the belly of the currach.

She holds on to the dog the whole trip. With her scarf pulled over her head in a protective veil and her face pressed into warm fur, she barely sees the green rock of the island moving away. Of her leaving, she will remember only the hiss of the oars, the list and promise of the boat as it moves over the sea.

CHAPTER 28

Vigil

February, March 1960

While she is sleeping, her son is still alive. She struggles to stay down beneath it, under the ground that is her slumber, where she can still smell him. He fills her nostrils first, then she can feel his body warm and wiggly and so tall he has to fold himself to fit in her lap. She holds tight, inhales, and he murmurs to her in Irish. *A chuisle mo chroí.* You are the pulse of my heart. His voice comes out all wrong, it is the graveled voice of an old man. It shocks her awake, he is ripped away, and all she can smell is the bread Rose brought going stale under a towel, the damp that lives on everything, the turf smoke backing up from the quiet chimney. All the odors of her life, choking her.

For the first few days she believed he would come back in. That a shadow of him, a Niall-shaped light, would come in to look at her while she was sitting up with his body and she would be able to snatch him back. That her greatest fear, her son stolen, has finally occurred, and she only needs to believe in his being returned to her. That he will get away, just as she told him how, just as she did, and come home.

But after they bury him, she knows that she shouldn't have worried about him being stolen. That wasn't anywhere near the worst thing, not at all. She was so afraid of him being stolen by fairies it had never occurred to her that his life, like anyone else's, could simply end. That, like all those children before him, he would die.

When she hears about Brigid leaving, she is livid, raging until she falls upon her bed and cries like a disappointed girl. At all the things she should have said, so that none of it would have happened. She spends most of her time now spinning it all in her head, changing what she did so the direction shifts and she saves her son. The night with Austin, the cursing stone, lying down with Brigid on her bed. Bringing the women into Brigid's home to burn her. Take away all of them, any of them, and fate could be reshuffled so he is not doomed.

Now of course she wants Austin's baby back. Wants it as fiercely as she wants her son to be alive. She didn't realize until now that the baby that Austin put in her was part of Niall as well.

She thinks often now of the way her mother sat by the fire after her son died, as if there was no life in her, as if she were already dead but her body still insisted on beating her heart and filling her lungs. Emer feels like this now. Buried inside herself but with skin so warm and flushed and healthy it insults her to be inside of it. She drugs herself to sleep only to have her child returned and taken away all over again.

Emer's neck doesn't plague her anymore. There is no pressure there, no threat; her breath comes in and out so easily it is offensive. There is nothing left for her to be afraid of.

She sleeps through the springtime. She is in Rose's house now, on the hearth bed. Rose puts her there on purpose, so Emer is forced to be aware of life going on around her as she lies like an invalid in the corner. Tea is set beside her, a bun, a bowl of spuds with new butter. Sometimes she sits up to eat, often she does not.

The weather barely lifts. The plans for evacuation seem to be di-

vided between a voice for leaving at the beginning of the summer
and those who want to stay to the end. They decide to abandon the
sowing they've started and get it over with. None of them wants to
be lulled into optimism by another glorious summer. In years to
come, they will talk as if this island was a paradise, but the truth
was, to live there required faith, courage and sheer stupid luck. As
well as the knowledge that all of them might fail you.

The bees, Fiona and Eve report before Rose can shush them,
Brigid's bees are awake again. They are busy making babies and
comb and honey, but there is no one left who dares to approach
them and pilfer a cup of sweetness from their home.

On the handful of days that give them a reprieve, Rose forces
Emer to sit on a stool in the sun, her back propped against the stone
wall of the house. The sunlight is insulting and she soon crawls back
inside, where it remains damp and cool and dark no matter what.

They won't leave her alone. Either Rose is there, or the other
women, or worse, her own mother like a carcass of disappointment
wrapped in a woolen shawl. She can't even look at her, her mother,
with her cruel, satisfied face, as if she is glad that this new generation has finally lost something. Emer would like to blame her for it
all, but she barely has the energy to keep upright in her chair. She
begs for sleep, deep and blackened sleep, and barely swims to the
surface to open her eyes, see that nothing has changed, and close
them again. She doesn't dream of him now. Only when she is first
awake, the split second before she opens her eyes, like when you're
sleeping in a strange bed but have forgotten and are expecting the
particular view from yours, does her heart leap, first in hope, then
plunge down again, so hard she thinks it will stop altogether. But
it doesn't, so she must roll over to a cooler spot on her pillow and
listen to the same wind and rain she's heard all her life, flinging at
the windows like a child in a tantrum, and dig her way back down
into the underworld beneath her consciousness. ·

After they have all gone to bed, when the house is dark and silent, she rises and sits by the glowing fire. She doesn't bother to try the door, padlocked from the inside by Rose who sleeps with the key. She sits for hours, her head aching and swimming with the effort of being upright, watching the fire as it slowly burns into the earth, trying with all its might to stay lit. She sits and pokes the fire and waits. She hasn't given up on him, but he never comes.

SHE FOOLS THE GIRLS in the end. Fiona and Eve, dumbed by grief themselves, are told to run after their mammy if they see Emer get up. She waits until Fiona goes out to milk the cows. Her mother is napping with the babies. Teresa and Bernie are minding the toddlers by the shore. She moves silently, getting her clothes on, not bothering with shoes, and puts a finger to her lips to signal Eve that she shouldn't say a thing.

"I'm to tell Mam when you wake up."

"I'm only going to get your mother. Which way is she?"

Eve, as gullible as Rose before her, looks relieved and says her mother has gone to move the sheep to the back field. Fiona would be more vigilant.

"I'll meet her on the road," Emer says. "Wait here, child, and wet the tea."

Emer walks the other way, unsteady on legs that haven't held her up in a fortnight. The wind has gone; the island is preternaturally calm, as if the whole place is listening. The fog is close; she can't see the next house on the road, let alone the mainland. Emer slips into the fog easily, following the green road at her feet, and no one comes after her.

She walks toward Brigid's house, meeting no one, not even a dog. She wonders where they all are, then remembers it is Sunday, and in sea this calm they'll have gone over to Mass before the fog.

The fog will keep them now. For all she knows it is only herself and Rose and the girls on the island, the rest of them meeting with the priest and the government official about the evacuation. She overheard something, stretches of conversation floated into her as she lay, heavy as a stone in her bed. Plans that once would have left her jubilant with success. She won't be going with them.

At Brigid's house the door opens without resistance and she slips inside. It still smells of her, and of the dog. Emer heard she took the dog with her, tying a rope to its neck and dragging it into a boat. The priest had spoken of it, of how the doctor was annoyed but Brigid had insisted. She loved that stupid creature as if it were her own child and not a dog at all.

Brigid has left the house as if she had merely gone for a walk. There are dirty dishes in the basin. A pair of knickers on the floor of the bedroom. The fire has burned without disturbance into ghost ash still holding the form of turf sods. She left the same way others left before her. Some tidied like they were merely going on holiday, others dropped it all where they stood and ran. If they were able to return, their lives would still be there for them. If not, what was the use of any of it? On the mainland, things could be procured easily, there were shops and post offices and trains and buses and butchers, and no need for the things you desperately hoarded on a remote island. There'd be nothing you couldn't replace if you wanted it dearly enough.

There is nothing here that Emer needs. A book of Yeats's poetry lies by her bedside, scraps of paper marking multiple pages. Emer flicks through bright clothing, sticks her finger into the face cream that Brigid once smoothed onto Emer's lips, which were chapped and happy from a long, brutal session of kissing.

She never should have left him alone. Not for an instant. Not to seduce his uncle, not to drown his father, not to come to this house and plunge herself into the body of another woman. She shouldn't have left him to milk the cows. All those moments she stole away from him were now stolen from her. In one of them, in any one of those thieving moments, she might have been let to keep him.

She lies down on Brigid's soft bed. She wants to sleep again. Sleep and sleep until her body forgets how to wake up. Except the problem is it keeps remembering. And will every day for the rest of her life. Which seems so unbearably long and yet empty, like an enormous sea with no land to row toward. The bed doesn't work, every time she wakes up it seems bigger, all this emptiness, than it did before. So she makes her legs stand up, weak and heavy as if the whole of her is a vessel filled with stone, and leaves by the back door and climbs through grass and bracken, so steep that every few moments she must grab on to a rock the color of jutting bone and pull herself forward.

SHE ALMOST MAKES IT to the top before Rose ruins it all. Huffing her way up the cliffs from the other side, calling Emer's name like a curse. Emer briefly hopes the fog will disguise her, but then Rose is there, her hand is on Emer's wrist, as tight and strong and full of hope as it was when she was a girl. As if she hasn't in all that time learned any better, doesn't know that faith will get her nowhere.

"Will you never leave me be, Rose," Emer says.

"You're soaked to the bone with the mist. You need the fire, so you do. And a cup of tea."

"I'll drown in any more tea," Emer barks. "Let go of my arm."

They struggle a bit, but Rose has always been stronger, and is immune to the hands that fill everyone else with hopelessness. Emer sinks exhausted to the wet ground. All she can hear is her angry breathing, and Rose's breath, which is determined and smooth.

"I won't let go of you," Rose says. "Not in your lifetime."

"You've no right."

"You're my sister."

"I AM NOTHING!" Emer screams, which startles Rose, but not enough to make her let go. "He was the only good in me and now he's gone."

"We'll leave the island, Emer. We'll start over. You'll have another child."

"I don't want one. And you don't want to leave."

"I don't mind, so long as we're together."

"I killed Austin."

"Ah, stop it, Emer."

"And Patch."

"That's enough. You didn't either."

"I did, Rose. I went to the cursing stone to get rid of Austin's baby."

Rose blinks, fine mist on her lashes. As if she can blink away anything that she does not want to see.

"Then it was Austin's fault," Rose says. "You didn't mean to. You didn't mean any of it."

"I did. I meant every bit. There's a terrible thing in me, Rose. A dark thing. Any love that was in me died with him."

"That's fear, Emer, nothing else. You've been scared witless for ages. Even as a girl, you were afraid of everything. Afraid of love."

The strength of Rose's grip weakens, enough for Emer to stand and wrench free, pushing toward the wind, the diving birds, the merciless rock and sea. Rose dives after her, holding on to her leg like a stubborn toddler.

"Take me over so. Orphan my children."

"Oh, for fuck's sake, Rose, let go!"

Rose gives a great yank and Emer falls, scraping her cheek on a stone, her face soaked by the wet grass and the onslaught of tears. Rose slides up to her and lays her whole self, heavy with milk and a lifetime of vigilant cheer, on top of Emer, like a wet woolen blanket, like the earth, like Austin, or Brigid, or Patch but with more desire, more loyalty, more regret, than all three of them put together.

Rose whispers, as angry as she gets which is still, underneath, kinder than it should be. "You'll break my heart so you will."

And Emer knows this is true, even as she is enraged by it. That somehow it won't be Austin drowning or Brigid leaving or her children going to America or her nephew dying right in front of her, but her sister, who she's held on to all this time, her sister going over that cliff will be the thing that breaks Rose. That she loves wretched Emer more than the lot of them. A miracle. Blasphemous, but a miracle nonetheless.

"How will I go on without him?" she croaks.

"Emer," Rose says, all semblance of optimism gone. "He was never yours to begin with."

Emer keens then, cries into the damp cushion of ground, into the yielding body of her twin. She wants to cry her life out. She won't even come close.

"I hate you, Rose," Emer says. And that's when Rose says something so manipulative and cruel that Emer knows they are related after all. And it works.

"If you take your own life, you'll go straight to hell. How will you ever see him then?"

CHAPTER 29

Birth

April 1960

One night, when the days have gotten so long it is nine o'clock before the purple leaves the sky, Emer, waiting by the fire, doesn't turn or start when she hears the door creak open behind her. It is not Niall but Brigid who steps into the light of the hearth. Emer has spent so much time sleeping, her dreams bleed into waking life with ease. She thinks this is another dream.

Brigid is in labor. She is pacing the room, grunting, one hand below her massive belly, the other pressing her lower back, stopping to squat and moan. Her movements and noises are crude, feral, like an animal, a cow giving birth in a field rather than a woman in a house.

"Emer," she pants between pains, and to Emer it is a breath of memory, Brigid lying beneath her and crying her name. "Emer, help me."

And though if she came to Emer in the daytime, in the world, Emer might scratch her eyes out, right now she does the only thing she can. Brigid holds her hand out and Emer takes it.

She leads her out the back door, not into the dark island night, but into a corridor. They walk on cold floors and enter a room full of women laboring, separated by linen partitions, so they each have a hell of their own. Nuns move back and forth in white habits, their faces pinched and void of emotion. The collective moan is deafening. It is the hospital on the mainland where she had Niall.

"In here," Brigid says, and she pulls Emer through a door into a white chamber with round brick walls, a spiral metal staircase in the middle leading up to a revolving light. A small oval window looks out on a violent sea.

"Where are we?" Emer asks.

There is a single bed with a metal frame and Brigid grabs hold of it and squats again. This time she screams. She is so drenched with sweat it looks as though she has gone swimming in her nightgown. Her features are distorted with fear and pain.

"Emer," she pants, when she can. "You'll need to catch the baby."

"I'll get a nun," Emer says.

"No," Brigid says. "They want to gie me the gas. I need you to do it."

"You can't have your baby in a lighthouse," Emer says. She almost laughs at how ridiculous this sounds.

"Please, Emer." Her breath is quickening again, her short break is over, another pain rising in her like a lethal wave.

"I can't! My hands. I'll hurt the baby."

Brigid roars this time, head back, hair dark and tangled, she howls toward the sky. She looks like some old druid warrior, queens who birthed babies standing in their castle bedrooms and then ran downstairs with their swords to join the fight.

"Now, Emer!" she thunders, and Emer darts forward. Brigid is lying half on the bed, her feet on the floor, her legs spread, thighs trembling from the effort. Emer lifts her nightgown and crouches in front of that dark, deep cavern between her legs and as Brigid screams again, screams like she's being murdered, a glistening wet mound slides out into Emer's waiting hands.

"It's in the caul," Emer whispers, and Brigid slumps onto the mattress, gulping for breath and sobbing and reaching out all at once. Emer lifts the silver sac, warm, jiggling like a jellyfish she has picked up from the sand, and hands it to Brigid. Brigid tears it open with her finger, liquid gushes out, and she peels the veil away from the tranquil face of a sleeping baby.

Not Niall. Not a monster or a saint or a changeling. Just a newborn baby, like any other. Except to Brigid, who looks at it as if it is a marvel.

Brigid lies back on the bed, wiping at the baby's face with her nightgown, pulling its arms and legs out of the pouch where it has grown. It's a girl. Brigid is crying and laughing at the same time. The baby breathes, opens its eyes, looks intently at her mother, then to Emer, as if waiting for instructions.

"Thank you," Brigid whispers, and Emer, who has no rage left, only regret, leans over and kisses her lover gently on her full, smiling mouth. She puts her hand out and cups the warm little head, so warm it is like she is made of soft skin and fire. She can hardly believe that Niall's head was once this size, that it fit so delicately in the palm of her cursed hand. That he was, however briefly, hers.

"Isn't she beautiful?" Brigid whispers.

Just before she wakes, sweaty and panting from the strange and vivid dream, Brigid wraps the silver mantle, the womb that was lent to her, in a piece of blue flannel, and gives it to Emer like a gift.

"There's no one left to save," Emer says.

"There's you," Brigid whispers. And then she is gone.

EMER WAKES IN BED, realizing she fell asleep before ever getting up to go to the fire at all. She peels back the blankets and looks around, but there is nothing, only damp sheets left from her thrashing, and a fierce hunger like she hasn't had in weeks. She eats the dinner Rose left for her and boils and eats six eggs, one after the other, spooning them hot and runny straight into her ravenous mouth. When her mother and Rose wake up, they find that Emer has made the tea and a loaf and already gone to the hens to replace the eggs she stole in the nighttime.

"You're up, so you are," their mother slurs.

"For all it's worth," Emer counters.

"You were always a keen little thing," her mother says.

This is not how Emer thinks of herself, not at all.

Rose has told Emer how their mother broke down at Niall's burial, how she wept as if it were her precious child laid to rest all over again. Emer doesn't know what to do with this. It is too late, for a lot of things.

She pulls a chair out for the woman as she always does, and sits with them, her mother, her sister, her nieces, and they pour the tea.

After that she is upright, anyway. Not agreeable, not overly useful, but upright. She does some household chores, stays hidden from the sun. On a close day she might walk down to the quay and back, a look of concentrated bearing on her face, as if she is walking off a cramp. There is nothing left of her that is fearsome. Her hands are as mild and scarred with life as the next woman's. Any power she once had over people's minds has gone inward. She keeps her hands close, wrapped around her waist under a shawl, and her one eye looking down. She is far from pleasant. But there's always Rose, by her side at every instant, for the smiling.

IN APRIL, THE WEATHER continues its desperate course, barely a breath between storms, battering the island with swells and wind. The sea rages, pummeling the rock, great chunks of green earth slide into the waves as it retreats. As though the island itself is trying to strip away generations of anger and remorse, holding them hostage at the same time that it laments their leaving.

CHAPTER 30

Evacuation

May 1960

On the first of May, on the feast of Bealtaine that marks the beginning of summer, one beautiful day is blown across the island as if from heaven. The sun shines high and bright, the water that has been rushing off the houses and stone walls into dikes dug by nuns long ago slows to a steady drip. The sea is as calm as glass. Islanders emerge, squinty as moles in the sunlight. The children run barefoot down to the water to greet the procession of boats.

All morning, while they empty their homes, they talk of the council houses that await them. With running water, toilets, electricity, gas cookers instead of a fire. Each family will be given a bicycle to go to the shops and pub only three miles up the road. The land is poor but they won't be as dependent on it. Their animals will have to learn to get out of the way of cars on the road.

The children squirm with excitement while they trap their pets in covered pots. The women tear up at every pause. The one old man lights his pipe and turns his face to the sea. They all wipe at their eyes and continue packing.

The children tell their mothers what they heard from the teacher: There will be dances, every Saturday at the hall in Cois Cuain.

Sure, they say, sounding like old immigrants already, *haven't island people always been great ones for the dancing.*

They wonder now if they ever truly had a say in it, whether they were let to stay or made to go. It may not have been the fairies or the saints, but the island itself that was in charge all along.

Before they go, most women take water from Saint Brigid's well. This has been done for generations, anyone leaving for work or war or marriage takes some of the holy water with them. Should they crave the blessings of home, they only need to pour a little out. If they have their babies far away, they can be sprinkled in it, just as they would be dipped on the island. Before Brigid came with her hands, the water had been the only one to ease things. It has flowed in the driest weather for as long as anyone can remember. They each take a swallow of it with them to ease their way into the world. Even the women who don't believe in it fill a bottle with this promise and seal it with wax. With superstition, it is better to stick to the thing than to stray. Better it doesn't work than you lose your chance at saving yourself altogether.

WHEN ROSE FINISHES CLEANING and almost everything is gone from the house, she ties up the mattress on Emer's bed into a roll for the men to bring down. It is made of the feathers of seabirds and would be expensive to replace. Under the mattress, wedged beneath the corner of the bed frame, she finds a small scrap of blue flannel, wrapped up and tied with butcher's string. She goes to open it, then decides not to. It isn't hers, it must belong to Emer. She'll bring it down to her at the boats, and let Emer decide what to do with it.

As she closes the door for the last time, she whispers their names: *Austin, Niall, Brigid.* She believes she is saying good-bye.

She walks down in the direction of the quay, where chaos reigns. Men are still carrying bedsteads and bureaus, transferring them to currachs that bring them to bigger boats waiting in the sea. She has never in her life seen so many boats in their water at once. They say one time when the fish were plenty, boats came from all over Europe, but most of them went to the harbor of Inis Muruch. There wasn't anything here for them. Brigid was the only tourist they'd ever had. It's like a regatta or a fair, all the excitement. There is far too much happiness surrounding their leaving. She'd like to smack the smiles off the faces of her children. As this is not a usual turn of her mind, she shakes it away and tries to lift her chin high and walk as if she knows which way she's going in the sunshine.

In the boat, ignoring the photographer feverishly snapping pictures of all the twins, she hands the flannel pouch to her sister. Emer stiffens, the little bit of color she has managed to gain drains instantly from her face. Like the worst moment of her life has just seared across her vision again.

"What is it?" Rose asks.

"Brigid gave this to me," Emer says. "I thought it was a dream."

Emer hands Rose the baby. Then she stands so quickly the boat threatens to tip. A man shouts at her to sit her bloody self down.

"Let me out," Emer says. "I've left something."

Rose tries to pull her back, the babies start crying, a sudden swell pitches the currach, one of the toddlers almost tumbles out of the boat. Finally, a man plucks Emer up by her armpits and plops her impatiently on the quay. She runs away from them all, up the green road and beyond. Rose has to negotiate and distribute children before she can be lifted out as well, her polite approach is not as immediately effective. By the time she's out, Emer has disappeared over the hill that leads to the cliffs. Rose follows after her.

Emer stumbles down the cliff path with no regard for the sheer drop. She ducks into the shrine and kneels at the opening to the well, her heart rising like it might leap out her throat any moment. She unwraps the flannel and finds a shriveled, vile, gorgeous thing, dried and brown and empty, a pouch knit out of blood and seaweed. It's bigger than a partial veil, it's the entire container, an enormous version of the mermaids' purses they collected from the coves as girls. Abandoned sacs where basking sharks grow before they break out one end and swim away.

She holds Brigid's caul just where the water flows thickest, until the sides of it soften and bellow out, until the sac where Brigid's child was formed is full again. Then she places it like a holy relic on top of the flannel and sets the offering in the cushion of grass and blue flowers. Flowers so tiny they've never, in all her life, seemed to belong to the human world. Fairy flowers, they called them as girls. A gift the good people presented to the blue-cloaked saint who came to their island. Emer lets go and holds her breath.

Inside the pouch, something moves. Thrashes and stretches, like a fish caught in a net. Then it swells and the whole thing grows, expands beyond its proportions, and Rose is there, her sister is beside her and Emer hasn't breathed yet, she mustn't breath yet though her lungs are crying for it, and finally, when she thinks her chest might burst holding it in, a hand tears at the membrane and tries to pull itself, slow and sticky and human, out of the place where it has grown.

Images rush at her, swarming, merciless. All those hands. The turnip stump and the curled-up, lichen remains of a miniature hand, her sister's fingers dripping with dangerous honey, her child swiping regret from her forehead, Brigid pulling her clothes away and dropping them, heavy as armor, to the ground. Her own hands and their insertion of misery, like a blade hidden in her palm.

The hand claws at the sides of the sac, and she can see the panic, the body behind it trapped in something so thick it cannot be pulled away. Emer has to go for her knife and slice it right down the middle, allowing what is within to straighten itself, and the husk of the membrane to fall away.

He is there, naked and fish-white and smeared with afterbirth, hot blue eyes opening to look at his mother whom he will, after this, always remember as smiling.

"Will you look at him," Rose hisses, and she crosses herself. "Saints alive."

Emer grabs hold of Niall, the whole slimy length of him, folding him almost in half to fit inside her arms. She wipes at his face and his eyes with her shawl, cleaning the clots off, kissing his skin and inhaling, he smells of salt and blood and milk and underneath it all, his glorious self.

"I didn't drink, Mammy. Not a drop."

"Good lad." She barely trusts herself to speak.

"It was Brigid," he says. "She told them to let me go."

"I know," Emer shushes him. "She gave me the caul."

"Not that Brigid."

Another hand returns to her, the first one, that woman, all those years ago, who peeled the curtain back to show her the world. Who held a scrap of blue fabric out to her like a gift, or a warning. Emer had thought she was something else altogether.

He is ice cold from the water, so she wraps him in her shawl and they climb, stumbling up again into the sun, to warm him.

"Mammy," he says, blinking in the unaccustomed brightness. He is looking beyond her toward the site of the evacuation.

"Look at all the boats in our sea."

She holds him for ages, murmuring the same way she did the day he was born the first time, *my boy, my boy, my boy.* He doesn't mind it, he lets her hold him for as long as she needs to, before they must rise and meet the boats and their new life on the other side. Where this day will fade in Niall's memory until all he recalls is a fevered dream. He won't even remember the woman who saved him, after first allowing him to die. Perhaps they will go farther than they planned, take their new bicycles and ride until they reach a place they have never seen, safe from the fairies, and themselves, where Emer's hands will be mild and forgettable, away from the opinions of the women who would rather she be punished than forgiven.

Go on, Emer's heart whispers, *go on. Find out where she has gone.*

Emer knows it as well as any of them. She doesn't deserve this. She who murdered their husbands and drove off the closest thing they had to a saint, who used her hands to insert hopelessness into any soul that seemed the slightest bit happier than she was. She who took their island away from them with the same vicious disregard as a fairy who steals a child right out of its mother's arms.

She doesn't deserve it—doesn't deserve a saint's absolution or a fairy's surrender, or the forgiveness of a woman scorned—and she will not be allowed to keep him, he will grow up and away from her, already on that walk down she can imagine his small hand letting go, but still she gets him back, her son, her bones, her soul, her pulse.

Mercy. He is given back to her, all the same.

ACKNOWLEDGMENTS

I suspect that no one aside from writers and people who hope to be mentioned by writers read the acknowledgments. But I always do, so I will try to make these as long and boring as possible. If I forget to thank you, please forgive me. It took five years to write this book, so chalk it up to age-related memory loss rather than ingratitude.

I am indebted to my fabulous agents, Grainne Fox and Christy Fletcher, for believing in me even when everyone else in the publishing world had forgotten me, as well as my editors, Arzu Tahsin and Jillian Verrillo, who saw my book for what it was and helped make it even more so.

I am profoundly grateful to the entire population of Inishbofin, Ireland, many of whom have housed me, fed me, shuttled me back and forth, answered my ignorant questions, and always greeted me and my son with love. For housing and feeding us: the Doonmore Hotel, the Beach Bar, the Dolphin Hotel, the Hostel, Caroline Coyne and Lorraine MacLean. Ann Prendergast for slagging my boy until he understood it, and, along with Claire, Veronica and countless babysitters, for making him feel safe when his mother had to work.

Cliodhna Hallissey for pirate stories under the picnic table, Michael Joe and Robbie for the bodhran lessons, Orla, Bernie and Lalage for *all that wine*, Padraic and Lisa McIntyre and their children for the craic, Tommy Burke for tours and history on Shark and Bofin, Tara, Audrey and the staff at the Community Centre for everything else. Thanks most of all to my dearest, oldest friends on the island: Susan and Joanne Elliott, who helped edit the final draft for inappropriate American phrases and ignorant farming details, and Desmond O'Halloran, who was always available for emergency lattes.

Kieran Concannon's film, *Death of an Island*, was the initial inspiration for the prologue of this book, and I will always be grateful for it, and to Kieran for smuggling me a copy meant for someone else.

Thanks to the MacDowell Colony, where I began this novel, and all the staff and office folk who make the running of a paradise appear effortless. Special thanks to Blake, for telling me about the women and their knives, and hanging a graduation balloon on my door after I finished the first draft.

I am grateful to the Virginia Center for the Creative Arts, where I wrestled with many later drafts, to Craig and Sheila Pleasants, Bea Booker and everyone in the office and staff, to all the artists who inspired me and made me laugh, in particular the ones who let me cry: Priyanka Champaneri and Kathryn Levy.

Thanks to my early readers: Gary Miller for tossing the hammer that stunned the poor pig, Sandra Miller for the popovers and truth telling, and Lacy Berman for loving Emer and reminding me to read poetry.

I am indebted to my friends (you know who you are) for remaining my friends even though I go to residencies and Ireland and don't talk to them for months at a time. Thanks to Breakwater school, the teachers, the children and the parents, for the reassurance that my son is with a family who loves him, even when I am not at home.

Thank you to my parents and my extended family; they have always supported my choice to be a writer, even when it means I am useless at calling them back.

Last and best, my husband, Tim, who made it possible for me to go away and write, and my son, Liam, who forgave me for leaving. I am thankful every day for my little family. You have made me happier than I ever suspected I would be.

About the author

2 Meet Lisa Carey

About the book

6 The Story Behind *The Stolen Child*

Read on

11 Author's Picks: My Favorite Books by Irish Authors

12 Have You Read? More by Lisa Carey

Insights,
Interviews
& More...

Meet Lisa Carey

© Timothy Spalding 2003

LISA CAREY was born in 1970 in Brookline, Massachusetts, to Irish American parents. Her father is a lawyer and law professor and her mother a nurse, and she has one younger brother, who works in the film industry. She has a large extended family of grandparents, aunts, uncles, and cousins and when she was a child they spent holidays and summers together on the south shore of Massachusetts. They still do, as much as they can.

From an early age, her favorite pastimes were reading, daydreaming, eavesdropping, and pretending to be the protagonist in a novel. At the age of nine she decided that her dream career would be to write copy for book jackets. She preferred writing assignments to all other schoolwork and became addicted to the feeling that came from creating an almost perfect sentence. She wrote melodramatic stories she never finished and preferred the lives of fictional characters to her own.

She attended public schools in Brookline and Hingham, Massachusetts, and then got her BA in English (reading novels) and philosophy (accidentally acquired by taking philosophy courses where they read novels) at Boston College. After graduation, she took a three-week trip to Ireland, where she cycled fifty miles to see the birthplace of her great-grandmother, in Connemara. She felt so at home in Ireland that she bought an electric kettle and continued to call everything "lovely" back in America. Since she preferred school to work (her only jobs thus far were medical secretary, barista, and bank teller), she had two graduate programs in mind: medical school (she loved hospitals) or creative writing. She ultimately chose to pursue the program that would allow more sleep and plenty of reading time. She applied to the MFA in fiction at Vermont College of Fine Arts, a low-residency program that was started before most people had heard of low-residency programs, which led her father to ask if she'd found it on the back of a matchbook.

She wrote short stories and mailed them (from the post office, in real envelopes) to her advisors every month, while also working at Brookline Booksmith, where she could buy novels at a discount. After she wrote a story that felt like it was the beginning of a novel, she left her job and apartment, borrowed extra money on her student loan, and moved to Ireland for four months to research and write it. She spent the majority of that summer on Inishbofin island, listening to accents in the pub and reading every Irish novel she could get her hands on. When she had ten days left before she had to fly home, she went to the Tyrone Guthrie Centre at Annaghmakerrig, an artist's residency in County Monaghan, and wrote the first hundred pages of the novel that had grown in her mind during all that listening and reading.

She returned to Brookline, immediately felt out of place, and moved back to Ireland as quickly as possible. She finished *The Mermaids Singing* in time for her MFA thesis, found an agent with the help of a friend in publishing, and got a two-book deal with Bard, a division of Avon Books, at the age of twenty-six. Since she had no plans for her next novel, she traveled to Annaghmakerrig to look for an idea. After a nightmare in Tyrone Guthrie's old Irish manor about a girl ghost in a nightgown, she wrote *In the Country of the Young.* ▶

When she was writing her third novel, *Love in the Asylum*, she returned to America with her Irish immigrant dog, Axel. She lived on Nantucket for a year before moving back to Brookline. In between books three and four she met Timothy Spalding, a classics scholar turned computer programmer, who read her second novel before their first date. After they were married, and while she was writing *Every Visible Thing*, they moved to Portland, Maine, where Tim started his website, Librarything .com. Just after her fourth novel was published, their son, Liam Patrick, was born. Lisa decided to take a year off from writing and stay home with Liam. Her delight in her son, combined with a baby brain that made writing less inviting than reading or sleep, turned one year into four. After her dog, Axel, died, she started a memoir about her life in Ireland, but she was much happier putting it in a drawer than having anyone read it.

In 2010, on a trip back to Inishbofin, she saw a documentary about the evacuation of an Irish island and knew she wanted to write another novel. Over the course of four years she wrote *The Stolen Child*, mostly during trips to Ireland and at artist residencies.

Tim, Lisa, and Liam have divided the last few years between Ireland, the United States, and Turkey. They built a library in their house in Portland to hold all their books, and now that their son is obsessed with reading, they might need to build another one. They have a large family of relatives and adopted friends.

Lisa, who can't bear to live away from the sea, is putting off having a "real" job for as long as she can, and she struggles with all the life crap that gets in the way of love and art. She reads more than she writes, spends more time in pajamas than clothes, worships the effortless creativity of her child, and still imagines that she is the protagonist in a novel she hasn't gotten around to finishing yet. She is currently writing a YA book and gathering ideas for her next adult novel.

Lisa is the author of five novels. Her books have been translated into twelve languages and optioned for film. *Every Visible Thing* won a Ferro-Grumley Award for Fiction; *Love in the Asylum* was the winner of a Massachusetts Book Award. She has been awarded fellowships at the Hawthornden Castle, the Tyrone Guthrie

Centre at Annaghmakerrig, the Virginia Center for the Creative Arts, and the MacDowell Colony. *The Stolen Child* is her newest novel.

This bio reads like a social media post, all happiness, success, and premeditated life choices with no breakdowns, failures, or existential despair. Lisa hopes no one is foolish enough to believe that's all there is, and that they read between the lines. ∾

The Story Behind
The Stolen Child

Inishbofin—an island off the west coast of Ireland, which translates as "island of the white cow,"—is a place I have returned to countless times since my first stay in 1995. During that initial visit I researched my first novel, and I based my fictional island on the landscape there. My second novel was also set on an island, this time in Maine. So by the time I went to write my fifth I had absolutely *no* intention of writing anything set on an island, certainly not one in Ireland. I safely could have said that's exactly what I *wouldn't* be writing. If every writer has only one story in them that they get to tell over and over again, then mine appears to be surrounded by water.

Fifteen years later, I visited Inishbofin with my four-year-old son. We met a group of American archaeologists who had a six-year-old, and they were kind enough to share their babysitter. One night, this allowed me the time to watch a documentary, *Death of an Island*, by a local man named Kieran Concannon. It was about the evacuation of a smaller neighboring island, Inishark, that was once home to hundreds of families. The combined blows of the famine, two world wars, and Irish emigration had dwindled the population down to twenty-three residents by 1960. Inishbofin, with its natural harbor and sandy beaches, attracted sailboats and visitors and would eventually build a thriving tourism business. But Inishark's harbor was a dangerous cove that could only be navigated during the right tide by experienced locals. It had no electricity, phone lines, or doctors, and it was on its own in an emergency. The government, which often provided social welfare to poor Irish villages, wanted to clear people off Inishark and so refused to set up the island with modern conveniences. What the government did offer were houses on the mainland if the islanders agreed to leave. After the sea killed three young men on their way back from Mass on Easter Sunday, the islanders had too few men to handle their boats. They left for a mainland village that overlooked their old home, and no one has lived on Inishark since. The documentary interviews people who have remembered the island in their dreams their entire lives. ▸

Not all novels come to you in a shivering flash, like a dream. This one did. I knew I would write about a community's final year on an Irish island, though my characters would not be the kind, generous, respectable people of that documentary, because, let's face it, I don't write characters like that. I would take the real evacuation and replace the community with one from my imagination. But the documentary remains, in my prologue, as a tribute to the real residents of Inishark.

I don't start writing a novel with one idea. I have to have at least five, all of which could be different novels and none of which has much in common. One woman from the documentary, whom I later met myself, told how she did not want to leave and refused to pack until the last minute. I started to imagine two sisters, one who hated her life on the island and the other who loved it. For some reason I had the Salem witch persecutions on my brain at the time, and I imagined a group of desperate, frightened islanders turning against an outsider. I was reading *Walk the Blue Fields* by Claire Keegan, one of my favorite Irish authors, about a female healer who moved into a desolate house in the west of Ireland. I couldn't get this character out of my mind, and she was my first inspiration for Brigid. I was also reading a book about Maine lighthouses and the families who lived in them before the lights were automated. I was reading Irish myths of changelings and stolen children to my son. Last I had an idea—left over from when I was researching my second novel—about a torrid affair between the Irish saints Patrick and Brigid. (I never worked out the details of this, thank goodness.)

So there I had it: evacuated islands, sisters, witch burning, healers, lighthouses, fairies, and saints. At least seven ideas, and many more that either ended up on the cutting-room floor or never made it into the room in the first place. Then, while I was writing the first draft, Emer and Brigid rejected my plans for friendship and became lovers. I hate it when writers talk about characters doing things on their own, because for me writing is extremely difficult and not one bit of it feels like it is being written by anyone else but miserable me, but in this case, they really did. I was the one who had to write it, but they told me to.

The Stolen Child is *not* an autobiographical novel; my abandoned memoir is proof that I fail when I try to write about myself. I included a few things from my memoir: my lovely Irish dog, and a baby who couldn't breast-feed. While writing it I was quite sure it had little to do with me, because the story was so difficult to manage and get a proper hold on. I have no healing powers, and I've never lived in a lighthouse or an orphanage, or anywhere without electricity or plumbing. I am not afraid of fairies and I have never had an affair with a woman. I wrote an entire draft that built toward one ending and then changed my mind while writing the last chapter and had to go back and redo the whole thing about five more times. But once I approached the final draft and read the entire story out loud, I was shocked. It may not be about me or my life, but its themes, particularly motherhood and all its backstories and consequences— pregnancy, miscarriage, abortion, love, loneliness, worship and resentment, the inability to live in the moment because you're ▶

too busy missing something else—had been in my life for years. So don't believe it when I say that my books aren't about me. They are nothing about me and everything, at the same time. Because, as my son said recently, "You are only able to have one perspective your whole life. Doesn't that make you the center of the universe?"

But still, it is other people's worlds that I fall in love with. I have been to Inishark every summer since I first saw the film, going for day trips in a local boat that drops you off and picks you up according to the tide. You have to leap off the boat while it's still running, just at the moment when it rises with a wave. There are only sheep there now, and sunbathing seals, and rabbits, and occasionally that group of archaeologists, who camp there for two weeks every year no matter the weather. It is one of the most beautiful places I have ever seen, yet I know, from being trapped on Inishbofin in a storm, how desolate it must have been at times. The houses are still there, their roofs fallen in, and if you visit with a local they will tell you who lived in each abandoned building, and where they ended up. You can almost hear the children in the school playground, or the bells announcing Mass in the church. Two years ago, a series of winter storms tore in half what remained of the cement quay that had lined the cove. The graveyard, set perilously on a cliffside, is beginning to release the bones of its ancestors as the land succumbs to erosion.

I never saw Inishark when it was populated, but I have visited its sister, Inishbofin, countless times over the last twenty-one years. I have been welcomed again and again by the wild landscape and the generous people; learned to understand the accents that required subtitles in the documentary; watched the babies from my first trip become adults manning the boat, serving Guinness, or playing music in the bar. I have spent lazy days sitting outside the pub, watching my son's silhouette run back and forth on the hillside against a sunset that lasts for hours. Although I have only seen Inishark as an abandoned village, I can imagine how heartbreaking it was to leave it, and I can see precisely what life would be like there now, if it weren't for the dangers of nature and the limited imagination of the outsiders who were in charge. ∾

Author's Picks: My Favorite Books by Irish Authors

Walk the Blue Fields by Claire Keegan
Foster by Claire Keegan
TransAtlantic by Colum McCann
The Green Road by Anne Enright
The China Factory by Mary Costello
There Are Little Kingdoms by Kevin Barry
Dubliners by James Joyce
The Woman Who Walked into Doors by
  Roddy Doyle
The Likeness by Tana French
Room by Emma Donoghue
The Country Girls by Edna O'Brien
The Butcher Boy by Patrick McCabe
Amongst Women by John McGahern
Tender by Belinda McKeon
The Testament of Mary by Colm Tóibín

Related links:
http://www.inishbofin.com

Inishark: Death of an Island:
https://youtu.be/VmXb2sIFJuY

Líonta na Cuimhne: Nets of Memory,
a documentary about emigration from
Inishark to Clinton, Massachusetts
https://vimeo.com/88290076

Have You Read?
More by Lisa Carey

THE MERMAIDS SINGING

There is an island off the west coast of Ireland called Inis Muruch—the Island of the Mermaids—a world where myth is more powerful than truth, and love can overcome even death. It is here that Lisa Carey sets her lyrical and sensual first novel, weaving together the voices and lives of three generations of Irish and Irish American women.

Years ago, the fierce and beautiful Grace stole away from the island with her small daughter, Gráinne, unable to bear its isolation. Now Gráinne is motherless at fifteen, and a grandmother she has never met has come to take her back. Her heart is pulled between a life in which she no longer belongs and a family she cannot remember. But only on Inis Muruch can she begin to understand the forces that have torn her family apart.

> "*Mermaids* combines the flinty Ireland of *Angela's Ashes* . . . and the long-delayed reunion of lost loves of *Cold Mountain*."
> —*New York* magazine

On a stormy November night in 1848, a ship carrying more than a hundred Irish emigrants ran aground twenty miles off the coast of Maine. Many were saved, but some were not—including a young girl who died crying out the name of her brother.

In the present day, the artist Oisin MacDara lives in self-imposed exile on Tiranogue, the small island where the shipwrecked Irish settled. The past is Oisin's curse, as memories of the twin sister who died tragically when he was a boy haunt him still.

Then, on a quiet All Hallows' Eve, a restless spirit is beckoned into his home by a candle flickering in the window: the ghost of the girl whose brief life ended on Tiranogue's shore more than a century earlier. In Oisin's house she seeks comfort and warmth, and a chance at the life that was denied her so long ago.

For a lonely man chained by painful memories, nothing will ever be the same again.

"A strange, wonder-filled book. . . . Every scene is gripping, every mood and movement . . . compellingly drawn, every new page an epiphany."
—*Washington Post Book World*

"[A] haunting, beautifully rendered, exquisitely doomy novel . . . the story builds inexorably, carried along by its own brand of otherworldly eroticism."
—Janet Maslin, *New York Times*

Have You Read? *(continued)*

LOVE IN THE ASYLUM

Can love save those who believe they are beyond redemption? In and out of a swank northeastern mental hospital more than a dozen times in ten years, Alba Elliot, a twenty-five-year-old children's book writer with bipolar disorder, believes she is a hopeless case. But an unlikely relationship with Oscar, a thirty-year-old drug addict whose "recreation" has cost him everything, and a century-old story hidden in the institution's library bring about changes that Alba could never have imagined.

Brought together by fate, influenced by forces as beautiful and powerful as they are unforeseen, Alba and Oscar will slowly rise from the ashes of despair and self-destruction and, in the midst of righting an old wrong, begin to heal their battered spirits. A beautifully crafted, heartfelt tale of tragedy and triumph, Lisa Carey's moving third novel is a testament to the surprising resilience of the human heart.

> "Compassionate [and] ambitious . . . [Carey] acutely perceives how families, which are meant to be our safe harbors, can harbor instead the rocks on which our psyches are shipwrecked."
> —*Boston Globe*

Five years ago the eldest Furey son, Hugh, ran off into the night and never returned. His parents, estranged by grief, are trying to put the tragedy behind them after a long, exhausting, and fruitless search. His mother, recovering from an emotional breakdown, has lost herself in a new career; Hugh's father, having abandoned his faith and his position as a theology professor, now cares halfheartedly for their two remaining children. Left more or less to fend for themselves, ten-year-old Owen and fifteen-year-old Lena struggle to hold on to their brother's memory—an increasingly self-destructive obsession that gives rise to angel fantasies, drug use, quixotic quests, and dangerous experimentation that will ultimately force a damaged family to confront its past and find a future.

> "Prose that blossoms like a bruise, both aching and vivid . . . heartbreaking and, ultimately, redemptive."
> —*Entertainment Weekly*

> "An emotionally compelling novel . . . bracing insight and sensitivity . . . A dramatic reminder of just what a corrosive mixture grief and silence can be."
> —*Washington Post Book World*